Acclaim for MERTON OF THE MOVIES

"At once satire and classic Hollywood tale, *Merton of the Movies* made me long for the Los Angeles cafeterias of John Fante, Nathaniel West's studio backlots, and the early days of Musso and Frank when Douglas Fairbanks and Charlie Chaplin would horse race down Hollywood Boulevard, the loser picking up the tab. A blistering, rollicking adventure in La La Land, before it got its Tinseltown fame."

— Liska Jacobs, author of *Catalina*

"Harry Leon Wilson's *Merton of the Movies* was the first great comic novel about Hollywood filmmaking in the 1920s, with all of its attendant artifice and illusion. It remains a prescient and hilarious examination of the performative nature of the modern self in a culture dominated by film and media images."

— John Parris Springer, author of *Hollywood Fictions: The Dream Factory in American Popular Literature*

"*Merton of the Movies* is and will always remain a delight of the American Dream run aground and a classic tale of the silent movie era. Dark and comic and darkly comic, it joyfully knocks down the façades of old Hollywood to reveal the desperation behind the scene while never ceasing to entertain."

— Ivy Pochoda, author of *Wonder Valley*

"It's notoriously hard to make comedy out of the movies. That whole world is so absurd, so improbable, so filled with grotesques that the reality is more fantastical than most writers can invent. *Merton of the Movies* succeeds by having at its center a naïve but likable everyman, whose apparently unrealistic fantasies, in some deeply ironic sense, come true.

For the author, and perhaps for any writer of comedy, style is everything. Harry Leon Wilson's prose is sometimes hilariously artificial, sometimes effortlessly satiric, sometimes downright postmodern. It has echoes of Perelman, Wodehouse, and Thurber, and is not shown up by those comparisons."

— Geoff Nicholson, author of *The Miranda*

MERTON OF THE MOVIES

MERTON

of the

MOVIES

HARRY LEON WILSON

Foreword by Mitra Jouhari
Introduction by Tom Lutz

This is a LARB Classics publication
Published by The Los Angeles Review of Books
6671 Sunset Blvd., Suite 1521, Los Angeles, CA 90028
www.larbbooks.org

Foreword copyright © 2019 by Mitra Jouhari
Introduction copyright © 2019 by Tom Lutz

ISBN 978-1-940660-60-8

Library of Congress Control Number 2019946192

Designed by Tom Comitta

FOREWORD

Mitra Jouhari

If you've watched any film about Hollywood in the last millennium or so, you probably know on some level that Hollywood is built on delusion, artifice, and big fat stacks of cash. It's a glossy, superficial place that draws in doe-eyed dreamers from all over the world armed with little more than vague plans to make it big, only to be unceremoniously chewed up and spat out before they've had a chance to unpack. One by one, these self-styled starlets get enough doors slammed in their face (if they make it to the room at all) that they decide it's time to head back to whatever life they thought they could beat. They drop their embossed headshots in the trash and leave their dignity somewhere between the studio lot and the bus station, where snide attendants are all too eager to sell them one-way tickets back home.

To Merton Gill, the not-so-humble hero of Harry Leon Wilson's 1920s classic, *Merton of the Movies*, Hollywood's got a Merton Gill-shaped hole that needs filling. In his mind, Hollywood is a meritocracy in which he's sure to succeed ... if he could just get there. Armed with what he believes to be a potent combination of good looks, dedication, and "humility," Merton Gill is counting the seconds until he can introduce the world to his glamorous alter ego: Clifford Armytage. Those who survive in Hollywood need confidence, and Merton's got more than enough to go around. He's a certified actor — with the mail-in diploma to prove it! — and is convinced he's destined for greatness.

As the saying goes, the first step is admitting you have a problem. The second, of course, is going to Los Angeles to try to become an actor.

He stakes out a studio that makes films starring a woman on whom he has a crush — one has to follow one's heart. The lucky lady is Beulah Baxter, and Merton's in love with her beauty and stunt-making before he even sets foot on set. But then, bit by bit, the walls on his beautifully constructed mental projection of Hollywood and those who live and work there come tumbling down. Merton eventually finds himself out of cash and squatting on a studio lot ... until Sarah Nevada "Flips" Montague, a comedienne and stunt woman, takes pity on him and finds him work. As filming begins, his co-stars make strange, almost comedic choices in their performances, but Merton acts up a storm in a dramatic role perfected for a Real Artist™ suited for straight man fame. And so it begins.

Not long after, Merton finds himself at the premiere of his big film and in a prison of his own making. Slowly but surely he realizes he's been duped. He is the unwitting star of the most disgusting film project an actor can be a party to: a big, broad comedy. Cynical Hollywood types have preyed on his naïvete, tricking him into being the butt of the joke. Back in Kansas, he had seen himself as a big-city star trapped in a joke of a small town. Now, in the big city, the joke isn't just *on* him, it *is* him.

Enter the heroine, Flips, who saves Merton from himself and gives him his only real chance at being a star. Behind every man there's a great woman, and behind every great woman there's a man who questions her every step of the way until he realizes that she was right all along. In 2019, as I write this, what is more timely than the tale of a man failing up, unable to acknowledge the comedy in how seriously he takes himself, thanks to his outsize ego?

And yet, through all of Merton's delusions of grandeur, through all his condescension, through all his stubborn insistence that he's destined for more, he remains sympathetic. There's something comforting about someone who believes in himself against all odds, who follows a dream blindly, who isn't scared of failing and doesn't care what others have to say. In the end, it makes sense that his performance makes people laugh. There is nothing funnier than wanting to become an actor. There is nothing more foolish than thinking that if you pick up stakes and go to Hollywood, things will work out. His flexibility (translation: inability to admit he was bamboozled) allows him to live a life of glamour and happiness (translation: wealth and complacency). He's a movie star, just not the way he thought he would be.

So what makes a movie star, anyway? As evidenced on the sets that Merton Gill frequents, it's not necessarily talent or beauty or intelligence or any of the things one might hope would lead to mainstream success. Judging by the Merton who walks up to the casting office day in and day out, success looks like dedication. Judging by the Merton who fantasized about his larger-than-life Hollywood persona back in Gashwiler's store, it might reek a bit of delusion. So for the hopeful young small-town wannabe, what's the key to Hollywood stardom? Dedication or delusion? If you ask Merton Gill, the answer might be: why choose?

INTRODUCTION

Tom Lutz

On her famous trip to the United States in 1934 and 1935, Gertrude Stein disappointed a lot of people. She didn't show up in Iowa City as scheduled, and 70 years later some of my Iowa friends still seemed upset about it. When she came to California, many of the state's then-famous writers hoping for an audience were also let down. Mabel Dodge Luhan wanted to introduce Stein to Robinson Jeffers and others at her Carmel artists' colony but was rebuffed. The people Stein wanted to meet instead were Dashiell Hammett and a writer named Harry Leon Wilson, who lived near Luhan and Jeffries in Carmel.

Harry Leon who? Wilson, however forgotten now, was then a popular writer. He had published over two dozen novels, many made into films (some cowritten with Booth Tarkington, another even more popular novelist). He had been editor of *Puck*, a regular contributor to *The Saturday Evening Post* and other magazines and newspapers, and even the national press reported on his comings and goings. Stein said that Wilson's 1923 novel *Merton of the Movies* was "the best book about twentieth-century American youth that has yet been done." This perhaps came as a surprise to F. Scott Fitzgerald, Ernest Hemingway, Willa Cather, Edith Wharton, Theodore Dreiser, Claude McKay, John Dos Passos, William Faulkner, Langston Hughes, Jessie Redmon Fauset, Edith Glasgow, Anita Loos, Jean Toomer, Sinclair Lewis, Anzia Yezierska, Edna Ferber, and the other novelists famous for chronicling American youth in the 1920s. Better than all of them, according to Stein, was Wilson, especially in *Merton of the Movies*. "I always give it to every one to read who reads English," she said, "and always have done ever since I first read it."

The shock, for the literati of the day ("A Snub, a Snub, a Snub," *The San Francisco Examiner* headline read, "Gertrude Stein Gives Carmel's Highbrows the Go-By"), was due to the fact that Wilson's was a popular reputation, not a literary one. But they should not have been surprised. As Karen Leick points out in *Gertrude Stein and the Making of an American Celebrity*, Stein told anyone who would listen that her favorite books were the pulp paperbacks. A few years after her visit she wrote to Thornton Wilder, one of her many mentees:

> And now Thornton about my literature not that I write but that I read. Could you instead of sending me books well thought of by historians could you go to a railway station or to the nearest drugstore and send me every few weeks or once a month four or five of the mystery stories that the man in charge recommends as the best, everybody when they send me reading matter consult not my tastes but my education, I suppose even when I give you the detail of the method of pleasing me you won't because after all to a good American principles are more important than pleasure.

The idea that a writer famous for being difficult loved easy reading took some getting used to, and various reporters and commentators worried it out in their columns. As Leick writes, Stein's tour of the United States transformed people's sense of her, and the laughter that attended her readings was also, it seems, the laughter of recognition — Stein's prose, some understood for the first time, was not difficult so much as it was playful, ludic. She wasn't trying to sound fancy, she was trying to make her prose sound like speech, trying to sound, as she wrote, "Amurican."

Not everyone had this realization. A. A. Van Duym, who had met Stein when he worked at the American Library in Paris in the early part of the century, told a New York paper that "strangest of all and a mystery to be solved by Stein devotees," was that "she always reserved ahead of time the forthcoming novels of Harold Bell Wright, James Oliver Curwood, Rex Beach," the pop fiction kings of the day. Wright, for instance, was reported to be the first author to sell a million copies of a book, and the first to make a million dollars from his novels. Van Duym couldn't process this fact because he, like many literary folk, was a snob, and he makes that snobbery clear: "Whether this [buying of commercial fiction] was to get close to the real soul of the American people," he speculated, "or merely to get books intended for the consumption of Alice or some other member of her household, I cannot tell."

Van Duym hadn't been paying attention. Stein spoke openly of her love for detective fiction. She had just written *Blood on the Dining-Room Floor*, which, however hard to detect with the naked eye, was her version of a murder mystery. And her relation to cultural levels went beyond literary taste. "I like ordinary people who don't bore me," she explained in turning down Mabel Dodge Luhan and her set. "Highbrows do, you know, always do."

In the meantime, scholars — who of course can be snobs as well — have come to recognize what Michael North calls the "common cause" of modernist and pulp literature. Both the modernist and the pulp writers rejected Victorian propriety, flowery diction, and puritanical morality, and were instead interested in crossing borders that the more demure literary lights — think William Dean Howells or Hamlin Garland or Fauset or Cather or Lewis — would have tiptoed around. Harry Leon Wilson was not at all sensationalist and kept things much lighter than, say, Joyce or Eliot (or, for that matter, Edgar Rice Burroughs, whose *The Girl from Hollywood* was published the same year), but he was thoroughly modern. You would be hard pressed to find a young female character as snappy and down-to-earth, as hip and post-Victorian as "Flips" Montague, our hero Merton's Virgil, his guide to Hollywood, his protector, and, eventually, his wife. She is a flapper with a heart of gold (Wilson's 1913 novel *Bunker Bean* is said to have been the first to popularize the term "flapper"), and she moves fluidly in the world, as irreverent with big directors as she is with cameramen and carpenters. Of all Wilson's contemporaries, only McKay and Loos managed to get as close to representing the young women who rejected everything the 19th century and the Genteel Tradition had to offer in exchange for the brave, new, transformed world of the 20th. Flips is as clear-sighted as Merton is addle-headed: "Say!" she says to him, "you're a real nut, aren't you? How'd you ever get this way?" She enjoys his hapless innocence and, in fact — without giving away too much of the plot — at times encourages it, for professional reasons. "You're so kind of ignorant and appealing," she says, and he is, both.

Harry Leon Wilson was born in Illinois right after the Civil War, and so was 20 years older than the generation of Pound and Eliot and the American modernists, 30 years older than the famous Lost Generation writers also associated with Stein. He grew up in Illinois, where his father was a printer, and he set type as a boy. He learned stenography, left home at 16, and wandered out west, where he worked as a researcher for Hubert Howe Bancroft's histories and a private secretary for Virgil Bogue, a major civil engineer. His first humor piece was published in *Puck* when he was 19, and by the time he was 25, he had moved to New York and become an assistant editor at the magazine, promoted to editor in chief just four years later. *Puck* was the country's premier humor outlet and so this position was among the best jobs in the magazine world of the day. But Wilson was not happy with it.

Perhaps nothing spells the difference between Wilson's literary culture and ours more than the fact that when he sold his first book, his advance enabled him to quit that plum job and become a full-time novelist. He was thrilled to return to the West — as his Associated Press obituary quotes him:

I had to live ten years in New York. It was then a simple town, with few street lights north of Forty-second street. Now the place is pretty terrible to me, perhaps the ugliest city in the world. I decided that the only way to get out of New York was to write a successful novel. So I tried with *The Spenders* and when I got a substantial advance from publishers, I quit my job and beat it for the high hills of Colorado.

He supported himself with novels and plays for the rest of his life.

Wilson is best known now as the author of *Ruggles of Red Gap* (1915), in which an English valet is won in a poker game by a crude new millionaire in the American West. *Ruggles* had an extensive afterlife, first as a stage musical that same year, then as a film in 1918, another in 1923 (with Edward Everett Horton as Ruggles), and an award-winning 1935 version with Charles Laughton. Later there was another film, several radio plays, and a television musical in 1957. *Merton of the Movies* was also adapted for film in 1924, in 1932 (with Joan Blondell and Zazu Pitts), and again in in 1947 with Red Skelton in the lead.

The film industry was still new and so, of course, was its role as the engine of celebrity. Hollywood's location as the center of that industry was newer still. The movie often cited as the first true feature, *The Great Train Robbery* (1903), arrived only 20 years earlier; the first film shot in Hollywood, D. W. Griffith's 17-minute *In Old California*, was made in 1910 for New Jersey's Biograph Company, and the first Hollywood studio film was made the next year, less than a dozen years before *Merton*. Wilson was briefly part of the business, having done "a stint in Hollywood" in the years before *Merton*, and so he writes of the industry with an insider's eye.

According to John Parris Springer, who first introduced me to *Merton* when he was writing *Hollywood Fictions: The Dream Factory in American Popular Literature* (2000), the Hollywood novel as a genre centers on the "confusion of illusion and reality." Springer sees *Merton* as Exhibit A. When the novel opens, we are introduced to "beautiful New York society girl" Estelle St. Clair, who has wandered off the ranch where she is a guest and has been kidnapped by an outlaw known as the Slimy Viper, down "on the border, where life is lightly held." He has started to "force his attention upon her" when Buck Benson arrives to save the day. Buck fights the villain, and eventually raises him over his head to dash him to the ground as Estelle watches in admiration. It is pure melodrama — until, that is, another voice intrudes: "Merton Gill, what in the sacred name of Time are you meanin' to do with that dummy? For the good land's sake! Have you gone plumb crazy, or what? Put that thing down!"

The entire scene "on the border," with all its stock characters and florid, melodramatic language, had been taking place in the imagination of young sales clerk Merton Gill, and the man yelling at him is his boss. The plot and language are pulled straight from the movies, and played out not in the Southwest, but in the back room of a clothing store in Ohio, where Merton is holding aloft not the Slimy Viper, but a dress dummy. Merton, it seems, has been preparing himself for a career as a movie star, seeing all the films, reading all the latest magazines (*Photo Land*, *Silver Screenings*, and *Camera*), posing for publicity photos, and plotting his meteoric rise with Tessie Kearns, a dressmaker who also dreams of a career in Hollywood, practicing the "difficult art" of screenwriting. Several studios have turned down her mailed-in screenplay *Passions Perils*, and the pals speculate that Tessie's sets — which include Westminster Abbey and a number of castles — must be too expensive. The two also agree that while the stories of film hero Buck Benson saving the day are glorious, and historical dramas were important, slapstick comedy was not worthy of their attention. Film comedy was a lower form, they thought, one that "degraded a fine and beautiful art," and so they would have nothing to do with it.

Merton and Tessie do not identify at all with their small-town jobs or origins, only with the roles they imagine for themselves in the film world. Cultural forms have always been schools for selfhood, and just as scripture and heroic epics and theater and novels had provided archetypes and templates and narrative structures, so movies, even in these early days of the industry, provided aspirational models, examples of how to act, quite literally, in everyday life. In the same way that Don Quixote lives in a delirium of fictional images he has absorbed from books of chivalry, so Merton lives in a cinematic montage, his sense of his own identity a comically exaggerated version of what Wilson presents as a new movie-based notion of selfhood. Eventually, in Erving Goffman's *The Presentation of Self in Everyday Life* (1956) and the host of performance theories that followed, this idea of the performative self would be normalized, would be part of our background understanding, its full impact part of what the historian Warren I. Susman has described as a shift from a culture of character (producer-capitalist, Judeo-Christian, traditional, inherent, fixed) to a culture of personality (mutable, adoptable, metamorphic, acquired, reinventable, fixable by self-help and therapy), or, in other words, more or less where we find ourselves today.

Gertrude Stein knew this — she knew that film was changing our relation to self and social life. Just before meeting Wilson, she visited Warner Brothers Studio and was shown the newsreel made of her arrival in New York. She found the experience of viewing herself on film "unaccountably alarming," according to biographer and historian James R. Mellow. In *Everybody's Autobiography*, she wrote, "I saw myself almost as large and moving around and talking I did not like it particularly the talking, it gave me a very funny feeling and I did not like that funny feeling."

I said earlier that when the novel opens we are in the film inside Merton's head, but in fact there is a brief introductory paragraph:

At the very beginning of the tale there comes a moment of puzzled hesitation. One way of approach is set beside another for choice, and a third contrived for better choice. Still the puzzle persists, all because the one precisely right way might seem — shall we say intense, high keyed, clamorous? Yet if one way is the only right way, why pause? Courage! Slightly dazed, though certain, let us be on, into the shrill thick of it. So, then —

This seems a moment of metafiction, with the author discussing his own problems as a writer — which of course would have given Stein a kick. Or is it? Perhaps Merton, about to call "action!" in the movie in his mind, was simply crafting decisions about the plot. Or perhaps, of course, both — both Wilson's metafiction and Merton's process — and more than that, as the invocation of "us" in the end suggests. The choice of how to be in the world, of how to present a self, of how to understand our own stories, had expanded dramatically — we, the readers then and now, no longer need to remain a store clerk in Ohio; we can be anything, anybody — and that imagining of ourselves and our possibilities, just as it had been directed by the epic and novel and theater for centuries, was now being shaped, for anyone with a nickel and nearby movie theater, by film. We have met Merton, and he is us.

And yet, at the same time, he is not. For most readers today, it will be depressing or distressing (or both) to read the casually brutal racism of yesteryear: "white" is a synonym for honesty, "Chinaman" for dishonesty, and Mexicans are invariably evil — witness the Slimy Viper himself, Snake le Vazquez. There is a "wooden Indian proffering cigars," a "cast-iron effigy of a small Negro" jockey on a front lawn, a "dozen villainous Asiatics," and stereotype after stereotype in unconcerned procession. Everyone from the Midwest is, invariably, a dullard, especially Merton himself, with only the cosmopolitans on the coasts, like Flips Montague, keyed into the new world. Wilson and his audience can congratulate themselves for being modern cosmopolitans and not oblivious hicks, can pat themselves on the back for overturning the cultural hierarchies of their Victorian predecessors, but as is always the case, they remain provincial still, and miles short of our current consensus.

When Merton first walks onto the studio lot, he is amazed at the wide world it represents, with outdoor sets that perfectly mimic New York, and others Baghdad.

> Then he explored farther and felt curiously disappointed at finding that these structures were to real houses what a dicky is to a sincere, genuine shirt. They were pretentiously false.

One had but to step behind them to discover them as poor shells.

At moments like this — and perhaps this is why Stein was impressed, too — Wilson seems aware that this new sense of self was doomed, that it was hollow, a false front. Actually seeing ourselves on film, rather than imagining ourselves in one, as Stein saw, produces estrangement. The age of anxiety, the age of the lonely crowd, is right around the next historical corner, and the performed self will start to be reinterpreted not as freedom, but as a burden, as a poor shell. But for the moment, still early in the 1920s, Merton's movie-made self was an exuberant comic corrective, a path away from a fusty past and into a future arriving fast.

MERTON OF THE MOVIES

CHAPTER I

DIRTY WORK AT THE BORDER

AT THE VERY BEGINNING of the tale there comes a moment of puzzled hesitation. One way of approach is set beside another for choice, and a third contrived for better choice. Still the puzzle persists, all because the one precisely right way might seem — shall we say intense, high keyed, clamorous? Yet if one way is the only right way, why pause? Courage! Slightly dazed, though certain, let us be on, into the shrill thick of it. So, then —

Out there in the great open spaces where men are men, a clash of primitive hearts and the coming of young love into its own! Well had it been for Estelle St. Clair if she had not wandered from the Fordyce ranch. A moment's delay in the arrival of Buck Benson, a second of fear in that brave heart, and hers would have been a fate worse than death.

Had she not been warned of Snake le Vasquez, the outlaw — his base threat to win her by fair means or foul? Had not Buck Benson himself, that strong, silent man of the open, begged her to beware of the half-breed? Perhaps she had resented the hint of mastery in Benson's cool, quiet tones as he said, "Miss St. Clair, ma'am, I beg you not to endanger your welfare by permitting the advances of this viper. He bodes no good to such as you."

Perhaps — who knows? — Estelle St. Clair had even thought to trifle with the feelings of Snake le Vasquez, then to scorn him for his presumption. Although the beautiful New York society girl had remained unsullied in the midst of a city's profligacy, she still liked "to play with fire," as she laughingly said, and at the quiet words of Benson — Two-Gun Benson his comrades of the border called him — she had drawn herself to her full height, facing him in all her blonde young beauty, and pouted adorably as she replied, "Thank you! But I can look out for myself."

Yet she had wandered on her pony farther than she meant to, and was not without trepidation at the sudden appearance of the picturesque halfbreed, his teeth flashing in an evil smile as he swept off his broad sombrero to her. Above her suddenly beating heart she sought to chat gayly, while the quick eyes of the outlaw took in the details of the smart riding costume that revealed every line of her lithe young figure. But suddenly she chilled under his hot glance that now spoke all too plainly.

"I must return to my friends," she faltered. "They will be anxious." But the fellow laughed with a sinister leer. "No — ah, no, the lovely señorita will come with me," he replied; but there was the temper of steel in his words. For Snake le Vasquez, on the border, where human life was lightly held, was known as the Slimy Viper. Of all the evil men in that inferno, Snake was the foulest. Steeped in vice, he feared neither God nor man, and respected no woman. And now, Estelle St. Clair, drawing-room pet, pampered darling of New York society, which she ruled with an iron hand from her father's Fifth Avenue mansion, regretted bitterly that she had not given heed to honest Buck Benson. Her prayers, threats, entreaties, were in vain. Despite her struggles, the blows her small fists rained upon the scoundrel's taunting face, she was borne across the border, on over the mesa, toward the lair of the outlaw.

"Have you no mercy?" she cried again and again. "Can you not see that I loathe and despise you, foul fiend that you are? Ah. God in heaven, is there no help at hand?" The outlaw remained deaf to these words that should have melted a heart of stone. At last over the burning plain was seen the ruined hovel to which the scoundrel was dragging his fair burden. It was but the work of a moment to dismount and bear her half-fainting form within the den. There he faced her, repellent with evil intentions.

"Ha, señorita, you are a beautiful wildcat, yes? But Snake le Vasquez will tame you! Ha, ha!" laughed he carelessly.

With a swift movement the beautiful girl sought to withdraw the small silver-mounted revolver without which she never left the ranch. But Snake le Vasquez, with a muttered oath, was too quick for her. He seized the toy and contemptuously hurled it across his vile den.

"Have a care, my proud beauty!" he snarled, and the next moment she was writhing in his grasp.

Little availed her puny strength. Helpless as an infant was the fair New York society girl as Snake le Vasquez, foulest of the viper breed, began to force his attention upon her. The creature's hot kisses seared her defenseless cheek. "Listen!" he hissed. "You are mine, mine at last. Here you shall remain a prisoner until you have consented to be my wife." All seemed, indeed, lost.

"Am I too late, Miss St. Clair?"

Snake le Vasquez started at the quiet, grim voice.

"Sapristi!" he snarled. "You!"

"Me!" replied Buck Benson, for it was, indeed, no other.

"Thank God, at last!" murmured Estelle St. Clair, freeing herself from the foul arms that had enfolded her slim young beauty and staggering back from him who would so basely have forced her into a distasteful marriage. In an instant she had recovered the St. Clair poise, had become every inch the New York society leader, as she replied, "Not too late, Mr. Benson! Just in time, rather. Ha, ha! This — this gentleman has become annoying. You are just in time to mete out the punishment he so justly deserves, for which I shall pray that heaven reward you."

She pointed an accusing finger at the craven wretch who had shrunk from her and now cowered at the far side of the wretched den. At that moment she was strangely thrilled. What was his power, this strong, silent man of the open with his deep reverence for pure American womanhood? True, her culture demanded a gentleman, but her heart demanded a man. Her eyes softened and fell before his cool, keen gaze, and a blush mantled her fair cheek. Could he but have known it, she stood then in meek surrender before this soft-voiced master. A tremor swept the honest rugged face of Buck Benson as heart thus called to heart. But his keen eyes flitted to Snake le Vasquez.

"Now, curse you, viper that you are, you shall fight me, by heaven! in American fashion, man to man, for, foul though you be, I hesitate to put a bullet through your craven heart."

The beautiful girl shivered with new apprehension; the eyes of Snake le Vasquez glittered with new hope. He faced his steely eyed opponent for an instant only, then with a snarl like that of an angry beast sprang upon him. Benson met the cowardly attack with the flash of a powerful fist, and the outlaw fell to the floor with a hoarse cry of rage and pain. But he was quickly upon his feet again, muttering curses, and again he attacked his grim-faced antagonist. Quick blows rained upon his defenseless face, for the strong, silent man was now fairly aroused. He fought like a demon, perhaps divining that here strong men battled for a good woman's love. The outlaw was proving to be no match for his opponent. Arising from the ground where a mighty blow had sent him, he made a lightning-like effort to recover the knife which Benson had taken from him.

"Have a care!" cried the girl in quick alarm. "That fiend in human form would murder you!"

But Buck Benson's cool eye had seen the treachery in ample time. With a muttered "Curse you, fiend that you are!" he seized the form of the outlaw in a powerful grasp, raised him high aloft as if he had been but a child, and was about to dash him to the ground when a new voice from the doorway froze him to immobility. Statute-like he stood there, holding aloft the now still form of Snake le Vasquez.

The voice from the doorway betrayed deep amazement and the profoundest irritation:

"Merton Gill, what in the sacred name of Time are you meanin' to do with that dummy? For the good land's sake! Have you gone plumb crazy, or what? Put that thing down!"

The newcomer was a portly man of middle age dressed in ill-fitting black. His gray hair grew low upon his brow and he wore a parted beard.

The conqueror of Snake le Vasquez was still frozen, though he had instantly ceased to be Buck Benson, the strong, silent, two-gun man of the open spaces. The irritated voice came again:

"Put that dummy down, you idiot! What you think you're doin', anyway? And say, what you got that other one in here for, when it ought to be out front of the store showin' that new line of gingham house frocks? Put that down and handle it careful! Mebbe you think I got them things down from Chicago just for you to play horse with. Not so! Not so at all! They're to help show off goods, and that's what I want 'em doin' right now. And for Time's sake, what's that revolver lyin' on the floor for? Is it loaded? Say, are you really out of your senses, or ain't you? What's got into you lately? Will you tell me that? Skyhootin' around in here, leavin' the front of the store unpertected for an hour or two, like your time was your own. And don't tell me you only been foolin' in here for three minutes, either, because when I come back from lunch just now there was Mis' Leffingwell up at the notions counter wanting some hooks and eyes, and she tells me she's waited there a good thutty minutes if she's waited one. Nice goin's on, I must say, for a boy drawin' down the money you be! Now you git busy! Take that one with the gingham frock out and stand her in front where she belongs, and then put one them new raincoats on the other and stand him out where he belongs, and then look after a few customers. I declare, sometimes I git clean out of patience with you! Now, for gosh's sake, stir your stumps!"

"Oh, all right — yes, sir," replied Merton Gill, though but half respectfully. The "Oh, all right" had been tainted with a trace of sullenness. He was tired of this continual nagging and fussing over small matters; some day he would tell the old grouch so.

And now, gone the vivid tale of the great out-of-doors, the wide plains of the West, the clash of primitive-hearted men for a good woman's love. Gone, perhaps, the greatest heart picture of a generation, the picture at which you laugh with a lump in your throat and smile with a tear in your eye, the story of plausible punches, a big, vital theme masterfully handled — thrills, action, beauty, excitement — carried to a sensational finish by the genius of that sterling star of the shadowed world, Clifford Armytage — once known as Merton Gill in the little hamlet of Simsbury, Illinois, where for a time, ere yet he was called to screen triumphs, he served as a humble clerk in the so-called emporium of Amos G. Gashwiler — Everything For The Home. Our Prices Always Right.

Merton Gill — so for a little time he must still be known — moodily seized the late Estelle St. Clair under his arm and withdrew from the dingy back storeroom. Down between the counters of the emporium he went with his fair burden and left her outside its portals, staring from her very definitely lashed eyes across the slumbering street at the Simsbury post office. She was tastefully arrayed in one of those new checked gingham house frocks so heatedly mentioned a moment since by her lawful owner, and across her chest Merton Gill now imposed, with no tenderness of manner, the appealing legend, "Our Latest for Milady; only $6.98." He returned for Snake le Vasquez. That outlaw's face, even out of the picture, was evil. He had been picked for the part because of this face — plump, pinkly tinted cheeks, lustrous, curling hair of some repellent composition, eyes with a hard glitter, each lash distinct in blue-black lines, and a small, tip-curled black mustache that lent the whole an offensive smirk. Garbed now in a raincoat, he, too, was posed before the emporium front, labeled "Rainproof or You Get Back Your Money." So frankly evil was his mien that Merton Gill, pausing to regard him, suffered a brief relapse into artistry.

"You fiend!" he muttered, and contemptuously smote the cynical face with an open hand.

Snake le Vasquez remained indifferent to the affront, smirking insufferably across the slumbering street at the wooden Indian proffering cigars before the establishment of Selby Brothers, Confectionery and Tobaccos.

Within the emporium the proprietor now purveyed hooks and eyes to an impatient Mrs. Leffingwell. Merton Gill, behind the opposite counter, waited upon a little girl sent for two and a quarter yards of stuff to match the sample crumpled in her damp hand. Over the suave amenities of this merchandising Amos Gashwiler glared suspiciously across the store at his employee. Their relations were still strained. Merton also glared at Amos, but discreetly, at moments when the other's back was turned or when he was blandly wishing to know of Mrs. Leffingwell if there would be something else today. Other customers entered. Trade was on.

Both Merton and Amos wore airs of cheerful briskness that deceived the public. No one could have thought that Amos was fearing his undoubtedly crazed clerk might become uncontrollable at any moment, or that the clerk was mentally parting from Amos forever in a scene of tense dramatic value in which his few dignified but scathing words would burn themselves unforgettably into the old man's brain. Merton, to himself, had often told Amos these things. Some day he'd say them right out, leaving his victim not only in the utmost confusion but in black despair of ever finding another clerk one half as efficient as Merton Gill.

The afternoon wore to closing time in a flurry of trade, during which, as Merton continued to behave sanely, the apprehension of his employer in a measure subsided. The last customer had departed from the emporium. The dummies were brought inside. The dust curtains were hung along the shelves of dry goods. There remained for Merton only the task of delivering a few groceries. He gathered these and took them out to the wagon in front. Then he changed from his store coat to his street coat and donned a rakish plush hat.

Amos was also changing from his store coat to his street coat and donning his frayed straw hat.

"See if you can't keep from actin' crazy while you make them deliveries," said Amos, not uncordially, as he lighted a choice cigar from the box which he kept hidden under a counter.

Merton wished to reply: "See here, Mr. Gashwiler, I've stood this abuse long enough! The time has come to say a few words to you —" But aloud he merely responded, "Yes, sir!"

The circumstance that he also had a cigar from the same box, hidden not so well as Amos thought, may have subdued his resentment. He would light the cigar after the first turn in the road had carried him beyond the eagle eye of its owner.

The delivery wagon outside was drawn by an elderly horse devoid of ambition or ideals. His head was sunk in dejection. He was gray at the temples, and slouched in the shafts in a loafing attitude, one forefoot negligently crossed in front of the other. He aroused himself reluctantly and with apparent difficulty when Merton Gill seized the reins and called in commanding tones, "Get on there, you old skate!" The equipage moved off under the gaze of Amos, who was locking the doors of his establishment.

Turning the first corner into a dusty side street, Merton dropped the reins and lighted the filched cigar. Other Gashwiler property was sacred to him. From all the emporium's choice stock he would have abstracted not so much as a pin; but the Gashwiler cigars, said to be "The World's Best 10c Smoke," with the picture of a dissipated clubman in evening dress on the box cover, were different, in that they were pointedly hidden from Merton. He cared little for cigars, but this was a challenge; the old boy couldn't get away with anything like that. If he didn't want his cigars touched let him leave the box out in the open like a man. Merton drew upon the lighted trophy, moistened and pasted back the wrapper that had broken when the end was bitten off, and took from the bottom of the delivery wagon the remains of a buggy whip that had been worn to half its length. With this he now tickled the bony ridges of the horse. Blows meant nothing to Dexter, but he could still be tickled into brief spurts of activity. He trotted with swaying head, sending up an effective dust screen between the wagon and a still possibly observing Gashwiler.

His deliveries made, Merton again tickled the horse to a frantic pace which continued until they neared the alley on which fronted the Gashwiler barn; there the speed was moderated to a mild amble, for Gashwiler believed his horse should be driven with tenderness, and his equally watchful wife believed it would run away if given the chance.

Merton drove into the barnyard, unhitched the horse, watered it at the half of a barrel before the iron pump, and led it into the barn, where he removed the harness. The old horse sighed noisily and shook himself with relief as the bridle was removed and a halter slipped over his venerable brow.

Ascertaining that the barnyard was vacant, Merton immediately became attentive to his charge. Throughout the late drive his attitude had been one of mild but contemptuous abuse.

More than once he had uttered the words "old skate" in tones of earnest conviction, and with the worn end of the whip he had cruelly tickled the still absurdly sensitive sides. Had beating availed he would with no compunction have beaten the drooping wreck. But now, all at once, he was curiously tender. He patted the shoulder softly, put both arms around the bony neck, and pressed his face against the face of Dexter. A moment he stood thus, then spoke in a tear-choked voice:

"Good-bye, old pal — the best, the truest pal a man ever had. You and me has seen some tough times, old pard; but you've allus brought me through without a scratch; allus brought me through." There was a sob in the speaker's voice, but he manfully recovered a clear tone of pathos. "And now, old pal, they're a-takin' ye from me — yes, we got to part, you an' me. I'm never goin' to set eyes on ye agin. But we got to be brave, old pal; we got to keep a stiff upper lip — no cryin' now; no bustin' down."

The speaker unclasped his arms and stood with head bowed, his face working curiously, striving to hold back the sobs.

For Merton Gill was once more Clifford Armytage, popular idol of the screen, in his great role of Buck Benson bidding the accustomed farewell to his four-footed pal that had brought him safely through countless dangers. How are we to know that in another couple of hundred feet of the reel Buck will escape the officers of the law who have him for that hold-up of the Wallahoola stage — of which he was innocent — leap from a second-story window of the sheriff's office onto the back of his old pal, and be carried safely over the border where the hellhounds can't touch him until his innocence is proved by Estelle St. Clair, the New York society girl, whose culture demanded a gentleman but whose heart demanded a man. How are we to know this? We only know that Buck Benson always has to kiss his horse good-bye at this spot in the drama.

Merton Gill is impressively Buck Benson. His sobs are choking him. And though Gashwiler's delivery horse is not a pinto, and could hardly get over the border ahead of a sheriff's posse, the scene is affecting.

"Good-bye, again, old pal, and God bless ye!" sobs Merton.

CHAPTER II

THAT NIGHT — THE APARTMENTS
OF CLIFFORD ARMYTAGE

MERTON GILL MEALED at the Gashwiler home. He ate his supper in moody silence, holding himself above the small gossip of the day that engaged Amos and his wife. What to him meant the announcement that Amos expected a new line of white goods on the morrow, or Mrs. Gashwiler's version of a regrettable incident occurring at that afternoon's meeting of the Entre Nous Five Hundred Club, in which the score had been juggled adversely to Mrs. Gashwiler, resulting in the loss of the first prize, a handsome fern dish, and concerning which Mrs. Gashwiler had thought it best to speak her mind? What importance could he attach to the disclosure of Metta Judson, the Gashwiler hired girl, who chatted freely during her appearances with food, that Doc Cummins had said old Grandma Foutz couldn't last out another day; that the Peter Swansons were sending clear to Chicago for Tilda's trousseau; and that Jeff Murdock had arrested one of the Giddings boys, but she couldn't learn if it was Ferd or Gus, for being drunk as a fool and busting up a bazaar out at the Oak Grove schoolhouse, and the fighting was something terrible.

Scarcely did he listen to these petty recitals. He ate in silence, and when he had finished the simple meal he begged to be excused. He begged this in a lofty, detached, somewhat weary manner, as a man of the world, excessively bored at the dull chatter but still the fastidious gentleman, might have begged it, breaking into one of the many repetitions by his hostess of just what she had said to Mrs. Judge Ellis. He was again Clifford Armytage, enacting a polished society man among yokels. He was so impressive, after rising, in his bow to Mrs. Gashwiler that Amos regarded him with a kindling suspicion.

"Say!" he called, as Merton in the hallway plucked his rakish plush hat from the mirrored rack. "You remember, now, no more o' that skylarkin' with them dummies! Them things cost money."

Merton paused. He wished to laugh sarcastically, a laugh of withering scorn. He wished to reply in polished tones, "Skylarkin'! You poor, dull clod, what do you know of my ambitions, my ideals? You, with your petty life devoted to gaining a few paltry dollars!" But he did not say this, or even register the emotion that would justly accompany such a subtitle. He merely rejoined, "All right, sir, I'm not going to touch them," and went quickly out. "Darned old grouch!" he muttered as he went down the concrete walk to the Gashwiler front gate.

Here he turned to regard the two-story brick house and the square of lawn with a concrete deer on one side of the walk, balanced by a concrete deer on the other. Before the gate was the cast-iron effigy of a small Negro in fantastic uniform, holding an iron ring aloft. The Gashwiler carriage horse had been tethered to this in the days before the Gashwiler touring car had been acquired.

"Dwelling of a country storekeeper!" muttered Merton. "That's all you are!"

This was intended to be scornful. Merton meant that on the screen it would be recognized as this and nothing more. It could not be taken for the mansion of a rich banker, or the country home of a Wall Street magnate. He felt that he had been keen in his dispraise, especially as old Gashwiler would never get the sting of it. Clod!

Three blocks brought him to the heart of the town, still throbbing faintly. He stood, irresolute, before the Giddings House. Chairs in front of this hostelry were now vacant of loafers, and a clatter of dishes came through the open windows of the dining room, where supper was on. Farther down the street Selby Brothers, Cigars and Confectionery, would be open; lights shone from the windows of the Fashion Pool Parlor across the way; the City Drug Store could still be entered; and the post office would stay open until after the mail from No. 4 was distributed. With these exceptions the shops along this mart of trade were tightly closed, including the Gashwiler Emporium, at the blind front of which Merton now glanced with the utmost distaste.

Such citizens as were yet abroad would be over at the depot to watch No. 4 go through. Merton debated joining these sightseers. Simsbury was too small to be noticed by many trains. It sprawled along the track as if it had been an afterthought of the railroad. Trains like No. 4 were apt to dash relentlessly by it without slackening speed, the mail bag being flung to the depot platform. But sometimes there would be a passenger for Simsbury, and the proud train would slow down and halt reluctantly, with a grinding of brakes, while the passenger alighted. Then a good view of the train could be had; a line of beautiful sleepers terminating in an observation car, its rear platform guarded by a brass-topped railing behind which the privileged lolled at ease; and up ahead a wonderful dining car, where dinner was being served; flitting white-clad waiters, the glitter of silver and crystal and damask, and favored beings feasting at their lordly ease, perhaps denying even a careless glance at the pitiful hamlet outside, or at most looking out impatient at the halt, or merely staring with incurious eyes while awaiting their choice foods.

Not one of these enviable persons ever betrayed any interest in Simsbury or its little group of citizens who daily gathered on the platform to do them honor. Merton Gill used to fancy that these people might shrewdly detect him to be out of place there — might perhaps take him to be an alien city man awaiting a similar proud train going the other way, standing, as he would, aloof from the obvious villagers, and having a manner, a carriage, an attire, such as further set him apart. Still, he could never be sure about this. Perhaps no one ever did single him out as a being patently of the greater world. Perhaps they considered that he was rightly of Simsbury and would continue to be a part of it all the days of his life; or perhaps they wouldn't notice him at all. They had been passing Simsburys all day, and all Simsburys and all their peoples must look very much alike to them. Very well — a day would come. There would be at Simsbury a momentous stop of No. 4 and another passenger would be in that dining car, disjoined forever from Simsbury, and he with them would stare out the polished windows at the gaping throng, and he would continue to stare with incurious eyes at still other Simsburys along the right of way, while the proud train bore him off to triumphs never dreamed of by natural-born villagers.

He decided now not to tantalize himself with a glance at this splendid means of escape from all that was sordid. He was still not a little depressed by the late unpleasantness with Gashwiler, who had thought him a crazy fool, with his revolver, his fiercely muttered words, and his holding aloft of a valuable dummy as if to threaten it with destruction. Well, some day the old grouch would eat his words; some day he would be relating to amazed listeners that he had known Merton Gill intimately at the very beginning of his astounding career. That was bound to come. But tonight Merton had no heart for the swift spectacle of No. 4. Nor even, should it halt, did he feel up to watching those indifferent, incurious passengers who little recked that a future screen idol in natty plush hat and belted coat amusedly surveyed them. Tonight he must be alone — but a day would come. Resistless Time would strike his hour!

Still he must wait for the mail before beginning his nightly study. Certain of his magazines would come tonight. He sauntered down the deserted street, pausing before the establishment of Selby Brothers. From the door of this emerged one Elmer Huff, clerk at the City Drug Store. Elmer had purchased a package of cigarettes and now offered one to Merton.

"'Lo, Mert! Have a little pill?"

"No, thanks," replied Merton firmly.

He had lately given up smoking — save those clandestine indulgences at the expense of Gashwiler — because he was saving money against his great day.

Elmer lighted one of his own little pills and made a further suggestion.

"Say, how about settin' in a little game with the gang tonight after the store closes — 10-cent limit?"

"No, thanks," replied Merton, again firmly.

He had no great liking for poker at any limit, and he would not subject his savings to a senseless hazard. Of course he might win, but you never could tell.

"Do you good," urged Elmer. "Quit at 12 sharp, with one round of roodles."

"No, I guess not," said Merton.

"We had some game last night, I'll tell the world! One hand we had four jacks out against four aces, and right after that I held four kings against an ace full. Say, one time there I was about 280 to the good, but I didn't have enough sense to quit. Hear about Gus Giddings? They got him over in the coop for breaking in on a social out at the Oak Grove schoolhouse last night. Say, he had a peach on when he left here, I'll tell the world! But he didn't get far. Them Grove lads certainly made a believer out of him. You ought to see that left eye of his!"

Merton listened loftily to this village talk, gossip of a rural sport who got a peach on and started something — And the poker game in the back room of the City Drug Store! What diversions were these for one who had a future? Let these clods live out their dull lives in their own way. But not Merton Gill, who held aloof from their low sports, studied faithfully the lessons in his film-acting course, and patiently bided his time.

He presently sauntered to the post office, where the mail was being distributed. Here he found the sightseers who had returned from the treat of No. 4's flight, and many of the less enterprising citizens who had merely come down for their mail. Gashwiler was among these, smoking one of his choice cigars. He was not allowed to smoke in the house. Merton, knowing this prohibition, strictly enforced by Mrs. Gashwiler, threw his employer a glance of honest pity. Briefly he permitted himself a vision of his own future home — a palatial bungalow in distant Hollywood, with expensive cigars in elaborate humidors and costly gold-tipped cigarettes in silver things on low tables. One might smoke freely there in every room.

Under more of the Elmer Huff sort of gossip, and the rhythmic clump of the cancelling stamp back of the drawers and boxes, he allowed himself a further glimpse of this luxurious interior. He sat on a low couch, among soft cushions, a magnificent bearskin rug beneath his feet. He smoked one of the costly cigarettes and chatted with a young lady interviewer from *Photo Land*.

"You ask of my wife," he was saying. "But she is more than a wife — she is my best pal, and, I may add, she is also my severest critic."

He broke off here, for an obsequious Japanese butler entered with a tray of cooling drinks. The tray would be gleaming silver, but he was uncertain about the drinks; something with long straws in them, probably. But as to anything alcoholic, now — while he was trying to determine this the general-delivery window was opened and the interview had to wait. But, anyway, you could smoke where you wished in that house, and Gashwiler couldn't smoke any closer to his house than the front porch. Even trying it there he would be nagged, and fussily asked why he didn't go out to the barn. He was a poor fish, Gashwiler; a country storekeeper without a future. A clod!

Merton, after waiting in line, obtained his mail, consisting of three magazines — *Photo Land, Silver Screenings*, and *Camera*. As he stepped away he saw that Miss Tessie Kearns stood three places back in the line. He waited at the door for her. Miss Kearns was the one soul in Simsbury who understood him. He had confided to her all his vast ambitions; she had sympathized with them, and her never-failing encouragement had done not a little to stiffen his resolution at odd times when the haven of Hollywood seemed all too distant. A certain community of ambitions had been the foundation of this sympathy between the two, for Tessie Kearns meant to become a scenario writer of eminence, and, like Merton, she was now both studying and practicing a difficult art. She conducted the millinery and dress-making establishment next to the Gashwiler Emporium, but found time, as did Merton, for the worthwhile things outside her narrow life.

She was a slight, spare little figure, sedate and mouselike, of middle age and, to the village, of a quiet, sober way of thought. But, known only to Merton, her real life was one of terrific adventure, involving crime of the most atrocious sort, and contact not only with the great and good, but with loathsome denizens of the underworld who would commit any deed for hire. Some of her scenarios would have profoundly shocked the good people of Simsbury, and she often suffered tremors of apprehension at the thought that one of them might be enacted at the Bijou Palace right there on Fourth Street, with her name brazenly announced as author. Suppose it were *Passion's Perils*! She would surely have to leave town after that! She would be too ashamed to stay. Still she would be proud, also, for by that time they would be calling her to Hollywood itself. Of course nothing so distressing — or so grand — had happened yet, for none of her dramas had been accepted; but she was coming on. It might happen any time.

She joined Merton, a long envelope in her hand and a brave little smile on her pinched face.

"Which one is it?" he asked, referring to the envelope.

"It's *Passion's Perils*," she answered with a jaunty affectation of amusement. "The Touchstone-Blatz people sent it back. The slip says its being returned does not imply any lack of merit."

"I should think it wouldn't!" said Merton warmly.

He knew *Passion's Perils*. A company might have no immediate need for it, but its rejection could not possibly imply a lack of merit, because the merit was there. No one could dispute that.

They walked on to the Bijou Palace. Its front was dark, for only twice a week, on Tuesdays and Saturdays, could Simsbury muster a picture audience; but they could read the bills for the following night. The entrance was flanked on either side by billboards, and they stopped before the first. Merton Gill's heart quickened its beats, for there was billed none other than Beulah Baxter in the ninth installment of her tremendous serial, *The Hazards of Hortense*.

It was going to be good! It almost seemed that this time the scoundrels would surely get Hortense. She was speeding across a vast open quarry in a bucket attached to a cable, and one of the scoundrels with an ax was viciously hacking at the cable's farther anchorage. It would be a miracle if he did not succeed in his hellish design to dash Hortense to the cruel rocks below. Merton, of course, had not a moment's doubt that the miracle would intervene; he had seen other serials. So he made no comment upon the gravity of the situation, but went at once to the heart of his ecstasy.

"The most beautiful woman on the screen," he murmured.

"Well, I don't know."

Miss Kearns appeared about to advance the claims of rival beauties, but desisted when she saw that Merton was firm.

"None of the rest can touch her," he maintained. "And look at her nerve! Would your others have as much nerve as that?"

"Maybe she has someone to double in those places," suggested the screen-wise Tessie Kearns.

"Not Beulah Baxter. Didn't I see her personal appearance that time I went to Peoria last spring on purpose to see it? Didn't she talk about the risks she took and how the directors were always begging her to use a double and how her artistic convictions wouldn't let her do any such thing? You can bet the little girl is right there in every scene!"

They passed to the other billboard. This would be the comedy. A painfully cross-eyed man in misfitting clothes was doing something supposed to be funny — pushing a lawn mower over the carpet of a palatial home.

"How disgusting!" exclaimed Miss Kearns.

"Ain't it?" said Merton. "How they can have one of those terrible things on the same bill with Miss Baxter — I can't understand it."

"Those censors ought to suppress this sort of buffoonery instead of scenes of dignified passion like they did in *Scarlet Sin*," declared Tessie. "Did you read about that?"

"They sure ought," agreed Merton. "These comedies make me tired. I never see one if I can help it."

Walking on, they discussed the wretched public taste and the wretched actors that pandered to it. The slapstick comedy, they held, degraded a fine and beautiful art. Merton was especially severe. He always felt uncomfortable at one of these regrettable exhibitions when people about him who knew no better laughed heartily. He had never seen anything to laugh at, and said as much.

They crossed the street and paused at the door of Miss Kearns's shop, behind which were her living rooms. She would tonight go over Passion's Perils once more and send it to another company.

"I wonder," she said to Merton, "if they keep sending it back because the sets are too expensive. Of course there's the one where the dissipated English nobleman, Count Blessingham, lures Valerie into Westminster Abbey for his own evil purposes on the night of the old earl's murder — that's expensive — but they get a chance to use it again when Valerie is led to the altar by young Lord Stonecliff, the rightful heir. And of course Stonecliff Manor, where Valerie is first seen as governess, would be expensive; but they use that in a lot of scenes, too. Still, maybe I might change the locations around to something they've got built."

"I wouldn't change a line," said Merton. "Don't give in to 'em. Make 'em take it as it is. They might ruin your picture with cheap stuff."

"Well," the authoress debated, "maybe I'll leave it. I'd especially hate to give up Westminster Abbey. Of course the scene where she is struggling with Count Blessingham might easily be made offensive — it's a strong scene — but it all comes right. You remember she wrenches herself loose from his grasp and rushes to throw herself before the altar, which suddenly lights up, and the scoundrel is afraid to pursue her there, because he had a thorough religious training when a boy at Oxford, and he feels it would be sacrilegious to seize her again while the light from the altar shines upon her that way, and so she's saved for the time being. It seems kind of a shame not to use Westminster Abbey for a really big scene like that, don't you think?"

"I should say so!" agreed Merton warmly. "They build plenty of sets as big as that. Keep it in!"

"Well, I'll take your advice. And I shan't give up trying with my other ones. And I'm writing to another set of people — see here." She took from her handbag a clipped advertisement which she read to Merton in the fading light, holding it close to her keen little eyes. "Listen! '5,000 photoplay ideas needed. Working girl paid $10,000 for ideas she had thought worthless. Yours may be worth more. Experience unnecessary. Information free. Producers' League 562, Piqua, Ohio.' Doesn't that sound encouraging? And it isn't as if I didn't have some experience. I've been writing scenarios for two years now."

"We both got to be patient," he pointed out. "We can't succeed all at once, just remember that."

"Oh, I'm patient, and I'm determined; and I know you are, too, Merton. But the way my things keep coming back — well, I guess we'd both get discouraged if it wasn't for our sense of humor."

"I bet we would," agreed Merton. "And good-night!"

He went on to the Gashwiler Emporium and let himself into the dark store. At the moment he was bewailing that the next installment of *The Hazards of Hortense* would be shown on a Saturday night, for on those nights the store kept open until nine and he could see it but once. On a Tuesday night he would have watched it twice, in spite of the so-called comedy unjustly sharing the bill with it.

Lighting a match, he made his way through the silent store, through the stock room that had so lately been the foul lair of Snake le Vasquez, and into his own personal domain, a square partitioned off from the stockroom in which were his cot, the table at which he studied the art of screen acting, and his other little belongings. He often called this his den. He lighted a lamp on the table and drew the chair up to it.

On the boards of the partition in front of him were pasted many presentments of his favorite screen actress, Beulah Baxter, as she underwent the nerve-racking *Hazards of Hortense*. The intrepid girl was seen leaping from the seat of her high-powered car to the cab of a passing locomotive, her chagrined pursuers in the distant background. She sprang from a high cliff into the chill waters of a storm-tossed sea. Bound to the back of a spirited horse, she was raced down the steep slope of a rocky ravine in the Far West. Alone in a foul den of the underworld she held at bay a dozen villainous Asiatics. Down the fire escape of a great New York hotel she made a perilous way. From the shrouds of a tossing ship she was about to plunge to a watery release from the persecutor who was almost upon her. Upon the roof of the Fifth Avenue mansion of her scoundrelly guardian in the great city of New York she was gaining the friendly projection of a cornice from which she could leap and again escape death — even a fate worse than death, for the girl was pursued from all sorts of base motives. This time, friendless and alone in profligate New York, she would leap from the cornice to the branches of the great eucalyptus tree that grew hard by. Unnerving performances like these were a constant inspiration to Merton Gill. He knew that he was not yet fit to act in such scenes — to appear opportunely in the last reel of each installment and save Hortense for the next one. But he was confident a day would come.

On the same wall he faced also a series of photographs of himself. These were stills to be one day shown to a director who would thereupon perceive his screen merits. There was Merton in the natty belted coat, with his hair slicked back in the approved mode and a smile upon his face; a happy, careless college youth. There was Merton in tennis flannels, his hair nicely disarranged, jauntily holding a borrowed racquet. Here he was in a trench coat and the cap of a lieutenant, grim of face, the jaw set, holding a revolver upon someone unpictured; there in a wide-collared sport shirt lolling negligently upon a bench after a hard game of polo or something. Again he appeared in evening dress, two straightened fingers resting against his left temple. Underneath this was written in a running, angular, distinguished hand, "Very truly yours, Clifford Armytage." This, and prints of it similarly inscribed, would one day go to unknown admirers who besought him for likenesses of himself.

But Merton lost no time in scanning these pictorial triumphs. He was turning the pages of the magazines he had brought, his first hasty search being for new photographs of his heroine. He was quickly rewarded. *Silver Screenings* proffered some fresh views of Beulah Baxter, not in dangerous moments, but revealing certain quieter aspects of her wondrous life. In her kitchen, apron clad, she stirred something. In her lofty music room she was seated at her piano. In her charming library she was shown "Among Her Books." More charmingly she was portrayed with her beautiful arms about the shoulders of her dear old mother. And these accompanied an interview with the actress.

The writer, one Esther Schwarz, professed the liveliest trepidation at first meeting the screen idol, but was swiftly reassured by the unaffected cordiality of her reception. She found that success had not spoiled Miss Baxter. A sincere artist, she yet absolutely lacked the usual temperament and mannerisms. She seemed more determined than ever to give the public something better and finer. Her splendid dignity, reserve, humanness, high ideals, and patient study of her art had but mellowed, not hardened, a gracious personality. Merton Gill received these assurances without surprise. He knew Beulah Baxter would prove to be these delightful things. He read on for the more exciting bits.

"I'm so interested in my work," prettily observed Miss Baxter to the interviewer; "suppose we talk only of that. Leave out all the rest — my Beverly Hills home, my cars, my jewels, my Paris gowns, my dogs, my servants, my recreations. It is work alone that counts, don't you think? We must learn that success, all that is beautiful and fine, requires work, infinite work and struggle. The beautiful comes only through suffering and sacrifice. And of course dramatic work broadens a girl's viewpoint, helps her to get the real, the worthwhile things out of life, enriching her nature with the emotional experience of her roles. It is through such pressure that we grow, and we must grow, must we not? One must strive for the ideal, for the art which will be but the pictorial expression of that, and for the emotion which must be touched by the illuminating vision of a well-developed imagination if the vital message of the film is to be felt.

"But of course I have my leisure moments from the grinding stress. Then I turn to my books — I'm wild about history. And how I love the great free out-of-doors! I should prefer to be on a simple farm, were I a boy. The public would not have me a boy, you say" — she shrugged prettily —" oh, of course, my beauty, as they are pleased to call it. After all, why should one not speak of that? Beauty is just a stock in trade, you know. Why not acknowledge it frankly? But do come to my delightful kitchen, where I spend many a spare moment, and see the lovely custard I have made for dear mamma's luncheon."

Merton Gill was entranced by this exposition of the quieter side of his idol's life. Of course he had known she could not always be making narrow escapes, and it seemed that she was almost more delightful in this staid domestic life. Here, away from her professional perils, she was, it seemed, "a slim little girl with sad eyes and a wistful mouth."

The picture moved him strongly. More than ever he was persuaded that his day would come. Even might come the day when it would be his lot to lighten the sorrow of those eyes and appease the wistfulness of that tender mouth. He was less sure about this. He had been unable to learn if Beulah Baxter was still unwed. *Silver Screenings*, in reply to his question, had answered, "Perhaps." *Camera*, in its answers to correspondents, had said, "Not now." Then he had written to *Photo Land*: "Is Beulah Baxter unmarried?" The answer had come, "Twice." He had been able to make little of these replies, enigmatic, ambiguous, at best. But he felt that some day he would at least be chosen to act with this slim little girl with the sad eyes and wistful mouth. He, it might be, would rescue her from the branches of the great eucalyptus tree growing hard by the Fifth Avenue mansion of the scoundrelly guardian. This, if he remembered well her message about hard work.

He recalled now the wondrous occasion on which he had travelled the nearly hundred miles to Peoria to see his idol in the flesh. Her personal appearance had been advertised. It was on a Saturday night, but Merton had silenced old Gashwiler with the tale of a dying aunt in the distant city. Even so, the old grouch had been none too considerate. He had seemed to believe that Merton's aunt should have died nearer to Simsbury, or at least have chosen a dull Monday.

But Merton had held with dignity to the point; a dying aunt wasn't to be hustled about as to either time or place. She died when her time came — even on a Saturday night — and where she happened to be, though it were a hundred miles from some point more convenient to an utter stranger. He had gone and thrillingly had beheld for five minutes his idol in the flesh, the slim little girl of the sorrowful eyes and wistful mouth, as she told the vast audience — it seemed to Merton that she spoke solely to him — by what narrow chance she had been saved from disappointing it. She had missed the train, but had at once leaped into her high-powered roadster and made the journey at an average of 65 miles an hour, braving death a dozen times. For her public was dear to her, and she would not have it disappointed, and there she was before them in her trim driving suit, still breathless from the wild ride.

Then she told them — Merton especially — how her directors had again and again besought her not to persist in risking her life in her dangerous exploits, but to allow a double to take her place at the more critical moments. But she had never been able to bring herself to this deception, for deception, in a way, it would be. The directors had entreated in vain. She would keep faith with her public, though full well she knew that at any time one of her dare-devil acts might prove fatal.

Her public was very dear to her. She was delighted to meet it here, face to face, heart to heart. She clasped her own slender hands over her own heart as she said this, and there was a pathetic little catch in her voice as she waved farewell kisses to the throng. Many a heart besides Merton's beat more quickly at knowing that she must rush out to the high-powered roadster and be off at 80 miles an hour to St. Louis, where another vast audience would the next day be breathlessly awaiting her personal appearance.

Merton had felt abundantly repaid for his journey. There had been inspiration in this contact. Little he minded the acid greeting, on his return, of a mere Gashwiler, spawning in his low mind a monstrous suspicion that the dying aunt had never lived.

Now he read in his magazines other intimate interviews by other talented young women who had braved the presence of other screen idols of both sexes. The interviewers approached them with trepidation, and invariably found that success had not spoiled them. Fine artists though they were, applauded and richly rewarded, yet they remained simple, unaffected, and cordial to these daring reporters. They spoke with quiet dignity of their work, their earnest efforts to give the public something better and finer. They wished the countless readers of the interviews to comprehend that their triumphs had come only with infinite work and struggle, that the beautiful comes only through suffering and sacrifice. At lighter moments they spoke gayly of their palatial homes, their domestic pets, their wives or husbands and their charming children. They all loved the great out-of-doors, but their chief solace from toil was in this unruffled domesticity where they could forget the worries of an exacting profession and lead a simple home life. All the husbands and wives were more than that — they were good pals; and of course they read and studied a great deal. Many of them were wild about books.

He was especially interested in the interview printed by *Camera* with that world favorite, Harold Parmalee. For this was the screen artist whom Merton most envied, and whom he conceived himself most to resemble in feature. The lady interviewer, Miss Augusta Blivens, had gone trembling into the presence of Harold Parmalee, to be instantly put at her ease by the young artist's simple, unaffected manner. He chatted of his early struggles when he was only too glad to accept the few paltry hundreds of dollars a week that were offered him in minor parts; of his quick rise to eminence; of his unceasing effort to give the public something better and finer; of his love for the great out-of-doors; and of his daily flight to the little nest that sheltered his pal wife and the kiddies. Here he could be truly himself, a man's man, loving the simple things of life. Here, in his library, surrounded by his books, or in the music room playing over some little Chopin prelude, or on the lawn romping with the giant police dog, he could forget the public that would not let him rest. Nor had he been spoiled in the least, said the interviewer, by the adulation poured out upon him by admiring women and girls in volume sufficient to turn the head of a less sane young man.

"There are many beautiful women in the world." pursued the writer, "and I dare say there is not one who meets Harold Parmalee who does not love him in one way or another. He has mental brilliancy for the intellectuals, good looks for the empty-headed, a strong vital appeal, a magnetism almost overwhelming to the susceptible, and an easy and supremely appealing courtesy for every woman he encounters."

Merton drew a long breath after reading these earnest words. Would an interviewer some day be writing as much about him? He studied the pictures of Harold Parmalee that abundantly spotted the article. The full face, the profile, the symmetrical shoulders, the jaunty bearing, the easy, masterful smile. From each of these he would raise his eyes to his own pictured face on the wall above him. Undoubtedly he was not unlike Harold Parmalee. He noted little similarities. He had the nose, perhaps a bit more jutting than Harold's, and the chin, even more prominent.

Possibly a director would have told him that his Harold Parmalee beauty was just a trifle overdone; that his face went just a bit past the line of pleasing resemblance and into something else. But at this moment the aspirant was reassured. His eyes were pale, under pale brows, yet they showed well in the prints. And he was slightly built, perhaps even thin, but a diet rich in fats would remedy that. And even if he were quite a little less comely than Parmalee, he would still be impressive. After all, a great deal depended upon the acting, and he was learning to act.

Months ago, the resolution big in his heart, he had answered the advertisement in *Silver Screenings*, urging him to "Learn Movie Acting, a fascinating profession that pays big. Would you like to know," it demanded, "if you are adapted to this work? If so, send 10 cents for our 10-Hour Talent-Prover, or Key to Movie-Acting Aptitude, and find whether you are suited to take it up."

Merton had earnestly wished to know this, and had sent 10 cents to the Film Incorporation Bureau, Station N, Stebbinsville, Arkansas. The Talent-Prover, or Key to Movie-Acting Aptitude, had come; he had mailed his answers to the questions and waited an anguished 10 days, fearing that he would prove to lack the required aptitude for this great art. But at last the cheering news had come. He had every aptitude in full measure, and all that remained was to subscribe to the correspondence course.

He had felt weak in the moment of his relief from this torturing anxiety. Suppose they had told him that he wouldn't do? And he had studied the lessons with unswerving determination. Night and day he had held to his ideal. He knew that when you did this your hour was bound to come.

He yawned now, thinking, instead of the anger expressions he should have been practicing, of the sordid things he must do tomorrow. He must be up at five, sprinkle the floor, sweep it, take down the dust curtains from the shelves of dry goods, clean and fill the lamps, then station outside the dummies in their raiment. All day he would serve customers, snatching a hasty lunch of crackers and cheese behind the grocery counter. And at night, instead of twice watching *The Hazards of Hortense*, he must still unreasonably serve late customers until the second unwinding of those delectable reels.

He suddenly sickened of it all. Was he not sufficiently versed in the art he had chosen to practice? And old Gashwiler every day getting harder to bear! His resolve stiffened. He would not wait much longer — only until the savings hidden out under the grocery counter had grown a bit. He made ready for bed, taking, after he had undressed, some dumbbell exercises that would make his shoulders a trifle more like Harold Parmalee's. This rite concluded, he knelt by his narrow cot and prayed briefly.

"Oh, God, make me a good movie actor! Make me one of the best! For Jesus'sake, amen!"

CHAPTER III

WESTERN STUFF

SATURDAY PROVED ALL that his black forebodings had pictured it — a day of sordid, harassing toil; toil, moreover, for which Gashwiler, the beneficiary, showed but the scantest appreciation. Indeed, the day opened with a disagreement between the forward-looking clerk and his hide-bound reactionary. Gashwiler had reached the store at his accustomed hour of 8:30 to find Merton embellishing the bulletin board in front with legends setting forth especial bargains of the day to be had within.

Chalk in hand, he had neatly written, "See our new importation of taffetas, $2.59 the yard." Below this he was in the act of putting down, "Try our choice Honey-dew spinach, 20 cts. the can." "Try our Preferred Chipped Beef, 58 cts. the pound."

He was especially liking that use of "the." It sounded modern. Yet along came Gashwiler, as if seeking an early excuse to nag, and criticized this.

"Why don't you say 'a yard,' 'a can,' 'a pound'?" he demanded harshly. "What's the sense of that there 'the' stuff? Looks to me like just putting on a few airs. You keep to plain language and our patrons'll like it a lot better." Viciously Merton Gill rubbed out the modern "the" and substituted the desired "a."

"Very well," he assented, "if you'd rather stick to the old-fashioned way; but I can tell you that's the way city stores do it. I thought you might want to be up to date, but I see I made a great mistake."

"Humph!" said Gashwiler, unbitten by this irony. "I guess the old way's good enough, long's our prices are always right. Don't forget to put on that canned salmon. I had that in stock for nearly a year now — and say it's 20 cents 'a' can, not 'the' can. Also say it's a grand reduction from 35 cents."

That was always the way. You never could please the old grouch. And so began the labor that lasted until nine that night. Merton must count out eggs and weigh butter that was brought in. He must do up sugar and grind coffee and measure dress goods and match silks; he must with the suavest gentility ask if there would not be something else today; and he must see that babies hazardously left on counters did not roll off.

He lived in a vortex of mental confusion, performing his tasks mechanically. When drawing a gallon of kerosene or refolding the shown dress goods, or at any task not requiring him to be genially talkative, he would be saying to Miss Augusta Blivens in far-off Hollywood, "Yes, my wife is more than a wife. She is my best pal, and, I may also add, my severest critic."

There was but one break in the dreary monotony, and that was when Lowell Hardy, Simsbury's highly artistic photographer, came in to leave an order for groceries. Lowell wore a soft hat with rakish brim, and affected low collars and flowing cravats, the artistic effect of these being heightened in his studio work by a purple velvet jacket. Even in Gashwiler's he stood out as an artist. Merton received his order, and noting that Gashwiler was beyond earshot bespoke his services for the following afternoon.

"Say, Lowell, be on the lot at two sharp tomorrow, will you? I want to shoot some Western stuff — some stills."

Merton thrilled as he used these highly technical phrases. He had not read his magazines for nothing.

Lowell Hardy considered, then consented. He believed that he, too, might some day be called to Hollywood after they had seen the sort of work he could turn out. He always finished his art studies of Merton with great care, and took pains to have the artist's signature entirely legible. "All right, Mert, I'll be there. I got some new patent paper I'll try out on these."

"On the lot at two sharp to shoot Western stuff," repeated Merton with relish.

"Right — o!" assented Lowell, and returned to more prosaic studio art.

The day wore itself to a glad end. The last exigent customer had gone, the curtains were up, the lights were out, and at five minutes past nine the released slave, meeting Tessie Kearns at her front door, escorted her with a high heart to the second show at the Bijou Palace. They debated staying out until after the wretched comedy had been run, but later agreed that they should see this, as Tessie keenly wished to know why people laughed at such things. The antics of the painfully cross-eyed man distressed them both, though the mental inferiors by whom they were surrounded laughed noisily. Merton wondered how any producer could bring himself to debase so great an art, and Tessie wondered if she hadn't, in a way, been aiming over the public's head with her scenarios. After all, you had to give the public what it wanted. She began to devise comedy elements for her next drama.

But *The Hazards of Hortense* came mercifully to soothe their annoyance. The slim little girl with a wistful smile underwent a rich variety of hazards, each threatening a terrible death. Through them all she came unscathed, leaving behind her a trail of infuriated scoundrels whom she had thwarted. She escaped from an underworld den in a Chicago slum just in the nick of time, cleverly concealing herself in the branches of the great eucalyptus tree that grew hard by, while her maddened pursuers scattered in their search for the prize. Again she was captured, this time to be conveyed by airplane, a helpless prisoner and subject to the most fiendish insults by Black Steve, to the frozen North. But in the far Alaskan wilds she eluded the fiends and drove swiftly over the frozen wastes with their only dog team. Having left her pursuers far behind, she decided to rest for the night in a deserted cabin along the way. Here a blizzard drove snow through the chinks between the logs, and a pack of fierce wolves besieged her. She tried to bar the door, but the bar was gone. At that moment she heard a call. Could it be Black Steve again? No, thank heaven! The door was pushed open and there stood Ralph Murdock, her fiancé. There was a quick embrace and words of cheer from Ralph. They must go on.

But no, the wind cut like a knife, and the wolves still prowled. The film here showed a running insert of cruel wolves exposing all their fangs. Ralph had lost his rifle. He went now to put his arm through the iron loops in place of the missing bar. The wolves sought to push open the door, but Ralph's arm foiled them.

Then the outside of the cabin was shown, with Black Steve and his three ugly companions furtively approaching. The wolves had gone, but human wolves, 10,000 times more cruel, had come in their place. Back in the cabin Ralph and Hortense discovered that the wolves had gone. It had an ugly look. Why should the wolves go? Ralph opened the door and they both peered out. There in the shadow of a eucalyptus tree stood Black Steve and his dastardly crew. They were about to storm the cabin. All was undoubtedly lost.

Not until the following week would the world learn how Hortense and her manly fiancé had escaped this trap. Again had Beulah Baxter striven and suffered to give the public something better and finer.

"A wonder girl," declared Merton when they were again in the open. "That's what I call her — a wonder girl. And she owes it all to hard, unceasing struggle and work and pains and being careful. You ought to read that new interview with her in this month's Silver Screenings."

"Yes, yes, she's wonderful," assented Tessie as they strolled to the door of her shop. "But I've been thinking about comedy. You know my new one I'm writing — of course it's a big, vital theme, all about a heartless wife with her mind wholly on society and bridge clubs and dancing and that sort of dissipation, and her husband is Hubert Glendenning, a studious young lawyer who doesn't like to go out evenings but would rather play with the kiddies a bit after their mother has gone to a party, or read over some legal documents in the library, which is very beautifully furnished; and her old school friend, Corona Bartlett, comes to stay at the house, a very voluptuous type, high colored, with black hair and lots of turquoise jewellery, and she's a bad woman through and through, and been divorced and everything by a man whose heart she broke, and she's become a mere adventuress with a secret vice — she takes perfume in her tea, like I saw that one did — and all her evil instincts are aroused at once by Hubert, who doesn't really care deeply for her, as she has only a surface appeal of mere sensuous beauty; but he sees that his wife is neglecting him and having an affair with an Italian count — I found such a good name for him, Count Ravioli — and staying out with him until all hours; so in a moment of weakness he gives himself to Corona Bartlett, and then sees that he must break up his home and get a divorce and marry Corona to make an honest woman of her; but of course his wife is brought to her senses, so she sees that she has been in the wrong and has a big scene with Corona in which she scorns her and Corona slinks away, and she forgives Hubert his one false step because it was her fault. It's full of big situations, but what I'm wondering — I'm wondering if I couldn't risk some comedy in it by having the faithful old butler a cross-eyed man. Nothing so outrageous as that creature we just saw, but still noticeably cross-eyed. Do you think it would lighten some of the grimmer scenes, perhaps, and wouldn't it be good pathos to have the butler aware of his infirmity and knowing the greatest surgeons in the world can't help him?"

"Well," Merton considered, "if I were you I shouldn't chance it. It would be mere acrobatic humor. And why do you want any one to be funny when you have a big gripping thing of love and hate like that? I don't believe I'd have him cross-eyed. I'd have him elderly and simple and dignified. And you don't want your audience to laugh, do you, when he holds up both hands to show how shocked he is at the way things are going on in that house?"

"Well, maybe I won't then. It was just a thought. I believe you have the right instinct in those matters, Merton. I'll leave him as he is."

"Good-night, then," said Merton. "I got to be on the lot tomorrow. My camera man's coming at two. Shooting some Western stuff."

"Oh, my! Really?"

Tessie gazed after him admiringly. He let himself into the dark store, so lately the scene of his torment, and on the way to his little room stopped to reach under the grocery counter for those hidden savings. Tonight he would add to them the 15 dollars lavished upon him by Gashwiler at the close of a week's toil. The money was in a tobacco pouch. He lighted the lamp on his table, placed the three new bills beside it and drew out the hoard. He would count it to confirm his memory of the grand total.

The bills were frayed, lacking the fresh green of new ones; weary looking, with an air of being glad to rest at last after much passing from hand to hand as symbols of wealth. Their exalted present owner tenderly smoothed out several that had become crumpled, secured them in a neat pile, adding the three recently acquired five-dollar bills, and proceeded to count, moistening the ends of a thumb and finger in defiance of the best sanitary teaching. It was no time to think of malignant bacteria.

By his remembered count he should now be possessed of 212 dollars. And there was the two-dollar bill, a limp, gray thing, abraded almost beyond identification. He placed this down first, knowing that the remaining bills should amount to 210 dollars. Slowly he counted, to finish with a look of blank, hesitating wonder. He made another count, hastily, but taking greater care. The wonder grew. Again he counted, slowly this time, so that there could be no doubt. And now he knew! He possessed 33 dollars more than he had thought. Knowing this was right, he counted again for the luxury of it: 245 obvious dollars!

How had he lost count? He tried to recall. He could remember taking out the money he had paid Lowell Hardy for the last batch of Clifford Armytage stills — for Lowell, although making professional rates to Merton, still believed the artist to be worth his hire — and he could remember taking some more out to send to the mail-order house in Chicago for the cowboy things; but it was plain that he had twice, at least, crowded a week's salary into the pouch and forgotten it.

It was a pleasurable experience; it was like finding 33 dollars. And he was by that much nearer to his goal; that much sooner would he be released from bondage; 33 dollars sooner could he look Gashwiler in the eye and say what he thought of him and his emporium. In his nightly prayer he did not neglect to render thanks for this.

He dressed the next morning with a new elation. He must be more careful about keeping tab on his money, but also it was wonderful to find more than you expected. He left the storeroom that reeked of kerosene and passed into the emporium to replace his treasure in its hiding place. The big room was dusky behind the drawn front curtains, but all the smells were there — the smell of ground coffee and spices at the grocery counter, farther on, the smothering smell of prints and woolens and new leather.

The dummies, waiting down by the door to be put outside, regarded each other in blank solemnity. A few big flies droned lazily about their still forms. Merton eyed the dusty floor, the gleaming counters, the curtains that shielded the shelves, with a new disdain. Sooner than he had thought he would bid them a last farewell. And today, at least, he was free of them — free to be on the lot at two, to shoot Western stuff. Let tomorrow, with its old round of degrading tasks, take care of itself.

At 10:30 he was in church. He was not as attentive to the sermon as he should have been, for it now occurred to him that he had no stills of himself in the garb of a clergyman. This was worth considering, because he was not going to be one of those one-part actors. He would have a wide range of roles. He would be able to play anything. He wondered how the Rev. Otto Carmichael would take the request for a brief loan of one of his pulpit suits. Perhaps he was not so old as he looked; perhaps he might remember that he, too, had once been young and fired with high ideals. It would be worth trying. And the things could be returned after a brief studio session with Lowell Hardy. He saw himself cast in such a part, the handsome young clergyman, exponent of a muscular Christianity. He comes to the toughest cattle town in all the great Southwest, determined to make honest men and good women of its sinning derelicts. He wins the hearts of these rugged but misguided souls. Though at first they treat him rough, they learn to respect him, and they call him the fighting parson. Eventually he wins the hand in marriage of the youngest of the dance hall denizens, a sweet young girl who despite her evil surroundings has remained as pure and good as she is beautiful.

Anyway, if he had those clothes for an hour or two while the artist made a few studies of him he would have something else to show directors in search of fresh talent.

After church he ate a lonely meal served by Metta Judson at the Gashwiler residence. The Gashwilers were on their accustomed Sabbath visit to the distant farm of Mrs. Gashwiler's father. But as he ate he became conscious that the Gashwiler influence was not wholly withdrawn. From above the mantel he was sternly regarded by a tinted enlargement of his employer's face entitled *Photographic Study* by Lowell Hardy. Lowell never took photographs merely. He made photographic studies, and the specimen at hand was one of his most daring efforts. Merton glared at it in free hostility — a clod, with ideals as false as the artist's pink on his leathery cheeks! He hurried his meal, glad to be relieved from the inimical scrutiny.

He was glad to be free from this and from the determined recital by Metta Judson of small-town happenings. What cared he that Gus Giddings had been fined ten dollars and costs by Squire Belcher for his low escapade, or that Gus's father had sworn to lick him within an inch of his life if he ever ketched him touching stimmilints again?

He went to the barn, climbed to the hayloft, and undid the bundle containing his Buck Benson outfit. This was fresh from the mail-order house in Chicago. He took out almost reverently a pair of high-heeled boots with purple tops, a pair of spurs, a gay shirt, a gayer neckerchief, a broad-brimmed hat, a leather holster, and — most impressive of all — a pair of goatskin chaps dyed a violent maroon. All these he excitedly donned, the spurs last. Then he clambered down the ladder from the loft, somewhat impeded by the spurs, and went into the kitchen. Metta Judson, washing dishes, gave a little cry of alarm. Nothing like this had ever before invaded the Gashwiler home by front door or back.

"Why, Mert' Gill, whatever you dressed up like that for? My stars, you look like a cowboy or something! Well, I must say!"

"Say, Metta, do me a favor. I want to see how these things look in a glass. It's a cowboy outfit for when I play regular Buck Benson parts, and everything's got to be just so or the audience writes to the magazines about it and makes fun of you."

"Go ahead," said Metta. "You can git a fine look at yourself in the tall glass in the old lady's bedroom."

Forthwith he went, profaning a sanctuary, to survey himself in a glass that had never reflected anything but the discreet arraying of his employer's lady. He looked long and earnestly. The effect was quite all he had hoped. He lowered the front of the broad-brimmed hat the least bit, tightened his belt another notch and moved the holster to a better line. He looked again. From feet to head he was perfect.

Then, slightly crouching, he drew his revolver from the holster and held it forward from the hip, wrist and forearm rigidly straight.

"Throw up your hands!"

He uttered the grim words in a low tone, but one facing him would not have been deceived by low tones. Steely-eyed, grim of face, relentless in all his bearing, the most desperate adversary would have quailed. Probably even Gashwiler himself would have quailed. When Buck Benson looked and spoke thus he meant it.

He held it a long, breathless moment before relaxing. Then he tiptoed softly from the hallowed confines of a good woman's boudoir and clattered down the back stairs to the kitchen. He was thinking: "I certainly got to get me another gun if I'm ever going to do Two-Gun Benson parts, and I got to get the draw down better. I ain't quick enough yet."

"Well, did you like your rig?" inquired Metta genially.

"Oh, it'll do for the stills we're shooting today," replied the actor. "Of course I ought to have a rattlesnake-skin band on my hat, and the things look too new yet. And say, Metta, where's the clothesline? I want to practice roping a little before my camera man gets here."

"My stars! You're certainly goin' to be a real one, ain't you?"

She brought him the clothesline, in use only on Mondays. He re-coiled it carefully and made a running noose in one end.

At two Lowell Hardy found his subject casting the rope at an inattentive Dexter. The old horse stood in the yard, head down, one foot crossed nonchalantly before the other. A slight tremor, a nervous flickering of his skin, was all that ensued when the rope grazed him. When it merely fell in his general neighborhood, as it oftener did, Dexter did not even glance up.

"Good stuff!" applauded the artist. "Now just stand that way, holding the noose out. I want to make a study of that."

He rapidly mounted his camera on a tripod and put in a plate. The study was made. Followed several studies of the fighting face of Two-Gun Benson, grim and rigid, about to shoot from the hip. But these were minor bits. More important would be Buck Benson and his old pal, Pinto. From the barn Merton dragged the saddle, blanket, and bridle he had borrowed from the Giddings House livery stable. He had never saddled a horse before, but he had not studied in vain. He seized Dexter by a wisp of his surviving mane and simultaneously planted a hearty kick in the beast's side, with a command, "Get around there, you old skate!" Dexter sighed miserably and got around as ordered. He was both pained and astonished. He knew that this was Sunday. Never had he been forced to work on this day. But he meekly suffered the protrusion of a bit between his yellow teeth, and shuddered but slightly when a blanket and then a heavy saddle were flung across his back. True, he looked up in some dismay when the girth was tightened. Not once in all his years had he been saddled. He was used to having things loose around his waist.

The girth went still tighter. Dexter glanced about with genuine concern. Someone was intending to harm him. He curved his swanlike neck and snapped savagely at the shoulder of his aggressor, who kicked him again in the side and yelled, "Whoa, there, dang you!"

Dexter subsided. He saw it was no use. Whatever queer thing they meant to do to him would be done despite all his resistance. Still his alarm had caused him to hold up his head now. He was looking much more like a horse.

"There!" said Merton Gill, and as a finishing touch he lashed the coiled clothesline to the front of the saddle. "Now, here! Get me this way. This is one of the best things I do — that is, so far." Fondly he twined his arms about the long, thin neck of Dexter, who tossed his head and knocked off the cowboy hat. "Never mind that — it's out," said Merton. "Can't use it in this scene." He laid his cheek to the cheek of his pet. "Well, old pal, they're takin' yuh from me, but we got to keep a stiff upper lip. You an' me has been through some purty lively times together, but we got to face the music at last — there, Lowell, did you get that?"

The artist had made his study. He made three others of the same affecting scene at different angles. Dexter was overwhelmed with endearments. Doubtless he was puzzled — to be kicked in the ribs at one moment, the next to be fondled. But Lowell Hardy was enthusiastic. He said he would have some corking studies. He made another of Buck Benson preparing to mount good old Pinto; though, as a matter of fact, Buck, it appeared, was not even half prepared to mount.

"Go on, jump on him now," suggested the artist. "I'll get a few more that way."

"Well, I don't know," Merton hesitated. He was 22 years old, and he had never yet been aboard a horse. Perhaps he shouldn't try to go too far in one lesson. "You see, the old boy's pretty tired from his week's work. Maybe I better not mount him. Say, I'll tell you, take me rolling a cigarette, just standing by him. I darned near forgot the cigarettes."

From the barn he brought a sack of tobacco and some brown papers. He had no intention of smoking, but this kind of cigarette was too completely identified with Buck Benson to be left out. Lolling against the side of Dexter, he poured tobacco from the sack into one of the papers. "Get me this way," he directed, "just pouring it out."

He had not yet learned to roll a cigarette, but Gus Giddings, the Simsbury outlaw, had promised to teach him. Anyway, it was enough now to be looking keenly out from under his hat while he poured tobacco into the creased paper against the background of good old Pinto. An art study of this pose was completed. But Lowell Hardy craved more action, more variety.

"Go on. Get up on him," he urged. "I want to make a study of that."

"Well" — again Merton faltered — "the old skate's tired out from a hard week, and I'm not feeling any too lively myself."

"Shucks! It won't kill him if you get on his back for a minute, will it? And you'll want one on him to show, won't you? Hurry up, while the light's right."

Yes, he would need a mounted study to show. Many times he had enacted a scene in which a director had looked over the art studies of Clifford Armytage and handed them back with the remark, "But you seem to play only society parts, Mr. Armytage. All very interesting, and I've no doubt we can place you very soon; but just at present we're needing a lead for a Western, a man who can look the part and ride."

Thereupon he handed these Buck Benson stills to the man, whose face would instantly relax into an expression of pleased surprise.

"The very thing," he would say. And among those stills, certainly, should be one of Clifford Armytage actually on the back of his horse. He'd chance it.

"All right; just a minute."

He clutched the bridle reins of Dexter under his drooping chin, and overcoming a feeble resistance dragged him alongside the watering trough. Dexter at first thought he was wished to drink, but a kick took that nonsense out of him. With extreme care Merton stood upon the edge of the trough and thrust a leg blindly over the saddle. With some determined clambering he was at last seated. His feet were in the stirrups. There was a strange light in his eyes. There was a strange light in Dexter's eyes. To each of them the experience was not only without precedent but rather unpleasant.

"Ride him out in the middle here, away from that well," directed the camera man.

"You — you better lead him out," suggested the rider. "I can feel him tremble already. He — he might break down under me."

Metta Judson, from the back porch, here came into the piece with lines that the author had assuredly not written for her.

"Giddap, there, you Dexter Gashwiler," called Metta loudly and with the best intentions.

"You keep still," commanded the rider severely, not turning his head. What a long way it seemed to the ground! He had never dreamed that horses were so lofty. "Better lead him," he repeated to his camera man.

Lowell Hardy grasped the bridle reins, and after many vain efforts persuaded Dexter to stumble away from the well. His rider grasped the horn of his saddle.

"Look out, don't let him buck," he called.

But Dexter had again become motionless, except for a recurrent trembling under this monstrous infliction.

"Now, there," began the artist. "Hold that. You're looking off over the Western hills. Atta boy! Wait till I get a side view."

"Move your camera," said the rider. "Seems to me he doesn't want to turn around."

But again the artist turned Dexter half around. That wasn't so bad. Merton began to feel the thrill of it. He even lounged in the saddle presently, one leg over the pommel, and seemed about to roll another cigarette while another art study was made. He continued to lounge there while the artist packed his camera. What had he been afraid of? He could sit a horse as well as the next man; probably a few little tricks about it he hadn't learned yet, but he'd get these, too.

"I bet they'll come out fine," he called to the departing artist. "Leave that to me. I dare say I'll be able to do something good with them. So long."

"So long," returned Merton, and was left alone on the back of a horse higher than people would think until they got on him. Indeed he was beginning to like it. If you just had a little nerve you needn't be afraid of anything. Very carefully he clambered from the saddle. His old pal shook himself with relief and stood once more with bowed head and crossed forelegs.

His late burden observed him approvingly. There was good old Pinto after a hard day's run over the mesa. He had borne his beloved owner far ahead of the sheriff's posse, and was now securing a moment's much-needed rest. Merton undid the riata and for half an hour practiced casting it at his immobile pet. Once the noose settled unerringly over the head of Dexter, who still remained immobile.

Then there was the lightning draw to be practiced. Again and again the trusty weapon of Buck Benson flashed from its holster to the damage of a slower adversary. He was getting that draw down pretty good. From the hip with straight wrist and forearm Buck was ready to shoot in no time at all. Throughout that villain-infested terrain along the border he was known for his quick draw. The most desperate of them would never molest him except they could shoot him from behind. With his back to a wall, they slunk from the encounter.

Elated from this practice and from the memory of that one successful rope cast, Merton became daring in the extreme. He considered nothing less than remounting his old pal and riding, in the cool of early evening, up and down the alley upon which the barnyard gave. He coiled the rope and again lashed it to the left front of the saddle. Then he curved an affectionate arm over the arched neck of Pinto, who sighed deeply.

"Well, old pal, you and me has still got some mighty long miles to git over between now and sunup tomorrow. I reckon we got to put a right smart of distance between us and that pesky sheriff's posse, but I know yuh ain't lost heart, old pal."

Dexter here tossed his head, being cloyed with these embraces, and Two-Gun Benson caught a look in the desperate eyes of his pet which he did not wholly like. Perhaps it would be better not to ride him any more today. Perhaps it would be better not to ride him again until next Sunday. After all, wasn't Dexter practically a wild horse, caught up from the range and broken to saddle only that afternoon? No use overdoing it. At this moment the beast's back looked higher than ever.

It was the cutting remark of a thoughtless, empty-headed girl that confirmed Merton in his rash resolve. Metta Judson, again on the back steps, surveyed the scene with kindling eyes.

"I bet you daresn't get on him again," said Metta.

These were strong words; not words to be flung lightly at Two-Gun Benson.

"You know a lot about it, don't you?" parried Merton Gill.

"Afraid of that old skate!" murmured Metta, counterfeiting the inflections of pity.

Her target shot her a glance of equal pity for her lack of understanding and empty-headed banter. He stalked to the barnyard gate and opened it. The way to his haven over the border was no longer barred. He returned to Dexter, firmly grasped the bridle reins under his weak chin and cajoled him again to the watering trough. Metta Judson was about to be overwhelmed with confusion. From the edge of the trough he again clambered into the saddle, the new boots groping a way to the stirrups. The reins in his left hand, he swept off his ideal hat with a careless gesture — he wished he had had an art study made of this, but you can't think of everything at one time. He turned loftily to Metta as one who had not even heard her tasteless taunts.

"Well, so long! I won't be out late." Metta was now convinced that she had in her heart done this hero a wrong.

"You better be here before the folks get back!" she warned.

Merton knew this as well as she did, but the folks wouldn't be back for a couple of hours yet, and all he meant to venture was a ride at sober pace the length of the alley.

"Oh, I'll take care of that!" he said. "A few miles' stiff gallop'll be all I want." He jerked Dexter's head up, snapped the reins on his neck, and addressed him in genial, comradely but authoritative tones.

"Git up there, old hoss!"

Dexter lowered his head again and remained as if posing conscientiously for the statue of a tired horse.

"Giddap, there, you old skate!" again ordered the rider.

The comradely unction was gone from his voice and the bony neck received a smarter wallop with the reins. Dexter stood unmoved. He seemed to be fearing that the worst was now coming, and that he might as well face it on that spot as elsewhere. He remained deaf to threats and entreaties alike. No hoof moved from its resting place.

"Giddap, there, you old Dexter Gashwiler!" ordered Metta, and was not rebuked. But neither would Dexter yield to a woman's whim.

"I'll tell you!" said Merton, now contemptuous of his mount. "Get the buggy whip and tickle his ribs."

Metta sped on his errand, her eyes shining with the lust for torture. With the frayed end of the whip from the delivery wagon she lightly scored the exposed ribs of Dexter, tormenting him with devilish cunning. Dexter's hide shuttled back and forth. He whinnied protestingly, but did not stir even one hoof.

"That's the idea," said Merton, feeling scornfully secure on the back of this spiritless animal. "Keep it up! I can feel him coming to life."

Metta kept it up. Her woman's ingenuity contrived new little tricks with the instrument of torture. She would doubtless have had a responsible post with the Spanish Inquisition. Face set, absorbed in her evil work, she tickled the ribs crosswise and tickled between them, up and down, always with the artist's light touch.

Dexter's frame grew tense, his head came up. Once more he looked like a horse. He had been brave to face destruction, but he found himself unable to face being tickled to death. If only they had chosen some other method for his execution he would have perished gamely, but this was exquisitely poignant — beyond endurance. He tossed his head and stepped into a trot toward the open gate.

Metta yelled in triumph. The rider tossed his own head in rhythm to Dexter's trot. His whole body tossed in the saddle; it was a fearsome pace; the sensations were like nothing he had ever dreamed of. And he was so high above the good firm ground! Dexter continued his jolting progress to the applause of Metta. The rider tried to command Metta to keep still, and merely bit his tongue.

Stirred to life by the tickling, Dexter now became more acutely aware of that strange, restless burden on his back, and was inspired to free himself from it. He increased his pace as he came to the gate, and managed a backward kick with both heels. This lost the rider his stirrups and left him less securely seated than he wished to be. He dropped the reins and grasped the saddle's pommel with both hands.

He strangely seemed to consider the pommel the steering wheel of a motor car. He seemed to be twisting it with the notion of guiding Dexter. All might have been well, but on losing his stirrups the rider had firmly clasped his legs about the waist of the animal. Again and again he tightened them, and now Dexter not only looked every inch a horse but very painfully to his rider felt like one, for the spurs were goring him to a most seditious behavior. The mere pace was slackened only that he might alarmingly kick and shake himself in a manner as terrifying to the rider as it was unseemly in one of Dexter's years.

But the thing was inevitable, because once in his remote, hot youth Dexter, cavorting innocently in an orchard, had kicked over a hive of busy bees which had been attending strictly to their own affairs until that moment. After that they had attended to Dexter with a thoroughness that had seared itself to this day across his memory. He now sincerely believed that he had over-turned another hive of bees, and that not but by the most strenuous exertion could he escape from their harrying. They were stinging him venomously along his sides, biting deeper with every jump. At last he would bear his rider safely over the border.

The rider clasped his mount ever more tightly. The deep dust of the alley road mounted high over the spirited scene, and through it came not only the hearty delight of Metta Judson in peals of womanly laughter, but the shrill cries of the three Ransom children whom Merton had not before noticed. These were Calvin Ransom, aged eight; Elsie Ransom, aged six; and little Woodrow Ransom, aged four. Their mother had lain down with a headache, having first ordered them to take their picture books and sit quietly in the parlor as good children should on a Sabbath afternoon. So they had noisily pretended to obtain the picture books and then quietly tiptoed out into the backyard, which was not so stuffy as the parlor.

Detecting the meritorious doings in the Gashwiler barnyard, they perched in a row on the alley fence and had been excited spectators from the moment that Merton had mounted his horse.

In shrill but friendly voices they had piped, "Oh, Merton Gill's a cowboy, Merton Gill's a cowboy! Oh, looka the cowboy on the big horse!"

For of course they were motion-picture experts and would know a cowboy when they saw one. Wide-eyed, they followed the perilous antics of Dexter as he issued from the alley gate, and they screamed with childish delight when the spurs had recalled to his memory that far-off dreadful day with the busy bees. They now balanced precariously on the alley fence, the better to trace Merton's flight through the dust cloud. "Merton's in a runaway, Merton's in a runaway, Merton's in a runaway!" they shrieked, but with none of the sympathy that would have become them. They appeared to rejoice in Merton's plight. "Merton's in a run-away," they joyously chanted.

Suddenly they ceased, frozen with a new and splendid wonder, for their descriptive phrase was now inexact. Merton was no longer in a runaway. But only for a moment did they hesitate before taking up the new chant.

"Looky, looky. He's throwed Merton right off into the dirt. He's throwed Merton right off into the dirt. Oh, looky Merton Gill right down there in the dirt!"

Again they had become exact. Merton was right down there in the dirt, and a frantic, flashing-heeled Dexter was vanishing up the alley at the head of a cloud of dust. The friendly Ransom tots leaped from the fence to the alley, forgetting on her bed of pain the mother who supposed them to be engrossed with picture books in the library. With one accord they ran toward the prostrate horseman, Calvin ahead and Elsie a close second, holding the hand of little Woodrow.

They were presently able to observe that the fleeing Dexter had narrowly escaped running down a motor car inopportunely turning at that moment into the alley. The gallant animal swerved in time, leaving the car's driver and his wife aghast at their slight margin of safety. Dexter vanished to the right up shaded Spruce Street on a Sabbath evening as the first call to evening worship pealed from a neighboring church tower.

His late rider had erected himself and was beating dust from the new chaps and the front of the new shirt. He picked up the ideal hat and dusted that. Underneath all the flurry of this adventure he was still the artist. He had been set afoot in the desert by a treacherous horse; he must find a water hole or perish with thirst. He replaced the hat, and it was then he observed the motor car bearing down the alley upon him.

"My good gosh!" he muttered.

The Gashwilers had returned a full two hours before their accustomed time. The car halted beside him and his employer leaned out a warmly hostile face.

"What's this mean?" he demanded.

The time was not one to tell Gashwiler what he thought of him. Not only was there a lady present, but he felt himself at a disadvantage. The lady saved him from an instant necessity for words.

"That was our new clothesline; I recognized it at once." The woman seemed to pride herself on this paltry feat.

"What's this mean?" again demanded Gashwiler. He was now a man of one idea.

Again was Merton Gill saved from the need of instant speech, though not in a way he would have chosen to be saved. The three Ransom children ran up, breathless, shouting.

"Oh, Merton, here's your pistol. I found it right in the road there." "We found your pistol right in the dirt there. I saw it first." "You did not; I saw it first. Merton, will you let me shoot it off, Merton? I found your pistol, didn't I, Merton? Didn't I find it right in the road there?" The friendly tots did little step dances while they were thus vocal.

"Be quiet, children," commanded Merton, finding a voice. But they were not to be quelled by mere tones.

"He throwed Merton right off into the dirt, didn't he, Merton? Merton, didn't he throw you right off into the dirt, Merton? Did he hurt you, Merton?" "Merton, will you let me shoot it off just once — just once, and I'll never ask again?" "He didn't either find it first, Merton." "He throwed you off right into the dirt — didn't he throw you right off into the dirt, Merton?"

With a harsher show of authority, or perhaps merely because he was bearded — so unreasoning are the inhibitions of the young — Gashwiler stilled the tumult. The dancing died. "What's this mean?" he repeated.

"We nearly had an accident," said the lady.

"What's this mean?"

An answer of sorts could no longer be delayed.

"Well, I thought I'd give Dexter a little exercise, so I saddled him up and was going to ride him around the block, when — when these kids here yelled and scared him so he ran away."

"Oh, what a story!" shouted the tots in unison. "What a bad story! You'll go to the bad place," intoned little Elsie.

"I swear, I don't know what's gettin' into you," declared Gashwiler. "Don't that horse get exercise enough during the week? Don't he like his day of rest? How'd you like me to saddle you up and ride you round the block? I guess you'd like that pretty well, wouldn't you?" Gashwiler fancied himself in this bit of sarcasm, brutal though it was. He toyed with it. "Next Sunday

I'll saddle you up and ride you round the block — see how you like that, young man."

"It was our clothesline," said the lady. "I could tell it right off."

With a womanish tenacity she had fastened to a minor inconsequence of the outrage. Gashwiler became practical.

"Well, I must say, it's a pretty how-de-do, That horse'll make straight back for the farm; we won't have any delivery horse tomorrow. Sue, you get out; I'll go down the road a piece and see if I can head him off."

"He turned the other way," said Merton.

"Well, he's bound to head around for the farm. I'll go up the road and you hurry out the way he went. Mebbe you can catch him before he gets out of town."

Mrs. Gashwiler descended from the car.

"You better have that clothesline back by seven o'clock tomorrow morning," she warned the offender.

"Yes, ma'am, I will."

This was not spoken in a Buck Benson manner.

"And say" — Gashwiler paused in turning the car — "what you doing in that outlandish rig, anyhow? Must think you're one o' them Wild West cowboys or something. Huh!" This last carried a sneer that stung.

"Well, I guess I can pick out my own clothes if I want to."

"Fine things to call clothes, I must say. Well, go see if you can pick out that horse if you're such a good picker-out."

Again Gashwiler was pleased with himself. He could play venomously with words.

"Yes, sir," said Merton, and plodded on up the alley, followed at a respectful distance by the Ransom kiddies, who at once resumed their vocal exercises.

"He throwed you off right into the dirt, didn't he, Merton? Mer-tun, didn't he throw you off right into the dirt?"

If it were inevitable he wished that they would come closer. He would even have taken little Woodrow by the hand. But they kept far enough back of him to require that their voices should be raised. Incessantly the pitiless rain fell upon him — "Mer-tun, he throwed you off right into the dirt, didn't he, Merton?"

He turned out of the alley up Spruce Street. The Ransom

children lawlessly followed, forgetting their good home, their poor, sick mother and the rules she had laid down for their Sabbath recreation. At every moment the shrill cry reached his burning ears, "Mer-tun, didn't he throw you off?" The kiddies appeared to believe that Merton had not heard them, but they were patient. Presently he would hear and reassure them that he had, indeed, been thrown off right into the dirt.

Now he began to meet or pass early churchgoers who would gaze at him in wonder or in frank criticism. He left the sidewalk and sought the center of the road, pretending that out there he could better search for a valuable lost horse. The Ransom children were at first in two minds about following him, but they soon found it more interesting to stay on the sidewalk. They could pause to acquaint the churchgoers with a matter of common interest. "He threw Merton off right into the dirt."

If the people they addressed appeared to be doubting this, or to find it not specific enough, they would call ahead to Merton to confirm their simple tale. With rapt, shining faces, they spread the glad news, though hurrying always to keep pace with the figure in the road.

Spruce Street was vacant of Dexter, but up Elm Street, slowly cropping the wayside herbage as he went, was undoubtedly Merton's good old pal. He quickened his pace. Dexter seemed to divine his coming and broke into a kittenish gallop until he reached the Methodist Church. Here, appearing to believe that he had again eluded pursuit, he stopped to graze on a carefully tended square of grass before the sacred edifice. He was at once shooed by two scandalized old ladies, but paid them no attention. They might perhaps even have tickled him, for this was the best grass he had found since leaving home. Other churchgoers paused in consternation, looking expectantly at the approaching Merton Gill. The three happy children who came up with him left no one in doubt of the late happening.

Merton was still the artist. He saw himself approach Dexter, vault into the saddle, put spurs to the beast, and swiftly disappear down the street. People would be saying that he should not be let to ride so fast through a city street. He was worse than Gus Giddings. But he saw this only with his artist's eye. In sordid fact he went up to Dexter, seized the trailing bridle reins and jerked savagely upon them. Back over the trail he led his good old pal. And for other later churchgoers there were the shrill voices of friendly children to tell what had happened — to appeal confidently to Merton, vaguely ahead in the twilight, to confirm their interesting story.

Dexter, the anarchist, was put to bed without his goodnight kiss. Good old Pinto had done his pal dirt. Never again would he be given a part in Buck Benson's company. Across the alley came the voices of tired, happy children, in the appeal for an encore. "Mer-tun, please let him do it to you again." "Mer-tun, please let him do it to you again."

And to the back porch came Mrs. Gashwiler to say it was a good thing he'd got that clothesline back, and came her husband wishing to be told what outlandish notion Merton Gill would next get into the thing he called his head. It was the beginning of the end.

Followed a week of strained relations with the Gashwiler household, including Dexter, and another week of relations hardly more cordial. But 30 dollars was added to the hoard which was now counted almost nightly. And the cruder wits of the village had made rather a joke of Merton's adventure. Some were tasteless enough to rally him coarsely upon the crowded street or at the post office while he awaited his magazines.

And now there were 275 dollars to put him forever beyond their jibes. He carefully rehearsed a scathing speech for Gashwiler. He would tell him what he thought of him. That merchant would learn from it some things that would do him good if he believed them, but probably he wouldn't believe them. He would also see that he had done his faithful employee grave injustices. And he would be left, in some humiliation, having found, as Merton Gill took himself forever out of retail trade, that two could play on words as well as one. It was a good warm speech, and its author knew every word of it from mumbled rehearsal during the two weeks, at times when Gashwiler merely thought he was being queer again.

At last came the day when he decided to recite it in full to the man for whom it had been composed. He confronted him, accordingly, at a dull moment on the third Monday morning, burning with his message.

He looked Gashwiler firmly in the eye and said in halting tones, "Mr. Gashwiler, now, I've been thinking I'd like to go West for a while — to California, if you could arrange to let me off, please." And Mr. Gashwiler had replied, "Well, now, that is a surprise. When was you wishing to go, Merton?"

"Why, I would be much obliged if you'd let me get off tonight on No. 4, Mr. Gashwiler, and I know you can get Spencer Grant to take my place, because I asked him yesterday."

"Very well, Merton. Send Spencer Grant in to see me, and you can get off tonight. I hope you'll have a good time."

"Of course, I don't know how long I'll be gone. I may locate out there. But then again —"

"That's all right, Merton. Any time you come back you can have your same old job. You've been a good man, and they ain't so plenty these days."

"Thank you, Mr. Gashwiler."

No. 4 was made to stop at Simsbury for a young man who was presently commanding a meal in the palatial diner, and who had, before this meal was eaten, looked out with compassion upon two Simsbury-like hamlets that the train rushed by, a blur of small-towners standing on their depot platforms to envy the inmates of that splendid structure.

At last it was Western Stuff and no fooling.

CHAPTER IV

THE WATCHER AT THE GATE

THE STREET LEADING to the Holden motion-picture studio, considered by itself, lacks beauty. Flanking it for most of the way from the boulevard to the studio gate are vacant lots labeled with their prices and appeals to the passer to buy them. Still their prices are high enough to mark the thoroughfare as one out of the common, and it is further distinguished by two rows of lofty eucalyptus trees. These have a real feathery beauty, and are perhaps a factor in the seemingly exorbitant prices demanded for the choice bungalow and home sites they shade. Save for a casual pioneer bungalow or two, there are no buildings to attract the notice until one reaches a high fence that marks the beginning of the Holden lot. Back of this fence is secreted a microcosmos, a world in little, where one may encounter strange races of people in their native dress and behold, by walking a block, cities actually apart by league upon league of the earth's surface and separated by centuries of time.

To penetrate this city of many cities, and this actual present of the remote past, one must be of a certain inner elect. Hardly may one enter by assuming the disguise of a native, as daring explorers have sometimes overcome the difficulty of entering other strange cities. Its gate, reached after passing along an impressive expanse of the reticent fence, is watched by a guardian. He is a stoatish man of middle age, not neatly dressed, and of forbidding aspect. His face is ruthless, with a very knowing cynicism.

He is there, it would seem, chiefly to keep people out of the delightful city, though from time to time he will bow an assent or wave it with the hand clutching his evening newspaper to one of the favored lawful inmates, who will then carelessly saunter or drive an expensive motor car through the difficult portal.

Standing across the street, one may peer through this portal into an avenue of the forbidden city. There is an exciting glimpse of greensward, flowering shrubbery, roses, vines, and a vista of the ends of enormous structures painted yellow. And this avenue is sprightly with the passing of enviable persons who are rightly there, some in alien garb, some in the duller uniform of the humble artisan, some in the pressed and garnished trappings of rich overlords.

It is really best to stand across the street for this clandestine view of heart-shaking delights. If you stand close to the gate to peer past the bulky shape of the warder he is likely to turn and give you a cold look. Further, he is averse to light conversation, being always morosely absorbed — yet with an eye ever alert for intrusive outlanders — in his evening paper. He never reads a morning paper, but has some means of obtaining at an early hour each morning a pink or green evening paper that shrieks with crimson headlines. Such has been his reading through all time, and this may have been an element in shaping his now inveterate hostility toward those who would engage him in meaningless talk. Even in accepting the gift of an excellent cigar he betrays only a bored condescension. There is no relenting of countenance, no genial relaxing of an ingrained suspicion toward all who approach him, no cordiality, in short, such as would lead you to believe that he might be glad to look over a bunch of stills taken by the most artistic photographer in all Simsbury, Illinois. So you let him severely alone after a bit, and go to stand across the street, your neatly wrapped art studies under your arm, and leaning against the trunk of a eucalyptus tree, you stare brazenly past him into the city of wonders.

It is thus we first observe that rising young screen actor, Clifford Armytage, beginning the 10th day of his determined effort to become much more closely identified with screen activities than hitherto. Ten days of waiting outside the guarded gate had been his, but no other 10 days of his life had seemed so eventful or passed so swiftly. For at last he stood before his goal, had actually fastened his eyes upon so much of it as might be seen through its gate. Never had he achieved so much downright actuality.

Back in Simsbury on a Sunday morning he had often strolled over to the depot at early train time for a sight of the two metal containers housing the films shown at the Bijou Palace the day before. They would be on the platform, pasted over with express labels. He would stand by them, even touch them, examine the padlocks, turn them over, heft them; actually hold within his grasp the film wraith of Beulah Baxter in a terrific installment of *The Hazards of Hortense*. Those metal containers imprisoned so much of beauty, of daring, of young love striving against adverse currents — held the triumphant fruiting of Miss Baxter's toil and struggle and sacrifice to give the public something better and finer. Often he had caressed the crude metal with a reverent hand, as if his wonder woman herself stood there to receive his homage.

That was actuality, in a way. But here it was in full measure, without mental subterfuge or vain imaginings. Had he not beheld from this post — he was pretty sure he had — Miss Baxter herself, swathed in costly furs, drive a robin's-egg-blue roadster through the gate without even a nod to the warder? Indeed, that one glimpse of reality had been worth his 10 days of waiting — worth all his watching of the gate and its keeper until he knew every dent in the keeper's derby hat, every bristle in his unkempt mustache, every wrinkle of his inferior raiment, and every pocket from which throughout the day he would vainly draw matches to relight an apparently fireproof cigar. Surely waiting thus rewarded could not be called barren. When he grew tired of standing he could cross the street and rest on a low bench that encircled one of the eucalyptus trees. Here were other waiters without the pale, usually men of strongly marked features, with a tendency to extremes in stature or hair or beards or noses, and not conspicuously neat in attire. These, he discovered, were extras awaiting employment, many of them Mexicans or strange-appearing mongrels, with a sprinkling of Negroes. Often he could have recruited there a band of outlaws for desperate deeds over the border. He did not fraternize with these waifs, feeling that his was another plane.

He had spent three days thus about the studio gate when he learned of the existence of another entrance. This was a door almost opposite the bench. He ventured through it and discovered a bare room with a wooden seat running about its sides. In a partition opposite the entrance was a small window and over it the words "Casting Director." One of the two other doors led to the interior, and through this he observed pass many of the chosen. Another door led to the office of the casting director, glimpses of which could be obtained through the little window.

The waiting room itself was not only bare as to floor and walls, but was bleak and inhospitable in its general effect. The wooden seat was uncomfortable, and those who sat upon it along the dull-toned walls appeared depressed and unhopeful, especially after they had braved a talk through the little window with someone who seemed always to be saying, "No, nothing today. Yes, perhaps next week. I have your address." When the aspirants were women, as they mostly were, the someone back of the window would add "dear" to the speech: "No, nothing today, dear."

There seemed never to be anything today, and Clifford Armytage spent very little of his waiting time in this room. It made him uncomfortable to be stared at by other applicants, whether they stared casually, incuriously, or whether they seemed to appraise him disparagingly, as if telling him frankly that for him there would never be anything today.

Then he saw that he, too, must undergo that encounter at the little window. Too apparently he was not getting anywhere by loitering about outside. It was exciting, but the producers would hardly look there for new talent.

He chose a moment for this encounter when the waiting room was vacant, not caring to be stared at when he took this first step in forming a connection that was to be notable in screen annals. He approached the window, bent his head, and encountered the gaze of a small, comely woman with warm brown eyes, neat reddish hair, and a quick manner. The gaze was shrewd; it seemed to read all that was needed to be known of this new candidate.

"Yes?" said the woman.

She looked tired and very businesslike, but her manner was not unkind. The novice was at once reassured. He was presently explaining to her that he wished to act in the pictures at this particular studio. No, he had not had much experience; that is, you could hardly call it experience in actual acting, but he had finished a course of study and had a diploma from the General Film Production Company of Stebbinsville, Arkansas, certifying him to be a competent screen actor. And of course he would not at first expect a big part. He would be glad to take a small part to begin with — almost any small part until he could familiarize himself with studio conditions. And here was a bunch of stills that would give any one an idea of the range of parts he was prepared to play, society parts in a full-dress suit, or soldier parts in a trench coat and lieutenant's cap, or juveniles in the natty suit with the belted coat, and in the storm-king model belted overcoat. And of course Western stuff — these would give an idea of what he could do — cowboy outfit and all that sort of thing, chaps and spurs and guns and so forth. And he was prepared to work hard and struggle and sacrifice in order to give the public something better and finer, and would it be possible to secure some small part at once? Was a good all-round actor by any chance at that moment needed in the company of Miss Beulah Baxter, because he would especially like such a part, and he would be ready to start to work at any time — tomorrow, or even today.

The tired little woman beyond the opening listened patiently to this, interrupting several times to say over an insistent telephone, "No, nothing today, dear." She looked at the stills with evident interest and curiously studied the face of the speaker as she listened. She smiled wearily when he was through and spoke briskly.

"Now, I'll tell you, son; all that is very nice, but you haven't had a lick of real experience yet, have you? — and things are pretty quiet on the lot just now. Today there are only two companies shooting. So you couldn't get anything today or tomorrow or probably for a good many days after that, and it won't be much when you get it. You may get on as an extra after a while when some of the other companies start shooting, but I can't promise anything, you understand. What you do now — leave me your name and address and telephone number."

"Yes, ma'am," said the applicant, and supplied these data.

"Clifford Armytage!" exclaimed the woman. "I'll say that's some warm name!"

"Well, you see" — he paused, but resolved to confide freely in this friendly seeming person — "you see, I picked that out for a good name to act under. It sounds good, doesn't it? And my own right name is only Merton Gill, so I thought I'd better have something that sounded a little more — well, you know."

"Sure!" said the woman. "All right, have any name you want; but I think I'll call you Merton when you come again. You needn't act with me, you know. Now, let's see — name, age, height, good general wardrobe, house address, telephone number — oh, yes, tell me where I can find you during the day."

"Right out here," he replied firmly. "I'm going to stick to this studio and not go near any of the others. If I'm not in this room I'll be just outside there, on that bench around the tree, or just across the street where you can see through the gate and watch the people go through."

"Say!" Again the woman searched his face and broke into her friendly smile. "Say, you're a real nut, aren't you? How'd you ever get this way?"

And again he was talking, telling now of his past and his struggles to educate himself as a screen actor — one of the best. He spoke of Simsbury and Gashwiler and of Lowell Hardy who took his stills, and of Tessie Kearns, whose sympathy and advice had done so much to encourage him. The woman was joyously attentive. Now she did more than smile. She laughed at intervals throughout the narrative, though her laughter seemed entirely sympathetic and in no way daunted the speaker.

"Well, Merton, you're a funny one — I'll say that. You're so kind of ignorant and appealing. And you say this Bughalter or Gigwater or whatever his name is will take you back into the store any time? Well, that's a good thing to remember, because the picture game is a hard game. I wouldn't discourage a nice clean boy like you for the world, but there are a lot of people in pictures right now that would prefer a steady job like that one you left."

"It's Gashwiler — that name."

"Oh, all right, just so you don't forget it and forget the address."

The new applicant warmly reassured her.

"I wouldn't be likely to forget that, after living there all those years."

When he left the window the woman was again saying into the telephone, "No, dear, nothing today. I'm sorry."

It was that night he wrote to Tessie Kearns:

Dear Friend Tessie:

Well, Tessie, here I am safe and sound in Hollywood after a long ride on the cars that went through many strange and interesting cities and different parts of the country, and I guess by this time you must have thought I was forgetting my old friends back in Simsbury; but not so, I can assure you, for I will never forget our long talks together and how you cheered me up often when the sacrifice and struggle seemed more than any man could bear. But now I feel repaid for all that sacrifice and struggle, for I am here where the pictures are made, and soon I will be acting different parts in them, though things are quiet on the lot now with only two companies shooting today; but more companies will be shooting in a few days more and then will come the great opportunity for me as soon as I get known, and my different capabilities, and what I can do and everything.

I had a long talk today with the lady out in front that hires the actors, and she was very friendly, but said it might be quite some time, because only two companies on the lot were shooting today, and she said if Gashwiler had promised to keep my old job for me to be sure and not forget his address, and it was laughable that she should say such a thing, because I would not be liable to forget his address when I lived there so long. She must have thought I was very forgetful, to forget that address.

There is some great scenery around this place, including many of the Rocky Mountains, etc. that make it look beautiful, and the city of Los Angeles is bigger than Peoria. I am quite some distance out of the center of town, and I have a nice furnished room about a mile from the Holden studios, where I will be hired after a few more companies get to shooting on the lot. There is an electric iron in the kitchen where one can press their clothes. And my furnished room is in the house of a Los Angeles society woman and her husband who came here from Iowa. Their little house with flowers in front of it is called a bungalow. The husband, Mr. Patterson, had a farm in Iowa, six miles out from Cedar Falls, and he cares little for society; but the wife goes into society all the time, as there is hardly a day just now that some society does not have its picnic, and one day it will be the Kansas Society picnic and the next day it will be the Michigan Society having a picnic, or some other state, and of course the Iowa Society that has the biggest picnic of all, and Mr. Patterson says his wife can go to all these society functions if she wants, but he does not care much for society, and he is thinking of buying a half interest in a good soft-drink place just to pass the time away, as he says after the busy life he has led he needs something to keep him busy, but his wife thinks only of society.

I take my meals out at different places, especially at drug stores. I guess you would be surprised to see these drug stores where you can go in and sit at the soda counter and order your coffee and sandwiches and custard pie and eat them right there in the drug store, but there are other places, too, like cafeterias, where you put your dishes on a tray and carry it to your own table. It is all quite different from Simsbury, and I have seen oranges growing on the trees, and there are palm trees, and it does not snow here; but the grass is green and the flowers bloom right through the winter, which makes it very attractive with the Rocky Mountains. standing up in the distance, etc.

Well, Tessie, you must excuse this long letter from your old friend, and write me if any company has accepted *Passion's Perils* and I might have a chance to act in that some day, and I will let you know when my first picture is released and the title of it so you can watch out for it when it comes to the Bijou Palace. I often think of the old town, and would like to have a chat with you and my other old friends, but I am not homesick, only sometimes I would like to be back there, as there are not many people to chat with here and one would almost be lonesome sometimes if they could not be at the studio. But I must remember that work and struggle and sacrifice are necessary to give the public something better and finer and become a good screen actor. So no more at present, from your old friend, and address Clifford Armytage at above number, as I am going by my stage name, though the lady at the Holden lot said she liked my old name better and called me that, and it sounded pretty good, as I have not got used to the stage name yet.

He felt better after this chat with his old friend, and the following morning he pressed a suit in the Patterson kitchen and resumed his vigil outside the gate. But now from time to time, at least twice a day, he could break the monotony of this by a call at the little window.

Sometimes the woman beyond it would be engrossed with the telephone and would merely look at him to shake her head. At others, the telephone being still, she would engage him in friendly talk. She seemed to like him as an occasional caller, but she remained smilingly skeptical about his immediate success in the pictures. Again and again she urged him not to forget the address of Giggenholder or Gooshswamp or whoever it might be that was holding a good job for him. He never failed to remind her that the name was Gashwiler, and that he could not possibly forget the address because he had lived at Simsbury a long time. This always seemed to brighten the woman's day. It puzzled him to note that for some reason his earnest assurance pleased her.

As the days of waiting passed he began to distinguish individuals among the people who went through the little outer room or sat patiently around its walls on the hard bench, waiting like himself for more companies to start shooting. Among the important-looking men that passed through would be actors that were now reaping the reward of their struggle and sacrifice; actors whom he thrilled to recognize as old screen friends. These would saunter in with an air of fine leisure, and their manner of careless but elegant dress would be keenly noted by Merton. Then there were directors. These were often less scrupulously attired and seemed always to be solving knotty problems. They passed hurriedly on, brows drawn in perplexity. They were very busy persons. Those on the bench regarded them with deep respect and stiffened to attention as they passed, but they were never observed by these great ones.

The waiting ones were of all ages; mostly women, with but a sprinkling of men. Many of the women were young or youngish, and of rare beauty, so Merton Gill thought. Others were elderly or old, and a few would be accompanied by children, often so young that they must be held on laps. They, too, waited with round eyes and in perfect decorum for a chance to act. Sometimes the little window would be pushed open and a woman beckoned from the bench. Some of them greeted the casting director as an old friend and were still gay when told that there was nothing today. Others seemed to dread being told this, and would wait on without daring an inquiry. Sometimes there would be a little flurry of actual business. Four society women would be needed for a bridge table at 8:30 the next morning on Stage Number Five. The casting director seemed to know the wardrobe of each of the waiters, and would select the four quickly. The gowns must be smart — it was at the country house of a rich New Yorker — and jewels and furs were not to be forgotten. There might be two days' work. The four fortunate ladies would depart with cheerful smiles. The remaining waiters settled on the bench, hoping against hope for another call.

Among the waiting-room hopefuls Merton had come to know by sight the Montague family. This consisted of a handsome elderly gentleman of most impressive manner, his wife, a portly woman of middle age, also possessing an impressive manner, and a daughter. Mr. Montague always removed his hat in the waiting room, uncovering an abundant cluster of iron-gray curls above a noble brow. About him there seemed ever to linger a faint spicy aroma of strong drink, and he would talk freely to those sharing the bench with him. His voice was full and rich in tone, and his speech, deliberate and precise, more than hinted that he had once been an ornament of the speaking stage. His wife, also, was friendly of manner, and spoke in a deep contralto somewhat roughened by wear but still notable.

The daughter Merton did not like. She was not unattractive in appearance, though her features were far off the screen-heroine model, her nose being too short, her mouth too large, her cheekbones too prominent, and her chin too square. Indeed, she resembled too closely her father, who, as a man, could carry such things more becomingly. She was a slangy chit, much too free and easy in her ways, Merton considered, and revealing a self-confidence that amounted almost to impudence. Further, her cheeks were brown, her brief nose freckled, and she did not take the pains with her face that most of the beautiful young women who waited there had so obviously taken. She was a harum-scarum baggage with no proper respect for any one, he decided, especially after the day she had so rudely accosted one of the passing directors. He was a more than usually absorbed director, and with drawn brows would have gone unseeing through the waiting room when the girl hailed him.

"Oh, Mr. Henshaw, one moment please!"

He glanced up in some annoyance, pausing with his hand to the door that led on to his proper realm.

"Oh, it's you, Miss Montague! Well, what is it? I'm very, very busy."

"Well, it's something I wanted to ask you." She quickly crossed the room to stand by him, tenderly flecking a bit of dust from his coat sleeve as she began, "Say, listen, Mr. Henshaw: Do you think beauty is a curse to a poor girl?"

Mr. Henshaw scowled down into the eyes so confidingly lifted to his.

"That's something you won't ever have to worry about," he snapped, and was gone, his brows again drawn in perplexity over his work.

"You're not angry with poor little me, are you, Mr. Henshaw?"

The girl called this after him and listened, but no reply came from back of the partition.

Mrs. Montague, from the bench, rebuked her daughter.

"Say, what do you think that kidding stuff will get you? Don't you want to work for him any more?"

The girl turned pleading eyes upon her mother.

"I think he might have answered a simple question," said she.

This was all distasteful to Merton Gill. The girl might, indeed, have deserved an answer to her simple question, but why need she ask it of so busy a man? He felt that Mr. Henshaw's rebuke was well merited, for her own beauty was surely not excessive.

Her father, from the bench, likewise admonished her.

"You are sadly prone to a spirit of banter," he declared, "though I admit that the so-called art of the motion picture is not to be regarded too seriously. It was not like that in my day. Then an actor had to be an artist; there was no position for the little he-doll whippersnapper who draws the big money today and is ignorant of even the rudiments of the actor's profession."

He allowed his glance to rest perceptibly upon Merton Gill, who felt uncomfortable.

"We were with Looey James five years," confided Mrs. Montague to her neighbors. "A hall show, of course — hadn't heard of movies then — doing *Virginius* and *Julius Caesar* and such classics, and then starting out with *The Two Orphans* for a short season. We were a knock-out, I'll say that. I'll never forget the night we opened the new opera house at Akron. They had to put the orchestra under the stage."

"And the so-called art of the moving picture robs us of our little meed of applause," broke in her husband. "I shall never forget a remark of the late Lawrence Barrett to me after a performance of *Richelieu* in which he had fairly outdone himself. 'Montague, my lad,' said he 'we may work for the money, but we play for the applause.' But now our finest bits must go in silence, or perhaps be interrupted by a so-called director who arrogates to himself the right to instill into us the rudiments of a profession in which we had grounded ourselves ere yet he was out of leading strings. Too often, naturally, the results are discouraging."

The unabashed girl was meantime having sprightly talk with the casting director, whom she had hailed through the window as Countess. Merton, somewhat startled, wondered if the little woman could indeed be of the nobility.

"Hello, Countess! Say, listen, can you give the camera a little peek at me today, or at pa or ma? 'No, nothing today, dear.'" She had imitated the little woman's voice in her accustomed reply. "Well, I didn't think there would be. I just thought I'd ask. You ain't mad, are you? I could have gone on in a harem tank scene over at the Bigart place, but they wanted me to dress the same as a fish, and a young girl's got to draw the line somewhere. Besides, I don't like that Hugo over there so much. He hates to part with anything like money, and he'll gyp you if he can. Say, I'll bet he couldn't play an honest game of solitaire. How'd you like my hair this way? Like it, eh? That's good. And me having the only freckles left in all Hollywood. Ain't I the little prairie flower, growing wilder every hour?

"Say, on the level, pa needs work. These days when he's idle he mostly sticks home and tries out new ways to make prime old Kentucky sour mash in eight hours. If he don't quit he is going to find himself seeing some moving pictures that no one else can. And he's all worried up about his hair going off on top, and trying new hair restorers. You know his latest? Well, he goes over to the Selig place one day and watches horse meat fed to the lions and says to himself that horses have plenty of hair, and it must be the fat under the skin that makes it grow, so he begs for a hunk of horse from just under the mane and he's rubbing that on. You can't tell what he'll bring home next. The old boy still believes you can raise hair from the dead. Do you want some new stills of me? I got a new one yesterday that shows my other expression. Well, so long, Countess."

The creature turned to her parents.

"Let's be on our way, old dears. This place is dead, but the Countess says they'll soon be shooting some tenement-house stuff up at the Consolidated. Maybe there'll be something in it for someone. We might as well have a look-in."

Merton felt relieved when the Montague family went out, the girl in the lead. He approved of the fine old father, but the daughter lacked dignity in speech and manner. You couldn't tell what she might say next.

The Montagues were often there, sometimes in full, sometimes represented by but one of their number. Once Mrs. Montague was told to be on Stage Six the next morning at 8:30 to attend a swell reception.

"Wear the gray georgette, dearie," said the casting director, "and your big pearls and the lorgnon."

"Not forgetting the gold cigarette case and the chinchilla neck piece," said Mrs. Montague. "The spare parts will all be there, Countess, and thanks for the word."

The elder Montague on the occasion of his calls often found time to regale those present with anecdotes of Lawrence Barrett.

"A fine artist in his day, sir; none finer ever appeared in a hall show."

And always about his once superb frock coat clung the scent of forbidden beverages. On one such day he appeared with an untidy sprouting of beard, accompanied by the talkative daughter.

"Pa's landed a part," she explained through the little window. "It's one of those we-uns mountaineer plays with revenooers and feuds; one of those plays where the city chap don't treat our Nell right — you know. And they won't stand for the crepe hair, so pop has got to raise a brush and he's mad. But it ought to give him a month or so, and after that he may be able to peddle the brush again; you can never tell in this business, can you, Countess?"

"It's most annoying," the old gentleman explained to the bench occupants. "In the true art of the speaking stage an artificial beard was considered above reproach. Nowadays one must descend to mere physical means if one is to be thought worthy."

CHAPTER V

A BREACH IN THE CITY WALLS

DURING THESE WEEKS of waiting outside the gate the little woman beyond the window had continued to be friendly but not encouraging to the aspirant for screen honors late of Simsbury, Illinois. For three weeks had he waited faithfully, always within call, struggling and sacrificing to give the public something better and finer, and not once had he so much as crossed the line that led to his goal.

Then on a Monday morning he found the waiting-room empty and his friend beyond the window suffering the pangs of headache. "It gets me something fierce right through here," she confided to him, placing her finger-tips to her temples.

"Ever use Eezo Pain Wafers?" he demanded in quick sympathy. She looked at him hopefully.

"Never heard of 'em."

"Let me get you some."

"You dear thing, fly to it!"

He was gone while she reached for her purse, hurrying along the eucalyptus-lined street of choice home sites to the nearest drug store. He was fearing someone else might bring the little woman another remedy; even that her headache might go before he returned with his. But he found her still suffering.

"Here they are." He was breathless. "You take a couple now and a couple more in half an hour if the ache hasn't stopped."

"Bless your heart! Come around inside." He was through the

door and in the dimly lit little office behind that secretive partition.

"And here's something else," he continued. "It's a menthol pencil and you take this cap off — see? — and rub your forehead with it. It'll be a help." She swallowed two of the magic wafers with the aid of water from the cooler, and applied the menthol.

"You're a dear," she said, patting his sleeve. "I feel better already. Sometimes these things come on me and stay all day." She was still applying the menthol to throbbing temples. "Say, don't you get tired hanging around outside there? How'd you like to go in and look around the lot? Would you like that?"

Would he! "Thanks!" He managed it without choking, "If I wouldn't be in the way."

"You won't. Go on — amuse yourself." The telephone rang. Still applying the menthol she held the receiver to her ear. "No, nothing today, dear. Say, Marie, did you ever take Eezo Pain Wafers for a headache? Keep 'em in mind — they're great. Yes, I'll let you know if anything breaks. Goo'-bye, dear."

Merton Gill hurried through a narrow corridor past offices where typewriters clicked and burst from gloom into the dazzling light of the Holden lot. He paused on the steps to reassure himself that the great adventure was genuine. There was the full stretch of greensward of which only an edge had shown as he looked through the gate. There were the vast yellow-brick, glass-topped structures of which he had seen but the ends. And there was the street up which he had looked for so many weeks, flanked by rows of offices and dressing rooms, and lively with the passing of many people. He drew a long breath and became calculating. He must see everything and see it methodically. He even went now along the asphalt walk to the corner of the office building from which he had issued for the privilege of looking back at the gate through which he had so often yearningly stared from across the street.

Now he was securely inside looking out. The watchman sat at the gate, bent low over his paper. There was, it seemed, more than one way to get by him. People might have headaches almost any time. He wondered if his friend the casting director were subject to them. He must carry a box of the Eezo wafers.

He strolled down the street between the rows of offices and the immense covered stages. Actors in costume entered two of these and through their open doors he could see into their shadowy interiors. He would venture there later. Just now he wished to see the outside of things. He contrived a pace not too swift but business-like enough to convey the impression that he was rightfully walking this forbidden street. He seemed to be going some place where it was of the utmost importance that he should be, and yet to have started so early that there was no need for haste.

He sounded the far end of that long street visible from outside the gate, discovering its excitements to wane gently into mere blacksmith and carpenter shops. He retraced his steps, this time ignoring the long row of offices for the opposite line of stages. From one dark interior came the slow, dulled strains of an orchestra and from another shots rang out. He met or passed strangely attired people, bandits, priests, choir boys, gentlemen in evening dress with blue-black eyebrows and careful hair. And he observed many beautiful young women, variously attired, hurrying to or from the stages. One lovely thing was in bridal dress of dazzling white, a veil of lace floating from her blonde head, her long train held up by a colored maid. She chatted amiably, as she crossed the street, with an evil-looking Mexican in a silver-corded hat — a veritable Snake de Vasquez.

But the stages could wait. He must see more streets. Again reaching the office that had been his secret gateway to these delights, he turned to the right, still with the air of having business at a certain spot to which there was really no need for him to hurry. There were fewer people this way, and presently, as if by magic carpet, he had left all that sunlight and glitter and cheerful noise and stood alone in the shadowy, narrow street of a frontier town. There was no bustle here, only an intense stillness. The street was deserted, the shop doors closed. There was a ghostlike, chilling effect that left him uneasy. He called upon himself to remember that he was not actually in a remote and desolate frontier town from which the inhabitants had fled; that back of him but a few steps was abounding life, that outside was the prosaic world passing and repassing a gate hard to enter. He whistled the fragment of a tune and went farther along this street of uncanny silence and vacancy, noting, as he went, the signs on the shop windows. There was the Busy Bee Restaurant, Jim's Place, the Hotel Renown, the Last Dollar Dance Hall, Hank's Pool Room. Upon one window was painted the terse announcement, "Joe – Buy or Sell." The Happy Days Bar adjoined the General Store.

He moved rapidly through this street. It was no place to linger. At the lower end it gave insanely upon a row of three-story brownstone houses which any picture patron would recognize as being wholly of New York. There were the imposing steps, the double-doored entrances, the broad windows, the massive lines of the whole. And beyond this he came to a many-colored little street out of Bagdad, overhung with gay balconies, vivacious with spindled towers and minarets, and small reticent windows, out of which veiled ladies would glance. And all was still with the stillness of utter desertion.

Then he explored farther and felt curiously disappointed at finding that these structures were to real houses what a dicky is to a sincere, genuine shirt. They were pretentiously false.

One had but to step behind them to discover them as poor shells.

Their backs were jutting beams carried but little beyond the fronts and their stout-appearing walls were revealed to be fragile contrivances of button-lath and thin plaster. The ghost quality departed from them with this discovery.

He left these cities of silence and came upon an open space and people. They were grouped before a railway station, a small red structure beside a line of railway track. At one end in black letters, on a narrow white board, was the name Boomerville.

The people were plainly Western: a dozen cowboys, a sprinkling of bluff ranchers and their families. An absorbed young man in cap and khaki and puttees came from a distant group surrounding a camera and readjusted the line of these people. He placed them to his liking. A wagon drawn by two horses was driven up and a rancher helped a woman and girl to alight. The girl was at once sought out by the cowboys. They shook hands warmly under megaphoned directions from a man back by the camera. The rancher and his wife mingled with the group. The girl was drawn aside by one of the cowboys. He had a nobler presence than the others; he was handsome and his accoutrements seemed more expensive. They looked into each other's eyes a long time, apparently pledging an eternal fidelity. One gathered that there would have been an embrace but for the cowboy's watchful companions. They must say good-bye with a mere handshake, though this was a slow, trembling, long-drawn clasp while they steadily regarded each other, and a second camera was brought to record it at a distance of six feet. Merton Gill thrilled with the knowledge that he was beholding his first close-up. His long study of the photo-drama enabled him to divine that the rancher's daughter was going to Vassar College to be educated, but that, although returning a year later a poised woman of the world, she would still long for the handsome cowboy who would marry her and run the Bar-X ranch. The scene was done. The camera would next be turned upon a real train at some real station, while the girl, with a final look at her lover, entered a real car, which the camera would show moving off to Vassar College. Thus conveying to millions of delighted spectators the impression that a real train had steamed out of the station, which was merely an imitation of one, on the Holden lot. The watcher passed on. He could hear the cheerful drone of a sawmill where logs were being cut. He followed the sound and came to its source. The saw was at the end of an oblong pool in which logs floated. Workmen were poling these toward the saw. On a raised platform at one side was a camera and a man who gave directions through a megaphone; a neighboring platform held a second camera. A beautiful young girl in a print dress and her thick hair in a braid came bringing his dinner in a tin pail to the handsomest of the actors. He laid down his pike-pole and took both the girl's hands in his as he received the pail. One of the other workmen, a hulking brute with an evil face, scowled darkly at this encounter and a moment later had insulted the beautiful young girl. But the first actor felled him with a blow. He came up from this, crouchingly, and the fight was on. Merton was excited by this fight, even though he was in no doubt as to which actor would win it. They fought hard, and for a time it appeared that the handsome actor must lose, for the bully who had insulted the girl was a man of great strength, but the science of the other told. It was the first fight Merton had ever witnessed. He thought these men must really be hating each other, so bitter were their expressions. The battle grew fiercer. It was splendid. Then, at the shrill note of a whistle, the panting combatants fell apart.

"Rotten!" said an annoyed voice through the megaphone. "Can't you boys give me a little action? Jazz it, jazz it! Think it's a love scene? Go to it, now — plenty of jazz — understand what I mean?" He turned to the camera man beside him. "Ed, you turn 10 — we got to get some speed some way. Jack" — to the other camera man — "you stay on 12. All ready! Get some life into it, now, and Lafe" — this to the handsome actor — "don't keep trying to hold your front to the machine. We'll get you all right. Ready, now. Camera!"

Again the fight was on. It went to a bitter finish in which the vanquished bully was sent with a powerful blow backward into the water, while the beautiful young girl ran to the victor and nestled in the protection of his strong arms.

Merton Gill passed on. This was the real thing. He would have a lot to tell Tessie Kearns in his next letter. Beyond the sawmill he came to an immense wooden structure like a cradle on huge rockers supported by scaffolding. From the ground he could make nothing of it, but a ladder led to the top. An hour on the Holden lot had made him bold. He mounted the ladder and stood on the deck of what he saw was a sea-going yacht. Three important-looking men were surveying the deckhouse forward. They glanced at the newcomer but with a cheering absence of curiosity or even of interest. He sauntered past them with a polite but not-too-keen interest. The yacht would be an expensive one. The deck fittings were elaborate. A glance into the captain's cabin revealed it to be fully furnished, with a chart and a sextant on the mahogany desk.

"Where's the bedding for this stateroom?" asked one of the men.

"I got a prop-rustler after it," one of the others informed him.

They strolled aft and paused by an iron standard ingeniously swung from the deck.

"That's Burke's idea," said one of the men. "I hadn't thought about a steady support for the camera; of course if we stood it on deck it would rock when the ship rocked and we'd get no motion. So Burke figures this out. The camera is on here and swings by that weight so it's always straight and the rocking registers. Pretty neat, what?"

"That was nothing to think of," said one of the other men, in apparent disparagement. "I thought of it myself the minute I saw it." The other two grinned at this, though Merton Gill, standing by, saw nothing to laugh at. He thought the speaker was pretty cheeky; for of course any one could think of this device after seeing it. He paused for a final survey of his surroundings from this elevation. He could see the real falseness of the sawmill he had just left, he could also look into the exposed rear of the railway station, and could observe beyond it the exposed skeleton of that New York street. He was surrounded by mockeries.

He clambered down the ladder and sauntered back to the street of offices. He was by this time confident that no one was going to ask him what right he had in there. Now, too, he became conscious of hunger and at the same moment caught the sign "Cafeteria" over a neat building hitherto unnoticed. People were entering this, many of them in costume. He went idly toward the door, glanced up, looked at his watch, and became, to any one curious about him, a man who had that moment decided he might as well have a little food. He opened the screen door of the cafeteria, half expecting it to prove one of those structures equipped only with a front. But the cafeteria was practicable. The floor was crowded with little square polished tables at which many people were eating. A railing along the side of the room made a passage to the back where food was served from a counter to the proffered tray. He fell into line. No one had asked him how he dared try to eat with real actors and actresses and apparently no one was going to. Toward the end of the passage was a table holding trays and napkins the latter wrapped about an equipment of cutlery. He took his tray and received at the counter the foods he designated. He went through this ordeal with difficulty because it was not easy to keep from staring about at other patrons. Constantly he was detecting some remembered face. But at last, with his laden tray he reached a vacant table near the center of the room and took his seat. He absently arranged the food before him. He could stare at leisure now. All about him were the strongly marked faces of the film people, heavy with makeup, interspersed with hungry civilians, who might be producers, directors, camera men, or mere artisans, for the democracy of the cafeteria seemed ideal.

At the table ahead of his he recognized the man who had been annoyed one day by the silly question of the Montague girl. They had said he was a very important director. He still looked important and intensely serious. He was a short, very plump man, with pale cheeks under dark brows, and troubled looking gray hair. He was very seriously explaining something to the man who sat with him and whom he addressed as Governor, a merry-looking person with a stubby gray mustache and little hair, who seemed not too attentive to the director.

"You see, Governor, it's this way: the party is lost on the desert — understand what I mean — and Kempton Ward and the girl stumble into this deserted tomb just at nightfall. Now here's where the big kick comes —"

Merton Gill ceased to listen for there now halted at his table, bearing a laden tray, none other than the Montague girl, she of the slangy talk and the regrettably free manner. She put down her tray and seated herself before it. She had not asked permission of the table's other occupant, indeed she had not even glanced at him, for cafeteria etiquette is not rigorous. He saw that she was heavily made up and in the costume of a gypsy, he thought, a short vivid skirt, a gay waist, heavy gold hoops in her ears, and dark hair massed about her small head. He remembered that this would not be her own hair. She fell at once to her food. The men at the next table glanced at her, the director without cordiality; but the other man smiled upon her cheerfully.

"Hello, Flips! How's the girl?"

"Everything's jake with me, Governor. How's things over at your shop?"

"So, so. I see you're working."

"Only for two days. I'm just atmosphere in this piece. I got some real stuff coming along pretty soon for Baxter. Got to climb down 10 stories of a hotel elevator cable, and ride a brake-beam and be pushed off a cliff and thrown to the lions, and a few other little things."

"That's good, Flips. Come in and see me some time. Have a little chat. Ma working?"

"Yeah — got a character bit with Charlotte King in *Her Other Husband*." "Glad to hear it. How's Pa Montague?"

"Pa's in bed. They've signed him for *Camillia of the Cumberlands*, providing he raises a brush, and just now it ain't long enough for whiskers and too long for anything else, so he's putterin' around with his new still."

"Well, drop over sometime, Flips, I'm keeping you in mind."

"Thanks, Governor. Say —" Merton glanced up in time to see her wink broadly at the man, and look toward his companion who still seriously made notes on the back of an envelope. The man's face melted to a grin which he quickly erased. The girl began again:

"Mr. Henshaw — could you give me just a moment, Mr. Henshaw?" The serious director looked up in quite frank annoyance.

"Yes, yes, what is it, Miss Montague?"

"Well, listen, Mr. Henshaw, I got a great idea for a story, and I was thinking who to take it to and I thought of this one and I thought of that one, and I asked my friends, and they all say take it to Mr. Henshaw, because if a story has any merit he's the one director on the lot that can detect it and get every bit of value out of it, so I thought — but of course if you're busy just now —"

The director thawed ever so slightly. "Of course, my girl, I'm busy — but then I'm always busy. They run me to death here. Still, it was very kind of your friends, and of course —"

"Thank you, Mr. Henshaw." She clasped her hands to her breast and gazed raptly into the face of her coy listener.

"Of course I'll have to have help on the details, but it starts off kind of like this. You see I'm a Hawaiian princess —" She paused, gazing aloft.

"Yes, yes, Miss Montague — a Hawaiian princess. Go on, go on!"

"Oh, excuse me; I was thinking how I'd dress her for the last spool in the big fire scene. Well, anyway, I'm this Hawaiian princess, and my father, old King Mauna Loa, dies and leaves me 21,000 volcanoes and a billiard cue —"

Mr. Henshaw blinked rapidly at this. For a moment he was dazed. "A billiard cue, did you say?" he demanded blankly.

"Yes. And every morning I have to go out and ram it down the volcanoes to see are they all right — and —"

"Tush, tush!" interrupted Mr. Henshaw scowling upon the playwright and fell again to his envelope, pretending thereafter to ignore her.

The girl seemed to be unaware that she had lost his attention. "And you see the villain is very wealthy; he owns the largest ukelele factory in the islands, and he tries to get me in his power, but he's foiled by my fiancé, a young native by the name of Herman Schwarz, who has invented a folding ukelele, so the villain gets his hired Hawaiian orchestra to shove Herman down one of the volcanoes and me down another, but I have the key around my neck, which Father put there when I was a babe and made me swear always to wear it, even in the bathtub, so I let myself out and unlock the other one and let Herman out and the orchestra discovers us and chases us over the cliff, and then along comes my old nurse who is now running a cigar store in San Pedro and she —" Here she affected to discover that Mr. Henshaw no longer listened.

"Why, Mr. Henshaw's gone!" she exclaimed dramatically. "Boy, boy, page Mr. Henshaw." Mr. Henshaw remained oblivious.

"Oh, well, of course I might have expected you wouldn't have time to listen to my poor little plot. Of course I know it's crude, but it did seem to me that something might be made out of it." She resumed her food. Mr. Henshaw's companion here winked at her and was seen to be shaking with emotion. Merton Gill could not believe it to be laughter, for he had seen nothing to laugh at. A busy man had been bothered by a silly girl who thought she had the plot for a photodrama, and even he, Merton Gill, could have told her that her plot was impossibly wild and inconsequent. If she were going into that branch of the art she ought to take lessons, the way Tessie Kearns did. She now looked so mournful that he was almost moved to tell her this, but her eyes caught his at that moment and in them was a light so curious, so alive with hidden meanings, so eloquent of some iron restraint she put upon her own emotions, that he became confused and turned his gaze from hers almost with the rebuking glare of Henshaw. She glanced quickly at him again, studying his face for the first time. There had been such a queer look in this young man's eyes; she understood most looks, but not that one.

Henshaw was treating the late interruption as if it had not been. "You see, Governor, the way we got the script now, they're in this tomb alone for the night — understand what I mean — and that's where the kick comes for the audience. They know he's a strong young fellow and she's a beautiful girl and absolutely in his power — see what I mean? — but he's a gentleman through and through and never lays a hand on her. Get that? Then later along comes this Ben Ali Ahab —"

The Montague girl glanced again at the face of the strange young man whose eyes had held a new expression for her, but she and Mr. Henshaw and the so-called governor and all those other diners who rattled thick crockery and talked unendingly had ceased to exist for Merton Gill. A dozen tables down the room and nearer the door sat none other than Beulah Baxter. Alone at her table, she gazed raptly aloft, meditating perhaps some daring new feat. Merton Gill stared, entranced, frozen. The Montague girl perfectly understood this look and traced it to its object. Then she surveyed Merton Gill again with something faintly like pity in her shrewd eyes. He was still staring, still rapt.

Beulah Baxter ceased to look aloft. She daintily reached for a wooden toothpick from the bowl before her and arose to pay her check at the near-by counter. Merton Gill arose at the same moment and stumbled a blind way through the intervening tables. When he reached the counter Miss Baxter was passing through the door. He was about to follow her when a cool but cynical voice from the counter said, "Hey, Bill — ain't you fergittin' somepin.'"

He looked for the check for his meal; it should have been in one hand or the other. But it was in neither. He must have left it back on his tray. Now he must return for it. He went as quickly as he could. The Montague girl was holding it up as he approached. "Here's the little joker, Kid," she said kindly.

"Thanks!" said Merton. He said it haughtily, not meaning to be haughty, but he was embarrassed and also fearful that Beulah Baxter would be lost. "Exit limping," murmured the girl as he turned away. He hurried again to the door, paid the check and was outside. Miss Baxter was not to be seen. His forgetfulness about the check had lost her to him. He had meant to follow, to find the place where she was working, and look and look and look! Now he had lost her. But she might be on one of those stages within the big barns. Perhaps the day was not yet lost. He crossed the street, forgetting to saunter, and ventured within the cavernous gloom beyond an open door. He stood for a moment, his vision dulled by the dusk. Presently he saw that he faced a wall of canvas backing. Beyond this were low voices and the sound of people moving. He went forward to a break in the canvas wall and at the same moment there was a metallic jar and light flooded the enclosure. From somewhere outside came music, principally the low, leisurely moan of a cello. A beautiful woman in evening dress was with suppressed emotion kneeling at the bedside of a sleeping child. At the doorway stood a dark, handsome gentleman in evening dress, regarding her with a cynical smile. The woman seemed to bid the child farewell, and arose with hands to her breast and quivering lips. The still-smiling gentleman awaited her. When she came to him, glancing backward to the sleeping child, he threw about her an elaborate fur cloak and drew her to him, his cynical smile changing to one of deceitful tenderness. The woman still glanced back at the child, but permitted herself to be drawn through the doorway by the insistent gentleman. From a door the other side of the bed came a kind-faced nurse. She looked first at the little one then advanced to stare after the departing couple. She raised her hands tragically and her face became set in a mask of sorrow and despair. She clasped the hands desperately.

Merton Gill saw his nurse to be the Montague mother. "All right," said an authoritative voice. Mrs. Montague relaxed her features and withdrew, while an unkempt youth came to stand in front of the still-grinding camera and held before it a placard on which were numbers. The camera stopped, the youth with the placard vanished. "Save it," called another voice, and with another metallic jar the flood of light was turned off. The cello ceased its moan in the middle of a bar.

The watcher recalled some of the girl's chat. Her mother had a character bit in Her Other Husband. This would be it, one of those moving tragedies not unfamiliar to the screen enthusiast. The beautiful but misguided wife had been saying goodbye to her little one and was leaving her beautiful home at the solicitation of the false friend in evening dress — forgetting all in one mad moment. The watcher was a tried expert, and like the trained faunal naturalist could determine a species from the shrewd examination of one bone of a photoplay. He knew that the wife had been ignored by a husband who permitted his vast business interests to engross his whole attention, leaving the wife to seek solace in questionable quarters. He knew that the shocked but faithful nurse would presently discover the little one to be suffering from a dangerous fever; that a hastily summoned physician would shake his head and declare in legible words, "Naught but a mother's love can win that tiny soul back from the brink of Eternity." The father would overhear this, and would see it all then: how his selfish absorption in Wall Street had driven his wife to another. He would pursue her, would find her ere yet it was too late. He would discover that her better nature had already prevailed and that she had started back without being sent for. They would kneel side by side, hand in hand, at the bedside of the little one, who would recover and smile and prattle, and together they would face an untroubled future.

This was all thrilling to Merton Gill; but Beulah Baxter was not here, her plays being clean and wholesome things of the great outdoors. Far down the great enclosure was another wall of canvas backing, a flood of light above it and animated voices from within. He stood again to watch. But this drama seemed to have been suspended. The room exposed was a bedroom with an open window facing an open door; the actors and the mechanical staff as well were busily hurling knives at various walls. They were earnest and absorbed in this curious pursuit. Sometimes they made the knife penetrate the wall, oftener it merely struck and clattered to the floor. Five knives at once were being hurled by five enthusiasts, while a harried-looking director watched and criticized.

"You're a clumsy bunch," he announced at last. "It's a simple thing to do, isn't it?" The knife-throwers redoubled their efforts, but they did not find it a simple thing to do.

"Let me try it, Mr. Burke." It was the Montague girl still in her gypsy costume. She had been standing quietly in the shadow observing the ineffective practice.

"Hello, Flips! Sure, you can try it. Show these boys something good, now. Here, Al, give Miss Montague that stickeree of yours." Al seemed glad to relinquish the weapon. Miss Montague hefted it, and looked doubtful.

"It ain't balanced right," she declared. "Haven't you got one with a heavier handle?"

"Fair enough," said the director. "Hey, Pickles, let her try that one you got." Pickles, too, was not unwilling to oblige.

"That's better," said the girl. "It's balanced right." Taking the blade by its point between thumb and forefinger she sent it with a quick flick of the wrist into the wall a dozen feet away. It hung there quivering.

"There! That's what we want. It's got to be quivering when Jack shoots at Ramon who threw it at him as he leaps through the window. Try it again, Flips." The girl obliged and bowed impressively to the applause.

"Now come here and try it through the doorway." He led her around the set. "Now stand here and see can you put it into the wall just to the right of the window. Good! Some little knife-thrower, I'll say. Now try it once with Jack coming through. Get set, Jack."

Jack made his way to the window through which he was to leap. He paused there to look in with some concern. "Say, Mr. Burke, will you please make sure she understands? She isn't to let go of that thing until I'm in and crouched down ready to shoot — understand what I mean? I don't want to get nicked nor nothing."

"All right, all right! She understands."

Jack leaped through the window to a crouch, weapon in hand. The knife quivered in the wall above him as he shot.

"Fine and dandy. Some class, I'll say. All right, Jack. Get back. We'll gun this little scene right here and now. All ready, Jack, all ready Miss Montague — camera! — one, two, three — come in, Jack." Again the knife quivered in the wall above his head even while he crouched to shoot at the treacherous Mexican who had thrown it.

"Good work, Flips. Thanks a whole lot. We'll do as much for you some time."

"You're entirely welcome, Mr. Burke. No trouble to oblige. How you coming?"

"Coming good. This thing's going to be a knockout. I bet it'll gross a million. Nearly done, too, except for some chase stuff up in the hills. I'll do that next week. What you doing?"

"Oh, everything's jake with me. I'm over on Number Four — *Toys of Destiny* — putting a little pep into the mob stuff. Laid out for two hours, waiting for something — I don't know what."

Merton Gill passed on. He confessed now to a reluctant admiration for the Montague girl. She could surely throw a knife. He must practice that himself sometime. He might have stayed to see more of this drama but he was afraid the girl would break out into more of her nonsense. He was aware that she swept him with her eyes as he turned away but he evaded her glance. She was not a person, he thought, that one ought to encourage.

He emerged from the great building and crossed an alley to another of like size. Down toward its middle was the usual wall of canvas with half-a-dozen men about the opening at one corner. A curious whirring noise came from within. He became an inconspicuous unit of the group and gazed in. The lights were on, revealing a long table elaborately set as for a banquet, but the guests who stood about gave him instant uneasiness. They were in the grossest caricatures of evening dress, both men and women, and they were not beautiful. The gowns of the women were grotesque and the men were lawless appearing, either as to hair or beards or both. He divined the dreadful thing he was stumbling upon even before he noted the sign in large letters on the back of a folding chair: "Jeff Baird's Buckeye Comedies." These were the buffoons who with their coarse pantomime, their heavy horse-play, did so much to debase a great art. There, even at his side, was the arch offender, none other than Jeff Baird himself, the man whose regrettable sense of so-called humor led him to make these low appeals to the witless. And even as he looked the cross-eyed man entered the scene. Garbed in the weirdly misfitting clothes of a waiter, holding aloft a loaded tray of dishes, he entered on roller skates, to halt before Baird with his uplifted tray at a precarious balance.

"All right, that's better," said Baird. "And, Gertie, listen: don't throw the chair in front of him. That's out. Now we'll have the entrance again. You other boys on the rollers, there —" Three other basely comic waiters on roller skates came to attention.

"Follow him in and pile up on him when he makes the grand spill — see what I mean? Get your trays loaded now and get off. Now you other people, take your seats. No, no, Annie, you're at the head, I told you. Tom, you're at the foot and start the roughhouse when you get the tray in the neck. Now, all set."

Merton Gill was about to leave this distressing scene but was held in spite of himself by the voice of a newcomer.

"Hello, Jeff! Atta boy!"

He knew without turning that the Montague girl was again at his elbow. He wondered if she could be following him.

"Hello, Flips! How's the kid?" The producer had turned cordially to her. "Just in time for the breakaway stuff. See how you like it."

"What's the big idea?"

"Swell reception at the Maison de Glue, with the waiters on roller skates in honor of rich Uncle Rollo Glue. The head waiter starts the fight by doing a fall with his tray. Tom gets the tray in the neck and soaks the nearest man — banquet goes flooey. Then we go into the chase stuff."

"Which is Uncle Rollo?"

"That's him at the table, with the herbaceous border under his chin."

"Is he in the fight?"

"I think so. I was going to rehearse it once more to see if I could get a better idea. Near as I can see now, everybody takes a crack at him."

"Well, maybe." Montague girl seemed to be considering. "Say, how about this, Jeff? He's awful hungry, see, and he's begun to eat the celery and everything he can reach, and when the mix-up starts he just eats on and pays no attention to it. Never even looks up, see what I mean? The fight spreads the whole length of the table; right around Rollo half-a-dozen murders are going on and he just eats and pays no attention. And he's still eating when they're all down and out, and don't know a thing till Charlie or someone crowns him with the punch-bowl. How about it? Ain't there a laugh in that?" Baird had listened respectfully and now patted the girl on a shoulder.

"Good work, Kid! That's a gag, all right. The little bean's sparking on all six, ain't it? Drop around again. We need folks like you. Now, listen, Rollo — you there, Rollo, come here and get this. Now, listen — when the fight begins —"

Merton Gill turned decisively away. Such coarse foolery as this was too remote from Beulah Baxter who, somewhere on that lot, was doing something really, as her interview had put it, distinctive and worth while.

He lingered only to hear the last of Baird's instructions to Rollo and the absurd guests, finding some sinister fascination in the man's talk. Baird then turned to the girl, who had also started off.

"Hang around, Flips. Why the rush?"

"Got to beat it over to Number Four."

"Got anything good there?"

"Nothing that will get me any billing. Been waiting two hours now just to look frenzied in a mob."

"Well, say, come around and see me some time."

"All right, Jeff. Of course I'm pretty busy. When I ain't working I've got to think about my art."

"No, this is on the level. Listen, now, sister, I got another two reeler to pull off after this one, then I'm goin' to do something new, see? Got a big idea. Probably something for you in it. Drop in t' the office and talk it over. Come in some time next week. 'F I ain't there I'll be on the lot some place. Don't forget, now."

Merton Gill, some distance from the Buckeye set, waited to note what direction the Montague girl would take. She broke away presently, glanced brazenly in his direction, and tripped lightly out the nearest exit. He went swiftly to one at the far end of the building, and was again in the exciting street. But the afternoon was drawing in and the street had lost much of its vivacity. It would surely be too late for any glimpse of his heroine. And his mind was already cluttered with impressions from his day's adventure. He went out through the office, meaning to thank the casting director for the great favor she had shown him, but she was gone. He hoped the headache had not driven her home. If she were to suffer again he hoped it would be some morning. He would have the Eezo wafers in one pocket and a menthol pencil in the other. And she would again extend to him the freedom of that wonderful city.

In his room that night he tried to smooth out the jumble in his dazed mind. Those people seemed to say so many things they considered funny but that were not really funny to any one else. And moving-picture plays were always waiting for something, with the bored actors lounging about in idle apathy. Still in his ears sounded the drone of the sawmill and the deep purr of the lights when they were put on. That was a funny thing. When they wanted the lights on they said "Kick it," and when they wanted the lights off they said "Save it!" And why did a boy come out after every scene and hold up a placard with numbers on it before the camera? That placard had never shown in any picture he had seen. And that queer Montague girl, always turning up when you thought you had got rid of her. Still, she had thrown that knife pretty well. You had to give her credit for that. But she couldn't be much of an actress, even if she had spoken of acting with Miss Baxter, of climbing down cables with her and falling off cliffs. Probably she was boasting, because he had never seen any one but Miss Baxter do these things in her pictures. Probably she had some very minor part. Anyway, it was certain she couldn't be much of an actress because she had almost promised to act in those terrible Buckeye comedies. And of course no one with any real ambition or capacity could consider such a thing — descending to rough horse-play for the amusement of the coarser element among screen patrons.

But there was one impression from the day's whirl that remained clear and radiant: He had looked at the veritable face of his heroine. He began his letter to Tessie Kearns. "At last I have seen Miss Baxter face to face. There was no doubt about its being her. You would have known her at once. And how beautiful she is! She was looking up and seemed inspired, probably thinking about her part. She reminded me of that beautiful picture of St. Cecelia playing on the piano...."

CHAPTER VI

UNDER THE GLASS TOPS

HE APPROACHED the office of the Holden studios the following morning with a new air of assurance. Formerly the mere approach had been an adventure; the look through the gate, the quick glimpse of the privileged ones who entered, the mingling, later, with the hopeful and the near-hopeless ones who waited. But now his feeling was that he had, somehow, become a part of that higher life beyond the gate. He might linger outside at odd moments, but rightfully he belonged inside. His novitiate had passed. He was one of those who threw knives or battled at the sawmill with the persecuter of golden-haired innocence, or lured beautiful women from their homes. He might be taken, he thought, for an actor resting between pictures.

At the gate he suffered a momentary regret at an error of tactics committed the evening before. Instead of leaving the lot by the office he should have left by the gate. He should have strolled to this exit in a leisurely manner and stopped, just inside the barrier, for a chat with the watchman; a chat, beginning with the gift of a cigar, which should have impressed his appearance upon that person. He should have remarked casually that he had had a hard day on Stage Number Four, and must now be off to a good night's rest because of the equally hard day tomorrow. Thus he could now have approached the gate with confidence and passed freely in, with a few more pleasant words to the watchman who would have no difficulty in recalling him.

But it was vain to wish this. For all the watchman knew this young man had never been beyond the walls of the forbidden city, nor would he know any reason why the besieger should not forever be kept outside. He would fix that next time.

He approached the window of the casting office with mingled emotions. He did not hope to find his friend again stricken with headache, but if it chanced that she did suffer he hoped to be the first to learn of it. Was he not fortified with the potent Eezo wafers, and a new menthol pencil, even with an additional remedy of tablets that the druggist had strongly recommended? It was, therefore, not with any actual, crude disappointment that he learned of his friend's perfect well-being. She smiled pleasantly at him, the telephone receiver at one ear. "Nothing today, dear," she said and put down the instrument.

Yes, the headache was gone, vanquished by his remedies. She was fine, thank you. No, the headaches didn't come often. It might be weeks before she had another attack. No, of course she couldn't be certain of this. And indeed she would be sure to let him know at the very first sign of their recurrence.

He looked over his patient with real anxiety, a solicitude from the bottom of which he was somehow unable to expel the last trace of a lingering hope that would have dismayed the little woman — not hope, exactly, but something almost like it which he would only translate to himself as an earnest desire that he might be at hand when the dread indisposition did attack her. Just now there could be no doubt that she was free from pain.

He thanked her profusely for her courtesy of the day before. He had seen wonderful things. He had learned a lot. And he wanted to ask her something, assuring himself that he was alone in the waiting room. It was this: did she happen to know — was Miss Beulah Baxter married?

The little woman sighed in a tired manner. "Baxter married? Let me see." She tapped her teeth with the end of a pencil, frowning into her vast knowledge of the people beyond the gate. "Now, let me think." But this appeared to be without result. "Oh, I really don't know; I forget. I suppose so. Why not? She often is."

He would have asked more questions, but the telephone rang and she listened a long time, contributing a "yes, yes," of under-

standing at brief intervals. This talk ended, she briskly demanded a number and began to talk in her turn. Merton Gill saw that
for the time he had passed from her life. She was calling an agen-
cy. She wanted people for a diplomatic reception in Washington.
She must have a Bulgarian general, a Serbian diplomat, two
French colonels, and a Belgian captain, all in uniform and all
good types. She didn't want just anybody, but types that would
stand out. Holden studios on Stage Number Two. Before noon,
if possible. All right, then. Another bell rang, almost before she
had hung up. "Hello, Grace. Nothing today, dear. They're out on
location, down toward Venice, getting some desert stuff. Yes, I'll
let you know."

Merton Gill had now to make way at the window for a youngish, weary-looking woman who had once been prettier, who led
an elaborately dressed little girl of five. She lifted the child to
the window. "Say good-morning to the beautiful lady, Toots.
Good-morning, Countess. I'm sure you got something for Toots
and me today because it's our birthday — both born on the same
day — what do you think of that? Any little thing will help us out
a lot — how about it?"

He went outside before the end of this colloquy, but presently
saw the woman and her child emerge and walk on disconsolate-
ly toward the next studio. Thus began another period of waiting
from which much of the glamour had gone. It was not so easy
now to be excited by those glimpses of the street beyond the
gate. A certain haze had vanished, leaving all too apparent the
circumstance that others were working beyond the gate while
Merton Gill loitered outside, his talent, his training, ignored.
His early air of careless confidence had changed to one not at
all careless or confident. He was looking rather desperate and
rather unbelieving. And it daily grew easier to count his savings.
He made no mistakes now. His hoard no longer enjoyed the addition of 15 dollars a week. Only subtractions were made.

There came a morning when but one bill remained. It was
a 10-dollar bill, bearing at its center a steel-engraved portrait
of Andrew Jackson. He studied it in consternation, though still
permitting himself to notice that Jackson would have made a
good motion-picture type — the long, narrow, severe face, the

stiff uncomprising mane of gray hair; probably they would have cast him for a feuding mountaineer, deadly with his rifle, or perhaps as an inventor whose device was stolen on his death-bed by his wicked Wall Street partner, thus leaving his motherless daughter at the mercy of Society's wolves.

But this was not the part that Jackson played in the gripping drama of Merton Gill. His face merely stared from the last money brought from Simsbury, Illinois, and the stare was not reassuring. It seemed to say that there was no other money in all the world. Decidedly things must take a turn. Merton Gill had a quite definite feeling that he had already struggled and sacrificed enough to give the public something better and finer. It was time the public realized this.

Still he waited, not even again reaching the heart of things, for his friend beyond the window had suffered no relapse. He came to resent a certain inconsequence in the woman. She might have had those headaches oftener. He had been led to suppose that she would, and now she continued to be weary but entirely well.

More waiting and the 10-dollar bill went for a five and some silver. He was illogically not sorry to be rid of Andrew Jackson, who had looked so tragically skeptical. The five-dollar bill was much more cheerful. It bore the portrait of Benjamin Harrison, a smooth, cheerful face adorned with whiskers that radiated success. They were little short of smug with success. He would almost rather have had Benjamin Harrison on five dollars than the grim-faced Jackson on 10. Still, facts were facts. You couldn't wait as long on five dollars as you could on 10.

Then on the afternoon of a day that promised to end as other days had ended, a wave of animation swept through the waiting room and the casting office. "Swell cabaret stuff" was the phrase that brought the applicants to a lively swarm about the little window. Evening clothes, glad wraps, cigarette cases, vanity-boxes — the Victor people doing *The Blight of Broadway* with Muriel Mercer — Stage Number Four at 8:30 tomorrow morning. There seemed no limit to the people desired. Merton Gill joined the throng about the window. Engagements were rapidly made, both through the window and over the telephone that was now ringing those people who had so long been told that there was nothing today. He did not push ahead of the women as some of the other men did. He even stood out of the line for the Montague girl who had suddenly appeared and who from the rear had been exclaiming: "Women and children first!"

"Thanks, old dear," she acknowledged the courtesy and beamed through the window. "Hullo, Countess!" The woman nodded briefly. "All right, Flips; I was just going to telephone you. Henshaw wants you for some baby-vamp stuff in the cabaret scene and in the gambling hell. Better wear that salmon-pink chiffon and the yellow curls. 8:30, Stage Four. Goo'-bye."

"Thanks, Countess! Me for the jumping tintypes at the hour named. I'm glad enough to be doing even third business. How about Ma?"

"Sure! Tell her grand-dame stuff, chaperone or something, the gray georgette and all her pearls and the cigarette case."

"I'll tell her. She'll be glad there's something doing once more on the perpendicular stage. Goo'-bye."

She stepped aside with "You're next, brother!" Merton Gill acknowledged this with a haughty inclination of the head. He must not encourage this hoyden. He glanced expectantly through the little window. His friend held a telephone receiver at her ear. She smiled wearily. "All right, son. You got evening clothes, haven't you? Of course, I remember now. Stage Four at 8:30. Goo'-bye."

"I want to thank you for this opportunity —" he began, but was pushed aside by an athletic young woman who spoke from under a broad hat. "Hullo, dearie! How about me and Ella?"

"Hullo, Maizie. All right. Stage Four, at 8:30, in your swellest evening stuff."

At the door the Montague girl called to an approaching group who seemed to have heard by wireless or occult means the report of new activity in the casting office. "Hurry, you troupers. You can eat tomorrow night, maybe!" They hurried. She turned to Merton Gill. "Seems like old times," she observed.

"Does it?" he replied coldly. Would this chit never understand that he disapproved of her trifling ways?

He went on, rejoicing that he had not been compelled to part, even temporarily, with a first-class full-dress suit, hitherto worn only in the privacy of Lowell Hardy's studio. It would have been awkward, he thought, if the demand for it had been much longer delayed. He would surely have let that go before sacrificing his Buck Benson outfit. He had traversed the eucalyptus avenue in this ecstasy, and was on a busier thoroughfare. Before a motion-picture theater he paused to study the billing of Muriel Mercer in *Hearts Aflame*. The beauteous girl, in an alarming gown, was at the mercy of a fiend in evening dress whose hellish purpose was all too plainly read in his fevered eyes. The girl writhed in his grasp. Doubtless he was demanding her hand in marriage. It was a tense bit. And tomorrow he would act with this petted idol of the screen. And under the direction of that Mr. Henshaw who seemed to take screen art with proper seriousness. He wondered if by any chance Mr. Henshaw would call upon him to do a quadruple transition, hate, fear, love, despair. He practiced a few transitions as he went on to press his evening clothes in the Patterson kitchen, and to dream, that night, that he rode his good old pal, Pinto, into the gilded cabaret to carry off Muriel Mercer, Broadway's pampered society pet, to the clean life out there in the open spaces where men are men.

At eight the following morning he was made up in a large dressing room by a grumbling extra who said that it was a dog's life plastering grease paint over the maps of dubs. He was presently on Stage Four in the prescribed evening regalia for gentlemen. He found the cabaret set, a gilded haunt of pleasure with small tables set about an oblong of dancing floor. Back of these on three sides were raised platforms with other tables, and above these discreet boxes, half masked by drapery, for the seclusion of more retiring merry-makers. The scene was deserted as yet, but presently he was joined by another early comer, a beautiful young woman of Spanish type with a thin face and eager, dark eyes. Her gown was glistening black set low about her polished shoulders, and she carried a red rose. So exotic did she appear he was surprised when she addressed him in the purest English.

"Say, listen here, old timer! Let's pick a good table right on the edge before the mob scene starts. Lemme see —" She glanced up and down the rows of tables. "The cam'ras'll be back there, so we can set a little closer, but not too close, or we'll be moved over.

How 'bout this here? Let's try it." She sat, motioning him to the other chair. Even so early in his picture career did he detect that in facing this girl his back would be to the camera. He hitched his chair about.

"That's right," said the girl, "I wasn't meaning to hog it. Say, we was just in time, wasn't we?"

Ladies and gentlemen in evening dress were already entering. They looked inquiringly about and chose tables. Those next to the dancing space were quickly filled. Many of the ladies permitted costly wraps of fur or brocade to spill across the backs of their chairs. Many of the gentlemen lighted cigarettes from gleaming metal cases. There was a lively interchange of talk.

"We better light up, too," said the dark girl. Merton Gill had neglected cigarettes and confessed this with some embarrassment. The girl presented an open case of gold attached to a chain pendent from her girdle. They both smoked. On their table were small plates, two wine glasses half filled with a pale liquid, and small coffee-cups. Spirals of smoke ascended over a finished repast. Of course if the part called for cigarettes you must smoke whether you had quit or not.

The places back of the prized first row were now filling up with the later comers. One of these, a masterful-looking man of middle age — he would surely be a wealthy club-man accustomed to command tables — regarded the filled row around the dancing space with frank irritation, and paused significantly at Merton's side. He seemed about to voice a demand, but the young actor glanced slowly up at him, achieving a superb transition — surprise, annoyance, and, as the invader turned quickly away, pitying contempt.

"Atta boy!" said his companion, who was, with the aid of a tiny gold-backed mirror suspended with the cigarette case, heightening the crimson of her full lips.

Two cameras were now in view, and men were sighting through them. Merton saw Henshaw, plump but worried looking, scan the scene from the rear. He gave hurried direction to an assistant who came down the line of tables with a running glance at their occupants. He made changes. A couple here and a couple there would be moved from the first row and other couples would come to take their places. Under the eyes of this assistant the Spanish girl had become coquettish. With veiled glances, with flashing smiles from the red lips, with a small gloved hand upon Merton Gill's sleeve, she allured him. The assistant paused before them. The Spanish girl continued to allure. Merton Gill stared moodily at the half-empty wine glass, then exhaled smoke as he glanced up at his companion in profound ennui. If it was *The Blight of Broadway* probably they would want him to look bored.

"You two stay where you are," said the assistant, and passed on.

"Good work," said the girl. "I knew you was a type the minute I made you."

Red-coated musicians entered an orchestra loft far down the set. The voice of Henshaw came through a megaphone: "Everybody that's near the floor fox-trot." In a moment the space was thronged with dancers. Another voice called "Kick it!" and a glare of light came on.

"You an' me both!" said the Spanish girl, rising.

Merton Gill remained seated. "Can't," he said. "Sprained ankle." How was he to tell her that there had been no chance to learn this dance back in Simsbury, Illinois, where such things were frowned upon by pulpit and press? The girl resumed her seat, at first with annoyance, then brightened. "All right at that," she said. "I bet we get more footage this way." She again became coquettish, luring with her wiles one who remained sunk in ennui.

A whistle blew, a voice called "Save it!" and the lights jarred off. Henshaw came trippingly down the line. "You people didn't dance. What's the matter?" Merton Gill glanced up, doing a double transition, from dignified surprise to smiling chagrin. "Sprained ankle," he said, and fell into the bored look that had served him with the assistant. He exhaled smoke and raised his tired eyes to the still luring Spanish girl. Weariness of the world and women was in his look. Henshaw scanned him closely.

"All right, stay there — keep just that way — it's what I want." He continued down the line, which had become hushed. "Now, people. I want some flashes along here, between dances — see what I mean? You're talking, but you're bored with it all. The hollowness of this night life is getting you; not all of you — most of you girls can keep on smiling — but *The Blight of Broadway* shows on many. You're beginning to wonder if this is all life has to offer — see what I mean?" He continued down the line.

From the table back of Merton Gill came a voice in speech to the retreating back of Henshaw: "All right, old top, but it'll take a good lens to catch any blight on this bunch — most of 'em haven't worked a lick in six weeks, and they're tickled pink." He knew without turning that this was the Montague girl trying to be funny at the expense of Henshaw who was safely beyond hearing. He thought she would be a disturbing element in the scene, but in this he was wrong, for he bent upon the wine glass a look more than ever fraught with jaded world-weariness. The babble of Broadway was resumed as Henshaw went back to the cameras.

Presently a camera was pushed forward. Merton Gill hardly dared look up, but he knew it was halted at no great distance from him. "Now, here's rather a good little bit," Henshaw was saying. "You, there, the girl in black, go on — tease him the way you were, and he's to give you that same look. Got that cigarette going? All ready. Lights! Camera!" Merton was achieving his first close-up. Under the hum of the lights he was thinking that he had been a fool not to learn dancing, no matter how the Reverend Otto Carmichael denounced it as a survival from the barbaric Congo. He was also thinking that the Montague girl ought to be kept away from people who were trying to do really creative things, and he was bitterly regretting that he had no silver cigarette case. The gloom of his young face was honest gloom. He was aware that his companion leaned vivaciously toward him with gay chatter and gestures. Very slowly he inhaled from a cigarette that was already distasteful — adding no little to the desired effect — and very slowly he exhaled as he raised to hers the bored eyes of a soul quite disillusioned. Here, indeed, was the blight of Broadway.

"All right, first rate!" called Henshaw. "Now get this bunch down here." The camera was pushed on.

"Gee, that was luck!" said the girl. "Of course it'll be cut to a flash, but I bet we stand out, at that." She was excited now, no longer needing to act.

From the table back of Merton came the voice of the Montague girl: "Yes, one must suffer for one's art. Here I got to be a baby-vamp when I'd rather be simple little Madelon, beloved by all in the village."

He restrained an impulse to look around at her. She was not serious and should not be encouraged. Farther down the set Henshaw was beseeching a table of six revelers to give him a little hollow gayety. "You're simply forcing yourselves to have a good time," he was saying; "remember that. Your hearts aren't in it. You know this night life is a mockery. Still, you're playing the game. Now, two of you raise your glasses to drink. You at the end stand up and hold your glass aloft. The girl next to you there, stand up by him and raise your face to his — turn sideways more. That's it. Put your hand up to his shoulder. You're slightly lit, you know, and you're inviting him to kiss you over his glass. You others, you're drinking gay enough, but see if you can get over that it's only half-hearted. You at the other end there — you're staring at your wine glass, then you look slowly up at your partner but without any life. You're feeling the blight, see? A chap down the line here just did it perfectly. All ready, now! Lights! Camera! You blonde girl, stand up, face raised to him, hand up to his shoulder. You others, drinking, laughing. You at the end, look up slowly at the girl, look away — about there — bored, weary of it all — cut! All right. Not so bad. Now this next bunch, Paul."

Merton Gill was beginning to loathe cigarettes. He wondered if Mr. Henshaw would mind if he didn't smoke so much, except, of course, in the close-ups. His throat was dry and rough, his voice husky. His companion had evidently played more smoking parts and seemed not to mind it.

Henshaw was now opposite them across the dancing floor, warning his people to be gay but not too gay. The glamour of this night life must be a little dulled.

"Now, Paul, get about three medium shots along here. There's a good table — get that bunch. And not quite so solemn, people; don't overdo it. You think you're having a good time, even if it does turn to ashes in your mouth — now, ready; lights! Camera!"

"I like Western stuff better," confided Merton to his companion. She considered this, though retaining her arch manner.

"Well, I don't know. I done a Carmencita part in a dance hall scene last month over to the Bigart, and right in the mi'st of the fight I get a glass of somethin' all over my gown that practically rooned it. I guess I rather do this refined cabaret stuff — at least you ain't so li'ble to roon a gown. Still and all, after you been warmin' the extra bench for a month one can't be choosy. Say, there's the princ'ples comin' on the set."

He looked around. There, indeed, was the beautiful Muriel Mercer, radiant in an evening frock of silver. At the moment she was putting a few last touches to her perfect face from a make-up box held by a maid. Standing with her was another young woman, not nearly so beautiful, and three men. Henshaw was instructing these. Presently he called through his megaphone: "You people are excited by the entrance of the famous Vera Vanderpool and her friends. You stop drinking, break off your talk, stare at her — see what I mean? — she makes a sensation. Music, lights, camera!"

Down the set, escorted by a deferential head-waiter, came Muriel Mercer on the arm of a middle-aged man who was elaborately garnished but whose thin dyed mustaches, partially bald head, and heavy eyes, proclaimed him to Merton Gill as one who meant the girl no good. They were followed by the girl who was not so beautiful and the other two men. These were young chaps of pleasing exterior who made the progress laughingly. The five were seated at a table next the dancing space at the far end. They chatted gayly as the older man ordered importantly from the head-waiter. Muriel Mercer tapped one of the younger men with her plumed fan and they danced. Three other selected couples danced at the same time, though taking care not to come between the star and the grinding camera. The older man leered at the star and nervously lighted a gold-tipped cigarette which he immediately discarded after one savage bite at it. It could be seen that Vera Vanderpool was the gayest of all that gay throng. Upon her as yet had come no blight of Broadway, though she shrank perceptibly when the partially bald one laid his hand on her slender wrist as she resumed her seat. Food and wine were brought. Vera Vanderpool drank, with a pretty flourish of her glass.

Now the two cameras were moved forward for close-ups. The older man was caught leering at Vera. It would surely be seen that he was not one to trust. Vera was caught with the mad light of pleasure in her beautiful eyes. Henshaw was now speaking in low tones to the group, and presently Vera Vanderpool did a transition. The mad light of pleasure died from her eyes and the smile froze on her beautiful mouth. A look almost of terror came into her eyes, followed by a pathetic lift of the upper lip. She stared intently above the camera. She was beholding some evil thing far from that palace of revels.

"Now they'll cut back to the tenement-house stuff they shot last week," explained the Spanish girl.

"Tenement house?" queried Merton. "But I thought the story would be that she falls in love with a man from the great wind-swept spaces out West, and goes out there to live a clean open life with him — that's the way I thought it would be — out there where she could forget the blight of Broadway."

"No, Mercer never does Western stuff. I got a little girl friend workin' with her and she told me about this story. Mercer gets into this tenement house down on the east side, and she's a careless society butterfly; but all at once she sees what a lot of sorrow there is in this world when she sees these people in the tenement house, starving to death, and sick kids and everything, and this little friend of mine does an Italian girl with a baby and this old man here, he's a rich swell and prominent in Wall Street and belongs to all the clubs, but he's the father of this girl's child, only Mercer don't know that yet. But she gets aroused in her better nature by the sight of all this trouble, and she almost falls in love with another gentleman who devotes all his time to relieving the poor in these tenements — it was him who took her there — but still she likes a good time as well as anybody, and she's stickin' around Broadway and around this old guy who's pretty good company in spite of his faults. But just now she got a shock at remembering the horrible sights she has seen; she can't get it out of her mind. And pretty soon she'll see this other gentleman that she nearly fell in love with, the one who hangs around these tenements doing good — he'll be over at one of them tables and she'll leave her party and go over to his table and say, 'Take me from this heartless Broadway to your tenements where I can relieve their suffering,' so she goes out and gets in a taxi with him, leaving the old guy with not a thing to do but pay the check. Of course he's mad, and he follows her down to the tenements where she's relieving the poor — just in a plain black dress — and she finds out he's the real father of this little friend of mine's child, and tells him to go back to Broadway while she has chosen the better part and must live her life with these real people. But he sends her a note that's supposed to be from a poor woman dying of something, to come and bring her some medicine, and she goes off alone to this dive in another street, and it's the old guy himself who has sent the note, and he has her there in this cellar in his power. But the other gentleman has found the note and has follered her, and breaks in the door and puts up a swell fight with the old guy and some toughs he has hired, and gets her off safe and sound, and so they're married and live the real life far away from the blight of Broadway. It's a swell story, all right, but Mercer can't act it. This little friend of mine can act all around her. She'd be a star if only she was better lookin'. You bet Mercer don't allow any lookers on the same set with her. Do you make that one at the table with her now? Just got looks enough to show Mercer off. Mercer's swell-lookin', I'll give her that, but for actin' — say, all they need in a piece for her is just some stuff to go in between her close-ups. Don't make much difference what it is. Oh, look! There comes the dancers. It's Luzon and Mario."

Merton Gill looked. These would be hired dancers to entertain the pleasure-mad throng, a young girl with vine leaves in her hair and a dark young man of barbaric appearance. The girl was clad in a mere whisp of a girdle and shining breast plates, while the man was arrayed chiefly in a coating of dark stain. They swirled over the dance floor to the broken rhythm of the orchestra, now clinging, now apart, working to a climax in which the man poised with his partner perched upon one shoulder. Through the megaphone came instructions to applaud the couple, and Broadway applauded — all but Merton Gill, who stared moodily into his coffee cup or lifted bored eyes to the scene of revelry. He was not bored, but his various emotions combined to produce this effect very plausibly. He was dismayed at this sudden revelation of art in the dance so near him. Imogene Pulver had once done an art dance back in Simsbury, at the cantata of Esther in the vestry of the Methodist church, and had been not a little criticized for her daring; but Imogene had been abundantly clad, and her gestures much more restrained. He was trying now to picture how Gashwiler would take a thing like this, or Mrs. Gashwiler, for that matter! One glimpse of those practically unclad bodies skipping and bounding there would probably throw them into a panic. They couldn't have sat it through. And here he was, right up in front of them, and not turning a hair.

This reflection permitted something of the contemptuous to show in the random glances with which he swept the dancers? He could not look at them steadily, not when they were close, as they often were. Also, he loathed the cigarette he was smoking. The tolerant scorn for the Gashwilers and his feeling for the cigarette brought him again into favorable notice. He heard Henshaw, but did not look up.

"Get another flash here, Paul. He's rather a good little bit." Henshaw now stood beside him. "Hold that," he said. "No, wait." He spoke to Merton's companion. "You change seats a minute with Miss Montague, as if you'd got tired of him — see what I mean? Miss Montague — Miss Montague." The Spanish girl arose, seeming not wholly pleased at this bit of directing. The Montague girl came to the table. She was a blithesome sprite in a salmon-pink dancing frock. Her blonde curls fell low over one eye which she now cocked inquiringly at the director.

"You're trying to liven him up," explained Henshaw. "That's all — baby-vamp him. He'll do the rest. He's quite a good little bit."

The Montague girl flopped into the chair, leaned roguishly toward Merton Gill, placed a small hand upon the sleeve of his coat and peered archly at him through beaded lashes, one eye almost hidden by its thatch of curls. Merton Gill sunk low in his chair, cynically tapped the ash from his tenth cigarette into the coffee cup and raised bored eyes to hers. "That's it — shoot it, Paul, just a flash."

The camera was being wheeled toward them. The Montague girl, with her hand still on his arm, continued her wheedling, though now she spoke.

"Why, look who's here. Kid, I didn't know you in your stepping-out clothes. Say, listen, why do you always upstage me? I never done a thing to you, did I? Go on, now, give me the fishy eye again. How'd you ace yourself into this first row, anyway? Did you have to fight for it? Say, your friend'll be mad at me putting her out of here, won't she? Well, blame it on the gelatin master. I never suggested it. Say, you got Henshaw going. He likes that blighted look of yours."

He made no reply to this chatter. He must keep in the picture. He merely favored her with a glance of fatigued indifference. The camera was focused.

"All ready, you people. Do like I said, now. Lights, camera!"

Merton Gill drew upon his cigarette with the utmost disrelish, raised the cold eyes of a disillusioned man to the face of the leering Montague girl, turned aside from her with every sign of apathy, and wearily exhaled the smoke. There seemed to be but this one pleasure left to him.

"Cut!" said Henshaw, and somewhere lights jarred off. "Just stick there a bit, Miss Montague. We'll have a couple more shots when the dancing begins."

Merton resented this change. He preferred the other girl. She lured him but not in so pronounced, so flagrant a manner. The blight of Broadway became more apparent than ever upon his face. The girl's hand still fluttered upon his sleeve as the music came and dancers shuffled by them.

"Say, you're the actin' kid, all right." She was tapping the floor with the heel of a satin slipper. He wished above all things that she wouldn't call him "Kid." He meditated putting a little of Broadway's blight upon her by saying in a dignified way that his real name was Clifford Armytage. Still, this might not blight her — you couldn't tell about the girl.

"You certainly are the actin'est kid on this set, I'll tell the lot that. Of course these close-ups won't mean much, just about one second, or half that maybe. Or some hick in the cuttin' room may kill 'em dead. Come on, give me the fish-eye again. That's it. Say, I'm glad I didn't have to smoke cigarettes in this scene. They wouldn't do for my type, standin' where the brook and river meet up. I hate a cigarette worse'n anything. You — I bet you'd give up food first."

"I hate 'em, too," he muttered grudgingly, glad to be able to say this, even though only to one whose attentions he meant to discourage. "If I have to smoke one more it'll finish me."

"Now, ain't that the limit? Too bad, Kid!"

"I didn't even have any of my own. That Spanish girl gave me these."

The Montague girl glanced over his shoulder at the young woman whose place she had usurped. "Spanish, eh? If she's Spanish I'm a Swede right out of Switzerland. Any-way, I never could like to smoke. I started to learn one summer when I was eight. Pa and Ma and I was out with a tent Tom-show, me doing Little Eva, and between acts I had to put on pants and come out and do a smoking song, all about a kid learning to smoke his first cigar and not doin' well with it, see? But they had to cut it out. Gosh, what us artists suffer at times! Pa had me try it a couple of years later when I was doin' Louise the blind girl in the *Two Orphans*, playin' 30 cents top. It was a good song, all right, with lots of funny gags. I'd 'a' been the laughing hit of the bill if I could 'a' learned not to swallow. We had to cut it out again after the second night. Talk about entering into your part. Me? I was too good."

If the distant camera glanced this way it caught merely the persistent efforts of a beautiful debutante who had not yet felt the blight of Broadway to melt the cynicism of one who suffered it more and more acutely each moment. Her hand fluttered on his sleeve and her left eye continuously beguiled him from under the overhanging curl. As often as he thought it desirable he put the bored glance upon her, though mostly he stared in dejection at the coffee cup or the empty wine glass. He was sorry that she had had that trouble with the cigar, but one who as Little Eva or poor persecuted Louise, the blind girl, had to do a song and dance between the acts must surely come from a low plane of art. He was relieved when, at megaphoned directions, an elderly fop came to whirl her off in the dance. Her last speech was: "That poor Henshaw — the gelatin master'll have mega-phone-lip by tonight."

He was left alone at his table. He wondered if they might want a close-up of him this way, uncompanioned, jaded, tired of it all, as if he would be saying: "There's always the river!" But nothing of this sort happened. There was more dancing, more close-ups of Muriel Mercer being stricken with her vision of tenement misery under the foul glare of a middle-aged roué inflamed with wine. And there was a shot of Muriel perceiving at last the blight of Broadway and going to a table at which sat a pale, noble-looking young man with a high forehead, who presently led her out into the night to the real life of the worthy poor. Later the deserted admirer became again a rouí inflamed with wine and submitted to a close-up that would depict his baffled rage. He clenched his hands in this and seemed to convey, with a snarling lift of his lip, that the girl would yet be his. Merton Gill had ceased to smoke. He had sounded on Broadway even the shallow pleasure of cigarettes. He was thoroughly blighted.

At last a megaphoned announcement from the assistant director dismissing the extras, keeping the star, the lead, and a few small-part people, to clean up medium shots, "dramatics," and other work requiring no crowd. "All you extra people here tomorrow morning, 8:30, same clothes and make-up." There was a quick breaking up of the revelry. The Broadway pleasure-seekers threw off the blight and stormed the assistant director for slips of paper which he was now issuing. Merton Gill received one, labeled "Talent check." There was fine print upon it which he took no pains to read, beyond gathering its general effect that the Victor Film-art Company had the full right to use any photographs of him that its agents might that day have obtained. What engrossed him to the exclusion of this legal formality was the item that he would now be paid seven dollars and fifty cents for his day's work — and once he had been forced to toil half a week for this sum! Emerging from the stage into the sunlight he encountered the Montague girl who hailed him as he would have turned to avoid her.

"Say, trouper, I thought I'd tell you in case you didn't know — we don't take our slips to that dame in that outside cafeteria any more. She always pinches off a quarter or may be four bits. They got it fixed now so the cash is always on tap in the office. I just thought I'd tell you."

"Thanks," he said, still with the jaded air of the disillusioned. He had only the vaguest notion of her meaning, but her intention had been kindly. "Thank you very much."

"Oh, don't mention it. I just thought I'd tell you." She glanced after him shrewdly.

Nearing the office he observed a long line of Broadway revelers waiting to cash their slips. Its head was lost inside the building and it trailed far outside. No longer was any blight to be perceived. The slips were ready in hand. Instead of joining the line Merton decided upon luncheon. It was two o'clock, and though waiters with trays had been abundant in the gilded cabaret, the best screen art had not seemed to demand a serving of actual food. Further, he would eat in the cafeteria in evening dress, his make-up still on, like a real actor. The other time he had felt conspicuous because nothing had identified him with the ordinary clientele of the place.

The room was not crowded now. Only a table here and there held late comers, and the choice of foods when he reached the serving counter at the back was limited. He permitted himself to complain of this in a practiced manner, but made a selection and bore his tray to the center of the room. He had chosen a table and was about to sit, when he detected Henshaw farther down the room, and promptly took the one next him. It was probable that Henshaw would recall him and praise the work he had done. But the director merely rolled unseeing eyes over him as he seated himself, and continued his speech to the man Merton had before seen him with, the grizzled dark man with the stubby gray mustache whom he called Governor. Merton wondered if he could be the governor of California, but decided not. Perhaps an ex-governor.

"She's working out well," he was saying. "I consider it one of the best continuities Belmore has done. Not a line of smut in it, but to make up for that we'll have over 30 changes of costume."

Merton Gill coughed violently, then stared moodily at his plate of baked beans. He hoped that this, at least, would recall him to Henshaw who might fix an eye on him to say: "And, by the way, here is a young actor that was of great help to me this morning." But neither man even glanced up. Seemingly this young actor could choke to death without exciting their notice. He stared less moodily at the baked beans. Henshaw would notice him sometime, and you couldn't do everything at once.

The men had finished their luncheon and were smoking. The animated Henshaw continued his talk. "And about that other thing we were discussing, Governor, I want to go into that with you. I tell you if we can do Robinson Crusoe, and do it right, a regular 5,000-foot program feature, the thing ought to gross a million. A good, clean, censor-proof picture — great kid show, run forever. Shipwreck stuff, loading the raft, island stuff, hut stuff, goats, finding the footprint, cannibals, the man Friday — can't you see it?"

The Governor seemed to see it. "Fine — that's so!" He stared above the director's head for the space of two inhalations from his cigarette, imbuing Merton Gill with gratitude that he need not smoke again that day. "But say, look here, how about your love interest?"

Henshaw waved this aside with his own cigarette and began to make marks on the back of an envelope. "Easy enough — Belmore can fix that up. We talked over one or two ways. How about having Friday's sister brought over with him to this island? The cannibals are going to eat her, too. Then the cannibals run to their canoes when they hear the gun, just the same as in the book. And Crusoe rescues the two. And when he cuts the girl's bonds he finds she can't be Friday's real sister, because she's white — see what I mean? Well, we work it out later that she's the daughter of an English Earl that was wrecked near the cannibal island, and they rescued her, and Friday's mother brought her up as her own child. She's saved the papers that came ashore, and she has the Earl's coat-of-arms tattooed on her shoulder blade, and finally, after Crusoe has fallen in love with her, and she's remembered a good deal of her past, along comes the old Earl, her father, in a ship and rescues them all. How about that?" Henshaw, brightly expectant, awaited the verdict of his chief.

"Well — I don't know." The other considered. "Where's your conflict, after the girl is saved from the savages? And Crusoe in the book wears a long beard. How about that? He won't look like anything — sort of hairy, and that's all."

Henshaw from the envelope on which he drew squares and oblongs appeared to gain fresh inspiration. He looked up with new light in his eyes. "I got it — got the whole thing. Modernize it. This chap is a rich young New Yorker, cruising on his yacht, and he's wrecked on this island and gets a lot of stuff ashore and his valet is saved, too — say there's some good comedy, see what I mean? — valet is one of these stiff English lads, never been wrecked on an island before and complains all the time about the lack of conveniences. I can see a lot of good gags for him, having to milk the goats, and getting scared of the other animals, and no place to press his master's clothes — things like that, you know. Well, the young fellow explores the island and finds another party that's been wrecked on the other side, and it's the girl and the man that got her father into his power and got all of his estate and is going to make beggars of them if the girl won't marry him, and she comes on the young fellow under some palms and they fall in love and fix it up to double-cross the villain — Belmore can work it out from there. How about that? And say, we can use a lot of trims from that South Sea piece we did last year, all that yacht and island stuff — see what I mean?"

The other considered profoundly. "Yes, you got a story there, but it won't be *Robinson Crusoe*, don't you see?"

Again Henshaw glanced up from his envelope with the light of inspiration. "Well, how about this? Call it *Robinson Crusoe, Junior*! There you are. We get the value of the name and do the story the way we want it, the young fellow being shaved every day by the valet, and he can invite the other party over to dine with him and receive them in evening dress and everything. Can't you see it? If that story wouldn't gross big then I don't know a story. And all easy stuff. We can use the trims for the long shots, and use that inlet, toward the other end of Catalina for the hut and the beach; sure-fire stuff, Governor — and *Robinson Crusoe, Junior* is a cinch title."

"Well, give Belmore as much dope as you've got, and see what he can work out."

They arose and stood by the counter to pay their checks.

"If you want to see the rushes of that stuff we shot this morning be over to the projection room at five," said Henshaw as they went out. Neither had observed the rising young screen actor, Clifford Armytage, though he had coughed violently again as they left. He had coughed most plausibly, moreover, because of the cigarettes.

At the cashier's window, no longer obstructed, he received his money, another five-dollar bill adorned with the cheerfully prosperous face of Benjamin Harrison and half that amount in silver coin. Then, although loath to do this, he went to the dressing room and removed his make-up. That grease paint had given him a world of confidence.

At the casting office he stopped to tell his friend of the day's camera triumph, how the director had seemed to single him out from a hundred or so revelers to portray facially the deadly effect of Broadway's night life.

"Good work!" she applauded. "Before long you'll be having jobs oftener. And don't forget, you're called again tomorrow morning for the gambling-house scene."

She was a funny woman; always afraid he would forget something he could not possibly forget. Once more in the Patterson kitchen he pressed his suit and dreamt of new eminences in his chosen art.

The following morning he was again the first to reach the long dressing room, the first to be made up by the grumbling extra, the first to reach the big stage. The cabaret of yesterday had overnight been transformed into a palatial gambling hell. Along the sides of the room and at its center were tables equipped for strange games of chance which only his picture knowledge enabled him to recognize. He might tarry at these tables, he thought, but he must remember to look bored in the near presence of Henshaw. The Spanish girl of yesterday appeared and he greeted her warmly. "I got some cigarettes this time," he said, "so let me pay you back all those I smoked of yours yesterday." Together they filled the golden case that hung from her girdle.

"It's swell, all right," said the girl, gazing about the vast room now filling with richly clad gamblers.

"But I thought it was all over except the tenement-house scenes where Vera Vanderpool has gone to relieve the poor," he said.

The girl explained. "This scene comes before the one we did yesterday. It's where the rich old boy first sees Vera playing roulette, and she loses a lot of money and is going to leave her string of pearls, but he says it's a mere trifle and let him pay her gambling losses, so in a weak moment she does, and that's how he starts to get her into his power. You'll see how it works out. Say, they spent some money on this set, all right."

It was indeed a rich set, as the girl had said. It seemed to Merton Gill that it would be called on the screen "One of those Plague Spots that Eat like a Cancer at the Heart of New York." He lighted a cigarette and leaned nonchalantly against a pillar to smile a tired little smile at the pleasure-mad victims of this life who were now grouping around the roulette and faro tables. He must try for his jaded look.

"Some swell shack!" The speaker was back of him, but he knew her for the Montague girl, and was instantly enabled to increase the blighted look for which he had been trying. "One natty little hovel, I'll tell the world," the girl continued. "Say, this puts it all over the Grand Central station, don't it? Must be right smack at the corner of Broadway and Fifth Avenue. Well, start the little ball rolling, so I can make a killing." He turned his head slightly and saw her dance off to one of the roulette tables, accompanied by the middle-aged fop who had been her companion yesterday.

Henshaw and his assistant now appeared and began grouping the players at the various tables. Merton Gill remained leaning wearily against his massive pillar, trying to appear blasé under the chatter of the Spanish girl. The groups were arranged to the liking of Henshaw, though only after many trials. The roulette ball was twirled and the lively rattle of chips could be heard. Scanning his scene, he noted Merton and his companion.

"Oh, there you are, you two. Sister, you go and stand back of that crowd around the faro table. Keep craning to look over their shoulders, and give us your side view. I want to use this man alone. Here." He led Merton to a round table on which were a deck of cards and some neatly stacked chips. "Sit here, facing the camera. Keep one hand on the cards, sort of toying with 'em, see what I mean?"

He scattered the piled chips loosely about the table, and called to a black waiter: "Here, George, put one of those wine glasses on his left."

The wine glass was placed. "Now kind of slump down in your chair, like you saw the hollowness of it all — see what I mean?"

Merton Gill thought he saw. He exhaled smoke, toyed contemptuously with the cards at his right hand and, with a gesture of repulsion, pushed the wine glass farther away. He saw the hollowness of it all. The spirit of wine sang in his glass but to deaf ears. Chance could no longer entice him. It might again have been suspected that cigarettes were ceasing to allure.

"Good work! Keep it up," said Henshaw and went back to his cameras.

The lights jarred on; desperate gaming was filmed. "More life at the roulette tables," megaphoned Henshaw. "Crowd closer around that left-hand faro table. You're playing for big stakes." The gaming became more feverish. The mad light of pleasure was in every eye, yet one felt that the blight of Broadway was real.

The camera was wheeled forward and Merton Gill joyously quit smoking while Henshaw secured flashes of various groups, chiefly of losers who were seeing the hollowness of it all. He did not, however, disdain a bit of comedy.

"Miss Montague."

"Yes, Mr. Henshaw." The Montague girl paused in the act of sprinkling chips over a roulette lay-out.

"Your escort has lost all his chips and you've lost all he bought for you —"

The girl and her escort passed to other players the chips before them, and waited.

"Your escort takes out his wallet, shows it to you empty, and shrugs his shoulders. You shrug, too, but turn your back on him, facing the camera, and take some bills out of your stocking — see what I mean? Give her some bills, someone."

"Never mind, Mr. Henshaw; I already got some there." The pantomime was done, the girl turned, stooped, withdrew flattened bills from one of the salmon-pink stockings and flourished them at her escort who achieved a transition from gloom to joy. Merton Gill, observing this shameless procedure, plumbed the nether depths of disgust for Broadway's night life.

The camera was now wheeled toward him and he wearily lighted another cigarette. "Get a flash of this chap," Henshaw was saying. The subject leaned forward in his chair, gazing with cynical eyes at the fevered throng. Wine, women, song, all had palled. Gambling had no charm — he looked with disrelish at the cigarette he had but just lighted.

"All right, Paul, that's good. Now get that bunch over at the crap table."

Merton Gill lost no time in relinquishing his cigarette. He dropped it into the wine glass which became a symbol of Broadway's dead-sea fruit. Thereafter he smoked only when he was in the picture. He felt that he was becoming screen wise. And Henshaw had remembered him. The cast of *The Blight of Broadway* might not be jeweled with his name, but his work would stand out. He had given the best that was in him.

He watched the entrance of Muriel Mercer, maddest of all the mad throng, accompanied by the two young men and the girl who was not so beautiful. He watched her lose steadily, and saw her string of pearls saved by the elderly scoundrel who had long watched the beautiful girl as only the Wolf of Wall Street could watch one so fair. He saw her leave upon his arm, perhaps for further unwholesome adventure along Broadway. The lights were out, the revelry done.

Merton Gill beyond a doubt preferred Western stuff, some heart-gripping tale of the open spaces, or perhaps of the frozen north, where he could be the hard-riding, straight-shooting, two-fisted wonder-man, and not have to smoke so many cigarettes — only one now and then, which he would roll himself and toss away after a few puffs. Still, he had shown above the mob of extra people, he thought. Henshaw had noticed him. He was coming on.

The Montague girl hailed him as he left the set. "Hullo, old trouper. I caught you actin' again today, right out before the

white folks. Well, so far so good. But say, I'm glad all that roulette and stuff was for the up-and-down stage and not on the level. I'd certainly have lost everything but my make-up. So long,
Kid!" She danced off to join a group of other women who were
leaving. He felt a kindly pity for the child. There could be little
future in this difficult art for one who took it so lightly; who
talked so frankly to strangers without being introduced.

At luncheon in the cafeteria he waited a long time in the hope
of encountering Henshaw, who would perhaps command his
further services in the cause of creative screen art. He meant to
be animated at this meeting, to show the director that he could
be something more than an actor who had probed the shams of
Broadway. But he lingered in vain. He thought Henshaw would
perhaps be doing without food in order to work on the scenario
for *Robinson Crusoe, Junior.*

He again stopped to thank his friend, the casting director, for
securing him his first chance. She accepted his thanks smilingly,
and asked him to drop around often. "Mind, you don't forget
our number," she said.

He was on the point of making her understand once for all
that he would not forget the number, that he would never forget Gashwiler's address, that he had been coming to this studio
too often to forget its location. But someone engaged her at the
window, so he was obliged to go on without enlightening the
woman. She seemed to be curiously dense.

CHAPTER VII

"NOTHING TODAY, DEAR!"

THE SAVINGS had been opportunely replenished. In two days he had accumulated a sum for which, back in Simsbury, he would have had to toil a week. Yet there was to be said in favor of the Simsbury position that it steadily endured. Each week brought its 15 dollars, pittance though it might be, while the art of the silver screen was capricious in its rewards, not to say jumpy. Never, for weeks at a stretch, had Gashwiler said with a tired smile, "Nothing today — sorry!" He might have been a grouch and given to unreasonable nagging, but with him there was always a very definite something today which he would specify, in short words if the occasion seemed to demand. There was not only a definite something every day but a definite if not considerable sum of money to be paid over every Saturday night, and in the meantime three very definite and quite satisfying meals to be freely partaken of at stated hours each day.

The leisure enforced by truly creative screen art was often occupied now with really moving pictures of Metta Judson placing practicable food upon the Gashwiler table. This had been no table in a gilded Broadway resort, holding empty coffee cups and half empty wine glasses, passed and repassed by apparently busy waiters with laden trays who never left anything of a practicable nature. Doubtless the set would not have appealed to Henshaw. He would never have been moved to take close-ups, even for mere flashes, of those who ate this food. And yet, more and more as the days went by, this old-time film would unreel itself before the eager eyes of Merton Gill. Often now it thrilled him as might have an installment of *The Hazards of Hortense,* for the food of his favorite pharmacy was beginning to pall and Metta Judson, though giving her shallow mind to base village gossip, was a good cook. She became the adored heroine of an apparently endless serial to be entitled *The Hazards of Clifford Armytage*, in which the hero had tragically little to do but sit upon a bench and wait while tempting repasts were served.

Sometimes on the little bench around the eucalyptus tree he would run an entire 5,000-foot program feature, beginning with the Sunday midday dinner of roast chicken, and abounding in tense dramatic moments such as corned-beef and cabbage on Tuesday night, and corned-beef hash on Wednesday morning. He would pause to take superb close-ups of these, the corned beef on its spreading platter hemmed about with boiled potatoes and turnips and cabbage, and the corned beef hash with its richly browned surface. The thrilling climax would be the roast of beef on Saturday night, with close-ups taken in the very eye of the camera, of the mashed potatoes and the apple pie drenched with cream. And there were close-ups of Metta Judson, who had never seriously contemplated a screen career, placing upon the table a tower of steaming hot cakes, while a platter of small sausages loomed eloquently in the foreground.

With eyes closed he would run this film again and again, cutting here, rearranging sequences, adding trims from suddenly remembered meals of the dead past, devising more intimate close-ups, such as the one of Metta withdrawing pies from the oven or smoothing hot chocolate caressingly over the top of a giant cake, or broiling chops, or saying in a large-lettered subtitle — artistically decorated with cooked foods — "How about some hot coffee, Merton?"

He became an able producer of this drama. He devised a hundred sympathetic little touches that Henshaw would probably never have thought of. He used footage on a mere platter of steak that another director might have ignored utterly. He made it gripping — the supreme heart-interest drama of his season a big thing done in a big way, and yet censor-proof. Not even the white-souled censors of the great state of Pennsylvania could have outlawed its realism, brutal though this was in such great moments as when Gashwiler carved the roast beef. So able was his artistry that Merton's nostrils would sometimes betray him — he could swear they caught rich aromas from that distant board.

Not only had the fare purveyed by his favorite pharmacy put a blight upon him equal to Broadway's blight, but even of this tasteless stuff he must be cautious in his buying. A sandwich, not too meaty at the center, coffee tasting strangely of other things sold in a pharmacy, a segment of pie fair — seeming on its surface, but lacking the punch, as he put it, of Metta Judson's pie, a standardized, factory-made, altogether formal and perfunctory pie — these were the meagre items of his accustomed luncheon and dinner.

He had abandoned breakfast, partly because it cost money and partly because a gentleman in eastern Ohio had recently celebrated his 103rd birthday by reason, so he confided to the press, of having always breakfasted upon a glass of clear cold water. Probably ham and eggs or corned beef hash would have cut him off at 90, and water from the tap in the Patterson kitchen was both clear and cold. It was not so much that he cared to live beyond 90 or so, but he wished to survive until things began to pick up on the Holden lot, and if this did bring him many more years, well and good. Further, if the woman in the casting office persisted, as she had for 10 days, in saying "Nothing yet" to inquiring screen artists, he might be compelled to intensify the regime of the Ohio centenarian. Perhaps a glass of clear cold water at night, after a hearty midday meal of drugstore sandwiches and pie, would work new wonders.

It seemed to be the present opinion of other waiters on the extra bench that things were never going to pick up on the Holden lot nor on any other lot. Strongly marked types, ready to add distinction to the screen of painted shadows, freely expressed a view that the motion-picture business was on the rocks. Unaffected by the optimists who wrote in the picture magazines, they saw no future for it. More than one of them threatened to desert the industry and return to previous callings. As they were likely to put it, they were going to leave the pictures flat and go back to type-writing or selling standard art-works or waiting on table or something where you could count on your little bit every week.

Under the eucalyptus tree one morning Merton Gill, making some appetizing changes in the fifth reel of *Eating at Gashwiler's*, was accosted by a youngish woman whom he could not at first recall. She had come from the casting office and paused when she saw him.

"Hello, I thought it was you, but I wasn't sure in them clothes. How they coming?"

He stared blankly, startled at the sudden transposition he had been compelled to make, for the gleaming knife of Gashwiler, standing up to carve, had just then hovered above the well-browned roast of beef. Then he placed the speaker by reason of her eyes. It was the Spanish girl, his companion of the gilded cabaret, later encountered in the palatial gambling hell that ate like a cancer at the heart of New York — probably at the corner of Broadway and Fifth Avenue.

He arose and shook hands cordially. He had supposed, when he thought of the girl at all, that she would always be rather Spanish, an exotic creature rather garishly dressed, nervously eager, craving excitement such as may be had in cabarets on Broadway, with a marked inclination for the lighter life of pleasure. But she wore not so much as a rose in her smoothly combed hair. She was not only not excited but she was not exciting. She was plainly dressed in skirt and shirtwaist of no distinction, her foot-gear was of the most ordinary, and well worn, and her face under a hat of no allure was without make-up, a commonplace, somewhat anxious face with lines about the eyes. But her voice as well as her eyes helped him to recall her.

She spoke with an effort at jauntiness after Merton had greeted her. "That's one great slogan, 'Business as Usual!' ain't it? Well, it's business as usual here, so I just found out from the Countess — as usual, rotten. I ain't had but three days since I seen you last."

"I haven't had even one," he told her.

"No? Say, that's tough. You're registered with the Service Bureau, ain't you?"

"Well, I didn't do that, because they might send me any place, and I sort of wanted to work on this particular lot." Instantly he saw himself saving Beulah Baxter, for the next installment, from a fate worse than death, but the one-time Spanish girl did not share this vision.

"Oh, well, little I care where I work. I had two days at the Bigart in a hop-joint scene, and one over at the United doin' some board-walk stuff. I could 'a' had another day there, but the director said I wasn't just the type for a chick bathing-suit. He was very nice about it. Of course I know my legs ain't the best part of me — I sure ain't one of them like the girl that says she's wasted in skirts." She grinned ruefully.

He felt that some expression of sympathy would be graceful here, yet he divined that it must be very discreetly, almost delicately, worded. He could easily be too blunt.

"I guess I'd be pretty skinny in a bathing-suit myself, right now. I know they won't be giving me any such part pretty soon if I have to cut down on the meals the way I been doing."

"Oh, of course I don't mean I'm actually skinny —"

He felt he had been blunt, after all.

"Not to say skinny." she went on, "but — well, you know — more like home-folks, I guess. Anyway, I got no future as a bathing beauty — none whatever. And this walkin' around to the different lots ain't helpin' me any, either. Of course it ain't as if I couldn't go back to the insurance office. Mr. Gropp, he's office manager, he was very nice about it. He says, 'I wish you all the luck in the world, girlie, and remember your job as filin' clerk will always be here for you.' Wasn't that gentlemanly of him? Still, I'd rather act than stand on my feet all day filing letters. I won't go back till I have to."

"Me either," said Merton Gill, struggling against the obsession of Saturday-night dinner at Gashwiler's.

Grimly he resumed his seat when the girl with a friendly "So long!" had trudged on. In spite of himself he found something base in his nature picturing his return to the emporium and to the thrice-daily encounter with Metta Judson's cookery. He let his lower instincts toy with the unworthy vision. Gashwiler would advance him the money to return, and the job would be there. Probably Spencer Grant had before this tired of the work and gone into insurance or some other line, and probably Gashwiler would be only too glad to have the wanderer back. He would get off No. 3 just in time for breakfast.

He brushed the monstrous scene from his eyes, shrugged it from his shoulders. He would not give up. They had all struggled and sacrificed, and why should he shrink from the common ordeal? But he wished the Spanish girl hadn't talked about going back to her job. He regretted not having stopped her with words of confident cheer that would have stiffened his own resolution. He could see her far down the street, on her way to the next lot, her narrow shoulders switching from light to shadow as she trudged under the line of eucalyptus trees. He hoped she wouldn't give up. No one should ever give up — least of all Merton Gill.

The days wore wearily on. He began to feel on his own face the tired little smile of the woman in the casting office as she would look up to shake her head, often from the telephone over which she was saying: "Nothing today, dear. Sorry!" She didn't exactly feel that the motion-picture business had gone on the rocks, but she knew it wasn't picking up as it should. And ever and again she would have Merton Gill assure her that he hadn't forgotten the home address, the town where lived Gighampton or Gumwash or whoever it was that held the good old job open for him. He had divined that it was a jest of some sort when she warned him not to forget the address and he would patiently smile at this, but he always put her right about the name of Gashwiler. Of course it was a name any one might forget, though the woman always seemed to make the most earnest effort to remember it.

Each day, after his brief chat with her in which he learned that there would be nothing today, he would sit on the waiting-room bench or out under the eucalyptus tree and consecrate himself anew to the art of the perpendicular screen. And each day, as the little hoard was diminished by even those slender repasts at the drug store, he ran his film of the Gashwiler dining room in action.

From time to time he would see the Montague girl, alone or with her mother, entering the casting office or perhaps issuing from the guarded gate. He avoided her when possible. She persisted in behaving as if they had been properly introduced and had known each other a long time. She was too familiar, and her levity jarred upon his more serious mood. So far as he could see, the girl had no screen future, though doubtless she was her own worst enemy. If someone had only taught her to be serious, her career might have been worthwhile. She had seemed not wholly negligible in the salmon-pink dancing frock, though of course the blonde curls had not been true.

Then the days passed until eating merely at a drugstore lunch counter became not the only matter of concern. There was the item of room rent. Mrs. Patterson, the Los Angeles society woman, had, upon the occasion of their first interview, made it all too clear that the money, trifling though it must seem for a well-furnished room with the privilege of electric iron in the kitchen, must be paid each week in advance. Strictly in advance. Her eye had held a cold light as she dwelt upon this.

There had been times lately when, upon his tree bench, he would try to dramatize Mrs. Patterson as a woman with a soft heart under that polished society exterior, chilled by daily contact with other society people at the Iowa or Kansas or other society picnics, yet ready to melt at the true human touch. But he had never quite succeeded in this bit of character work. Something told him that she was cold all through, a society woman without a flaw in her armor. He could not make her seem to listen patiently while he explained that only one company was now shooting on the lot, but that big things were expected to be on in another week or so. A certain skeptic hardness was in her gaze as he visioned it.

He decided, indeed, that he could never bring himself even to attempt this scene with the woman, so remote was he from seeing her eye soften and her voice warm with the assurance that a few weeks more or less need not matter. The room rent, he was confident, would have to be paid strictly in advance so long as their relations continued. She was the kind who would insist upon this formality even after he began to play, at an enormous salary, a certain outstanding part in the *Hazards of Hortense*. The exigencies, even the adversities, of art would never make the slightest appeal to this hardened soul. So much for that. And daily the hoard waned.

Yet his was not the only tragedy. In the waiting room, where he now spent more of his time, he listened one day to the Montague girl chat through the window with the woman she called Countess.

"Yeah, Pa was double-crossed over at the Bigart. He raised that lovely set of whiskers for *Camillia of the Cumberlands* and what did he get for it? — just two weeks. Fact! What do you know about that? Hugo has him killed off in the second spool with a squirrel rifle from ambush, and Pa thinking he would draw pay for at least another three weeks. He kicked, but Hugo says the plot demanded it. I bet, at that, he was just trying to cut down his salary list. I bet that continuity this minute shows Pa drinking his corn out of a jug and playing a fiddle for the dance right down to the last scene. Don't artists get the razz, though. And that Hugo, he'd spend a week in the hot place to save a thin dime. Let me tell you, Countess, don't you ever get your lemon in his squeezer."

There were audible murmurs of sympathy from the Countess.

"And so the old trouper had to start out Monday morning to peddle the brush. Took him three days to land anything at all, and then it's nothing but a sleeping souse in a Western bar-room scene. In here now he is — something the Acme people are doing. He's had three days, just lying down with his back against a barrel sleeping. He's not to wake up even when the fight starts, but sleep right on through it, which they say will be a good gag. Well, maybe. But it's tough on his home. He gets all his rest daytimes and keeps us restless all night making a new kind of beer and tending his still, and so on. You bet Ma and I, the minute he's through with this piece, are going pronto to get that face of his as naked as the day he was born. Pa's so temperamental — like that time he was playing a Bishop and never touched a drop for five weeks, and in bed every night at nine-thirty. Me? Oh, I'm having a bit of my own in this Acme piece — *God's Great Outdoors*, I think it is — anyway, I'm to be a little blonde hussy in the bar-room, sitting on the miners' knees and all like that, so they'll order more drinks. It certainly takes all kinds of art to make an artist. And next week I got some shipwreck stuff for Baxter, and me with bronchial pneumonia right this minute, and hating tank stuff, anyway. Well, Countess, don't take any counterfeit money. So long."

She danced through a doorway and was gone — she was one who seldom descended to plain walking. She would manage a dance step even in the short distance from the casting office door to the window. It was not of such material, Merton Gill was sure, that creative artists were molded. And there was no question now of his own utter seriousness. The situation hourly grew more desperate. For a week he had foregone the drug-store pie, so that now he recalled it as very wonderful pie indeed, but he dared no longer indulge in this luxury. An occasional small bag of candy and as much sugar as he could juggle into his coffee must satisfy his craving for sweets. Stoically he awaited the end — some end. The moving-picture business seemed to be still on the rocks, but things must take a turn.

He went over the talk of the Montague girl. Her father had perhaps been unfairly treated, but at least he was working again. And there were other actors who would go unshaven for even a sleeping part in the bar-room scene of *God's Great Outdoors*. Merton Gill knew one, and rubbed his shaven chin. He thought, too, of the girl's warning about counterfeit money. He had not known that the casting director's duties required her to handle money, but probably he had overlooked this item in her routine. And was counterfeit money about? He drew out his own remaining bill and scrutinized it anxiously. It seemed to be genuine. He hoped it was, for Mrs. Patterson's sake, and was relieved when she accepted it without question that night.

Later he tested the handful of silver that remained to him and prayed earnestly that an increase of prosperity be granted to producers of the motion picture. With the silver he eked out another barren week, only to face a day the evening of which must witness another fiscal transaction with Mrs. Patterson. And there was no longer a bill for this heartless society creature. He took a long look at the pleasant little room as he left it that morning. The day must bring something but it might not bring him back that night.

At the drug store he purchased a bowl of vegetable soup, loaded it heavily with ketchup at intervals when the attendant had other matters on his mind, and seized an extra half-portion of crackers left on their plate by a satiated neighbor. He cared little for ketchup, but it doubtless bore nourishing elements, and nourishment was now important. He crumpled his paper napkin and laid upon the marble slab a trifling silver coin. It was the last of his hoard. When he should eat next and under what circumstances were now as uncertain as where he should sleep that night, though he was already resolving that ketchup would be no part of his meal. It might be well enough in its place, but he had abundantly proved that it was not, strictly speaking, a food.

He reached the Holden studios and loitered outside for half an hour before daring the daily inquiry at the window. Yet, when at last he did approach it, his waning faith in prayer was renewed, for here in his direst hour was cheering news. It seemed even that his friend beyond the window had been impatient at his coming.

"Just like you to be late when there's something doing!" she called to him with friendly impatience. "Get over to the dressing rooms on the double-quick. It's the Victor people doing some Egyptian stuff — they'll give you a costume. Hurry along!"

And he had lingered over a bowl of soggy crackers soaked, at the last, chiefly in ketchup! He hurried, with a swift word of thanks.

In the same dressing room where he had once been made up as a Broadway pleasure seeker he now donned the flowing robe and burnoose of a Bedouin, and by the same grumbling extra his face and hands were stained the rich brown of children of the desert. A dozen other men of the paler race had undergone the same treatment. A sheik of great stature and noble mien smoked an idle cigarette in the doorway. He was accoutered with musket and with pistols in his belt.

An assistant director presently herded the desert men down an alley between two of the big stages and to the beginning of the oriental street that Merton had noticed on his first day within the Holden walls. It was now peopled picturesquely with other Bedouins. Banners hung from the walls and veiled ladies peeped from the latticed balconies. A camel was led excitedly through the crowded way, and donkeys and goats were to be observed. It was a noisy street until a whistle sounded at the farther end, then all was silence while the voice of Henshaw came through the megaphone.

It appeared that long shots of the street were Henshaw's first need. Up and down it Merton Gill strolled in a negligent manner, stopping perhaps to haggle with the vendor who sold sweetmeats from a tray, or to chat with a tribal brother fresh from the sandy wastes, or to purchase a glass of milk from the man with the goats. He secured a rose from the flower seller, and had the inspiration to toss it to one of the discreet balconies above him, but as he stepped back to do this he was stopped by the watchful assistant director who stood just inside a doorway. "Hey, Bill, none of that! Keep your head down, and pay no attention to the dames. It ain't done."

He strolled on with the rose in his hand. Later, and much nearer the end of the street where the cameras were, he saw the sheik of noble mien halt the flower seller, haggle for another rose, place this daintily behind his left ear and stalk on, his musket held over one shoulder, his other hand on a belted pistol. Merton disposed of his rose in the same manner. He admired the sheik for his stature, his majestic carriage, his dark, handsome, yet sinister face with its brooding eyes. He thought this man, at least, would be a true Arab, some real son of the desert who had wandered afar. His manner was so much more authentic than that of the extra people all about.

A whistle blew and the street action was suspended. There was a long wait while cameras were moved up and groups formed under the direction of Henshaw and his assistant. A band of Bedouins were now to worship in the porch of a mosque. Merton Gill was among these. The assistant director initiated them briefly into Moslem rites. Upon prayer rugs they bowed their foreheads to earth in the direction of Mecca.

"What's the idea of this here?" demanded Merton Gill's neighbor in aggrieved tones.

"Ssh!" cautioned Merton. "It's Mass or something like that." And they bent in unison to this noon-tide devotion.

When this was done Henshaw bustled into the group. "I want about a dozen or 15 good types for the cafe," he explained to his assistant. Merton Gill instinctively stood forward, and was presently among those selected. "You'll do," said Henshaw, nodding. The director, of course, had not remembered that this was the actor he had distinguished in *The Blight of Broadway*, yet he had again chosen him for eminence. It showed, Merton felt, that his conviction about the screen value of his face was not ill founded.

The selected types were now herded into a dark, narrow, low-ceiled room with a divan effect along its three walls. A grizzled Arab made coffee over a glowing brazier. Merton Gill sat cross-legged on the divan and became fearful that he would be asked to smoke the narghileh which the assistant director was now preparing. To one who balked at mere cigarettes, it was an evil-appearing device. His neighbor who had been puzzled at prayer-time now hitched up his flowing robe to withdraw a paper of cigarettes from the pocket of a quite occidental garment.

"Go on, smoke cigarettes," said the assistant director.

"Have one?" said Merton's neighbor, and he took one. It seemed you couldn't get away from cigarettes on the screen. East and West were here one. He lighted it, though smoking warily. The noble sheik, of undoubtedly Asiatic origin, came to the doorway overlooking the assistant director's work on the narghileh. A laden camel halted near him, sneered in an evil manner at the bystanders, and then, lifting an incredible length of upper lip, set his yellow teeth in the nearest shoulder. It was the shoulder of the noble sheik, who instantly rent the air with a plaintive cry: "For the love of Mike! — keep that man-eater off'n me, can't you?"

His accent had not been that of the Arabian waste-land. Merton Gill was disappointed. So the fellow was only an actor, after all. If he had felt sympathy at all, it would now have been for the camel. The beast was jerked back with profane words and the sheik, rubbing his bitten shoulder, entered the cafe, sitting cross-legged at the end of the divan nearest the door.

"All right, Bob." The assistant director handed him the tube of the water pipe, and the sheik smoked with every sign of enjoyment. Merton Gill resolved never to play the part of an Arab sheik — at the mercy of man-eating camels and having to smoke something that looked murderous.

Under Henshaw's direction the grizzled proprietor now served tiny cups of coffee to the sheik and his lesser patrons. Two of these played dominoes, and one or two reclined as in sleep. Cameras were brought up. The interior being to his satisfaction, Henshaw rehearsed the entrance of a little band of European tourists. A beautiful girl in sports garb, a beautiful young man in khaki and puttees, a fine old British father with gray side whiskers shaded by a sun-hat with a flowing veil twined about it. These people sat and were served coffee, staring in a tourist manner at their novel surroundings. The Bedouins, under stern command, ignored them, conversing among themselves over their coffee — all but the sheik.

The sheik had been instantly struck by the fair young English girl. His sinister eyes hung constantly upon her, shifting only when she regarded him, furtively returning when she ceased. When they left the cafe, the sheik arose and placed himself partly in the girl's way. She paused while his dark eyes caught and held hers. A long moment went before she seemed able to free herself from the hypnotic tension he put upon her. Then he bowed low, and the girl with a nervous laugh passed him.

It could be seen that the sheik meant her no good. He stepped to the door and looked after the group. There was evil purpose in his gaze.

Merton Gill recalled something of Henshaw's words the first day he had eaten at the cafeteria: "They find this deserted tomb just at nightfall, and he's alone there with the girl, and he could do anything, but the kick for the audience is that he's a gentleman and never lays a finger on her."

This would be the story. Probably the sheik would now arrange with the old gentleman in the sunhat to guide the party over the desert, and would betray them in order to get the beautiful girl into his power. Of course there would be a kick for the audience when the young fellow proved to be a gentleman in the deserted tomb for a whole night — any moving-picture audience would expect him under these propitious circumstances to be quite otherwise, if the girl were as beautiful as this one. But there would surely be a greater kick when the sheik found them in the tomb and bore the girl off on his camel, after a fight in which the gentleman was momentarily worsted. But the girl would be rescued in time. And probably the piece would be called *Desert Passion*.

He wished he could know the ending of the story. Indeed he sincerely wished he could work in it to the end, not alone because he was curious about the fate of the young girl in the bad sheik's power. Undoubtedly the sheik would not prove to be a gentleman, but Merton would like to work to the end of the story because he had no place to sleep and but little assurance of wholesome food. Yet this, it appeared, was not to be. Already word had run among the extra people. Those hired today were to be used for today only. Tomorrow the desert drama would unfold without them.

Still, he had a day's pay coming. This time, though, it would be but five dollars — his dress suit had not been needed. And five dollars would appease Mrs. Patterson for another week. Yet what would be the good of sleeping if he had nothing to eat? He was hungry now. Thin soup, ever so plenteously spiced with ketchup, was inadequate provender for a working artist. He knew, even as he sat there cross-legged, an apparently self-supporting and care-free Bedouin, that this ensuing five dollars would never be seen by Mrs. Patterson.

There were a few more shots of the cafe's interior during which one of the inmates carefully permitted his half-consumed cigarette to go out. After that a few more shots of the lively street which, it was now learned, was a street in Cairo. Earnest efforts were made by the throngs in these scenes to give the murderous camel plenty of head room. Some close-ups were taken of the European tourists while they bargained with a native merchant for hammered brassware and rare shawls.

The bad sheik was caught near the group bending an evil glare upon the beauteous English girl, and once the camera turned while she faced him with a little shiver of apprehension. Later the sheik was caught bargaining for a camel train with the innocent-looking old gentleman in the sun-hat. Undoubtedly the sheik was about to lead them into the desert for no good purpose. A dreadful fate seemed in store for the girl, but she must be left to face it without the support of Merton Gill.

The lately hired extras were now dismissed. They trooped back to the dressing room to doff their flowing robes and remove the Bedouin make-up. Merton Gill went from the dressing room to the little window through which he had received his robe and his slip was returned to him signed by the assistant director. It had now become a paper of value, even to Mrs. Patterson; but she was never to know this, for its owner went down the street to another window and relinquished it for a five-dollar bill.

The bill was adorned with a portrait of Benjamin Harrison smugly radiating prosperity from every hair in his beard. He was clearly one who had never gone hungry nor betrayed the confidence of a society woman counting upon her room rent strictly in advance. The portrait of this successful man was borne swiftly to the cafeteria where its present owner lavishly heaped a tray with excellent food and hastened with it to a table. He ate with but slight regard for his surroundings. Beulah Baxter herself might have occupied a neighboring table without coming to his notice at once. He was very hungry. The ketchup-laden soup had proved to be little more than an appetizer.

In his first ardor he forgot his plight. It was not until later in the meal that the accusing face of Mrs. Patterson came between him and the last of his stew which he secured with blotters of bread. Even then he ignored the woman. He had other things to think of. He had to think of where he should sleep that night. But for once he had eaten enough; his optimism was again enthroned.

Sleeping, after all, was not like eating. There were more ways to manage it. The law of sleep would in time enforce itself, while eating did nothing of the sort. You might sleep for nothing, but someone had to be paid if you ate. He cheerfully paid 80 cents for his repast. The ketchup as an appetizer had been ruinous.

It was late in the afternoon when he left the cafeteria and the cheerful activities of the lot were drawing to a close. Extra people from the various stages were hurrying to the big dressing room, whence they would presently stream, slips in hand, toward the cashier's window. Belated principals came in from their work to resume their choice street garments and be driven off in choice motor cars.

Merton Gill in deep thought traversed the street between the big stages and the dressing rooms. Still in deep thought he retraced his steps, and at the front office turned off to the right on a road that led to the deserted street of the Western town. His head bowed in thought he went down this silent thoroughfare, his footsteps echoing along the way lined by the closed shops. The Happy Days Saloon and Joe-Buy-or-Sell, the pool-room and the restaurant, alike slept for want of custom. He felt again the eeriness of this desertion, and hurried on past the silent places.

Emerging from the lower end of this street he came upon a log cabin where activity still survived. He joined the group before its door. Inside two cameras were recording some drama of the rude frontier. Over glowing coals in the stone fireplace a beautiful young girl prepared food in a long-handled frying pan. At a table in the room's center two bearded miners seemed to be appraising a buckskin pouch of nuggets, pouring them from hand to hand. A candle stuck in a bottle flickered beside them. They were honest, kindly faced miners, roughly dressed and heavily bearded, but it could be seen that they had hearts of gold. The beautiful young girl, who wore a simple dress of blue calico, and whose hair hung about her fair face in curls of a radiant buff, now served them food and poured steaming coffee from a large pot.

The miners seemed loath to eat, being excited by the gold nuggets. They must have struck it rich that day, Merton Gill divined, and now with wealth untold they would be planning to send the girl East to school. They both patted her affectionately, keeping from her the great surprise they had in store.

The girl was arch with them, and prettily kissed each upon his bald head. Merton at once saw that she would be the daughter of neither; she would be their ward. And perhaps they weren't planning to send her to school. Perhaps they were going to send her to fashionable relatives in the East, where she would unwittingly become the rival of her beautiful but cold-hearted cousin for the hand of a rich young stock-broker, and be ill-treated and long for the old miners who would get word of it and buy some fine clothes from Joe-Buy-or-Sell, and go East to the consternation of the rich relatives and see that their little mountain flower was treated right.

As he identified this photo-play he studied the interior of the cabin, the rough table at which the three now ate, the makeshift chairs, the rifle over the fireplace, the picks and shovels, the shelf along the wall with its crude dishes, the calico curtain screening off what would be the dressing room of the little mountain flower. It was a home-like room, for all its roughness. Along one wall were two bunks, one above the other, well supplied with blankets.

The director, after a final shot of one of the miners being scalded by his coffee which he drank from a saucer, had said, "All right, boys! We'll have the fight first thing in the morning."

Merton Gill passed on. He didn't quite know what the fight would be about. Surely the two miners wouldn't fight. Perhaps another miner of loose character would come along and try to jump their claim, or attempt some dirty work with the little girl. Something like that. He carried with him the picture of the homey little ulterior, the fireplace with its cooking utensils, the two bunks with their ample stock of blankets — the crude door closed with a wooden bar and a leather latch-string, which hung trustfully outside.

In other circumstances — chiefly those in which Merton Gill had now been the prominent figure in the film world he meant one day to become — he would on this night have undoubtedly won public attention for his mysterious disappearance. The modest room in the Patterson home, to which for three months he had unfailingly come after the first picture show, on this night went untenanted. The guardian at the Holden gate would have testified that he had not passed out that way, and the way through the offices had been closed at five, subsequent to which hour several witnesses could have sworn to seeing him still on the lot.

In the ensuing search even the tank at the lower end of the lot might have been dragged — without result.

Being little known to the public, however, and in the Patterson home it being supposed that you could never tell about motion-picture actors, his disappearance for the night caused absolutely no slightest ripple. Public attention as regarded the young man remained at a mirror-like calm, unflawed by even the mildest curiosity. He had been seen, perhaps, though certainly not noted with any interest, to be one of the group watching a night scene in front of one of the Fifth Avenue mansions.

Lights shone from the draped windows of this mansion and from its portals issued none other than Muriel Mercer, who, as Vera Vanderpool, freed at last from the blight of Broadway, was leaving her palatial home to cast her lot finally with the ardent young tenement worker with the high forehead. She descended the brownstone steps, paused once to look back upon the old home where she had been taught to love pleasure above the worthwhile things of life, then came on to the waiting limousine, being greeted here by the young man with the earnest forehead who had won her to the better way.

The missing youth might later have been observed, but probably was not, walking briskly in the chill night toward the gate that led to the outer world. But he wheeled abruptly before reaching this gate, and walked again briskly, this time debouching from the main thoroughfare into the black silence of the Western village. Here his pace slackened, and halfway down the street he paused irresolutely. He was under the wooden porch of the Fashion Restaurant — Give our Tamales a Trial. He lingered here but a moment, however, then lurked on down the still thoroughfare, keeping well within the shadow of the low buildings. Just beyond the street was the log cabin of the big-hearted miners. A moment later he could not have been observed even by the keenest eye.

Nothing marked his disappearance, at least nothing that would have been noted by the casual minded. He had simply gone. He was now no more than the long-vanished cowboys and sheriffs and gamblers and petty tradesmen who had once peopled this street of silence and desolation.

A night watchman came walking presently, flashing an electric torch from side to side. He noticed nothing. He was, indeed, a rather imaginative man, and he hoped he would not notice anything. He did not like coming down this ghostly street, which his weak mind would persist in peopling with phantom crowds from long-played picture dramas. It gave him the creeps, as he had more than once confessed. He hurried on, flashing his torch along the blind fronts of the shops in a perfunctory manner. He was especially nervous when he came to corners. And he was glad when he issued from the little street into the wider one that was well lighted.

How could he have been expected to notice a very trifling incongruous detail as he passed the log cabin? Indeed many a keener-eyed and entirely valorous night watchman might have neglected to observe that the leathern latch-string of the cabin's closed door was no longer hanging outside.

CHAPTER VIII

CLIFFORD ARMYTAGE, THE OUTLAW

DAN BROUGHT the wide stretches of the Holden lot into gray relief. It lightened the big yellow stages and crept down the narrow street of the Western town where only the ghosts of dead plays stalked. It burnished the rich fronts of the Fifth Avenue mansions and in the next block illumined the rough sides of a miner's cabin.

With more difficulty it seeped through the blurred glass of the one window in this structure and lightened the shadows of its interior to a pale gray. The long-handled frying-pan rested on the hearth where the little girl had left it. The dishes of the overnight meal were still on the table; the vacant chairs sprawled about it; and the rifle was in its place above the rude mantel; the picks and shovels awaited the toil of a new day. All seemed as it had been when the director had closed the door upon it the previous night.

But then the blankets in the lower bunk were seen to heave and to be thrust back from the pale face of Merton Gill. An elbow came into play, and the head was raised. A gaze still vague with sleep travelled about the room in dull alarm. He was waking up in his little room at the Patterson house and he couldn't make it look right. He rubbed his eyes vigorously and pushed himself farther up. His mind resumed its broken threads. He was where he had meant to be from the moment he had spied the blankets in those bunks.

In quicker alarm, now, he reached for his watch. Perhaps he had slept too late and would be discovered — arrested, jailed! He found his watch on the floor beside the bunk. Seven o'clock. He was safe. He could dress at leisure, and presently be an early-arriving actor on the Holden lot. He wondered how soon he could get food at the cafeteria. Sleeping in this mountain cabin had cursed him with a ravenous appetite, as if he had indeed been far off in the keen air of the North Woods.

He crept from the warm blankets, and from under the straw mattress — in which one of the miners had hidden the pouch of nuggets — he took his newly pressed trousers. Upon a low bench across the room was a battered tin wash — basin, a bucket of water brought by the little girl from the spring, and a bar of yellow soap. He made a quick toilet, and at 7:30, a good hour before the lot would wake up, he was dressed and at the door.

It might be chancy, opening that door; so he peered through a narrow crack at first, listening intently. He could hear nothing and no one was in sight. He pushed the latch — string through its hole, then opened the door enough to emit his slender shape.

A moment later, 10 feet from the closed door, he stood at ease, scanning the log cabin as one who, passing by, had been attracted by its quaint architecture. Then glancing in both directions to be again sure that he was unobserved, he walked away from his new home.

He did not slink furtively. He took the middle of the street and there was a bit of swagger to his gait. He felt rather set up about this adventure. He reached what might have been called the lot's civic center and cast a patronizing eye along the ends of the big stages and the long, low dressing — room building across from them. Before the open door of the warehouse he paused to watch a truck being loaded with handsome furniture — a drawing room was evidently to be set on one of the stages. Rare rugs and beautiful chairs and tables were carefully brought out. He had rather a superintending air as he watched this process. He might have been taken for the owner of these costly things, watching to see that no harm befell them. He strolled on when the truck had received its load. Such people as he had met were only artisans, carpenters, electricians, property-men.

He faced them all confidently, with glances of slightly amused tolerance. They were good men in their way but they were not actors — not artists.

In the neatly landscaped little green place back of the office building a climbing rose grew on a trellis. He plucked a pink bud, fixed it in his lapel, and strolled down the street past the dressing rooms. Across from these the doors of the big stages were slid back, and inside he could see that sets were being assembled. The truckload of furniture came to one of these doors and he again watched it as the stuff was carried inside.

For all these workmen knew, he might presently be earning a princely salary as he acted amid these beautiful objects, perhaps attending a reception in a Fifth Avenue mansion where the father of a beautiful New York society girl would tell him that he must first make good before he could aspire to her hand. And he would make good — out there in the great open spaces, where the girl would come to him after many adventures and where they would settle to an untroubled future in the West they both loved.

He had slept; he knew where — with luck — he could sleep again; and he had money in his pocket for several more ample meals. At this moment he felt equal to anything. No more than pleasantly aware of his hunger, sharpened by the walk in this keen morning air, he made a nonchalant progress toward the cafeteria. Motor cars were now streaming through the gate, disgorging other actors — trim young men and beautiful young women who must hurry to the dressing rooms while he could sit at ease in a first-class cafeteria and eat heavily of sustaining foods. Inside he chose from the restricted menu offered by the place at this early hour and ate in a leisurely, almost condescending manner. Half-a-dozen other early comers wolfed their food as if they feared to be late for work, but he suffered no such anxiety. He consumed the last morsel that his tray held, drained his cup of coffee, and jingled the abundant silver coin in his pocket.

True, underneath it, as he plumed himself upon his adventure, was a certain pestering consciousness that all was not so well with him as observers might guess. But he resolutely put this away each time it threatened to overwhelm him. He would cross no bridge until he came to it. He even combated this undercurrent of sanity by wording part of an interview with himself some day to appear in *Photo Land*:

"Clifford Armytage smiled that rare smile which his admirers have found so winning on the silver screen — a smile reminiscent, tender, eloquent of adversities happily surmounted. 'Yes,' he said frankly in the mellow tones that are his, 'I guess there were times when I almost gave up the struggle. I recall one spell, not so many years ago, when I camped informally on the Holden lot, sleeping where I could find a bed and stinting myself in food to eke out my little savings. Yet I look back upon that time' — he mischievously pulled the ears of the magnificent Great Dane that lolled at his feet — 'as one of the happiest in my career, because I always knew that my day would come. I had done only a few little bits, but they had stood out, and the directors had noticed me. Not once did I permit myself to become discouraged, and so I say to your readers who may feel that they have in them the stuff for truly creative screen art — '"

He said it, dreaming above the barren tray, said it as Harold Parmalee had said it in a late interview extorted from him by Augusta Blivens for the refreshment of his host of admirers who read *Photo Land*. He was still saying it as he paid his check at the counter, breaking off only to reflect that 55 cents was a good deal to be paying for food so early in the day. For of course he must eat again before seeking shelter of the humble miner's cabin.

It occurred to him that the blankets might be gone by nightfall. He hoped they would have trouble with the fight scene. He hoped there would be those annoying delays that so notoriously added to the cost of producing the screen drama — long waits, when no one seemed to know what was being waited for, and bored actors lounged about in apathy. He hoped the fight would be a long fight. You needed blankets even in sunny California.

He went out to pass an enlivening day, fairly free of misgiving. He found an abundance of entertainment. On one stage he overlooked for half an hour a fragment of the desert drama which he had assisted the previous day. A covered incline led duskily down to the deserted tomb in which the young man and the beautiful English girl were to take shelter for the night. They would have eluded the bad sheik for a little while, and in the tomb the young man would show himself to be a gentleman by laying not so much as a finger upon the defenseless girl.

But this soon palled upon the watching connoisseur. The actual shots were few and separated by barren intervals of waiting for that mysterious something which photoplays in production seemed to need. Being no longer identified with this drama he had lost much of his concern over the fate in store for the girl, though he knew she would emerge from the ordeal as pure as she was beautiful — a bit foolish at moments, perhaps, but good.

He found that he was especially interested in bedroom scenes. On Stage Four a sumptuous bedroom, vacant for the moment, enchained him for a long period of contemplation. The bed was of some rare wood ornately carved, with a silken canopy, spread with finest linen and quilts of down, its pillows opulent in their embroidered cases. The hide of a polar bear, its head mounted with open jaws, spread over the rich rug beside the bed. He wondered about this interestingly. Probably the stage would be locked at night. Still, at a suitable hour, he could discreetly find out. On another stage a bedroom likewise intrigued him, though this was a squalid room in a tenement and the bed was a cheap thing sparsely covered and in sad disorder. People were working on this set, and he presently identified the play, for Muriel Mercer in a neat black dress entered to bring comfort to the tenement dwellers. But this play, too, had ceased to interest him. He knew that Vera Vanderpool had escaped the blight of Broadway to choose the worthwhile, the true, the vital things of life, and that was about all he now cared to know of the actual play. This tenement bed had become for him its outstanding dramatic value. He saw himself in it for a good night's rest, waking refreshed in plenty of time to be dressed and out before the tenement people would need it. He must surely learn if the big sliding doors to these stages were locked overnight.

He loitered about the stages until late afternoon, with especial attention to sleeping apartments. In one gripping drama he felt cheated. The set showed the elaborately fitted establishment of a fashionable modiste. Mannequins in wondrous gowns came through parted curtains to parade before the shop's clientele, mostly composed of society butterflies. One man hovered attentive about the most beautiful of these, and whispered entertainingly as she scanned the gowns submitted to her choice. He was a dissolute — looking man, although faultlessly arrayed. His hair was thin, his eyes were cruel, and his face bespoke self-indulgence.

The expert Merton Gill at once detected that the beautiful young woman he whispered to would be one of those light-headed wives who care more for fashionable dress than for the good name of their husbands. He foresaw that the creature would be trapped into the power of this villain by her love of finery, though he was sure that the end would find her still a good woman. The mannequins finished their parade and the throng of patrons broke up. The cameras were pushed to an adjoining room where the French proprietor of the place figured at a desk. The dissolute pleasure-seeker came back to question him. His errant fancy had been caught by one of the mannequins — the most beautiful of them, a blonde with a flowerlike face and a figure whose perfection had been boldly attested by the gowns she had worn. The unprincipled proprietor at once demanded from a severe-faced forewoman that this girl be sent for, after which he discreetly withdrew. The waiting scoundrel sat and complacently pinched the ends of his small dark mustache. It could be seen that he was one of those who believe that money will buy anything.

The fair girl entered and was leeringly entreated to go out to dinner with him. It appeared that she never went out to dinner with anyone, but spent her evenings with her mother who was very, very ill. Her unworthy admirer persisted. Then the telephone on the manager's desk called her. Her mother was getting worse. The beautiful face was now suffused with agony, but this did not deter the man from his loathsome advances. There was another telephone call. She must come at once if she were to see her mother alive. The man seized her. They struggled. All seemed lost, even the choice gown she still wore; but she broke away to be told over the telephone that her mother had died. Even this sad news made no impression upon the wretch. He seemed to be a man of one idea. Again he seized her, and the maddened girl stabbed him with a pair of long gleaming shears that had lain on the manager's desk. He fell lifeless at her feet, while the girl stared in horror at the weapon she still grasped.

Merton Gill would not have lingered for this. There were tedious waits, and scenes must be rehearsed again and again. Even the agony of the girl as she learned of her mother's passing must be done over and over at the insistence of a director who seemed to know what a young girl should feel at these moments. But Merton had watched from his place back of the lights with fresh interest from the moment it was known that the girl's poor old mother was an invalid, for he had at first believed that the mother's bedroom would be near by. He left promptly when it became apparent that the mother's bedroom would not be seen in this drama. They would probably show the doctor at the other telephone urging the girl to hurry home, and show him again announcing that all was over, but the expense of mother and her deathbed had been saved. He cared little for the ending of this play. Already he was becoming a little callous to the plight of beautiful young girls threatened with the loss of that which they held most dear.

Purposely all day he had avoided the neighborhood of his humble miner's home. He thought it as well that he should not be seen much around there. He ate again at four o'clock, heartily and rather expensively, and loafed about the stages until six. Then he strolled leisurely down the village street and out the lower end to where he could view the cabin. Work for the day was plainly over. The director and his assistant lingered before the open door in consultation. A property man and an electrician were engaged inside, but a glance as he passed showed that the blankets were still in the bunks. He did not wait to see more, but passed on with all evidences of disinterest in this lowly abode.

He ascertained that night that the fight must have been had. The table was overturned, one of the chairs wrecked, and there were other signs of disorder. Probably it had been an excellent fight; probably these primitive men of the woods had battled desperately. But he gave little consideration to the combat, and again slept warmly under the blankets. Perhaps they would fight again tomorrow, or perhaps there would be less violent bits of the drama that would secure him another night of calm repose.

The following morning found him slightly disturbed by two unforeseen needs arising from his novel situation. He looked carefully at his collar, wondering how many days he would be able to keep it looking like a fresh collar, and he regretted that he had not brought his safety-razor to this new home. Still the collar was in excellent shape as yet, and a scrutiny of his face in the cracked mirror hanging on the log wall determined that he could go at least another day without shaving. His beard was of a light growth, gentle in texture, and he was yet far from the plight of Mr. Montague. Eventually, to be sure, he would have to go to the barber shop on the lot and pay money to be shaved, which seemed a pity, because an actor could live indefinitely unshaven but could live without food for the merest fragment of time.

He resolved to be on the lookout that day for a barber-shop set. He believed they were not common in the photodrama, still one might be found.

He limited himself to the lightest of breakfasts. He had timidly refrained from counting his silver but he knew he must be frugal. He rejoiced at this economy until late afternoon when, because of it, he simply had to eat a heavier dinner than he had expected to need. There was something so implacable about this demand for food. If you skimped in the morning you must make amends at the next meal. He passed the time as on the previous day, a somewhat blasé actor resting between pictures, and condescending to beguile the tedium by overlooking the efforts of his professional brethren. He could find no set that included a barber shop, although they were beds on every hand. He hoped for another night in the cabin, but if that were not to be, there was a bed easy of access on Stage Three. When he had observed it, a ghastly old father was coughing out his life under its blankets, nursed only by his daughter, a beautiful young creature who sewed by his bedside, and who would doubtless be thrown upon the world in the very next reel, though — Merton was glad to note — probably not until the next day.

Yet there was no need for this couch of the tubercular father, for action in the little cabin was still on. After making the unhappy discovery in the cafeteria that his appetite could not be hoodwinked by the clumsy subterfuge of calling coffee and rolls a breakfast some six hours previously, he went boldly down to stand before his home. Both miners were at work inside. The room had been placed in order again, though the little mountain flower was gone. A letter, he gathered, had been received from her, and one of the miners was about to leave on a long journey.

Merton could not be sure, but he supposed that the letter from the little girl told that she was unhappy in her new surroundings, perhaps being ill-treated by the supercilious Eastern relatives. The miner who was to remain helped the other to pack his belongings in a quaint old carpet sack, and together they undid a bundle which proved to contain a splendid new suit. Not only this, but now came a scene of eloquent appeal to the watcher outside the door. The miner who was to remain expressed stern disapproval of the departing miner's beard. It would never do, he was seen to intimate, and when the other miner portrayed helplessness a new package was unwrapped and a safety razor revealed to his shocked gaze.

At this sight Merton Gill felt himself growing too emotional for a mere careless bystander, and withdrew to a distance where he could regain better control of himself. When he left the miner to be shorn was betraying comic dismay while the other pantomimed the correct use of the implement his thoughtfulness had provided. When he returned after half-an-hour's rather nervous walk up another street, the departing miner was clean shaven and one might note the new razor glittering on the low bench beside the battered tin basin.

They worked late in his home that night; trifling scenes were taken and retaken. The departing miner had to dress in his splendid but ill-fitting new garments and to bid an affectionate farewell to his partner, then had to dress in his old clothes again for some bit that had been forgotten, only to don the new suit for close-ups. At another time Merton Gill might have resented this tediously drawn-out affair which was keeping him from his rest, for he had come to look upon this structure as one having rights in it after a certain hour, but a sight of the razor which had not been touched allayed any possible feeling of irritation.

It was 9:30 before the big lights jarred finally off and the director said, "That's all, boys." Then he turned to call, "Jimmie! Hey, Jimmie! Where's that prop-rustler gone to now?"

"Here, Mr. Burke, yes, sir."

"We've finished the shack stuff. Let's see," — he looked at the watch on his wrist — "That'll be all for tonight. Strike this first thing tomorrow morning."

"Yes, sir," said Jimmie. The door was closed and the men walked away. Merton trailed them a bit, not remaining too pointedly near the cabin. He circled around through Fifth Avenue to regain the place.

Softly he let himself in and groped through the dark until his hand closed upon the abandoned razor. Satisfying himself that fresh blades had accompanied it, he made ready for bed. He knew it was to be his last night in this shelter. The director had told Jimmie to strike it first thing in the morning. The cabin would still be there, but it would contain no homely furniture, no chairs, no table, no wash-basin, no safety-razor and, most vital of lacks — it would be devoid of blankets.

Yet this knowledge did not dismay him. He slept peacefully after praying that something good would happen to him. He put it that way very simply. He had placed himself, it seemed, where things could only happen to him. He was, he felt, beyond bringing them about.

CHAPTER IX

MORE WAYS THAN ONE

EARLY HE WAS UP to bathe and shave. He shaved close to make it last longer, until his tender face reddened under the scraping. Probably he would not find another cabin in which a miner would part with his beard for an Eastern trip. Probably he would have to go to the barber the next time. He also succeeded, with soap and water, in removing a stain from his collar. It was still a decent collar; not immaculate, perhaps, but entirely possible.

This day he took eggs with his breakfast, intending to wheedle his appetite with a lighter second meal than it had demanded the day before. He must see if this would not average better on the day's overhead.

After breakfast he was irresistibly drawn to view the moving picture of his old home being dismantled. He knew now that he might stand brazenly there without possible criticism. He found Jimmie and a companion property-boy already busy. Much of the furniture was outside to be carted away. Jimmie, as Merton lolled idly in the doorway, emptied the blackened coffee pot into the ashes of the fireplace and then proceeded to spoon into the same refuse heap half a kettle of beans upon which the honest miners had once feasted. The watcher deplored that he had not done more than taste the beans when he had taken his final survey of the place this morning. They had been good beans, but to do more than taste them would have been stealing. Now he saw them thrown away and regretted that he could not have known what their fate was to be. There had been enough of them to save him a day's expenses.

He stood aside as the two boys brought out the cooking utensils, the rifle, the miners' tools, to stow them in a waiting handcart. When they had loaded this vehicle they trundled it on up the narrow street of the Western town. Yet they went only a little way, halting before one of the street's largest buildings. A sign above its wooden porch flaunted the name Crystal Palace Hotel. They unlocked its front door and took the things from the cart inside.

From the street the watcher could see them stowing these away. The room appeared to contain a miscellaneous collection of articles needed in the ruder sort of photodrama. Emptying their cart, they returned with it to the cabin for another load. Merton Gill stepped to the doorway and peered in from apparently idle curiosity. He could see a row of saddles on wooden supports; there were kitchen stoves, lamps, painted chairs, and heavy earthenware dishes on shelves. His eyes wandered over these articles until they came to rest upon a pile of blankets at one side of the room. They were neatly folded, and they were many.

Down before the cabin he could see the handcart being reloaded by Jimmie and his helper. Otherwise the street was empty. The young man at the doorway stepped lightly in and regarded the windows on either side of the door. He sauntered to the street and appeared to be wondering what he would examine next in this curious world. He passed Jimmie and the other boy returning with the last load from the cabin. He noted at the top of the load the mattress on which he had lain for three nights and the blankets that had warmed him. But he was proved not to be so helpless as he had thought. Again he knew where a good night's rest might be had by one using ordinary discretion.

Again that day, the fourth of his double life, he went the mad pace, a well-fed, carefree youth, sauntering idly from stage to stage, regarding nonchalantly the joys and griefs, the twistings of human destiny there variously unfolded. Not only was he this to the casual public notice; to himself he was this, at least consciously. True, in those nether regions of the mind so lately discovered and now being so expertly probed by Science, in the mind's dark basement, so to say, a certain unlovely fronted dragon of reality would issue from the gloom where it seemed to have been lurking and force itself upon his notice.

This would be at oddly contented moments when he least feared the future, when he was most successfully being to himself all that he must seem to others. At such times when he leisurely walked a world of plenty and fruition, the dragon would half-emerge from its subconscious lair to chill him with its head composed entirely of repellent facts. Then a stout effort would be required to send the thing back where it belonged, to those lower, decently hidden levels of the mind — life.

And the dragon was cunning. From hour to hour, growing more restive, it employed devices of craft and subtlety. As when Merton Gill, carefree to the best of his knowledge, strolling lightly to another point of interest, graciously receptive to the pleasant life about him, would suddenly discover that a part of his mind without superintendence had for some moments been composing a letter, something that ran in effect:

"Mr. Gashwiler, dear sir, I have made certain changes in my plans since I first came to sunny California and getting quite a little homesick for good old Simsbury and I thought I would write you about taking back my old job in the emporium, and now about the money for the ticket back to Simsbury, the railroad fare is —"

He was truly amazed when he found this sort of thing going on in that part of his mind he didn't watch. It was scandalous. He would indignantly snatch the half-finished letter and tear it up each time he found it unaccountably under way.

It was surely funny the way your mind would keep doing things you didn't want it to do. As, again, this very morning when, with his silver coin out in his hand, he had merely wished to regard it as a great deal of silver coin, a store of plenty against famine, which indeed it looked to be under a not-too-minute scrutiny. It looked like as much as two dollars and 50 cents, and he would have preferred to pocket it again with this impression. Yet that rebellious other part of his mind had basely counted the coin even while he eyed it approvingly, and it had persisted in shouting aloud that it was not two dollars and 50 cents but one dollar and 85 cents.

The counting part of the mind made no comment on this discrepancy; it did not say that this discovery put things in a very different light. It merely counted, registered the result, and ceased to function, with an air of saying that it would ascertain the facts without prejudice and you could do what you liked about them. It didn't care.

That night a solitary guest enjoyed the quiet hospitality of the Crystal Palace Hotel. He might have been seen — but was not — to effect a late evening entrance to this snug inn by means of a front window which had, it would seem, at some earlier hour of the day, been unfastened from within. Here a not-too-luxurious but sufficing bed was contrived on the floor of the lobby from a pile of neatly folded blankets at hand, and a second night's repose was enjoyed by the lonely patron, who again at an early hour of the morning, after thoughtfully refolding the blankets that had protected him, was at some pains to leave the place as he had entered it without attracting public notice, perchance of unpleasant character.

On this day it would not have been possible for any part of the mind whatsoever to misvalue the remaining treasure of silver coin. It had become inconsiderable, and even if kept from view could be, and was, counted again and again by mere blind fingertips. They contracted, indeed, a senseless habit of confining themselves in a trousers pocket to count the half-dollar, the quarter, and the two dimes long after the total was too well known to its owner.

Nor did this total, unimpressive at best, long retain even these poor dimensions. A visit to the cafeteria, in response to the imperious demands of a familiar organic process, resulted in less labor, by two dimes, for the stubbornly reiterative fingertips.

An ensuing visit to the Holden lot barber, in obedience to social demands construed to be equally imperious with the physical, reduced all subsequent counting, whether by fingertips or a glance of the eye, to barest mechanical routine. A single half-dollar is easy to count. Still, on the following morning there were two coins to count. True, both were dimes.

A diligent search among the miscellany of the Crystal Palace Hotel had failed to reveal a single razor. The razor used by the miner should in all reason have been found, but there was neither that nor any other. The baffled seeker believed there must have been crooked work somewhere. Without hesitation he found either Jimmie or his companion to be guilty of malfeasance in office. But at least one item of more or less worried debate was eliminated. He need no longer weigh mere surface gentility against the stern demands of an active metabolism. A shave cost a quarter. Twenty cents would not buy a shave, but it would buy at the cafeteria something more needful to anyone but a fop.

He saw himself in the days to come — if there were very many days to come, of which he was now not too certain — descending to the unwholesome artistic level of the elder Montague. He would, in short, be compelled to peddle the brush. And of course as yet it was nothing like a brush — nothing to kindle the eye of a director needing genuine brushes. In the early morning light he fingered a somewhat gaunt chin and wondered how long "they" would require to grow. Not yet could he be taken for one of those actors compelled by the rigorous exactions of creative screen art to let Nature have its course with his beard. At present he merely needed a shave.

And the collar had not improved with usage. Also, as the day wore on, coffee with one egg proved to have been not long-enduring fare for this private in the army of the unemployed. Still, his morale was but slightly impaired. There were always ways, it seemed. And the later hours of the hungry afternoon were rather pleasantly occupied in dwelling upon one of them.

The sole guest of the Crystal Palace Hotel entered the hostelry that night somewhat earlier than was usual; indeed at the very earliest moment that foot traffic through the narrow street seemed to have diminished to a point where the entry could be effected without incurring the public notice which he at these moments so sincerely shunned. After a brief interval inside the lobby he issued from his window with certain objects in hand, one of which dropped as he clambered out. The resulting clamor seemed to rouse far echoes along the dead street, and he hastily withdrew, with a smothered exclamation of dismay, about the nearest corner of the building until it could be ascertained that echoes alone had been aroused.

After a little breathless waiting he slunk down the street, keeping well within friendly shadows, stepping softly, until he reached the humble cabin where so lately the honest miners had enacted their heart-tragedy. He jerked the latch-string of the door and was swiftly inside, groping a way to the fireplace. Here he lighted matches, thoughtfully appropriated that morning from the cafeteria counter. He shielded the blaze with one hand while with the other he put to use the articles he had brought from his hotel.

Into a tin cooking pot with a long handle he now hastily ladled well-cooked beans from the discarded heap in the fireplace, by means of an iron spoon. He was not too careful. More or less ashes accompanied the nutritious vegetables as the pot grew to be half full. That was a thing to be corrected later, and at leisure. When the last bean had been salvaged the flame of another match revealed an unsuspected item — a half-loaf of bread nestled in the ashes at the far corner of the fireplace. It lacked freshness; was, in truth, withered and firm to the touch, but doubtless more wholesome than bread freshly baked.

He was again on his humble cot in the seclusion of the Crystal Palace Hotel. Half-reclining, he ate at leisure. It being inadvisable to light matches here he ate chiefly by the touch system. There was a marked alkaline flavor to the repast, not unpleasantly counteracted by a growth of vegetable mold of delicate lavender tints which Nature had been decently spreading over the final reduction of this provender to its basic elements. But the time was not one in which to cavil about minor infelicities. Ashes wouldn't hurt any one if taken in moderation; you couldn't see the mold in a perfectly dark hotel; and the bread was good.

The feast was prolonged until a late hour, but the fingertips that had accurately counted money in a dark pocket could ascertain in a dark hotel that a store of food still remained. He pulled the blankets about him and sank comfortably to rest. There was always some way.

Breakfast the next morning began with the promise of only moderate enjoyment. Somehow in the gray light sifting through the windows the beans did not look as good as they had tasted the night before, and the early mouthfuls were less blithesome on the palate than the remembered ones of yesterday. He thought perhaps he was not so hungry as he had been at his first encounter with them. He delicately removed a pocket of ashes from the center, and tried again. They tasted better now. The mold of tender tints was again visible but he made no effort to avoid it. For his appetite had reawakened. He was truly hungry, and ate with an entire singleness of purpose.

Toward the last of the meal his conscious self feebly prompted him to quit, to save against the inevitable hunger of the night. But the voice was ignored. He was now clay to the molding of the subconscious. He could have saved a few of the beans when reason was again enthroned, but they were so very few that he fatuously thought them not worth saving. Might as well make a clean job of it. He restored the stewpan and spoon to their places and left his hotel. He was fed. Today something else would have to happen.

The plush hat cocked at a rakish angle, he walked abroad with something of the old confident swagger. Once he doubtfully fingered the sprouting beard, but resolutely dismissed a half-formed notion of finding out how the Holden lot barber would regard a proposition from a new patron to open a charge account. If nothing worse than remaining unshaven was going to happen to him, what cared he? The collar was still pretty good. Why let his beard be an incubus? He forgot it presently in noticing that the people arriving on the Holden lot all looked so extremely well fed. He thought it singular that he should never before have noticed how many well-fed people one saw in a day.

Late in the afternoon his explorations took him beyond the lower end of his little home street, and he was attracted by sounds of the picture drama from a rude board structure labeled the High Gear Dance Hall. He approached and entered with that calm ease of manner which his days on the lot had brought to a perfect bloom. No one now would ever suppose that he was a mere sightseer or chained to the Holden lot by circumstances over which he had ceased to exert the slightest control.

The interior of the High Gear Dance Hall presented nothing new to his seasoned eye. It was the dance hall made familiar by many a smashing five-reel Western. The picture was, quite normally, waiting. Electricians were shoving about the big light standards, cameras were being moved, and bored actors were loafing informally at the round tables or chatting in groups about the set.

One actor alone was keeping in his part. A ragged, bearded, unkempt elderly man in red shirt and frayed overalls, a repellent felt hat pulled low over his brow, reclined on the floor at the end of the bar, his back against a barrel. Apparently he slept. A flash of remembrance from the Montague girl's talk identified this wretched creature. This was what happened to an actor who had to peddle the brush. Perhaps for days he had been compelled to sleep there in the interests of dance hall atmosphere.

He again scanned the group, for he remembered, too, that the Montague girl would also be working here in God's Great Outdoors. His eyes presently found her. She was indeed a blonde hussy, short-skirted, low-necked, pitifully rouged, depraved beyond redemption. She stood at the end of the piano, and in company with another of the dance hall girls who played the accompaniment, she was singing a ballad the refrain of which he caught as "God calls them Angels in Heaven, we call them Mothers here."

The song ended, the Montague girl stepped to the center of the room, looked aimlessly about her, then seized an innocent bystander, one of the rough characters frequenting this unsavory resort, and did a dance with him among the tables. Tiring of this, she flitted across the room and addressed the bored director who impatiently awaited the changing of lights. She affected to consider him a reporter who had sought an interview with her. She stood erect, facing him with one hand on a hip, the other patting and readjusting her blonde coiffure.

"Really," she began in a voice of pained dignity, "I am at a loss to understand why the public should be so interested in me. What can I say to your readers — I who am so wholly absorbed in my art that I can't think of hardly anything else? Why will not the world let us alone? Hold on — don't go!"

She had here pretended that the reporter was taking her at her word. She seized him by a lapel to which she clung while with her other arm she encircled a post, thus anchoring the supposed intruder into her private affairs. "As I was saying," she resumed, "all this publicity is highly distasteful to the artist, and yet since you have forced yourself in here I may as well say a few little things about how good I am and how I got that way. Yes, I have nine motor cars, and I just bought a lace tablecloth for 12,000 bones —"

She broke off inconsequently, poor victim of her constitutional frivolity. The director grinned after her as she danced away, though Merton Gill had considered her levity in the worst of taste. Then her eye caught him as he stood modestly back of the working electricians and she danced forward again in his direction. He would have liked to evade her but saw that he could not do this gracefully.

She greeted him with an impudent grin. "Why, hello, trouper! As I live, the actin' Kid!" She held out a hand to him and he could not well refuse it. He would have preferred to "up-stage" her once more, as she had phrased it in her low jargon, but he was cornered. Her grip of his hand quite astonished him with its vigor.

"Well, how's everything with you? Everything jake?" He tried for a show of easy confidence. "Oh, yes, yes, indeed, everything is."

"Well, that's good, Kid." But she was now without the grin, and was running a practiced eye over what might have been called his production. The hat was jaunty enough, truly a hat of the successful, but all below that, the not-too-fresh collar, the somewhat rumpled coat, the trousers crying for an iron despite their nightly compression beneath their slumbering owner, the shoes not too recently polished, and, more than all, a certain hunted though still-defiant look in the young man's eyes, seemed to speak eloquently under the shrewd glance she bent on him.

"Say, listen here, Old-timer, remember I been trouping man and boy for over 40 year and it's hard to fool me — you working?"

He resented the persistent levity of manner, but was coerced by the very apparent real kindness in her tone. "Well," he looked about the set vaguely in his discomfort, "you see, right now I'm between pictures — you know how it is."

Again she searched his eyes and spoke in a lower tone: "Well, all right — but you needn't blush about it, Kid." The blush she detected became more flagrant.

"Well, I — you see —" he began again, but he was saved from being explicit by the call of an assistant director.

"Miss Montague. Miss Montague — where's that Flips girl — on the set, please." She skipped lightly from him. When she returned a little later to look for him he had gone.

He went to bed that night when darkness had made this practicable, and under his blankets whiled away a couple of wakeful hours by running tensely dramatic films of breakfast, dinner, and supper at the Gashwiler home. It seemed that you didn't fall asleep so quickly when you had eaten nothing since early morning. Never had he achieved such perfect photography as now of the Gashwiler corned-beef hash and light biscuits, the Gashwiler hot cakes and sausage, and never had Gashwiler so impressively carved the Saturday night four-rib roast of tender beef. Gashwiler achieved a sensational triumph in the scene, being accorded all the closeups that the most exacting of screen actors could wish. His knife-work was perfect. He held his audience enthralled by his technique.

Mrs. Gashwiler, too, had a small but telling part in the drama tonight; only a character bit, but one of those poignant bits that stand out in the memory. The subtitle was, "Merton, won't you let me give you another piece of the mince pie?" That was all, and yet, as screen artists say, it got over. There came very near to being not a dry eye in the house when the simple words were flashed beside an insert of thick, flaky-topped mince pies with quarters cut from them to reveal their noble interiors

Sleep came at last while he was regretting that lawless orgy of the morning. He needn't have cleaned up those beans in that silly way. He could have left a good half of them. He ran what might have been considered a split-reel comedy of the stew-pan's bottom still covered with perfectly edible beans lightly protected with Nature's own pastel-tinted shroud for perishing vegetable matter and diversified here and there with casual small deposits of ashes.

In the morning something good really did happen. As he folded his blankets in the gray light a hard object rattled along the floor from them. He picked this up before he recognized it as a mutilated fragment from the stale half-loaf of bread he had salvaged. He wondered how he could have forgotten it, even in the plenitude of his banquet. There it was, a mere nubbin of crust and so hard it might almost have been taken for a petrified specimen of prehistoric bread. Yet it proved to be rarely palatable. It's flavor was exquisite. It melted in the mouth.

Somewhat refreshed by this modest cheer, he climbed from the window of the Crystal Palace with his mind busy on two tracks. While the letter to Gashwiler composed itself, with especially clear directions about where the return money should be sent, he was also warning himself to remain throughout the day at a safe distance from the door of the cafeteria. He had proved the wisdom of this even the day before that had started with a bounteous breakfast. Today the aroma of cooked food occasionally wafted from the cafeteria door would prove, he was sure, to be more than he could bear.

He rather shunned the stages today, keeping more to himself. The collar, he had to confess, was no longer, even to the casual eye, what a successful screen-actor's collar should be. The sprouting beard might still be misconstrued as the whim of a director sanctified to realism — every day it was getting to look more like that — but no director would have commanded the wearing of such a collar except in actual work where it might have been a striking detail in the apparel of an underworldling, one of those creatures who became the tools of rich but unscrupulous roués who are bent upon the moral destruction of beautiful young screen heroines. He knew it was now that sort of collar. No use now in pretending that it had been worn yesterday for the first time.

CHAPTER X

OF SHATTERED ILLUSIONS

THE NEXT MORNING he sat a long time in the genial sunlight watching carpenters finish a scaffolding beside the pool that had once floated logs to a sawmill. The scaffolding was a stout affair supporting an immense tank that would, evidently for some occult reason important to screen art, hold a great deal of water. The sawmill was gone; at one end of the pool rode a small sail-boat with one mast, its canvas flapping idly in a gentle breeze. Its deck was littered with rigging upon which two men worked. They seemed to be getting things shipshape for a cruise.

When he had tired of this he started off toward the High Gear Dance Hall. Something all day had been drawing him there against his will. He hesitated to believe it was the Montague girl's kindly manner toward him the day before, yet he could identify no other influence. Probably it was that. Yet he didn't want to face her again, even if for a moment she had quit trying to be funny, even if for a moment her eyes had searched his quite earnestly, her broad, amiable face glowing with that sudden friendly concern. It had been hard to withstand this yesterday; he had been in actual danger of confiding to her that engagements of late were not plentiful — something like that. And it would be harder today. Even the collar would make it harder to resist the confidence that he was not at this time overwhelmed with offers for his art.

He had for what seemed like an interminable stretch of time been solitary and an outlaw. It was something to have been spoken to by a human being who expressed ever so fleeting an interest in his affairs, even by someone as inconsequent, as negligible in the world of screen artistry as this lightsome minx who, because of certain mental infirmities, could never hope for the least enviable eminence in a profession demanding seriousness of purpose. Still it would be foolish to go again to the set where she was. She might think he was encouraging her.

So he passed the High Gear, where a four-horse stage, watched by two cameras, was now releasing its passengers who all appeared to be direct from New York, and walked on to an outdoor set that promised entertainment. This was the narrow street of some quaint European village, Scotch he soon saw from the dress of its people. A large automobile was invading this remote hamlet to the dismay of its inhabitants. Rehearsed through a megaphone they scurried within doors at its approach, ancient men hobbling on sticks and frantic mothers grabbing their little ones from the path of the monster. Two trial trips he saw the car make the length of the little street.

At its lower end, brooding placidly, was an ancient horse rather recalling Dexter in his generously exposed bones and the jaded droop of his head above a low stone wall. Twice the car sped by him, arousing no sign of apprehension nor even of interest. He paid it not so much as the tribute of a raised eyelid.

The car went back to the head of the street where its entrance would be made. "All right — ready!" came the megaphoned order. Again the peaceful street was thrown into panic by this snorting dragon from the outer world. The old men hobbled affrightedly within doors, the mothers saved their children. And this time, to the stupefaction of Merton Gill, even the old horse proved to be an actor of rare merits. As the car approached he seemed to suffer a painful shock. He tossed his aged head, kicked viciously with his rear feet, stood absurdly aloft on them, then turned and fled from the monster. As Merton mused upon the genius of the trainer who had taught his horse not only to betray fright at a motor car but to distinguish between rehearsals and the actual taking of a scene, he observed a man who emerged from a clump of near-by shrubbery. He carried a shotgun. This was broken at the breech and the man was blowing smoke from the barrels as he came on.

So that was it. The panic of the old horse had been but a simple reaction to a couple of charges of — perhaps rock — salt. Merton Gill hoped it had been nothing sterner. For the first time in his screen career he became cynical about his art. A thing of shame, of machinery, of subterfuge. Nothing would be real, perhaps not even the art.

It is probable that lack of food conduced to this disparaging outlook; and he recovered presently, for he had been smitten with a quick vision of Beulah Baxter in one of her most daring exploits. She, at least, was real. Deaf to entreaty, she honestly braved her hazards. It was a comforting thought after this late exposure of a sham.

In this slightly combative mood he retraced his steps and found himself outside the High Gear Dance Hall, fortified for another possible encounter with the inquiring and obviously sympathetic Montague girl. He entered and saw that she was not on the set. The bar-room dance hall was for the moment deserted of its ribald crew while an honest inhabitant of the open spaces on a balcony was holding a large revolver to the shrinking back of one of the New York men who had lately arrived by the stage. He forced this man, who was plainly not honest, to descend the stairs and to sign, at a table, a certain paper. Then, with weapon still in hand, the honest Westerner forced the cowardly New Yorker in the direction of the front door until they had passed out of the picture.

On this the bored director of the day before called loudly, "Now, boys, in your places. You've heard a shot — you're running outside to see what's the matter. On your toes, now — try it once." From rear doors came the motley frequenters of the place, led by the elder Montague.

They trooped to the front in two lines and passed from the picture. Here they milled about, waiting for further orders.

"Rotten!" called the director. "Rotten and then some. Listen. You came like a lot of children marching out of a public school. Don't come in lines, break it up, push each other, fight to get ahead, and you're noisy, too. You're shouting. You're saying, 'What's this? What's it all about? What's the matter? Which way did he go?' Say anything you want to, but keep shouting — anything at all. Say 'Thar's gold in them hills!' if you can't think of anything else. Go on, now, boys, do it again and pep it, see. Turn the juice on, open up the old mufflers."

The men went back through the rear doors. The late caller would here have left, being fed up with this sort of stuff, but at that moment he descried the Montague girl back behind a light-standard. She had not noted him, but was in close talk with a man he recognized as Jeff Baird, arch perpetrator of the infamous Buckeye comedies. They came toward him, still talking, as he looked.

"We'll finish here tomorrow afternoon, anyway," the girl was saying.

"Fine," said Baird. "That makes everything jake. Get over on the set whenever you're through. Come over tonight if they don't shoot here, just to give us a look-in."

"Can't," said the girl. "Soon as I get out o' this dump I got to eat on the lot and everything and be over to Baxter's layout — she'll be doing tank stuff till all hours — shipwreck and murder and all like that. Gosh, I hope it ain't cold. I don't mind the water, but I certainly hate to get out and wait in wet clothes while Sig Rosenblatt is thinking about a retake."

"Well" — Baird turned to go — "take care of yourself — don't dive and forget to come up. Come over when you're ready."

"Sure! S'long!" Here the girl, turning from Baird, noted Merton Gill beside her. "Well, well, as I live, the actin' kid once more! Say, you're getting to be a regular studio hound, ain't you?"

For the moment he had forgotten his troubles. He was burning to ask her if Beulah Baxter would really work in a shipwreck scene that night at the place where he had watched the carpenters and the men on the sailboat; but as he tried to word this he saw that the girl was again scanning him with keen eyes. He knew she would read the collar, the beard, perhaps even a look of mere hunger that he thought must now be showing.

"Say, see here, Trouper, what's the shootin' all about, anyway? You up against it — yes." There was again in her eye the look of warm concern, and she was no longer trying to be funny. He might now have admitted a few little things about his screen career, but again the director interrupted.

"Miss Montague — where are you? Oh! Well, remember you're behind the piano during that gun play just now, and you stay hid till after the boys get out. We'll shoot this time, so get set."

She sped off, with a last backward glance of questioning. He waited but a moment before leaving. He was almost forgetting his hunger in the pretty certain knowledge that in a few hours he would actually behold his wonder-woman in at least one of her daring exploits. Shipwreck! Perhaps she would be all but drowned. He hastened back to the pool that had now acquired this high significance. The carpenters were still puttering about on the scaffold. He saw that platforms for the cameras had been built out from its side.

He noted, too, and was puzzled by an airplane propeller that had been stationed close to one corner of the pool, just beyond the stern of the little sailing-craft. Perhaps there would be an airplane wreck in addition to a shipwreck. Now he had something besides food to think of. And he wondered what the Montague girl could be doing in the company of a really serious artist like Beulah Baxter. From her own story she was going to get wet, but from what he knew of her she would be some character not greatly missed from the cast if she should, as Baird had suggested, dive and forget to come up. He supposed that Baird had meant this to be humorous, the humor typical of a man who could profane a great art with the atrocious Buckeye comedies, so called.

He put in the hours until nightfall in aimless wandering and idle gazing, and was early at the poolside where his heroine would do her sensational acting. It was now a scene of thrilling activity. Immense lights, both from the scaffolding and from a tower back of the sailing-craft, flooded its deck and rigging from time to time as adjustments were made. The rigging was slack and the deck was still littered, intentionally so, he now perceived. The gallant little boat had been cruelly buffeted by a gale. Two sailors in piratical dress could be seen to emerge at intervals from the cabin.

Suddenly the gale was on with terrific force, the sea rose in great waves, and the tiny ship rocked in a perilous manner. Great billows of water swept its decks. Merton Gill stared in amazement at these phenomena so dissonant with the quiet starlit night. Then he traced them without difficulty to their various sources. The gale issued from the swift revolutions of that airplane propeller he had noticed a while ago. The flooding billows were spilled from the big tank at the top of the scaffold and the boat rocked in obedience to the tugging of a rope — tugged from the shore by a crew of helpers — that ran to the top of its mast. Thus had the storm been produced.

A spidery, youngish man from one of the platforms built out from the scaffold, now became sharply vocal through a megaphone to assistants who were bending the elements to the need of this particular hazard of Hortense. He called directions to the men who tugged the rope, to the men in control of the lights, and to another who seemed to create the billows. Among other items he wished more action for the boat and more water for the billows. "See that your tank gets full-up this time," he called, whereupon an engine under the scaffold, by means of a large rubber hose reaching into the pool, began to suck water into the tank above.

The speaker must be Miss Baxter's director, the enviable personage who saw her safely through her perils. When one of the turning reflectors illumined him Merton saw his face of a keen Semitic type. He seemed to possess not the most engaging personality; his manner was aggressive, he spoke rudely to his doubtless conscientious employees, he danced in little rages of temper, and altogether he was not one with whom the watcher would have cared to come in contact. He wondered, indeed, that so puissant a star as Beulah Baxter should not be able to choose her own director, for surely the presence of this unlovely, waspishly tempered being could be nothing but an irritant in the daily life of the wonder-woman. Perhaps she had tolerated him merely for one picture. Perhaps he was especially good in shipwrecks.

If Merton Gill were in this company he would surely have words with this person, director or no director. He hastily wrote a one-reel scenario in which the man so far forgot himself as to speak sharply to the star, and in which a certain young actor, a new member of the company, resented the ungentlemanly words by pitching the offender into a convenient pool and earned even more than gratitude from the starry-eyed wonder-woman.

The objectionable man continued active, profuse of gesture and loud through the megaphone. Once more the storm. The boat rocked threateningly, the wind roared through its slack rigging, and giant billows swept the frail craft. Light as from a half-clouded moon broke through the mist that issued from a steam pipe. There was another lull, and the Semitic type on the platform became increasingly offensive. Merton saw himself saying, "Allow me, Miss Baxter, to relieve you of the presence of this bounder." The man was impossible. Constantly he had searched the scene for his heroine. She would probably not appear until they were ready to shoot, and this seemed not to be at once if the rising temper of the director could be thought an indication.

The big hose again drew water from the pool to the tank, whence, at a sudden release, it would issue in billows. The big lights at last seemed to be adjusted to the director's whim. The airplane propeller whirred and the gale was found acceptable. The men at the rope tugged the boat into grave danger. The moon lighted the mist that overhung the scene.

Then at last Merton started, peering eagerly forward across the length of the pool. At the far end, half illumined by the big lights, stood the familiar figure of his wonder-woman, the slim little girl with the wistful eyes. Plainly he could see her now as the mist lifted. She was chatting with one of the pirates who had stepped ashore from the boat. The wonderful golden hair shone resplendent under the glancing rays of the arcs. A cloak was about her shoulders, but at a word of command from the director she threw it off and stepped to the boat's deck. She was dressed in a short skirt, her trim feet and ankles lightly shod and silken clad. The sole maritime touch in her garb was a figured kerchief at her throat similar to those worn by the piratical crew.

"All ready, Hortense — all ready Jose and Gaston, get your places."

Miss Baxter acknowledged the command with that characteristic little wave of a hand that he recalled from so many of her pictures, a half-humorous, half-mocking little defiance. She used it often when escaping her pursuers, as if to say that she would see them in the next installment.

The star and the two men were now in the cabin, hidden from view. Merton Gill was no seaman, but it occurred to him that at least one of the crew would be at the wheel in this emergency. Probably the director knew no better. Indeed the boat, so far as could be discerned, had no wheel. Apparently when a storm came up all hands went down into the cabin to get away from it.

The storm did come up at this moment, with no one on deck. It struck with the full force of a tropic hurricane. The boat rocked, the wind blew, and billows swept the deck. At the height of the tempest Beulah Baxter sprang from the cabin to the deck, clutching wildly at a stanchion. Buffeted by the billows she groped a painful way along the side, at risk of being swept off to her death.

She was followed by one of the crew who held a murderous knife in his hand, then by the other sailor who also held a knife. They, too, were swept by the billows, but seemed grimly determined upon the death of the heroine. Then, when she reached mid-ship and the foremost fiend was almost upon her, the mightiest of all the billows descended and swept her off into the cruel waters. Her pursuers, saving themselves only by great effort, held to the rigging and stared after the girl. They leaned far over the ship's rocking side and each looked from under a spread hand.

For a distressing interval the heroine battled with the waves, but her frail strength availed her little. She raised a despairing face for an instant to the camera and its agony was illumined. Then the dread waters closed above her. The director's whistle blew, the waves were stilled, the tumult ceased. The head of Beulah Baxter appeared halfway down the tank. She was swimming toward the end where Merton stood.

He had been thrilled beyond words at this actual sight of his heroine in action, but now it seemed that a new emotion might overcome him. He felt faint. Beulah Baxter would issue from the pool there at his feet. He might speak to her, might even help her to climb out. At least no one else had appeared to do this. Seemingly no one now cared where Miss Baxter swam to or whether she were offered any assistance in landing. She swam with an admirable crawl stroke, reached the wall, and put up a hand to it. He stepped forward, but she was out before he reached her side. His awe had delayed him. He drew back then, for the star, after vigorously shaking herself, went to a tall brazier in which glowed a charcoal fire.

Here he now noticed for the first time the prop-boy Jimmie, he who had almost certainly defaulted with an excellent razor. Jimmie threw a blanket about the star's shoulders as she hovered above the glowing coals. Merton had waited for her voice. He might still venture to speak to her — to tell her of his long and profound admiration for her art. Her voice came as she shivered over the fire:

"Murder! That water's cold. Rosenblatt swore he'd have it warmed but I'm here to say it wouldn't boil an egg in four minutes."

He could not at first identify this voice with the remembered tones of Beulah Baxter. But of course she was now hoarse with the cold. Under the circumstances he could hardly expect his heroine's own musical clearness. Then as the girl spoke again something stirred among his more recent memories. The voice was still hoarse, but he placed it now. He approached the brazier. It was undoubtedly the Montague girl. She recognized him, even as she squeezed water from the hair of wondrous gold.

"Hello, again, Kid. You're everywhere, ain't you? Say, wha'd you think of that Rosenblatt man? Swore he'd put the steam into that water and take off the chill. And he never." She threw aside the blanket and squeezed water from her garments, then began to slap her legs, arms, and chest.

"Well, I'm getting a gentle glow, anyhow. Wha'd you think of the scene?"

"It was good — very well done, indeed." He hoped it didn't sound patronizing, though that was how he felt. He believed now that Miss Baxter would have done it much better. He ventured a question. "But how about Miss Baxter — when does she do something? Is she going to be swept off the boat, too?"

"Baxter? Into that water? Quit your kidding!"

"But isn't she here at all — won't she do anything here?"

"Listen here, Kid; why should she loaf around on the set when she's paying me good money to double for her?"

"You — double for Beulah Baxter?" It was some more of the girl's nonsense, and a blasphemy for which he could not easily forgive her.

"Why not? Ain't I a good stunt actress? I'll tell the lot she hasn't found any one yet that can get away with her stuff better than what I do."

"But she — I heard her say herself she never allowed any one to double for her — she wouldn't do such a thing."

Here sounded a scornful laugh from Jimmie, the prop — boy. "Bunk!" said he at the laugh's end. "How long you been doublin' for her, Miss Montague? Two years, ain't it? — I know it was before I come here, and I been on the lot a year and a half. Say, he ought to see some the stuff you done for her out on location, like jumpin' into the locomotive engine from your auto and catchin' the brake beams when the train's movin', and goin' across that quarry on the cable, and ridin' down that lumber flume 60 miles per hour and ridin' some them outlaw buckjumpers — he'd ought to seen some that stuff, hey, Miss Montague?"

"That's right, Jimmie, you tell him all about me. I hate to talk of myself." Very wonderfully Merton Gill divined that this was said with a humorous intention. Jimmie was less sensitive to values. He began to obey.

"Well, I dunno — there's that motorcycle stuff. Purty good, I'll say. I wouldn't try that, no, sir, not for a cool million dollars. And that chase stuff on the roofs down town where you jumped across that court that wasn't any too darned narrow, an' say, I wisht I could skin up a tree the way you can. An' there was that time —"

"All right, all right, Jimmie. I can tell him the rest sometime. I don't really hate to talk about myself — that's on the level. And say, listen here, Jimmie, you're my favorite sweetheart, ain't you?"

"Yes, ma'am," assented Jimmie, warmly.

"All right. Beat it up and get me about two quarts of that hot coffee and about four ham sandwiches, two for you and two for me. That's a good kid."

"Sure!" exclaimed Jimmie, and was off.

Merton Gill had been dazed by these revelations, by the swift and utter destruction of his loftiest ideal. He hardly cared to know, now, if Beulah Baxter were married. It was the Montague girl who had most thrilled him for two years. Yet, almost as if from habit, he heard himself asking, "Is — do you happen to know if Beulah Baxter is married?"

"Baxter married? Sure! I should think you'd know it from the way that Sig Rosenblatt bawls everybody out."

"Who is he?"

"Who is he? Why, he's her husband, of course — he's Mr. Beulah Baxter."

"That little director up on the platform that yells so?" This unspeakable person to be actually the husband of the wonder-woman, the man he had supposed she must find intolerable even as a director. It was unthinkable, more horrible, somehow, than her employment of a double. In time he might have forgiven that — but this!

"Sure, that's her honest-to-God husband. And he's the best one out of three that I know she's had. Sig's a good scout even if he don't look like Buffalo Bill. In fact, he's all right in spite of his rough ways. He'd go farther for you than most of the men on this lot. If I wanted a favor I'd go to Sig before a lot of Christians I happen to know. And he's a bully director if he is noisy. Baxter's crazy about him, too. Don't make any mistake there."

"I won't," he answered, not knowing what he said.

She shot him a new look. "Say, Kid, as long as we're talking, you seem kind of up against it. Where's your overcoat a night like this, and when did you last —"

"Miss Montague! Miss Montague!" The director was calling.

"Excuse me," she said. "I got to go entertain the white folks again." She tucked up the folds of her blanket and sped around the pool to disappear in the mazes of the scaffolding. He remained a moment staring dully into the now quiet water. Then he walked swiftly away.

Beulah Baxter, his wonder-woman, had deceived her public in Peoria, Illinois, by word of mouth. She employed a double at critical junctures. "She'd be a fool not to," the Montague girl had said. And in private life, having been unhappily wed twice before, she was Mrs. Sigmund Rosenblatt. And crazy about her husband!

A little while ago he had felt glad he was not to die of starvation before seeing his wonder-woman. Reeling under the first shock of his discoveries he was now sorry. Beulah Baxter was no longer his wonder-woman. She was Mr. Rosenblatt's. He would have preferred death, he thought, before this heart-withering revelation.

CHAPTER XI

THE MONTAGUE GIRL INTERVENES

He came to life the next morning, shivering under his blankets. It must be cold outside. He glanced at his watch and reached for another blanket, throwing it over himself and tucking it in at the foot. Then he lay down again to screen a tense bit of action that had occurred late the night before. He had plunged through the streets for an hour, after leaving the pool, striving to recover from the twin shocks he had suffered. Then, returning to his hotel, he became aware that *The Hazards of Hortense* were still on. He could hear the roar of the airplane propeller and see the lights over the low buildings that lined his street.

Miserably he was drawn back to the spot where the most important of all his visions had been rent to tatters. He went to the end of the pool where he had stood before. Mr. Rosenblatt — hardly could he bring his mind to utter the hideous syllables — was still dissatisfied with the sea's might. He wanted bigger billows and meant to have them if the company stayed on the set all night. He was saying as much with peevish inflections. Merton stood warming himself over the fire that still glowed in the brazier.

To him from somewhere beyond the scaffold came now the Montague girl and Jimmie. The girl was in her blanket, and Jimmie bore a pitcher, two tin cups, and a package of sandwiches. They came to the fire and Jimmie poured coffee for the girl. He produced sugar from a pocket.

"Help yourself, James," said the girl, and Jimmie poured coffee for himself. They ate sandwiches as they drank. Merton drew a little back from the fire. The scent of the hot coffee threatened to make him forget he was not only a successful screen actor but a gentleman.

"Did you have to do it again?" he asked.

"I had to do it twice again," said the girl from over her tin cup. "They're developing the strips now, then they'll run them in the projection room, and they won't suit Sig one little bit, and I'll have to do it some more. I'll be swimming here till daylight doth appear."

She now shot that familiar glance of appraisal at Merton. "Have a sandwich and some coffee, Kid — give him your cup, Jimmie."

It was Merton Gill's great moment, a heart-gripping climax to a two-days' drama that had at no time lacked tension. Superbly he arose to it. Consecrated to his art, Clifford Armytage gave the public something better and finer. He drew himself up and spoke lightly, clearly, with careless ease:

"No, thanks — I couldn't eat a mouthful." The smile with which he accompanied the simple words might be enigmatic, it might hint of secret sorrows, but it was plain enough that these could not ever so distantly relate to a need for food.

Having achieved this sensational triumph, with all the quietness of method that should distinguish the true artist, he became seized with stage fright amounting almost to panic. He was moved to snatch the sandwich that Jimmie now proffered, the cup that he had refilled with coffee. Yet there was but a moment of confusion. Again he wielded an iron restraint. But he must leave the stage. He could not tarry there after his big scene, especially under that piercing glance of the girl. Somehow there was incredulity in it.

"Well, I guess I'll have to be going," he remarked jauntily, and turned for his exit.

"Say, Kid." The girl halted him a dozen feet away.

"Say, listen here. This is on the level. I want to have a talk with you tomorrow. You'll be on the lot, won't you?"

He seemed to debate this momentarily, then replied, "Oh, yes. I'll be around here somewhere."

"Well, remember, now. If I don't run into you, you come down to that set where I was working today. See? I got something to say to you."

"All right. I'll probably see you sometime during the day."

He had gone on to his hotel. But he had no intention of seeing the Montague girl on the morrow, nor of being seen by her. He would keep out of that girl's way whatever else he did. She would ask him if everything was jake, and where was his overcoat, and a lot of silly questions about matters that should not concern her.

He was in two minds about the girl now. Beneath an unreasonable but very genuine resentment that she should have doubled for Beulah Baxter — as if she had basely cheated him of his most cherished ideal — there ran an undercurrent of reluctant but very profound admiration for her prowess. She had done some thrilling things and seemed to make nothing of it. Through this admiration there ran also a thread of hostility because he, himself, would undoubtedly be afraid to attempt her lightest exploit. Not even the trifling feat he had just witnessed, for he had never learned to swim. But he clearly knew, despite this confusion, that he was through with the girl. He must take more pains to avoid her. If met by chance, she must be snubbed-up-staged, as she would put it.

Under his blankets now, after many appealing close-ups of the sandwich which Jimmie had held out to him, he felt almost sorry that he had not taken the girl's food. All his being, save that part consecrated to his art, had cried out for it. Art, had triumphed, and now he was near to regretting that it had not been beaten down. No good thinking about it, though.

He reached again for his watch. It was 7:30 and time to be abroad. Once more he folded his blankets and placed them on the pile, keeping an alert glance, the while, for another possible bit of the delicious bread. He found nothing of this sort. The Crystal Palace Hotel was bare of provender. Achieving a discreet retirement from the hostelry he stood irresolute in the street. This morning there was no genial sun to warm him. A high fog overcast the sky, and the air was chill. At intervals he shivered violently. For no reason, except that he had there last beheld actual food, he went back to the pool.

Evidently Mr. Rosenblatt had finally been appeased. The place was deserted and lay bare and ugly in the dull light. The gallant ship of the night before was seen to be a poor, flimsy make-shift. No wonder Mr. Rosenblatt had wished billows to engulf it and mist to shroud it. He sat on a beam lying at the ship end of the pool and stared moodily at the pitiful make-believe.

He rounded his shoulders and pulled up the collar of his coat. He knew he should be walking, but doubted his strength. The little walk to the pool had made him strangely breathless. He wondered how long people were in starving to death. He had read of fasters who went for weeks without food, but he knew he was not of this class. He lacked talent for it. Doubtless another day would finish him. He had no heart now for visions of the Gashwiler table. He descended tragically to recalling that last meal at the drug store-the bowl of soup with its gracious burden of rich, nourishing ketchup.

He began to alter the scenario of his own life. Suppose he had worked two more weeks for Gashwiler. That would have given him 30 dollars. Suppose he had worked a month. He could have existed a long time on 60 dollars. Suppose he had even stuck it out for one week more — 15 dollars at this moment! He began to see a breakfast, the sort of meal to be ordered by a hungry man with 15 dollars to squander.

The shivering seized him again and he heard his teeth rattle. He must move from this spot, forever now to be associated with black disillusion. He arose from his seat and was dismayed to hear a hail from the Montague girl. Was he never to be free from her? She was poised at a little distance, one hand raised to him, no longer the drenched victim of a capricious Rosenblatt, but the beaming, joyous figure of one who had triumphed over wind and wave. He went almost sullenly to her while she waited. No good trying to escape her for a minute or so.

"Hello, old Trouper! You're just in time to help me hunt for something." She was in the familiar street suit now, a skirt and jacket of some rough brown goods and a cloth hat that kept close to her small head above hair that seemed of no known shade whatever, though it was lighter than dark. She flashed a smile at him from her broad mouth as he came up, though her knowing gray eyes did not join in this smile. He knew instantly that she was taking him in.

This girl was wise beyond her years, he thought, but one even far less knowing could hardly have been in two minds about his present abject condition. The pushed-up collar of his coat did not entirely hide the once-white collar beneath it, the beard had reached its perhaps most distressing stage of development, and the suit was rumpled out of all the nattiness for which it had been advertised. Even the plush hat had lost its smart air.

Then he plainly saw that the girl would, for the moment at least, ignore these phenomena. She laughed again, and this time the eyes laughed, too. "C'mon over and help me hunt for that bar pin I lost. It must be at this end, because I know I had it on when I went into the drink. Maybe it's in the pool, but maybe I lost it after I got out. It's one of Baxter's that she wore in the scene just ahead of last night, and she'll have to have it again today. Now —" She began to search the ground around the cold brazier. "It might be along here." He helped her look. Pretty soon he would remember an engagement and get away. The search at the end of the pool proved fruitless. The girl continued to chatter. They had worked until one-thirty before that grouch of a Rosenblatt would call it a day. At that she'd rather do water stuff than animal stuff-especially lions. "Lions? I should think so!" He replied to this. "Dangerous, isn't it?"

"Oh, it ain't that. They're nothing to be afraid of if you know 'em, but they're so hot and smelly when you have to get close to 'em. Anything I really hate, it's having to get up against a big, hot, hairy, smelly lion."

He murmured a sympathetic phrase and extended his search for the lost pin to the side of the pool. Almost under the scaffold he saw the shine of precious stones and called to her as he picked up the pin, a bar pin splendidly set with diamonds. He was glad that he had found it for her. It must have cost a great deal of money and she would doubtless be held responsible for its safe-keeping.

She came dancing to him. "Say, that's fine-your eyes are working, ain't they? I mighta been set back a good six dollars if you hadn't found that." She took the bauble and fastened it inside her jacket. So the pin, too, had been a tawdry makeshift. Nothing was real any more. As she adjusted the pin he saw his moment for escape. With a gallant striving for the true Clifford Armytage manner he raised the plush hat.

"Well, I'm glad you found Mrs. Rosenblatt's pin — and I guess I'll be getting on."

The manner must have been defective. She looked through him and said with great firmness, "Nothing like that, old pippin." Again he was taken with a violent fit of shivering. He could not meet her eyes. He was turning away when she seized him by the wrist. Her grip was amazingly forceful. He doubted if he could break away even with his stoutest effort. He stood miserably staring at the ground. Suddenly the girl reached up to pat his shoulder. He shivered again and she continued to pat it. When his teeth had ceased to be castanets she spoke:

"Listen here, old Kid, you can't fool any one, so quit trying. Don't you s'pose I've seen 'em like you before? Say, boy, I was trouping while you played with marbles. You're up against it. Now, c'mon" — with the arm at his shoulder she pulled him about to face her — "c'mon and be nice, tell mother all about it."

The late Clifford Armytage was momentarily menaced by a complete emotional overthrow. Another paroxysm of shivering perhaps averted this humiliation. The girl dropped his wrist, turned, stooped, and did something. He recalled the scene in the gambling hell, only this time she fronted away from the camera. When she faced him again he was not surprised to see bills in her hand. It could only have been the chill he suffered that kept him from blushing. She forced the bills into his numb fingers and he stared at them blankly. "I can't take these," he muttered.

"There, now, there, now! Be easy. Naturally I know you're all right or I wouldn't give up this way. You're just having a run of hard luck. The Lord knows, I've been helped out often enough in my time. Say, listen, I'll never forget when I went out as a kid with Her First False Step-they had lions in that show. It was a frost from the start. No salaries, no nothing. I got a big laugh one day when I was late at rehearsal. The manager says: 'You're fined two dollars, Miss Montague.' I says, 'All right, Mr. Gratz, but you'll have to wait till I can write home for the money.' Even Gratz had to laugh. Anyway, the show went bust and I never would 'a' got any place if two or three parties hadn't of helped me out here and there, just the same as I'm doing with you this minute. So don't be foolish."

"Well, you see, I don't —" He broke off from nervous weakness. In his mind was a jumble of incongruous sentences and he seemed unable to manage any of them.

The girl now sent a clean shot through his armor. "When'd you eat last?"

He looked at the ground again in painful embarrassment. Even in the chill air he was beginning to feel hot. "I don't remember," he said at last quite honestly.

"That's what I thought. You go eat. Go to Mother Haggin's, that cafeteria just outside the gate. She has better breakfast things than the place on the lot." Against his will the vision of a breakfast enthralled him, yet even under this exaltation an instinct of the wariest caution survived.

"I'll go to the one on the lot, I guess. If I went out to the other one I couldn't get in again."

She smiled suddenly, with puzzling lights in her eyes. "Well, of all things! You want to get in again, do you? Say, wouldn't that beat the hot place a mile? You want to get in again? All right, Old-timer, I'll go out with you and after you've fed I'll cue you on to the lot again."

"Well-if it ain't taking you out of your way." He knew that the girl was somehow humoring him, as if he were a sick child. She knew, and he knew, that the lot was no longer any place for him until he could be rightly there.

"No, c'mon, I'll stay by you." They walked up the street of the Western village. The girl had started at a brisk pace and he was presently breathless.

"I guess I'll have to rest a minute," he said. They were now before the Crystal Palace Hotel and he sat on the steps.

"All in, are you? Well, take it easy."

He was not only all in, but his mind still played with incongruous sentences. He heard himself saying things that must sound foolish.

"I've slept in here a lot," he volunteered. The girl went to look through one of the windows.

"Blankets!" she exclaimed. "Well, you got the makings of a trouper in you, I'll say that. Where else did you sleep?"

"Well, there were two miners had a nice cabin down the street here with bunks and blankets, and they had a fight, and half a kettle of beans and some bread, and one of them shaved and I used his razor, but I haven't shaved since because I only had 20 cents day before yesterday, and anyway they might think I was growing them for a part, the way your father did, but I moved up here when I saw them put the blankets in, and I was careful and put them back every morning. I didn't do any harm, do you think? And I got the rest of the beans they'd thrown into the fireplace, and if I'd only known it I could have brought my razor and overcoat and some clean collars, but somehow you never seem to know when —"

He broke off, eyeing her vaguely. He had little notion what he had been saying or what he would say next.

"This is going to be good," said the Montague girl. "I can see that from here. But now you c'mon-we'll walk slow-and you tell me the rest when you've had a little snack."

She even helped him to rise, with a hand under his elbow, though he was quick to show her that he had not needed this help. "I can walk all right," he assured her.

"Of course you can. You're as strong as a horse. But we needn't go too fast." She took his arm in a friendly way as they completed the journey to the outside cafeteria.

At this early hour they were the only patrons of the place. Miss Montague, a little with the air of a solicitous nurse, seated her charge at a corner table and took the place opposite him.

"What's it going to be?" she demanded.

Visions of rich food raced madly through his awakened mind, wide platters heaped with sausage and steaks and ham and corned-beef hash.

"Steak," he ventured, "and something like ham and eggs and some hot cakes and coffee and —" He broke off. He was becoming too emotional under this golden spread of opportunity. The girl glanced up from the bill of fare and appraised the wild light in his eyes.

"One minute, Kid, let's be more restful at first. You know, kind of ease into the heavy eats. It'll prob'ly be better for you."

"Anything you say," he conceded. Her words of caution had stricken him with a fear that this was a dream; that he would wake up under blankets back in the Crystal Palace. It was like that in dreams. You seemed able to order all sorts of food, but something happened; it never reached the table. He would take no further initiative in this scene, whether dream or reality. "You order something," he concluded. His eyes trustfully sought the girl's.

"Well, I think you'll start with one orange, just to kind of hint to the old works that something good is coming. Then — lemme see" — she considered gravely. "Then I guess about two soft-boiled eggs — no, you can stand three — and some dry toast and some coffee. Maybe a few thin strips of bacon wouldn't hurt. We'll see can you make the grade." She turned to give the order to a waitress. "And shoot the coffee along, sister. A cup for me, too."

Her charge shivered again at the mere mention of coffee. The juncture was critical. He might still be dreaming, but in another moment he must know. He closely, even coolly, watched the two cups of coffee that were placed before them. He put a benumbed hand around the cup in front of him and felt it burn. It was too active a sensation for mere dreaming. He put sugar into the cup and poured in the cream from a miniature pitcher, inhaling a very real aroma. Events thus far seemed normal. He stirred the coffee and started to raise the cup. Now, after all, it seemed to be a dream. His hand shook so that the stuff spilled into the saucer and even out on to the table. Always in dreams you were thwarted at the last moment.

The Montague girl had noted the trembling and ineffective hand. She turned her back upon him to chat with the waitress over by the food counter. With no eye upon him, he put both hands about the cup and succeeded in raising it to his lips. The hands were still shaky, but he managed some sips of the stuff, and then a long draught that seemed to scald him. He wasn't sure if it scalded or not. It was pretty hot, and fire ran through him. He drained the cup — still holding it with both hands. It was an amazing sensation to have one's hand refuse to obey so simple an order. Maybe he would always be that way now, practically a cripple.

The girl turned back to him. "Atta boy," she said. "Now take the orange. And when the toast comes you can have some more coffee." A dread load was off his mind. He did not dream this thing. He ate the orange, and ate wonderful toast to the accompaniment of another cup of coffee. The latter half of this he managed with but one hand, though it was not yet wholly under control. The three eggs seemed like but one. He thought they must have been small eggs. More toast was commanded and more coffee.

"Easy, easy!" cautioned his watchful hostess from time to time. "Don't wolf it — you'll feel better afterwards."

"I feel better already," he announced.

"Well," the girl eyed him critically, "you certainly got the main chandelier lighted up once more."

A strange exhilaration flooded all his being. His own thoughts babbled to him, and he presently began to babble to his new friend.

"You remind me so much of Tessie Kearns," he said as he scraped the sides of the egg cup.

"Who's she?"

"Oh, she's a scenario writer I know. You're just like her." He was now drunk — maudlin drunk — from the coffee. Sober, he would have known that no human beings could be less alike than Tessie Kearns and the Montague girl. Other walls of his reserve went down.

"Of course I could have written to Gashwiler and got some money to go back there —"

"Gashwiler, Gashwiler?" The girl seemed to search her memory. "I thought I knew all the tank towns, but that's a new one. Where is it?"

"It isn't a town; it's a gentleman I had a position with, and he said he'd keep it open for me." He flew to another thought with the inconsequence of the drunken. "Say, Kid" — He had even caught that form of address from her — "I'll tell you. You can keep this watch of mine till I pay you back this money." He drew it out. "It's a good solid-gold watch and everything. My uncle Sylvester gave it to me for not smoking, on my 18th birthday. He smoked, himself; he even drank considerable. He was his own worst enemy. But you can see it's a good solid-gold watch and keeps time, and you hold it till I pay you back, will you?"

The girl took the watch, examining it carefully, noting the inscription engraved on the case. There were puzzling glints in her eyes as she handed it back to him. "No; I'll tell you, it'll be my watch until you pay me back, but you keep it for me. I haven't any place to carry it except the pocket of my jacket, and I might lose it, and then where'd we be?"

"Well, all right." He cheerfully took back the watch. His present ecstasy would find him agreeable to all proposals.

"And say," continued the girl, "what about this Gashweiler, or whatever his name is? He said he'd take you back, did he? A farm?"

"No, an emporium — and you forgot his name just the way that lady in the casting office always does. She's funny. Keeps telling me not to forget the address, when of course I couldn't forget the town where I lived, could I? Of course it's a little town, but you wouldn't forget it when you lived there a long time — not when you got your start there."

"So you got your start in this town, did you?"

He wanted to talk a lot now. He prattled of the town and his life there, of the eight-hour talent-tester and the course in movie-acting. Of Tessie Kearns and her scenarios, not yet prized as they were sure to be later. Of Lowell Hardy, the artistic photographer, and the stills that he had made of the speaker as Clifford Armytage. Didn't she think that was a better stage name than Merton Gill, which didn't seem to sound like so much? Anyway, he wished he had his stills here to show her. Of course some of them were just in society parts, the sort of thing that Harold Parmalee played — had she noticed that he looked a good deal like Harold Parmalee? Lots of people had.

Tessie Kearns thought he was the dead image of Parmalee. But he liked Western stuff better — a lot better than cabaret stuff where you had to smoke one cigarette after another — and he wished she could see the stills in the Buck Benson outfit, chaps and sombrero and spurs and holster. He'd never had two guns, but the one he did have he could draw pretty well. There would be his hand at his side, and in a flash he would have the gun in it, ready to shoot from the hip. And roping — he'd need to practice that some. Once he got it smack over Dexter's head, but usually it didn't go so well.

Probably a new clothesline didn't make the best rope — too stiff. He could probably do a lot better with one of those hair ropes that the real cowboys used. And Metta Judson — she was the best cook anywhere around Simsbury. He mustn't forget to write to Metta, and to Tessie Kearns, to be sure and see The Blight of Broadway when it came to the Bijou Palace. They would be surprised to see those close-ups that Henshaw had used him in. And he was in that other picture. No close-ups in that, still he would show pretty well in the cage-scene — he'd had to smoke a few cigarettes there, because Arabs smoke all the time, and he hadn't been in the later scene where the girl and the young fellow were in the deserted tomb all night and he didn't lay a finger on her because he was a perfect gentleman.

He didn't know what he would do next. Maybe Henshaw would want him in *Robinson Crusoe, Junior,* where Friday's sister turned out to be the daughter of an English earl with her monogram tattooed on her left shoulder. He would ask Henshaw, anyway.

The Montague girl listened attentively to the long, wandering recital. At times she would seem to be strongly moved, to tears or something. But mostly she listened with a sympathetic smile, or perhaps with a perfectly rigid face, though at such moments there would be those curious glints of light far back in her gray eyes. Occasionally she would prompt him with a question.

In this way she brought out his version of the Sabbath afternoon experience with Dexter. He spared none of the details, for he was all frankness now. He even told how ashamed he had felt having to lead Dexter home from his scandalous grazing before the Methodist Church. He had longed to leap upon the horse and ride him back at a gallop, but he had been unable to do this because there was nothing from which to climb on him, and probably he would have been afraid to gallop the beast, anyway.

This had been one of the bits that most strangely moved his listener. Her eyes were moist when he had finished, and some strong emotion seemed about to overpower her, but she had recovered command of herself, and become again the sympathetic provider and counsellor.

He would have continued to talk, apparently, for the influence of strong drink had not begun to wane, but the girl at length stopped him.

"Listen here, Merton —" she began; her voice was choked to a peculiar hoarseness and she seemed to be threatened with a return of her late strong emotion. She was plainly uncertain of her control, fearing to trust herself to speech, but presently, after efforts which he observed with warmest sympathy, she seemed to recover her poise. She swallowed earnestly several times, wiped her moisture — dimmed eyes with her handkerchief, and continued, "It's getting late and I've got to be over at the show shop. So I'll tell you what to do next. You go out and get a shave and a haircut and then go home and get cleaned up — you said you had a room and other clothes, didn't you?"

Volubly he told her about the room at Mrs. Patterson's, and, with a brief return of lucidity, how the sum of ten dollars was now due this heartless society woman who might insist upon its payment before he would again enjoy free access to his excellent wardrobe.

"Well, lemme see —" She debated a moment, then reached under the table, fumbled obscurely, and came up with more money. "Now, here, here's 20 more besides that first I gave you, so you can pay the dame her money and get all fixed up again, fresh suit and clean collar and a shine and everything. No, no — this is my scene; you stay out."

He had waved protestingly at sight of the new money, and now again he blushed.

"That's all understood," she continued. "I'm staking you to cakes till you get on your feet, see? And I know you're honest, so I'm not throwing my money away. There — sink it and forget it. Now, you go out and do what I said, the barber first. And lay off the eats until about noon. You had enough for now. By noon you can stoke up with meat and potatoes — anything you want that'll stick to the merry old slats. And I'd take milk instead of any more coffee. You've thinned down some — you're not near so plump as Harold Parmalee. Then you rest up for the balance of the day, and you show here tomorrow morning about this time. Do you get it? The Countess'll let you in. Tell her I said to, and come over to the office building. See?"

He tried to tell her his gratitude, but instead he babbled again of how much she was like Tessie Kearns. They parted at the gate.

With a last wondering scrutiny of him, a last reminder of her very minute directions, she suddenly illumined him with rays of a compassion that was somehow half-laughter. "You poor, feckless dub!" she pronounced as she turned from him to dance through the gate. He scarcely heard the words; her look and tone had been so warming.

Ten minutes later he was telling a barber that he had just finished a hard week on the Holden lot, and that he was glad to get the brush off at last. From the barber's he hastened to the Patterson house, rather dreading the encounter with one to whom he owed so much money. He found the house locked. Probably both of the Pattersons had gone out into society. He let himself in and began to follow the directions of the Montague girl. The bath, clean linen, the other belted suit, already pressed, the other shoes, the buttoned, cloth-topped ones, already polished! He felt now more equal to the encounter with a heartless society woman. But, as she did not return, he went out in obedience to a new hunger.

In the most sumptuous cafeteria he knew of, one patronized only in his first careless days of opulence, he ate for a long time. Roast beef and potatoes he ordered twice, nor did he forget to drink the milk prescribed by his benefactress. Plenty of milk would make him more than ever resemble Harold Parmalee. And he commanded an abundance of dessert: lemon pie and apple pie and a double portion of chocolate cake with ice-cream. His craving for sweets was still unappeased, so at a near-by drug store he bought a pound box of candy.

The world was again under his feet. Restored to his rightful domain, he trod it with lightness and certainty. His mind was still a pleasant jumble of money and food and the Montague girl. Miles of gorgeous film flickered across his vision. An experienced alcoholic would have told him that he enjoyed a coffee "hang-over." He wended a lordly way to the nearest motion-picture theater.

Billed there was the 10th installment of *The Hazards of Hortense*. He passed before the lively portrayal in colors of Hortense driving a motor car off an open drawbridge. The car was already halfway between the bridge and the water beneath. He sneered openly at the announcement: "Beulah Baxter in the Sensational Surprise Picture of the Century." A surprise picture indeed, if those now entering the theater could be told what he knew about it! He considered spreading the news, but decided to retain the superiority his secret knowledge gave him.

Inside the theater, eating diligently from his box of candy, he was compelled to endure another of the unspeakable Buckeye comedies. The cross-eyed man was a lifeguard at a beach and there were social entanglements involving a bearded father, his daughter in an inconsiderable bathing suit, a confirmed dipsomaniac, two social derelicts who had to live by their wits, and a dozen young girls also arrayed in inconsiderable bathing suits. He could scarcely follow the chain of events, so illogical were they, and indeed made little effort to do so. He felt far above the audience that cackled at these dreadful buffooneries. One subtitle read: "I hate to kill him — murder is so hard to explain."

This sort of thing, he felt more than ever, degraded an art where earnest people were suffering and sacrificing in order to give the public something better and finer. Had he not, himself, that very day, completed a perilous ordeal of suffering and sacrifice? And he was asked to laugh at a cross-eyed man posing before a camera that fell to pieces when the lens was exposed, shattered, presumably, by the impact of the afflicted creature's image! This, surely, was not art such as Clifford Armytage was rapidly fitting himself, by trial and hardship, to confer upon the public.

It was with curiously conflicting emotions that he watched the ensuing Hazards of Hortense. He had to remind himself that the slim little girl with the wistful eyes was not only not performing certain feats of daring that the film exposed, but that she was Mrs. Sigmund Rosenblatt and crazy about her husband. Yet the magic had not wholly departed from this wronged heroine. He thought perhaps this might be because he now knew, and actually liked, that talkative Montague girl who would be doing the choice bits of this drama. Certainly he was loyal to the hand that fed him.

Black Steve and his base crew, hirelings of the scoundrelly guardian who was "a Power in Wall Street," again and again seemed to have encompassed the ruin, body and soul, of the persecuted Hortense. They had her prisoner in a foul den of Chinatown, whence she escaped to balance precariously upon the narrow cornice of a skyscraper, hundreds of feet above a crowded thoroughfare. They had her, as the screen said, "Depressed by the Grim Menace of Tragedy that Impended in the Shadows." They gave her a brief respite in one of those gilded resorts "Where the Clink of Coin Opens Wide the Portals of Pleasure, Where Wealth Beckons with Golden Fingers," but this was only a trap for the unsuspecting girl, who was presently, sewed in a plain sack, tossed from the stern of an ocean liner far out at sea by creatures who would do anything for money — who, so it was said, were Remorseless in the Mad Pursuit of Gain.

At certain gripping moments it became apparent to one of the audience that Mrs. Sigmund Rosenblatt herself was no longer in jeopardy. He knew the girl who was, and profoundly admired her artistry as she fled along the narrow cornice of the skyscraper. For all purposes she was Beulah Baxter. He recalled her figure as being — not exactly stubby, but at least not of marked slenderness. Yet in the distance she was indeed all that an audience could demand. And she was honest, while Mrs. Rosenblatt, in the Majestic Theater at Peoria, Illinois, had trifled airily with his faith in women and deceived him by word of mouth.

He applauded loudly at the sensational finish, when Hortense, driving her motor car at high speed across the great bridge, ran into the draw, that opened too late for her to slow down, and plunged to the cruel waters far below.

Mrs. Rosenblatt would possibly have been a fool to do this herself. The Montague girl had been insistent on that point;

there were enough things she couldn't avoid doing, and all stars very sensibly had doubles for such scenes when distance or action permitted. At the same time, he could never again feel the same toward her. Indeed, he would never have felt the same even had there been no Rosenblatt. Art was art!

It was only five o'clock when he left the picture theater, but he ate again at the luxurious cafeteria. He ate a large steak, drank an immense quantity of milk, and bought another box of candy on his way to the Patterson home. Lights were on there, and he went in to face the woman he had so long kept out of her money. She would probably greet him coldly and tell him she was surprised at his actions.

Yet it seemed that he had been deceived in this society woman. She was human, after all. She shook hands with him warmly and said they were glad to see him back; he must have been out on location, and she was glad they were not to lose him, because he was so quiet and regular and not like some other motion-picture actors she had known.

He told her he had just put in a hard week on the Holden lot, where things were beginning to pick up. He was glad she had missed him, and he certainly had missed his comfortable room, because the accommodations on the lot were not of the best. In fact, they were pretty unsatisfactory, if you came right down to it, and he hoped they wouldn't keep him there again. And, oh, yes — he was almost forgetting. Here was 10 dollars — he believed there were two weeks' rent now due. He passed over the money with rather a Clifford Armytage flourish.

Mrs. Patterson accepted the bill almost protestingly. She hadn't once thought about the rent, because she knew he was reliable, and he was to remember that any time convenient to him would always suit her in these matters. She did accept the bill, still she was not the heartless creature he had supposed her to be.

As he bade her good-night at the door she regarded him closely and said, "Somehow you look a whole lot older, Mr. Armytage."

"I am," replied Mr. Armytage.

Miss Montague, after parting with her protege had walked quickly, not without little recurrent dance steps — as if some excess of joy would ever and again overwhelm her — to the long office building on the Holden lot, where she entered a door marked "Buckeye Comedies. Jeff Baird, Manager." The outer office was vacant, but through the open door to another room she observed Baird at his desk, his head bent low over certain sheets of yellow paper. He was a bulky, rather phlegmatic looking man, with a parrot-like crest of gray hair. He did not look up as the girl entered. She stood a moment as if to control her excitement, then spoke.

"Jeff, I found a million dollars for you this morning."

"Thanks!" said Mr. Baird, still not looking up. "Chuck it down in the coal cellar, will you? We're littered with the stuff up here."

"On the level, Jeff."

Baird looked up. "On the level?"

"You'll say so."

"Shoot!"

"Well, he's a small-town hick that saved up 72 dollars to come here from Goosewallow, Michigan, to go into pictures-took a correspondence course in screen — acting and all that, and he went broke and slept in a property room down in the village all last week; no eats at all for three, four days. I'd noticed him around the lot on different sets; something about him that makes you look a second time. I don't know what it is — kind of innocent and bug-eyed the way he'd rubber at things, but all the time like as if he thought he was someone. Well, I keep running across him and pretty soon I notice he's up against it. He still thinks he's someone, and is very up-stage if you start to kid him the least bit, but the signs are there, all right. He's up against it good and hard.

"All last week he got to looking worse and worse. But he still had his stage presence. Say, yesterday he looked like the juvenile lead of a busted road show that has walked in from Albany and was just standing around on Broadway wondering who he'd consent to sign up with for 40 weeks — see what I mean? — hungry but proud. He was over on the Baxter set last night while I was doing the water stuff, and you'd ought to see him freeze me when I suggested a sandwich and a cup o' coffee. It was grand.

"Well, this morning I'm back for a bar pin of Baxter's I'd lost, and there he is again, no overcoat, shivering his teeth loose, and all in. So I fell for him. Took him up for some coffee and eggs, staked him to his room rent, and sent him off to get cleaned and barbered. But before he went he cut loose and told me his history from the cradle to Hollywood.

"I'd 'a' given something good if you'd been at the next table. I guess he got kind of jagged on the food, see? He'd tell me anything that run in his mind, and most of it was good. You'll say so. I'll get him to do it for you sometime. Of all the funny nuts that make this lot! Well, take my word for it; that's all I ask. And listen here, Jeff — I'm down to cases. There's something about this kid, like when I tell you I'd always look at him twice. And it's something rich that I won't let out for a minute or two. But here's what you and me do, right quick:

"The kid was in that cabaret and gambling-house stuff they shot last week for *The Blight of Broadway*, and this something that makes you look at him must of struck Henshaw the way it did me, for he let him stay right at the edge of the dance floor and took a lot of close-ups of him looking tired to death of the gay night life. Well, you call up the Victor folks and ask can you get a look at that stuff because you're thinking of giving a part to one of the extras that worked in it. Maybe we can get into the projection room right away and you'll see what I mean. Then I won't have to tell you the richest thing about it. Now!" — she took a long breath — "will you?"

Baird had listened with mild interest to the recital, occasionally seeming not to listen while he altered the script before him. But he took the telephone receiver from its hook and said briefly to the girl: "You win. Hello! Give me the Victor office. Hello! Mr. Baird speaking —"

The two were presently in the dark projection room watching the scenes the girl had told of.

"They haven't started cutting yet," she said delightedly. "All his close-ups will be in. Goody! There's the lad-get him? Ain't he the actin'est thing you ever saw? Now wait-you'll see others."

Baird watched the film absorbedly. Three times it was run for the sole purpose of exposing to this small audience Merton Gill's notion of being consumed with ennui among pleasures that had palled. In the gambling-hall bit it could be observed that he thought not too well of cigarettes. "He screens well, too," remarked the girl. "Of course I couldn't be sure of that."

"He screens all right," agreed Baird.

"Well, what do you think?"

"I think he looks like the first plume on a hearse."

"He looks all of that, but try again. Who does he remind you of? Catch this next one in the gambling hell — get the profile and the eyebrows and the chin — there!"

"Why —" Baird chuckled. "I'm a Swede if he don't look like —"

"You got it!" the girl broke in excitedly. "I knew you would. I didn't at first, this morning, because he was so hungry and needed a shave, and he darned near had me bawling when he couldn't hold his cup o' coffee except with two hands. But what d'you think? — pretty soon he tells me himself that he looks a great deal like Harold Parmalee and wouldn't mind playing parts like Parmalee, though he prefers Western stuff. Wouldn't that get you?"

The film was run again so that Baird could study the Gill face in the light of this new knowledge.

"He does, he does, he certainly does — if he don't look like a No. 9 company of Parmalee I'll eat that film. Say, Flips, you did find something."

"Oh, I knew it; didn't I tell you so?"

"But, listen — does he know he's funny?"

"Not in a thousand years! He doesn't know anything's funny, near as I can make him."

They were out in the light again, walking slowly back to the Buckeye offices.

"Get this," said Baird seriously. "You may think I'm kidding, but only yesterday I was trying to think if I couldn't dig up some guy that looked more like Parmalee than Parmalee himself does — just enough more to get the laugh, see? And you spring this lad on me. All he needs is the eyebrows worked up a little bit. But how about him — will he handle? Because if he will I'll use him in the new five-reeler."

"Will he handle?" Miss Montague echoed the words with deep emphasis. "Leave him to me. He's got to handle. I already got 25 bucks invested in his screen career. And, Jeff, he'll be easy to work, except he don't know he's funny. If he found out he was, it might queer him — see what I mean? He's one of that kind — you can tell it. How will you use him? He could never do Buckeye stuff."

"Sure not. But ain't I told you? In this new piece Jack is stage struck and gets a job as valet to a ham that's just about Parmalee's type, and we show Parmalee acting in the screen, but all straight stuff, you understand. Unless he's a wise guy he'll go all through the piece and never get on that it's funny. See, his part's dead straight and serious in a regular drama, and the less he thinks he's funny the bigger scream he'll be. He's got to be Harold Parmalee acting right out, all over the set, as serious as the lumbago — get what I mean?"

"I got you," said the girl, "and you'll get him tomorrow morning. I told him to be over with his stills. And he'll be serious all the time, make no mistake there. He's no wise guy. And one thing, Jeff, he's as innocent as a cup-custard, so you'll have to keep that bunch of Buckeye roughnecks from riding him. I can tell you that much. Once they started kidding him, it would be all off."

"And, besides —" She hesitated briefly. "Somehow I don't want him kidded. I'm pretty hard-boiled, but he sort of made me feel like a 50-year-old mother watching her only boy go out into the rough world. See?"

"I'll watch out for that," said Baird.

CHAPTER XII

ALIAS HAROLD PARMALEE

Merton Gill awoke to the comforting realization that he was between sheets instead of blankets, and that this morning he need not obscurely leave his room by means of a window. As he dressed, however, certain misgivings, to which he had been immune the day before, gnawed into his optimism. He was sober now. The sheer intoxication of food after fasting, of friendly concern after so long a period when no one had spoken him kindly or otherwise, had evaporated. He felt the depression following success.

He had been rescued from death by starvation, but had anything more than this come about? Had he not fed upon the charity of a strange girl, taking her money without seeing ways to discharge the debt? How could he ever discharge it? Probably before this she had begun to think of him as a cheat. She had asked him to come to the lot, but had been vague as to the purpose. Probably his ordeal of struggle and sacrifice was not yet over. At any rate, he must find a job that would let him pay back the borrowed 25 dollars.

He would meet her as she had requested, assure her of his honest intentions, and then seek for work. He would try all the emporiums in Hollywood. They were numerous and some one of them would need the services of an experienced assistant. This plan of endeavor crystallized as he made his way to the Holden lot. He had brought his package of stills, but only because the girl had insisted on seeing them.

The Countess made nothing of letting him in. She had missed him, she said, for what seemed like months, and was glad to hear that he now had something definite in view, because the picture game was mighty uncertain and it was only the lucky few nowadays that could see something definite. He did not confide to her that the definite something now within his view would demand his presence at some distance from her friendly self.

He approached the entrance to Stage Five with head bent in calculation, and not until he heard her voice did he glance up to observe that the Montague girl was dancing from pleasure, it would seem, at merely beholding him. She seized both his hands in her strong grasp and revolved him at the center of a circle she danced. Then she held him off while her eyes took in the details of his restoration.

"Well, well, well! That shows what a few ham and eggs and sleep will do. Kid, you gross a million at this minute. New suit, new shoes, snappy cravat right from the Men's Quality Shop, and all shaved and combed slick and everything! Say — and I was afraid maybe you wouldn't show."

He regarded her earnestly. "Oh, I would have come back, all right; I'd never forget that 25 dollars I owe you; and you'll get it all back, only it may take a little time. I thought I'd see you for a minute, then go out and find a job — you know, a regular job in a store."

"Nothing of the sort, old Trouper!" She danced again about him, both his hands in hers, which annoyed him because it was rather loud public behavior, though he forgave her in the light of youth and kindliness. "No regular job for you, old Pippin — nothing but acting all over the place — real acting that people come miles to see."

"Do you think I can really get a part?" Perhaps the creature had something definite in view for him.

"Sure you can get a part! Yesterday morning I simply walked into a part for you. Come along over to the office with me. Goody — I see you brought the stills. I'll take a peek at 'em myself before Baird gets here." "Baird? Not the Buckeye comedy man?" He was chilled by a sudden fear.

"Yes, Jeff Baird. You see he is going to do some five-reelers and this first one has a part that might do for you. At least, I told him some things about you, and he thinks you can get away with it."

He went moodily at her side, thinking swift thoughts. It seemed ungracious to tell her of his loathing for the Buckeye comedies, those blasphemous caricatures of worthwhile screen art. It would not be fair. And perhaps here was a quick way to discharge his debt and be free of obligation to the girl. Of course he would always feel a warm gratitude for her trusting kindness, but when he no longer owed her money he could choose his own line of work. Rather bondage to some Hollywood Gashwiler than clowning in Baird's infamies!

"Well, I'll try anything he gives me," he said at last, striving for the enthusiasm he could not feel.

"You'll go big, too," said the girl. "Believe, me Kid, you'll go grand."

In Baird's offices he sat at the desk and excitedly undid the package of stills. "We'll give 'em the once-over before he comes," she said, and was presently exclaiming with delight at the art study of Clifford Armytage in evening dress, two straight fingers pressing the left temple, the face in three-quarter view.

"Well, now, if that ain't Harold Parmalee to the life! If it wasn't for that Clifford Armytage signed under it, you'd had me guessing. I knew yesterday you looked like him, but I didn't dream it would be as much like him as this picture is. Say, we won't show Baird this at first. We'll let him size you up and see if your face don't remind him of Parmalee right away. Then we'll show him this and it'll be a cinch. And my, look at these others — here you're a soldier, and here you're a-a-a polo player — that is polo, ain't it, or is it tennis? And will you look at these stunning Westerns! These are simply the best of all — on horseback, and throwing a rope, and the fighting face with the gun drawn, and rolling a cigarette — and, as I live, saying good-bye to the horse. Wouldn't that get you — Buck Benson to the life!"

Again and again she shuffled over the stills, dwelling on each with excited admiration. Her excitement was pronounced. It seemed to be a sort of nervous excitement. It had caused her face to flush deeply, and her manner, especially over the Western pictures, at moments oddly approached hysteria. Merton was deeply gratified. He had expected the art studies to produce no such impression as this. The Countess in the casting office had certainly manifested nothing like hysteria at beholding them. It must be that the Montague girl was a better judge of art studies.

"I always liked this one, after the Westerns," he observed, indicating the Harold Parmalee pose.

"It's stunning," agreed the girl, still with her nervous manner. "I tell you, sit over there in Jeff's chair and take the same pose, so I can compare you with the photo."

Merton obliged. He leaned an elbow on the chair-arm and a temple on the two straightened fingers. "Is the light right?" he asked, as he turned his face to the pictured angle.

"Fine," applauded the girl. "Hold it." He held it until shocked by shrill laughter from the observer. Peal followed peal. She had seemed oddly threatened with hysteria; perhaps now it had come. She rocked on her heels and held her hands to her sides. Merton arose in some alarm, and was reassured when the victim betrayed signs of mastering her infirmity. She wiped her eyes presently and explained her outbreak.

"You looked so much like Parmalee I just couldn't help thinking how funny it was — it just seemed to go over me like anything, like a spasm or something, when I got to thinking what Parmalee would say if he saw someone looking so much like him. See? That was why I laughed."

He was sympathetic and delighted in equal parts. The girl had really seemed to suffer from her paroxysm, yet it was a splendid tribute to his screen worth.

It was at this moment that Baird entered. He tossed his hat on a chair and turned to the couple.

"Mr. Baird, shake hands with my friend Merton Gill. His stage name is Clifford Armytage."

"Very pleased to meet you," said Merton, grasping the extended hand. He hoped he had not been too dignified, too condescending. Baird would sometime doubtless know that he did not approve of those so-called comedies, but for the present he must demean himself to pay back some money borrowed from a working girl.

"Delighted," said Baird; then he bent a suddenly troubled gaze upon the Gill lineaments. He held this a long moment, breaking it only with a sudden dramatic turning to Miss Montague.

"What's this, my child? You're playing tricks on the old man." Again he incredulously scanned the face of Merton. "Who is this man?" he demanded.

"I told you, he's Merton Gill from Gushwomp, Ohio," said the girl, looking pleased and expectant.

"Simsbury, Illinois," put in Merton quickly, wishing the girl could be better at remembering names.

Baird at last seemed to be convinced. He heavily smote an open palm with a clenched fist. "Well, I'll be swoshed! I thought you must be kidding. If I'd seen him out on the lot I'd 'a' said he was the twin brother of Harold Parmalee."

"There!" exclaimed the girl triumphantly. "Didn't I say he'd see it right quick? You can't keep a thing from this old bey. Now you just came over here to this desk and look at this fine batch of stills he had taken by a regular artist back in Cranberry."

"Ah!" exclaimed Baird unctuously, "I bet they're good. Show me." He went to the desk. "Be seated, Mr. Gill, while I have a look at these."

Merton Gill, under the eye of Baird which clung to him with something close to fascination, sat down. He took the chair with fine dignity, a certain masterly deliberation. He sat easily, and seemed to await a verdict confidently foreknown. Baird's eyes did not leave him for the stills until he had assumed a slightly Harold Parmalee pose. Then his head with the girl's bent over the pictures, he began to examine them.

Exclamations of delight came from the pair. Merton Gill listened amiably. He was not greatly thrilled by an admiration which he had long believed to be his due. Had he not always supposed that things of precisely this sort would be said about those stills when at last they came under the eyes of the right people?

Like the Montague girl, Baird was chiefly impressed with the Westerns. He looked a long time at them, especially at the one where Merton's face was emotionally averted from his old pal, Pinto, at the moment of farewell. Regarding Baird, as he stood holding this art study up to the light, Merton became aware for the first time that Baird suffered from some nervous affliction, a peculiar twitching of the lips, a trembling of the chin, which he had sometimes observed in senile persons. All at once Baird seemed quite overcome by this infirmity. He put a handkerchief to his face and uttered a muffled excuse as he hastily left the room. Outside, the noise of his heavy tread died swiftly away down the hall.

The Montague girl remained at the desk. There was a strange light in her eyes and her face was still flushed. She shot a glance of encouragement at Merton.

"Don't be nervous, old Kid; he likes 'em all right." He reassured her lightly: "Oh, I'm not a bit nervous about him. It ain't as if he was doing something worth while, instead of mere comedies."

The girl's color seemed to heighten. "You be sure to tell him that; talk right up to him. Be sure to say 'mere comedies.' It'll show him you know what's what. And as a matter of fact, Kid, he's trying to do something worth while, right this minute, something serious. That's why he's so interested in you."

"Well, of course, that's different." He was glad to learn this of Baird. He would take the man seriously if he tried to be serious, to do something fine and distinctive.

Baird here returned, looking grave. The Montague girl seemed more strangely intense. She beckoned the manager to her side.

"Now, here, Jeff, here was something I just naturally had to laugh at."

Baird had not wholly conquered those facial spasms, but he controlled himself to say, "Show me!"

"Now, Merton," directed the girl, "take that same pose again, like you did for me, the way you are in this picture."

As Merton adjusted himself to the Parmalee pose she handed the picture to Baird. "Now, Jeff, I ask you — ain't that Harold to the life — ain't it so near him that you just have to laugh your head off?"

It was even so. Baird and the girl both laughed convulsively, the former with rumbling chuckles that shook his frame. When he had again composed himself he said, "Well, Mr. Gill, I think you and I can do a little business. I don't know what your idea about a contract is, but —"

Merton Gill quickly interrupted. "Well, you see I'd hardly like to sign a contract with you, not for those mere comedies you do. I'll do anything to earn a little money right now so I can pay back this young lady, but I wouldn't like to go on playing in such things, with cross-eyed people and waiters on roller skates, and all that. What I really would like to do is something fine and worth while, but not clowning in mere Buckeye comedies."

Mr. Baird, who had devoted the best part of an active career to the production of Buckeye comedies, and who regarded them as at least one expression of the very highest art, did not even flinch at these cool words. He had once been an actor himself. Taking the blow like a man, he beamed upon his critic. "Exactly, my boy; don't you think I'll ever ask you to come down to clowning. You might work with me for years and I'd never ask you to do a thing that wasn't serious. In fact, that's why I'm hoping to engage you now. I want to do a serious picture, I want to get out of all that slapstick stuff, see? Something fine and worth while, like you say. And you're the very actor I need in this new piece."

"Well, of course, in that case —" This was different; he made it plain that in the case of a manager striving for higher things he was not one to withhold a helping hand. He was beginning to feel a great sympathy for Baird in his efforts for the worth while. He thawed somewhat from the reserve that Buckeye comedies had put upon him. He chatted amiably. Under promptings from the girl he spoke freely of his career, both in Simsbury and in Hollywood. It was 12 o'clock before they seemed willing to let him go, and from time to time they would pause to gloat over the stills.

At last Baird said cheerily, "Well, my lad, I need you in my new piece. How'll it be if I put you on my payroll, beginning today, at 40 a week? How about it, hey?"

"Well, I'd like that first rate, only I haven't worked any today; you shouldn't pay me for just coming here."

The manager waved a hand airily. "That's all right, my boy; you've earned a day's salary just coming here to cheer me up.

These mere comedies get me so down in the dumps sometimes. And besides, you're not through yet. I'm going to use you some more. Listen, now —" The manager had become coldly businesslike. "You go up to a little theater on Hollywood Boulevard — you can't miss it — where they're running a Harold Parmalee picture. I saw it last night and I want you to see it today. Better see it afternoon and evening both."

"Yes, sir," said Merton.

"And watch Parmalee. Study him in this picture. You look like him already, but see if you can pick up some of his tricks, see what I mean? Because it's a regular Parmalee part I'm going to have you do, see? Kind of a society part to start with, and then we work in some of your Western stuff at the finish. But get Parmalee as much as you can. That's all now. Oh, yes, and can you leave these stills with me? Our publicity man may want to use them later."

"All right, Mr. Baird, I'll do just what you say, and of course you can keep the stills as long as I got an engagement with you, and I'm very glad you're trying to do something really worth while."

"Thanks," said Baird, averting his face.

The girl followed him into the hall. "Great work, boy, and take it from me, you'll go over. Say, honest now, I'm glad clear down into my boots." She had both his hands again, and he could see that her eyes were moist. She seemed to be an impressionable little thing, hysterical one minute while looking at a bunch of good stills, and sort of weepy the next. But he was beginning to like her, in spite of her funny talk and free ways.

"And say," she called after him when he had reached the top of the stairs, "you know you haven't had much experience yet with a bunch of hard-boiled troupers; many a one will be jealous of you the minute you begin to climb, and maybe they'll get fresh and try to kid you, see? But don't you mind it — give it right back to them. Or tell me if they get too raw. Just remember I got a mean right when I swing free."

"All right, thank you," he replied, but his bewilderment was plain.

She stared a moment, danced up to him, and seized a hand in both of hers. "What I mean son, if you feel bothered any time

— by anything — just come to me with it, see? I'm in this piece, and I'll look out for you. Don't forget that." She dropped his hand, and was back in the office while he mumbled his thanks for what he knew she had meant as a kindness.

So she was to be in the Baird piece; she, too, would be trying to give the public something better and finer. Still, he was puzzled at her believing he might need to be looked out for. An actor drawing forty dollars a week could surely look out for himself. He emerged into the open of the Holden lot as one who had at last achieved success after long and grueling privation. He walked briefly among the scenes of this privation, pausing in reminiscent mood before the Crystal Palace Hotel and other outstanding spots where he had so stoically suffered the torments of hunger and discouragement.

He remembered to be glad now that no letter of appeal had actually gone to Gashwiler. Suppose he had built up in the old gentleman's mind a false hope that he might again employ Merton Gill? A good thing he had held out! Yesterday he was starving and penniless; today he was fed and on someone's payroll for probably as much money a week as Gashwiler netted from his entire business. From sheer force of association, as he thus meditated, he found himself hungry, and a few moments later he was selecting from the food counter of the cafeteria whatever chanced to appeal to the eye — no weighing of prices now.

Before he had finished his meal Henshaw and his so-called Governor brought their trays to the adjoining table. Merton studied with new interest the director who would some day be telling people that he had been the first to observe the aptitude of this new star — had, in fact, given him a lot of footage and close-ups and medium shots and "dramatics" in *The Blight of Broadway* when he was a mere extra — before he had made himself known to the public in Jeff Baird's first worthwhile piece.

He was strongly moved, now, to bring himself to Henshaw's notice when he heard the latter say, "It's a regular Harold Parmalee part, good light comedy, plenty of heart interest, and that corking fight on the cliff."

He wanted to tell Henshaw that he himself was already engaged to do a Harold Parmalee part, and had been told, not two hours ago, that he would by most people be taken for Parmalee's twin brother. He restrained this impulse, however, as Henshaw went on to talk of the piece in hand.

It proved to be *Robinson Crusoe*, which he had already discussed. Or, rather, not *Robinson Crusoe* any longer. Not even *Robinson Crusoe, Junior*. It was to have been called *Island Passion*, he learned, but this title had been amended to *Island Love*.

"They're getting fed up on that word 'passion,'" Henshaw was saying, "and anyhow, 'love' seems to go better with 'island,' don't you think, Governor? '*Desert Passion*' was all right — there's something strong and intense about a desert. But 'island' is different."

And it appeared that *Island Love*, though having begun as *Robinson Crusoe*, would contain few of the outstanding features of that tale. Instead of Crusoe's wrecked sailing-ship, there was a wrecked steam yacht, a very expensive yacht stocked with all modern luxuries, nor would there be a native Friday and his supposed sister with the tattooed shoulder, but a wealthy young New Yorker and his valet who would be good for comedy on a desert island, and a beautiful girl, and a scoundrel who would in the last reel be thrown over the cliffs.

Henshaw was vivacious about the effects he would get. "I've been wondering, Governor," he continued, "if we're going to kill off the heavy, whether we shouldn't plant it early that besides wanting this girl who's on the island, he's the same scoundrel that wronged the young sister of the lead that owns the yacht. See what I mean? — it would give more conflict."

"But here —" The Governor frowned and spoke after a moment's pause. "Your young New Yorker is rich, isn't he? Fine old family, and all that, how could he have a sister that would get wronged? You couldn't do it. If he's got a wronged sister, he'd have to be a workingman or a sailor or something. And she couldn't be a New York society girl; she'd have to be working some place, in a store or office — don't you see? How could you have a swell young New Yorker with a wronged sister? Real society girls never get wronged unless their father loses his money, and then it's never anything serious enough to kill a heavy for. No — that's out." "Wait, I have it." Henshaw beamed with a new inspiration. "You just said a sailor could have his sister wronged, so why not have one on the yacht, a good strong type, you know, and his little sister was wronged by the heavy, and he'd never known who it was, because the little girl wouldn't tell him, even on her death-bed, but he found the chap's photograph in her trunk, and on the yacht he sees that it was this same heavy — and there you are. Revenge — see what I mean? He fights with the heavy on the cliff, after showing him the little sister's picture, and pushes him over to death on the rocks below — get it? And the lead doesn't have to kill him. How about that?" Henshaw regarded his companion with pleasant anticipation.

The Governor again debated before he spoke. He still doubted. "Say, whose show is this, the lead's or the sailor's that had the wronged sister? You'd have to show the sailor and his sister, and show her being wronged by the heavy — that'd take a big cabaret set, at least — and you'd have to let the sailor begin his stuff on the yacht, and then by the time he'd kept it up a bit after the wreck had pulled off the fight, where would your lead be? Can you see Parmalee playing second to this sailor? Why, the sailor'd run away with the piece. And that cabaret set would cost money when we don't need it — just keep those things in mind a little."

"Well," Henshaw submitted gracefully, "anyway, I think my suggestion of *Island Love* is better than *Island Passion* — kind of sounds more attractive, don't you think?"

The Governor lighted a cigarette. "Say, Howard, it's a wonderful business, isn't it? We start with poor old *Robinson Crusoe* and his goats and parrot and man Friday, and after dropping Friday's sister who would really be the Countess of Kleig, we wind up with a steam-yacht and a comic butler and call it *Island Love*. Who said the art of the motion picture is in its infancy? In this case it'll be plumb senile. Well, go ahead with the boys and dope out your hogwash. Gosh! Sometimes I think I wouldn't stay in the business if it wasn't for the money. And remember, don't you let a single solitary sailor on that yacht have a wronged sister that can blame it on the heavy, or you'll never have Parmalee playing the lead."

Again Merton Gill debated bringing himself to the notice of these gentlemen. If Parmalee wouldn't play the part for any reason like a sailor's wronged sister, he would. It would help him to be known in Parmalee parts. Still, he couldn't tell how soon they might need him, nor how soon Baird would release him. He regretfully saw the two men leave, however. He might have missed a chance even better than Baird would give him.

He suddenly remembered that he had still a professional duty to perform. He must that afternoon, and also that evening, watch a Harold Parmalee picture. He left the cafeteria, swaggered by the watchman at the gate-he had now the professional standing to silence that fellow-and made his way to the theater Baird had mentioned.

In front he studied the billing of the Parmalee picture. It was *Object, Matrimony — a Smashing Comedy of Love and Laughter.* Harold Parmalee, with a gesture of mock dismay, seemed to repulse a bevy of beautiful maidens who wooed him. Merton took his seat with a dismay that was not mock, for it now occurred to him that he had no experience in love scenes, and that an actor playing Parmalee parts would need a great deal of such experience. In Simsbury there had been no opportunity for an intending actor to learn certain little niceties expected at sentimental moments. Even his private life had been almost barren of adventures that might now profit him.

He had sometimes played kissing games at parties, and there had been the more serious affair with Edwina May Pulver — nights when he had escorted her from church or sociables to the Pulver gate and lingered in a sort of nervously worded ecstasy until he could summon courage to kiss the girl. Twice this had actually happened, but the affair had come to nothing, because the Pulvers had moved away from Simsbury and he had practically forgotten Edwina May; forgotten even the scared haste of those embraces. He seemed to remember that he had grabbed her and kissed her, but was it on her cheek or nose?

Anyway, he was now quite certain that the mechanics of this dead amour were not those approved of in the best screen circles. Never had he gathered a beauteous girl in his arms and very slowly, very accurately, very tenderly, done what Parmalee and other screen actors did in their final fade-outs. Even when Beulah Baxter had been his screen ideal he had never seen himself as doing more than save her from some dreadful fate. Of course, later, if he had found out that she was unwed —

He resolved now to devote special study to Parmalee's methods of wooing the fair creature who would be found in his arms at the close of the present film. Probably Baird would want some of that stuff from him.

From the very beginning of *Object, Matrimony* it was apparent that the picture drama would afford him excellent opportunities for studying the Parmalee technique in what an early subtitle called "The Eternal Battle of the Sexes." For Parmalee in the play was Hubert Throckmorton, popular screen idol and surfeited with the attentions of adoring women. Cunningly the dramatist made use of Parmalee's own personality, of his screen triumphs, and of the adulation lavished upon him by discriminating fair ones. His breakfast tray was shown piled with missives amply attesting the truth of what the interviewer had said of his charm. All women seemed to adore Hubert Throckmorton in the drama, even as all women adored Harold Parmalee in private life.

The screen revealed Throckmorton quite savagely ripping open the letters, glancing at their contents and flinging them from him with humorous shudders. He seemed to be asking why these foolish creatures couldn't let an artist alone. Yet he was kindly, in this half-humorous, half-savage mood. There was a blending of chagrin and amused tolerance on his face as the screen had him murmur, casting the letter aside, "Poor, Silly Little Girls!"

From this early scene Merton learned Parmalee's method of withdrawing the gold cigarette case, of fastidiously selecting a cigarette, of closing the case and of absently — thinking of other matters — tamping the gold-tipped thing against the cover. This was an item that he had overlooked. He should have done that in the cabaret scene. He also mastered the Parmalee trick of withdrawing the handkerchief from the cuff of the perfectly fitting morning coat. That was something else he should have done in *The Blight of Broadway*. Little things like that, done right, gave the actor his distinction.

The drama progressed. Millionaire Jasper Gordon, "A Power in Wall Street," was seen telephoning to Throckmorton. He was entreating the young actor to spend the week-end at his palatial Long Island country home to meet a few of his friends. The grim old Wall Street magnate was perturbed by Throckmorton's refusal, and renewed his appeal. He was one of those who always had his way in Wall Street, and he at length prevailed upon Throckmorton to accept his invitation. He than manifested the wildest delight, and he was excitedly kissed by his beautiful daughter who had been standing by his side in the sumptuous library while he telephoned. It could be seen that the daughter, even more than her grim old father, wished Mr. Throckmorton to be at the Long Island country home.

Later Throckmorton was seen driving his high-powered roadster, accompanied only by his valet, to the Gordon country home on Long Island, a splendid mansion surrounded by its landscaped grounds where fountains played and roses bloomed against the feathery background of graceful eucalyptus trees. Merton Gill here saw that he must learn to drive a high-powered roadster. Probably Baird would want some of that stuff, too.

A round of country-house gaieties ensued, permitting Throckmorton to appear in a series of perfectly fitting sports costumes. He was seen on his favorite hunter, on the tennis courts, on the first tee of the golf course, on a polo pony, and in the mazes of the dance. Very early it was learned that the Gordon daughter had tired of mere social triumphs and wished to take up screen acting in a serious way. She audaciously requested Throckmorton to give her a chance as leading lady in his next great picture.

He softened his refusal by explaining to her that acting was a difficult profession and that suffering and sacrifice were necessary to round out the artist. The beautiful girl replied that within ten days he would be compelled to admit her rare ability as an actress, and laughingly they wagered a kiss upon it. Merton felt that this was the sort of thing he must know more about.

Throckmorton was courteously gallant in the scene. Even when he said, "Shall we put up the stakes now, Miss Gordon?" it could be seen that he was jesting. He carried this light manner through minor scenes with the beautiful young girl friends of Miss Gordon who wooed him, lay in wait for him, ogled and sighed. Always he was the laughingly tolerant conqueror who had but a lazy scorn for his triumphs.

He did not strike the graver note until it became suspected that there were crooks in the house bent upon stealing the famous Gordon jewels. That it was Throckmorton who averted this catastrophe by sheer nerve and by use of his rare histrionic powers — as when he disguised himself in the coat and hat of the arch crook whom he had felled with a single blow and left bound and gagged, in order to receive the casket of jewels from the thief who opened the safe in the library, and that he laughed away the thanks of the grateful millionaire, astonished no one in the audience, though it caused Merton Gill to wonder if he could fell a crook with one blow. He must practice up some blows.

Throckmorton left the palatial country home wearied by the continuous adulation. The last to speed him was the Gordon daughter, who reminded him of their wager; within ten days he would acknowledge her to be an actress fit to play as his leading woman.

Throckmorton drove rapidly to a simple farm where he was not known and would be no longer surfeited with attentions. He dressed plainly in shirts that opened wide at the neck and assisted in the farm labors, such as pitching hay and leading horses into the barn. It was the simple existence that he had been craving — away from it all! No one suspected him to be Hubert Throckmorton, least of all the simple country maiden, daughter of the farmer, in her neat print dress and heavy braid of golden hair that hung from beneath her sunbonnet. She knew him to be only a man among men, a simple farm laborer, and Hubert Throckmorton, wearied by the adulation of his feminine public, was instantly charmed by her coy acceptance of his attentions.

That this charm should ripen to love was to be expected. Here was a child, simple, innocent, of a wild-rose beauty in her print dress and sunbonnet, who would love him for himself alone. Beside a blossoming orange tree on the simple Long Island farm he declared his love, warning the child that he had nothing to offer her but two strong arms and a heart full of devotion.

The little girl shyly betrayed that she returned his love but told him that he must first obtain the permission of her grandmother without which she would never consent to wed him. She hastened into the old farmhouse to prepare Grandmother for the interview.

Throckmorton presently faced the old lady who sat huddled in an armchair, her hands crooked over a cane, a ruffled cap above her silvery hair. He manfully voiced his request for the child's hand in marriage. The old lady seemed to mumble an assent. The happy lover looked about for his fiancé when, to his stupefaction, the old lady arose briskly from her chair, threw off cap, silvery wig, gown of black, and stood revealed as the child herself, smiling roguishly up at him from beneath the sunbonnet. With a glad cry he would have seized her, when she stayed him with lifted hand. Once more she astounded him. Swiftly she threw off sunbonnet, blonde wig, print dress, and stood before him revealed as none other than the Gordon daughter.

Hubert Throckmorton had lost his wager. Slowly, as the light of recognition dawned in his widening eyes, he gathered the beautiful girl into his arms. "Now may I be your leading lady?" she asked.

"My leading lady, not only in my next picture, but for life," he replied.

There was a pretty little scene in which the wager was paid. Merton studied it. Twice again, that evening, he studied it. He was doubtful. It would seem queer to take a girl around the waist that way and kiss her so slowly. Maybe he could learn. And he knew he could already do that widening of the eyes. He could probably do it as well as Parmalee did.

Back in the Buckeye office, when the Montague girl had returned from her parting with Merton, Baird had said:

"Kid, you've brightened my whole day."

"Didn't I tell you?"

"He's a lot better than you said."

"But can you use him?"

"You can't tell. You can't tell till you try him out. He might be good, and he might blow up right at the start."

"I bet he'll be good. I tell you, Jeff, that boy is just full of acting. All you got to do — keep his stuff straight, serious. He can't help but be funny that way."

"We'll see. Tomorrow we'll kind of feel him out. He'll see this Parmalee film today — I caught it last night — and there's some stuff in it I want to play horse with, see? So I'll start him tomorrow in a quiet scene, and find out does he handle. If he does, we'll go right into some hokum drama stuff. The more serious he plays it the better. It ought to be good, but you can't ever tell in our trade. You know that as well as I do."

The girl was confident. "I can tell about this lad," she insisted.

CHAPTER XIII

GENIUS COMES INTO ITS OWN

Merton Gill, enacting the part of a popular screen idol, as in the play of yesterday, sat at breakfast in his apartments on Stage Number Five. Outwardly he was cool, wary, unperturbed, as he peeled the shell from a hard-boiled egg and sprinkled salt upon it. For the breakfast consisted of hard-boiled eggs and potato salad brought on in a wooden dish.

He had been slightly disturbed by the items of this meal; it was not so elegant a breakfast as Hubert Throckmorton's, but he had been told by Baird that they must be a little different.

He had been slightly disturbed, too, at discovering the faithful valet who brought on the simple repast was the cross-eyed man. Still, the fellow had behaved respectfully, as a valet should. He had been quietly obsequious of manner, revealing only a profound admiration for his master and a constant solicitude for his comfort. Probably he, like Baird, was trying to do something distinctive and worth while.

Having finished the last egg — glad they had given him no more than three — the popular screen idol at the prompting of Baird, back by the cameras, arose, withdrew a metal cigarette case, purchased that very morning with this scene in view, and selected a cigarette. He stood negligently, as Parmalee had stood, tapped the end of the cigarette on the side of the case, as Parmalee had done, lighted a match on the sole of his boot, and idly smoked in the Parmalee manner.

Three times the day before he had studied Parmalee in this bit of business. Now he idly crossed to the center-table upon which reposed a large photograph album. He turned the pages of this, pausing to admire the pictures there revealed. Baird had not only given him general instructions for this scene, but now prompted him in low, encouraging tones.

"Turn over slowly; you like 'em all. Now lift the album up and hold it for a better light on that one. It's one of the best, it pleases you a lot. Look even more pleased — smile! That's good. Put down the album; turn again, slowly; turn twice more, that's it; pick it up again. This one is fine —"

Baird took him through the album in this manner, had him close it when all the leaves were turned, and stand a moment with one hand resting on it. The album had been empty. It had been deemed best not to inform the actor that later close-ups of the pages would show him to have been refreshed by studying photographs of himself — copies, in fact, of the stills of Clifford Armytage at that moment resting on Baird's desk.

As he stood now, a hand affectionately upon the album, a trace of the fatuously admiring smile still lingering on his expressive face, a knock sounded upon the door. "Come in," he called.

The valet entered with the morning mail. This consisted entirely of letters. There were hundreds of them, and the valet had heaped them in a large clothes-basket which he now held respectfully in front of him.

The actor motioned him, with an authentic Parmalee gesture, to place them by the table. The valet obeyed, though spilling many letters from the top of the overflowing basket. These, while his master seated himself, he briskly swept up with a broom.

The chagrined amusement of Harold Parmalee, the half-savage, half-humorous tolerance for this perhaps excusable weakness of woman, was here accurately manifested. The actor yawned slightly, lighted another cigarette with flawless Parmalee technique, withdrew a handkerchief from his sleeve-cuff, lightly touched his forehead with it, and began to open the letters. He glanced at each one in a quick, bored manner, and cast it aside.

When a dozen or so had been thus treated he was aroused by another knock at the door. It opened to reveal the valet with another basket overflowing with letters. Upon this the actor arose, spread his arms wide in a gesture of humorous helplessness. He held this briefly, then drooped in humorous despair.

He lighted another cigarette, eyed the letters with that whimsical lift of the brows so characteristic of Parmalee, and lazily blew smoke toward them. Then, regarding the smoke, he idly waved a hand through it. "Poor, silly little girls!" But there was a charming tolerance in his manner. One felt his generous recognition that they were not wholly without provocation.

This appeared to close the simple episode. The scenes, to be sure, had not been shot without delays and rehearsals, and a good two hours of the morning had elapsed before the actor was released from the glare of light and the need to remember that he was Harold Parmalee. His peeling of an egg, for example, had not at first been dainty enough to please the director, and the scene with the album had required many rehearsals to secure the needed variety of expressions, but Baird had been helpful in his promptings, and always kind.

"Now, this one you've turned over — it's someone you love better than anybody. It might be your dear old mother that you haven't seen for years. It makes you kind of solemn as you show how fond you were of her. You're affected deeply by her face. That's it, fine! Now the next one, you like it just as much, but it pleases you more. It's someone else you're fond of, but you're not so solemn.

"Now turn over another, but very slow — slow — but don't let go of it. Stop a minute and turn back as if you had to have another peek at the last one, see what I mean? Take plenty of time. This is a great treat for you. It makes you feel kind of religious. Now you're getting it — that's the boy! All right —"

The scene where he showed humorous dismay at the quantity of his mail had needed but one rehearsal. He had here been Harold Parmalee without effort. Also he had not been asked to do again the Parmalee trick of lighting a cigarette nor of withdrawing the handkerchief from its cuff to twice touch his forehead in moments of amused perplexity. Baird had merely uttered a low "Fine!" at beholding these bits.

He drew a long breath of relief when released from the set. Seemingly he had met the test. Baird had said that morning,

"Now we'll just run a little kind of test to find out a few things about you," and had followed with a general description of the scenes. It was to be of no great importance — a minor detail of the picture. Perhaps this had been why the wealthy actor breakfasted in rather a plainly furnished room on hard-boiled eggs and potato salad. Perhaps this had been why the costume given him had been not too well fitting, not too nice in detail. Perhaps this was why they had allowed the cross-eyed man to appear as his valet. He was quite sure this man would not do as a valet in a high-class picture. Anyway, however unimportant the scene, he felt that he had acquitted himself with credit.

The Montague girl, who had made him up that morning, with close attention to his eyebrows, watched him from back of the cameras, and she seized both his hands when he left the set. "You're going to land," she warmly assured him. "I can tell a trouper when I see one."

She was in costume. She was apparently doing the part of a society girl, though slightly overdressed, he thought.

"We're working on another set for this same picture," she explained, "but I simply had to catch you acting. You'll probably be over with us tomorrow. But you're through for the day, so beat it and have a good time."

"Couldn't I come over and watch you?"

"No, Baird doesn't like to have his actors watching things they ain't in; he told me specially that you weren't to be around except when you're working. You see, he's using you in kind of a special part in this multiple-reeler, and he's afraid you might get confused if you watched the other parts. I guess he'll start you tomorrow. You're to be in a good, wholesome heart play. You'll have a great chance in it."

"Well, I'll go see if I can find another Parmalee picture for this afternoon. Say, you don't think I was too much like him in that scene, do you? You know it's one thing if I look like him — I can't help that — but I shouldn't try to imitate him too closely, should I? I got to think about my own individuality, haven't I?"

"Sure, sure you have! But you were fine — your imitation wasn't a bit too close. You can think about your own individuality this afternoon when you're watching him."

Late that day in the projection room Baird and the Montague girl watched the "rush" of that morning's episode.

"The squirrel's done it," whispered the girl after the opening scene. It seemed to her that Merton Gill on the screen might overhear her comment.

Even Baird was low-toned. "Looks so," he agreed.

"If that ain't Parmalee then I'll eat all the hard-boiled eggs on the lot."

Baird rubbed his hands. "It's Parmalee plus," he corrected.

"Oh, Mother, Mother!" murmured the girl while the screen revealed the actor studying his photographs.

"He handled all right in that spot," observed Baird.

"He'll handle right — don't worry. Ain't I told you he's a natural born trouper?"

The mail was abandoned in humorous despair. The cigarette lighted in a flawless Parmalee manner, the smoke idly brushed aside. "Poor, silly little girls," the actor was seen to say. The girl gripped Baird's arm until he winced. "There, old Pippin! There's your million, picked right up on the lot!"

"Maybe," assented the cooler Baird, as they left the projection room.

"And say," asked the girl, "did you notice all morning how he didn't even bat an eye when you spoke to him, if the camera was still turning? Not like a beginner that'll nearly always look up and get out of the picture."

"What I bet," observed Baird, "I bet he'd 'a' done that album stuff even better than he did if I'd actually put his own pictures in, the way I'm going to for the close-ups. I was afraid he'd see it was kidding if I did, or if I told him what pictures they were going to be. But I'm darned now if I don't think he'd have stood for it. I don't believe you'll ever be able to peeve that boy by telling him he's good."

The girl glanced up defensively as they walked.

"Now don't get the idea he's conceited, because he ain't. Not one bit."

"How do you know he ain't?"

She considered this, then explained brightly, "Because I wouldn't like him if he was. No, no — now you listen here" as

Baird had grinned. "This lad believes in himself, that's all. That's different from conceit. You can believe a whole lot in yourself, and still be as modest as a new — hatched chicken. That's what he reminds me of, too."

The following morning Baird halted him outside the set on which he would work that day. Again he had been made up by the Montague girl, with especial attention to the eyebrows so that they might show the Parmalee lift.

"I just want to give you the general dope of the piece before you go on," said Baird, in the shelter of high canvas backing. "You're the only son of a widowed mother and both you and she are toiling to pay off the mortgage on the little home. You're the cashier of this business establishment, and in love with the proprietor's daughter, only she's a society girl and kind of looks down on you at first. Then, there's her brother, the proprietor's only son. He's the clerk in this place. He doesn't want to work, but his father has made him learn the business, see? He's kind of a no-good; dissipated; wears flashy clothes and plays the races and shoots craps and drinks. You try to reform him because he's idolized by his sister that you're in love with.

"But you can't do a thing with him. He keeps on and gets in with a rough crowd, and finally he steals a lot of money out of the safe, and just when they are about to discover that he's the thief you see it would break his sister's heart so you take the crime on your own shoulders. After that, just before you're going to be arrested, you make a getaway — because, after all, you're not guilty — and you go out West to start all over again —"

"Out there in the big open spaces?" suggested Merton, who had listened attentively.

"Exactly," assented Baird, with one of those nervous spasms that would now and again twitch his lips and chin. "Out there in the big open spaces where men are men — that's the idea. And you build up a little gray home in the West for yourself and your poor old mother who never lost faith in you. There'll be a lot of good Western stuff in this — Buck Benson stuff, you know, that you can do so well — and the girl will get out there some way and tell you that her brother finally confessed his crime, and everything'll be Jake, see what I mean?"

"Yes, sir; it sounds fine, Mr. Baird. And I certainly will give the best that is in me to this part." He had an impulse to tell the manager, too, how gratified he was that one who had been content with the low humor of the Buckeye comedies should at last have been won over to the better form of photodrama. But Baird was leading him on to the set; there was no time for this congratulatory episode.

Indeed the impulse was swept from his mind in the novelty of the set now exposed, and in the thought that his personality was to dominate it. The scene of the little drama's unfolding was a delicatessen shop. Counters and shelves were arrayed with cooked foods, salads, cheeses, the latter under glass or wire protectors. At the back was a cashier's desk, an open safe beside it. He took his place there at Baird's direction and began to write in a ledger.

"Now your old mother's coming to mop up the place," called Baird. "Come on, Mother! You look up and see her, and rush over to her. She puts down her bucket and mop, and takes you in her arms. She's weeping; you try to comfort her; you want her to give up mopping, and tell her you can make enough to support two, but she won't listen because there's the mortgage on the little flat to be paid off. So you go back to the desk, stopping to give her a sad look as she gets down on the floor. Now, try it."

A very old, bent, feeble woman with a pail of water and cloths tottered on. Her dress was ragged, her white hair hung about her sad old face in disorderly strands. She set down her bucket and raised her torn apron to her eyes.

"Look up and see her," called Baird. "A glad light comes into her eyes. Rush forward — say 'Mother' distinctly, so it'll show. Now the clench. You're crying on his shoulder, Mother, and he's looking down at you first, then off, about at me. He's near crying himself. Now he's telling you to give up mopping places, and you're telling him every little helps.

"All right, break. Get to mopping, Mother, but keep on crying. He stops for a long look at you. He seems to be saying that some day he will take you out of such work. Now he's back at his desk. All right. But we'll do it once more. And a little more pathos, Merton, when you take the old lady in your arms. You can broaden it. You don't actually break down, but you nearly do."

The scene was rehearsed again, to Baird's satisfaction, and the cameras ground. Merton Gill gave the best that was in him. His glad look at first beholding the old lady, the yearning of his eyes when his arms opened to enfold her, the tenderness of his embrace as he murmured soothing words, the lingering touch of his hand as he left her, the manly determination of the last look in which he showed a fresh resolve to release her from this toil, all were eloquent of the deepest filial devotion and earnestness of purpose.

Back at his desk he was genuinely pitying the old lady. Very lately, it was evident, she had been compelled to play in a cabaret scene, for she smelled strongly of cigarettes, and he could not suppose that she, her eyes brimming with anguished mother love, could have relished these. He was glad when it presently developed that his own was not to be a smoking part.

"Now the dissipated brother's coming on," explained Baird. "He'll breeze in, hang up his hat, offer you a cigarette, which you refuse, and show you some money that he won on the third race yesterday. You follow him a little way from the desk, telling him he shouldn't smoke cigarettes, and that money he gets by gambling will never do him any good. He laughs at you, but you don't mind. On your way back to the desk you stop by your mother, and she gets up and embraces you again.

"Take your time about it — she's your mother, remember."

The brother entered. He was indeed dissipated appearing, loudly dressed, and already smoking a cigarette as he swaggered the length of the shop to offer Merton one. Merton refused in a kindly but firm manner. The flashy brother now pulled a roll of bills from his pocket and pointed to his winning horse in a racing extra. The line in large type was there for the close-up — "Pianola Romps Home in Third Race."

Followed the scene in which Merton sought to show this youth that cigarettes and gambling would harm him. The youth remained obdurate. He seized a duster and, with ribald action, began to dust off the rows of cooked food on the counters. Again the son stopped to embrace his mother, who again wept as she enfolded him. The scene was shot.

Step by step, under the patient coaching of Baird, the simple drama unfolded. It was hot beneath the lights, delays were frequent and the rehearsals tedious, yet Merton Gill continued to give the best that was in him. As the day wore on, the dissipated son went from bad to worse. He would leave the shop to place money on a horse race, and he would seek to induce the customers he waited on to play at dice with him. A few of them consented, and one, a colored man who had come to purchase pigs'-feet, won at this game all the bills which the youth had shown to Merton on entering.

There were moments during this scene when Merton wondered if Baird were not relapsing into Buckeye comedy depths, but he saw the inevitable trend of the drama and the justification for this bit of gambling. For the son, now penniless, became desperate. He appealed to Merton for a loan, urging it on the ground that he had a sure thing 30-to-one shot at Latonia. At least these were the words of Baird, as he directed Merton to deny the request and to again try to save the youth from his inevitable downfall. Whereupon the youth had sneered at Merton and left the place in deep anger.

There followed the scene with the boy's sister, only daughter of the rich delicatessen merchant, who Merton was pleased to discover would be played by the Montague girl. She entered in a splendid evening gown, almost too splendid, Merton thought, for street wear in daylight, though it was partially concealed by a rich opera cloak. The brother being out, Merton came forward to wait upon her.

"It's like this," Baird explained. "She's just a simple New York society girl, kind of shallow and heartless, because she has never been aroused nor anything, see? You're the first one that's really touched her heart, but she hesitates because her father expects her to marry a count and she's come to get the food for a swell banquet they're giving for him. She says where's her brother, and if anything happened to him it would break her heart. Then she orders what she wants and you do it up for her, looking at her all the time as if you thought she was the one girl in the world.

"She kind of falls for you a little bit, still she is afraid of what her father would say. Then you get bolder, see? You come from behind the counter and begin to make love, talking as you come out — so-and-so, so-and-so, so-and-so — Miss Hoffmeyer, I have loved you since the day I first set eyes on you — so-and-so, so-and-so, so-and-so, I have nothing to offer but the love of an honest man — she's falling for it, see? So you get up close and grab her — cave-man stuff. Do a good hard clench — she's yours at last; she just naturally sags right down on to you. You've got her.

"Do a regular Parmalee. Take your time. You're going to kiss her and kiss her right. But just as you get down to it the father busts in and says what's the meaning of this, so you fly apart and the father says you're discharged, because his daughter is the affianced wife of this Count Aspirin, see? Then he goes back to the safe and finds all the money has been taken, because the son has sneaked in and grabbed out the bundle and hid it in the ice-box on his way out, taking only a few bills to get down on a horse. So he says call the police — but that's enough for now. Go ahead and do that love scene for me."

Slowly the scene was brought to Baird's liking. Slowly, because Merton Gill at first proved to be diffident at the crisis. For three rehearsals the muscular arm of Miss Montague had most of the clenching to do. He believed he was being rough and masterful, but Baird wished a greater show of violence. They had also to time this scene with the surreptitious entrance of the brother, his theft of the money which he stuffed into a paper sack and placed in the ice-box, and his exit.

The leading man having at last proved that he could be Harold Parmalee even in this crisis, the scene was extended to the entrance of the indignant father. He was one of those self-made men of wealth, Merton thought, a short, stout gentleman with fiery whiskers, not at all fashionably dressed. He broke upon the embrace with a threatening stick. The pair separated, the young lover facing him, proud, erect, defiant, the girl drooping and confused.

The father discharged Merton Gill with great brutality, then went to the safe at the back of the room, returning to shout the news that he had been robbed by the man who would have robbed him of his daughter. It looked black for Merton. Puzzled at first, he now saw that the idolized brother of the girl must have taken the money. He seemed about to declare this when his nobler nature compelled him to a silence that must be taken for guilt.

The erring brother returned, accompanied by several customers. "Bring a detective to arrest this man," ordered the father. One of the customers stepped out to return with a detective. Again Merton was slightly disquieted at perceiving that the detective was the cross-eyed man. This person bustled about the place, tapping the cooked meats and the cheeses, and at last placed his hand upon the shoulder of the supposed thief. Merton, at Baird's direction, drew back and threatened him with a blow. The detective cringed and said: "I will go out and call a policeman."

The others now turned their backs upon the guilty man. Even the girl drew away after one long, agonized look at the lover to whose embrace she had so lately submitted. He raised his arms to her in mute appeal as she moved away, then dropped them at his side.

"Give her all you got in a look," directed Baird. "You're saying: 'I go to a felon's cell, but I do it all for you.' Dream your eyes at her." Merton Gill obeyed.

The action progressed. In this wait for the policeman the old mother crept forward. She explained to Merton that the money was in the ice-box where the real thief had placed it, and since he had taken the crime of another upon his shoulders he should also take the evidence, lest the unfortunate young man be later convicted by that; she also urged him to fly by the rear door while there was yet time. He did these things, pausing for a last embrace of the weeping old lady, even as the hand of the arriving policeman was upon the door.

"All for today, except some close-ups," announced Baird when this scene had been shot. There was a breaking up of the group, a relaxation of that dramatic tension which the heart-values of the piece had imposed. Only once, while Merton was doing some of his best acting, had there been a kind of wheezy tittering from certain members of the cast and the group about the cameras.

Baird had quickly suppressed this. "If there's any kidding in this piece it's all in my part," he announced in cold, clear tones, and there had been no further signs of levity. Merton was pleased by this manner of Baird's. It showed that he was finely in earnest in the effort for the worthwhile things. And Baird now congratulated him, seconded by the Montague girl. He had, they told him, been all that could be expected.

"I wasn't sure of myself," he told them, "in one scene, and I wanted to ask you about it, Mr. Baird. It's where I take that money from the ice-box and go out with it. I couldn't make myself feel right. Wouldn't it look to other people as if I was actually stealing it myself? Why couldn't I put it back in the safe?"

Baird listened respectfully, considering. "I think not," he announced at length. "You'd hardly have time for that, and you have a better plan. It'll be brought out in the subtitles, of course. You are going to leave it at the residence of Mr. Hoffmeyer, where it will be safe. You see, if you put it back where it was, his son might steal it again. We thought that out very carefully."

"I see," said Merton. "I wish I had been told that. I feel that I could have done that bit a lot better. I felt kind of guilty."

"You did it perfectly," Baird assured him.

"Kid, you're a wonder," declared the Montague girl. "I'm that tickled with you I could give you a good hug," and with that curious approach to hysteria she had shown while looking at his stills, she for a moment frantically clasped him to her. He was somewhat embarrassed by this excess, but pardoned it in the reflection that he had indeed given the best that was in him. "Bring all your Western stuff to the dressing room tomorrow," said Baird.

Western stuff — the real thing at last! He was slightly amazed later to observe the old mother outside the set. She was not only smoking a cigarette with every sign of relish, but she was singing as she did a little dance step. Still she had been under a strain all day, weeping, too, almost continuously. He remembered this, and did not judge her harshly as she smoked, danced, and lightly sang,

> *Her mother's name was Cleo,*
> *Her father's name was Pat;*
> *They called her Cleopatra,*
> *And let it go at that.*

CHAPTER XIV

OUT THERE WHERE MEN ARE MEN

From the dressing room the following morning, arrayed in the Buck Benson outfit, unworn since that eventful day on the Gashwiler lot, Merton accompanied Baird to a new set where he would work that day. Baird was profuse in his admiration of the cowboy embellishments, the maroon chaps, the new boots, the hat, the checked shirt and gay neckerchief.

"I'm mighty glad to see you so sincere in your work," he assured Merton. "A lot of these hams I hire get to kidding on the set and spoil the atmosphere, but don't let it bother you. One earnest leading man, if he'll just stay earnest, will carry the piece. Remember that — you got a serious part."

"I'll certainly remember," Merton earnestly assured him.

"Here we are; this is where we begin the Western stuff," said Baird. Merton recognized the place. It was the High Gear Dance Hall where the Montague girl had worked. The name over the door was now "The Come All Ye," and there was a hitching rack in front to which were tethered half-a-dozen saddled horses.

Inside, the scene was set as he remembered it. Tables for drinking were about the floor, and there was a roulette wheel at one side. A red-shirted bartender, his hair plastered low over his brow, leaned negligently on the bar. Scattered around the room were dance hall girls in short skirts, and a number of cowboys.

"First, I'll wise you up a little bit," said Baird. "You've come out here to work on a ranch in the great open spaces, and these cowboys all love you and come to town with you every time, and they'll stand by you when the detective from New York gets here. Now — let's see — I guess first we'll get your entrance. You come in the front door at the head of them. You've ridden in from the ranch. We get the horseback stuff later. You all come in yelling and so on, and the boys scatter, some to the bar and some to the wheel, and some sit down to the tables to have their drinks and some dance with the girls. You distribute money to them from a paper sack. Here's the sack." From a waiting property boy he took a paper sack. "Put this in your pocket and take it out whenever you need money.

"It's the same sack, see, that the kid put the stolen money in, and you saved it after returning the money. It's just a kind of an idea of mine," he vaguely added, as Merton looked puzzled at this.

"All right, sir." He took the sack, observing it to contain a rude imitation of bills, and stuffed it into his pocket.

"Then, after the boys scatter around, you go stand at the end of the bar. You don't join in their sports and pastimes, see? You're serious; you have things on your mind. Just sort of look around the place as if you were holding yourself above such things, even if you do like to give the boys a good time. Now we'll try the entrance."

Cameras were put into place, and Merton Gill led through the front door his band of rollicking good fellows. He paused inside to give them bills from the paper sack. They scattered to their dissipations. Their leader austerely posed at one end of the bar and regarded the scene with disapproving eyes. Wine, women, and the dance were not for him. He produced again the disillusioned look that had won Henshaw.

"Fine," said Baird. "Gun it, boys."

The scene was shot, and Baird spoke again: "Hold it, everybody; go on with your music, and you boys keep up the dance until Mother's entrance, then you quit and back off."

Merton was puzzled by this speech, but continued his superior look, breaking it with a very genuine shock of surprise when his old mother tottered in at the front door. She was still the disconsolate creature of the day before, bedraggled, sad-eyed, feeble, very aged, and still she carried her bucket and the bundle of rags with which she had mopped. Baird came forward again.

"Oh, I forgot to tell you. Of course you had your old mother follow you out here to the great open spaces, but the poor old thing has cracked under the strain of her hard life, see what I mean? All her dear ones have been leaving the old nest and going out over the hills one by one-you were the last to go-and now she isn't quite right, see?

"You have a good home on the ranch for her, but she won't stay put. She follows you around, and the only thing that keeps her quiet is mopping, so you humor her; you let her mop. It's the only way. But of course it makes you sad. You look at her now, then go up and hug her the way you did yesterday; you try to get her to give up mopping, but she won't, so you let her go on. Try it."

Merton went forward to embrace his old mother. Here was tragedy indeed, a bit of biting pathos from a humble life. He gave the best that was in him as he enfolded the feeble old woman and strained her to his breast, murmuring to her that she must give it up-give it up.

The old lady wept, but was stubborn. She tore herself from his arms and knelt on the floor. "I just got to mop, I just got to mop," she was repeating in a cracked voice. "If I ain't let to mop I git rough till I'm simply a scandal."

It was an affecting scene, marred only by one explosive bit of coarse laughter from an observing cowboy at the close of the old mother's speech. Merton Gill glanced up in sharp annoyance at this offender. Baird was quick in rebuke.

"The next guy that laughs at this pathos can get off the set," he announced, glaring at the assemblage. There was no further outbreak and the scene was filmed.

There followed a dramatic bit that again involved the demented mother. "This ought to be good if you can do it the right way," began Baird. "Mother's mopping along there and slashes some water on this Mexican's boot-where are you, Pedro? Come here and get this. The old lady sloshes water on you while you're playing monte here, so you yell Caramba or something, and kick at her. You don't land on her, of course, but her son rushes up and grabs your arm — here, do it this way." Baird demonstrated. "Grab his wrist with one hand and his elbow with the other and make as if you broke his arm across your knee-you know, like you were doing joojitsey. He slinks off with his broken arm, and you just dust your hands off and embrace your mother again.

"Then you go back to the bar, not looking at Pedro at all. See? He's insulted your mother, and you've resented it in a nice, dignified, gentlemanly way. Try it."

Pedro sat at the table and picked up his cards. He was a foul-looking Mexican and seemed capable even of the enormity he was about to commit. The scene was rehearsed to Baird's satisfaction, then shot. The weeping old lady, blinded by her tears, awkward with her mop, the brutal Mexican, his prompt punishment.

The old lady was especially pathetic as she glared at her insulter from where she lay sprawled on the floor, and muttered, "Caramba, huh? I dare you to come outside and say that to me!"

"Good work," applauded Baird when the scene was finished. "Now we're getting into the swing of it. In about three days here we'll have something that exhibitors can clean up on, see if we don't."

The three days passed in what for Merton Gill was a whirlwind of dramatic intensity. If at times he was vaguely disquieted by a suspicion that the piece was not wholly serious, he had only to remember the intense seriousness of his own part and the always serious manner of Baird in directing his actors. And indeed there were but few moments when he was even faintly pricked by this suspicion. It seemed a bit incongruous that Hoffmeyer, the delicatessen merchant, should arrive on a bicycle, dressed in cowboy attire save for a badly dented derby hat, and carrying a bag of golf clubs; and it was a little puzzling how Hoffmeyer should have been ruined by his son's mad act, when it would have been shown that the money was returned to him. But Baird explained carefully that the old man had been ruined some other way, and was demented, like the poor old mother who had gone over the hills after her children had left the home nest. And assuredly in Merton's own action he found nothing that was not deeply earnest as well as strikingly dramatic. There was the tense moment when a faithful cowboy broke upon the festivities with word that a New York detective was coming to search for the man who had robbed the Hoffmeyer establishment. His friends gathered loyally about Merton and swore he would never be taken from them alive. He was induced to don a false mustache until the detective had gone. It was a long, heavy black mustache with curling tips, and in this disguise he stood aloof from his companions when the detective entered.

The detective was the cross-eyed man, himself now disguised as Sherlock Holmes, with a fore-and-aft cloth cap and drooping blond mustache. He smoked a pipe as he examined those present. Merton was unable to overlook this scene, as he had been directed to stand with his back to the detective. Later it was shown that he observed in a mirror the Mexican whom he had punished creeping forward to inform the detective of his man's whereabouts. The coward's treachery cost him dearly. The hero, still with his back turned, drew his revolver and took careful aim by means of the mirror.

This had been a spot where for a moment he was troubled. Instead of pointing the weapon over his shoulder, aiming by the mirror, he was directed to point it at the Mexican's reflection in the glass, and to fire at this reflection. "It's all right," Baird assured him. "It's a camera trick, see? It may look now as if you were shooting into the mirror but it comes perfectly right on the film. You'll see. Go on, aim carefully, right smack at that looking-glass — fire!" Still somewhat doubting, Merton fired. The mirror was shattered, but a dozen feet back of him the treacherous Mexican threw up his arms and fell lifeless, a bullet through his cowardly heart. It was a puzzling bit of trick-work, he thought, but Baird of course would know what was right, so the puzzle was dismissed. Buck Benson, silent man of the open, had got the scoundrel who would have played him false.

A thrilling struggle ensued between Merton and the hellhound of justice. Perceiving who had slain his would-be informant, the detective came to confront Merton. Snatching off his cap and mustache he stood revealed as the man who had not dared to arrest him at the scene of his crime. With another swift movement he snatched away the mustache that had disguised his quarry. Buck Benson, at bay, sprang like a tiger upon his antagonist. They struggled while the excited cowboys surged about them. The detective proved to be no match for Benson. He was borne to earth, then raised aloft and hurled over the adjacent tables.

This bit of acting had involved a trick which was not obscure to Merton like his shot into the mirror that brought down a man back of him. Moreover, it was a trick of which he approved. When he bore the detective to earth the cameras halted their grinding while a dummy in the striking likeness of the detective was substituted. It was a light affair, and he easily raised it for the final toss of triumph.

"Throw it high as you can over those tables and toward the bar," called Baird. The figure was thrown as directed.

"Fine work! Now look up, as if he was still in the air, now down, now brush your left sleeve lightly with your right hand, now brush your right sleeve lightly with your left hand.

"All right — cut. Great, Merton! If that don't get you a hand I don't know what will. Now all outside for the horseback stuff!"

Outside, the faithful cowboys leaped into their saddles and urged their beloved leader to do the same. But he lingered beside his own horse, pleading with them to go ahead. He must remain in the place of danger yet awhile for he had forgotten to bring out his old mother. They besought him to let them bring her out, but he would not listen. His alone was the task.

Reluctantly the cowboys galloped off. As he turned to reenter the dance hall he was confronted by the detective, who held two frowning weapons upon him. Benson was at last a prisoner.

The detective brutally ordered his quarry inside. Benson, seeing he was beaten, made a manly plea that he might be let to bid his horse good-bye. The detective seemed moved. He relented. Benson went to his good old pal.

"Here's your chance for a fine bit," called Baird. "Give it to us now the way you did in that still. Broaden it all you want to. Go to it."

Well did Merton Gill know that here was his chance for a fine bit. The horse was strangely like Dexter upon whom he had so often rehearsed this bit. He was a bony, drooping, sad horse with a thin neck. "They're takin' ye frum me, old pal — takin' ye frum me. You an' me has seen some tough times an' I sort o' figgered we'd keep on together till the last — an' now they got me, old pal, takin' me far away where ye won't see me no more —"

"Go to it, cowboy — take all the footage you want!" called Baird in a curiously choked voice.

The actor took some more footage. "But we got to keep a stiff upper lip, old pal, you and me both. No cryin', no bustin' down. We had our last gallop together, an' we're at the forkin' of th' trail. So we got to be brave — we got to stand the gaff."

Benson released his old pal, stood erect, dashed a bit of moisture from his eyes, and turned to the waiting detective who, it seemed, had also been strangely moved during this affecting farewell. Yet he had not forgotten his duty. Benson was forced to march back into the Come All Ye Dance Hall. As he went he was wishing that Baird would have him escape and flee on his old pal.

And Baird was a man who seemed to think of everything, or perhaps he had often seen the real Buck Benson's play, for it now appeared that everything was going to be as Merton Gill wished. Baird had even contrived an escape that was highly spectacular.

Locked by the detective in an upper room, the prisoner went to the window and glanced out to find that his loyal horse was directly beneath him. He would leap from the window, alight in the saddle after a 20-foot drop, and be off over the border. The window scene was shot, including a flash of the horse below. The mechanics of the leap itself required more time. Indeed, it took the better part of a morning to satisfy Baird that this thrilling exploit had been properly achieved. From a lower window, quite like the high one, Merton leaped, but only to the ground a few feet below.

"That's where we get your take-off," Baird explained.

"Now we get you lighting in the saddle." This proved to be a more delicate bit of work. From a platform built out just above the faithful horse Merton precariously scrambled down into the saddle. He glanced anxiously at Baird, fearing he had not alighted properly after the supposed 20-foot drop, but the manager appeared to be delighted with his prowess after the one rehearsal, and the scene was shot.

"It's all jake," Baird assured him. "Don't feel worried. Of course we'll trick the bit where you hit the saddle; the camera'll look out for that."

One detail only troubled Merton. After doing the leap from the high window, and before doing its finish where he reached the saddle, Baird directed certain changes in his costume. He was again to don the false mustache, to put his hat on, and also a heavy jacket lined with sheep's wool worn by one of the cowboys in the dance hall. Merton was pleased to believe he had caught the manager napping here. "But Mr. Baird, if I leap from the window without the hat or mustache or jacket and land on my horse in them, wouldn't it look as if I had put them on as I was falling?"

Baird was instantly overcome with confusion. "Now, that's so! I swear I never thought of that, Merton. I'm glad you spoke about it in time. You sure have shown me up as a director. You see I wanted you to disguise yourself again — I'll tell you; get the things on, and after we shoot you lighting in the saddle we'll retake the window scene. That'll fix it."

Not until long afterward, on a certain dread night when the earth was to rock beneath him, did he recall that Baird had never retaken that window scene. At present the young actor was too engrossed by the details of his daring leap to remember small things. The leap was achieved at last. He was in the saddle after a 20-foot drop. He gathered up the reins, the horse beneath him coughed plaintively, and Merton rode him out of the picture. Baird took a load off his mind as to this bit of riding.

"Will you want me to gallop?" he asked, recalling the unhappy experience with Dexter.

"No; just walk him beyond the camera line. The camera'll trick it up all right." So, safely, confidently, he had ridden his steed beyond the lens range at a curious shuffling amble, and his work at the Come All Ye Dance Hall was done.

Then came some adventurous days in the open. In motor cars the company of artists was transported to a sunny nook in the foothills beyond the city, and here in the wild, rough, open spaces, the drama of mother-love, sacrifice, and thrills was further unfolded.

First to be done here was the continuation of the hero's escape from the dance hall. Upon his faithful horse he ambled along a quiet road until he reached the shelter of an oak tree. Here he halted at the roadside.

"You know the detective is following you," explained Baird, "and you're going to get him. Take your nag over a little so the tree won't mask him too much. That's it. Now, you look back, lean forward in the saddle, listen! You hear him coming. Your face sets — look as grim as you can. That's the stuff — the real Buck Benson stuff when they're after him. That's fine. Now you get an idea. Unlash your rope, let the noose out, give it a couple of whirls to see is everything all right. That's it — only you still look grim — not so worried about whether the rope is going to act right. We'll attend to that. When the detective comes in sight give about three good whirls and let her fly. Try it once. Good! Now coil her up again and go through the whole thing. Never mind about whether you're going to get him or not. Remember, Buck Benson never misses. We'll have a later shot that shows the rope falling over his head."

Thereupon the grim-faced Benson, strong, silent man of the open, while the cameras ground, waited the coming of one who hounded him for a crime of which he was innocent. His iron face was relentless. He leaned forward, listening. He uncoiled the rope, expertly ran out the noose, and grimly waited. Far up the road appeared the detective on a galloping horse. Benson twirled the rope as he sat in his saddle. It left his hand, to sail gracefully in the general direction of his pursuer.

"Cut!" called Baird. "That was bully. Now you got him. Ride out into the road. You're dragging him off his horse, see? Keep on up the road; you're still dragging the hound. Look back over your shoulder and light your face up just a little — that's it, use Benson's other expression. You got it fine. You're treating the skunk rough, but look what he was doing to you, trying to pinch you for something you never did. That's fine — go ahead. Don't look back any more."

Merton was chiefly troubled at this moment by the thought that someone would have to double for him in the actual casting of the rope that would settle upon the detective's shoulders.

Well, he must practice roping. Perhaps, by the next picture, he could do this stuff himself. It was exciting work, though sometimes tedious. It had required almost an entire morning to enact this one simple scene, with the numerous close-ups that Baird demanded.

The afternoon was taken up largely in becoming accustomed to a pair of old Spanish spurs that Baird now provided him with. Baird said they were very rare old spurs which he had obtained at a fancy price from an impoverished Spanish family who had treasured them as heirlooms. He said he was sure that Buck Benson in all his vast collection did not possess a pair of spurs like these. He would doubtless, after seeing them worn by Merton Gill in this picture, have a pair made like them.

The distinguishing feature of these spurs was their size. They were enormous, and their rowels extended a good 12 inches from Merton's heels after he had donned them.

"They may bother you a little at first," said Baird, "but you'll get used to them, and they're worth a little trouble because they'll stand out."

The first effort to walk in them proved bothersome indeed, for it was made over ground covered with a low-growing vine and the spurs caught in this. Baird was very earnest in supervising this progress, and even demanded the presence of two cameras to record it.

"Of course I'm not using this stuff," he said, "but I want to make a careful study of it. These are genuine hidalgo spurs. Mighty few men in this line of parts could get away with them. I bet Benson himself would have a lot of trouble. Now, try it once more."

Merton tried once more, stumbling as the spurs caught in the undergrowth. The cameras closely recorded his efforts, and Baird applauded them. "You're getting it — keep on. That's better. Now try to run a few steps — go right toward that left-hand camera."

He ran the few steps, but fell headlong. He picked himself up, an expression of chagrin on his face.

"Never mind," urged Baird. "Try it again. We must get this right." He tried again to run; was again thrown. But he was determined to please the manager, and he earnestly continued his efforts. Benson himself would see the picture and probably marvel that a new man should have mastered, apparently with ease, a pair of genuine hidalgos.

"Maybe we better try smoother ground," Baird at last suggested after repeated falls had shown that the undergrowth was difficult. So the cameras were moved on to the front of a ranch house now in use for the drama, and the spur lessons continued. But on smooth ground it appeared that the spurs were still troublesome. After the first mishap here Merton discovered the cause. The long shanks were curved inward so that in walking their ends clashed. He pointed this out to Baird, who was amazed at the discovery.

"Well, well, that's so! They're bound to interfere. I never knew that about hidalgo spurs before."

"We might straighten them," suggested the actor.

"No, no," Baird insisted, "I wouldn't dare try that. They cost too much money, and it might break 'em. I tell you what you do, stand up and try this: just toe in a little when you walk — that'll bring the points apart. There — that's it; that's fine."

The cameras were again recording so that Baird could later make his study of the difficulties to be mastered by the wearer of genuine hidalgos. By toeing in Merton now succeeded in walking without disaster, though he could not feel that he was taking the free stride of men out there in the open spaces.

"Now try running," directed Baird, and he tried running; but again the spurs caught and he was thrown full in the eyes of the grinding camera. He had forgotten to toe in. But he would not give up. His face was set in Buck Benson grimness. Each time he picked himself up and earnestly resumed the effort. The rowels were now catching in the long hair of his chaps.

He worked on, directed and cheered by the patient Baird, while the two camera men, with curiously strained faces, recorded his failures. Baird had given strict orders that other members of the company should remain at a distance during the spur lessons, but now he seemed to believe that a few other people might encourage the learner. Merton was directed to run to his old mother who, bucket at her side and mop in hand, knelt on the ground at a little distance. He was also directed to run toward the Montague girl, now in frontier attire of fringed buckskin. He made earnest efforts to keep his feet during these essays, but the spurs still proved treacherous.

"Just pick yourself up and go on," ordered Baird, and had the cameras secure close shots of Merton picking himself up and going carefully on, toeing in now, to embrace his weeping old mother and the breathless girl who had awaited him with open arms.

He was tired that night, but the actual contusions he had suffered in his falls were forgotten in the fear that he might fail to master the hidalgos. Baird himself seemed confident that his pupil would yet excite the jealousy of Buck Benson in this hazardous detail of the screen art. He seemed, indeed, to be curiously satisfied with his afternoon's work. He said that he would study the film carefully and try to discover just how the spurs could be mastered.

"You'll show 'em yet how to take a joke," he declared when the puzzling implements were at last doffed. The young actor felt repaid for his earnest efforts. No one could put on a pair of genuine hidalgos for the first time and expect to handle them correctly.

There were many days in the hills. Until this time the simple drama had been fairly coherent in Merton Gill's mind. So consecutively were the scenes shot that the story had not been hard to follow. But now came rather a jumble of scenes, not only at times bewildering in themselves, but apparently unrelated.

First it appeared that the Montague girl, as Miss Rebecca Hoffmeyer, had tired of being a mere New York society butterfly, had come out into the big open spaces to do something real, something worth while. The ruin of her father, still unexplained, had seemed to call out unsuspected reserves in the girl. She was stern and businesslike in such scenes as Merton was permitted to observe. And she had not only brought her ruined father out to the open spaces but the dissipated brother, who was still seen to play at dice whenever opportunity offered. He played with the jolly cowboys and invariably won.

Off in the hills there were many scenes which Merton did not overlook. "I want you to have just your own part in mind,"

Baird told him. And, although he was puzzled later, he knew that Baird was somehow making it right in the drama when he became again the successful actor of that first scene, which he had almost forgotten. He was no longer the Buck Benson of the open spaces, but the foremost idol of the shadowed stage, and in Harold Parmalee's best manner he informed the aspiring Montague girl that he could not accept her as leading lady in his next picture because she lacked experience. The wager of a kiss was laughingly made as she promised that within 10 days she would convince him of her talent.

Later she herself, in an effective scene, became the grimfaced Buck Benson and held the actor up at the point of her two guns. Then, when she had convinced him that she was Benson, she appeared after an interval as her own father; the fiery beard, the derby hat with its dents, the chaps, the bicycle, and golf bag. In this scene she seemed to demand the actor's intentions toward the daughter, and again overwhelmed him with confusion, as Parmalee had been overwhelmed when she revealed her true self under the baffling disguise. The wager of a kiss was prettily paid. This much of the drama he knew. And there was an affecting final scene on a hillside.

The actor, arrayed in chaps, spurs, and boots below the waist was, above this, in faultless evening dress. "You see, it's a masquerade party at the ranch," Baird explained, "and you've thought up this costume to sort of puzzle the little lady."

The girl herself was in the short, fringed buckskin skirt, with knife and revolvers in her belt. Off in the hills day after day she had worn this costume in those active scenes he had not witnessed. Now she was merely coy. He followed her out on the hillside with only a little trouble from the spurs — indeed he fell but once as he approached her — and the little drama of the lovers, at last united, was touchingly shown.

In the background, as they stood entwined, the poor demented old mother was seen. With mop and bucket she was cleansing the side of a cliff, but there was a happier look on the worn old face.

"Glance around and see her," railed Baird. "Then explain to the girl that you will always protect your mother, no matter what happens. That's it. Now the clench — kiss her — slow! That's it. Cut!"

Merton's part in the drama was ended. He knew that the company worked in the hills another week and there were more close-ups to take in the dance hall, but he was not needed in these. Baird congratulated him warmly.

"Fine work, my boy! You've done your first picture, and with Miss Montague as your leading lady I feel that you're going to land ace-high with your public. Now all you got to do for a couple of weeks is to take it easy while we finish up some rough ends of this piece. Then we'll be ready to start on the new one. It's pretty well doped out, and there's a big part in it for you — big things to be done in a big way, see what I mean."

"Well, I'm glad I suited you," Merton replied. "I tried to give the best that was in me to a sincere interpretation of that fine part. And it was a great surprise to me. I never thought I'd be working for you, Mr. Baird, and of course I wouldn't have been if you had kept on doing those comedies. I never would have wanted to work in one of them."

"Of course not," agreed Baird cordially. "I realized that you were a serious artist, and you came in the nick of time, just when I was wanting to be serious myself, to get away from that slapstick stuff into something better and finer. You came when I needed you. And, look here, Merton, I signed you on at 40 a week —"

"Yes, sir: I was glad to get it."

"Well, I'm going to give you more. From the beginning of the new picture you're on the payroll at 75 a week. No, no, not a word —" as Merton would have thanked him. "You're earning the money. And for the picture after that — well, if you keep on giving the best that's in you, it will be a whole lot more. Now take a good rest till we're ready for you."

At last he had won. Suffering and sacrifice had told. And Baird had spoken of the Montague girl as his leading lady — quite as if he were a star. And 75 dollars a week! A sum Gashwiler had made him work five weeks for. Now he had something big to write to his old friend, Tessie Kearns. She might spread the news in Simsbury, he thought. He contrived a close-up of Gashwiler hearing it, of Mrs. Gashwiler hearing it, of Metta Judson hearing it.

They would all be incredulous until a certain picture was shown at the Bijou Palace, a gripping drama of mother-love, of a clean-limbed young American type wrongfully accused of a crime and taking the burden of it upon his own shoulders for the sake of the girl he had come to love; of the tense play of elemental forces in the great West, the regeneration of a shallow society girl when brought to adversity by the ruin of her old father; of the lovers reunited in that West they both loved.

And somehow — this was still a puzzle — the very effective weaving in and out of the drama of the world's most popular screen idol, played so expertly by Clifford Armytage who looked enough like him to be his twin brother.

Fresh from joyous moments in the projection room, the Montague girl gazed at Baird across the latter's desk, Baird spoke.

"Sis, he's a wonder."

"Jeff, you're a wonder. How'd you ever keep him from getting wise?"

Baird shrugged. "Easy! We caught him fresh."

"How'd you ever win him to do all those falls on the trick spurs, and get the close-ups of them? Didn't he know you were shooting?"

"Oh!" Baird shrugged again. "A little talk made that all jake. But what bothers me — how's he going to act when he's seen the picture?"

The girl became grave. "I'm scared stiff every time I think of it. Maybe he'll murder you, Jeff."

"Maybe he'll murder both of us. You got him into it."

She did not smile, but considered gravely, absently.

"There's something else might happen," she said at last. "That boy's got at least a couple of sides to him. I'd rather he'd be crazy mad than be what I'm thinking of now, and that's that all this stuff might just fairly break his heart. Think of it — to see his fine honest acting turned into good old Buckeye slapstick! Can't you get that? How'd you like to think you were playing Romeo, and act your heart out at it, and then find out they'd slipped in a cross-eyed Juliet in a comedy make-up on you? Well, you can laugh, but maybe it won't be funny to him. Honest, Jeff, that kid gets me under the ribs kind of. I hope he takes it standing up, and goes good and crazy mad."

"I'll know what to say to him if he does that. If he takes it the other way, lying down, I'll be too ashamed ever to look him in the eye again. Say, it'll be like going up to a friendly baby and soaking it with a potato masher or something."

"Don't worry about it, Kid. Anyway, it won't be your fault so much as mine. And you think there's only two ways for him to take it, mad or heartbroken? Well, let me tell you something about that lad — he might fool you both ways. I don't know just how, but I tell you he's an actor, a born one. What he did is going to get over big. And I never yet saw a born actor that would take applause lying down, even if it does come for what he didn't know he was doing. Maybe he'll be mad — that's natural enough. But maybe he'll fool us both. So cheerio, old Pippin! and let's fly into the new piece. I'll play safe by shooting the most of that before the other one is released. And he'll still be playing straight in a serious heart drama. Fancy that, Armand!"

CHAPTER XV

A NEW TRAIL

One genial morning a few days later the sun shone in across the desk of Baird while he talked to Merton Gill of the new piece. It was a sun of fairest promise. Mr. Gill's late work was again lavishly commended, and confidence was expressed that he would surpass himself in the drama shortly to be produced.

Mr. Baird spoke in enthusiastic terms of this, declaring that if it did not prove to be a knock-out — a clean-up picture — then he, Jeff Baird, could safely be called a Chinaman. And during the time that would elapse before shooting on the new piece could begin he specified a certain study in which he wished his actor to engage.

"You've watched the Edgar Wayne pictures, haven't you?"

"Yes, I've seen a number of them."

"Like his work? — that honest country-boy-loving-his — mother-and-little-sister stuff, wearing overalls and tousled hair in the first part, and coming out in city clothes and eight dollar neckties at the last, with his hair slicked back same as a seal?"

"Oh, yes, I like it. He's fine. He has a great appeal."

"Good! That's the kind of a part you're going to get in this new piece. Lots of managers in my place would say 'No-he's a capable young chap and has plenty of talent, but he lacks the experience to play an Edgar Wayne part.' That's what a lot of these Wisenheimers would say. But me — not so. I believe you can get away with this part, and I'm going to give you your chance."

"I'm sure I don't know how to thank you, Mr. Baird, and I'll try to give you the very best that is in me —"

"I'm sure of that, my boy; you needn't tell me. But now — what I want you to do while you got this lay-off between pieces, chase out and watch all the Edgar Wayne pictures you can find. There was one up on the Boulevard last week I'd like you to watch half-a-dozen times. It may be at another house down this way, or it may be out in one of the suburbs. I'll have someone outside call up and find where it is today and they'll let you know. It's called *Happy Homestead* or something snappy like that, and it kind of suggests a layout for this new piece of mine, see what I mean? It'll suggest things to you.

"Edgar and his mother and little sister live on this farm and Edgar mixes in with a swell dame down at the summer hotel, and a villain tries to get his old mother's farm and another villain takes his little sister off up to the wicked city, and Edgar has more trouble than would patch Hell a mile, see? But it all comes right in the end, and the city girl falls for him when she sees him in his stepping-out clothes.

"It's a pretty little thing, but to my way of thinking it lacks strength; not enough punch to it. So we're sort of building up on that general idea, only we'll put in the pep that this piece lacked. If I don't miss my guess, you'll be able to show Wayne a few things about serious acting — especially after you've studied his methods a little bit in this piece."

"Well, if you think I can do it," began Merton, then broke off in answer to a sudden thought. "Will my mother be the same actress that played it before, the one that mopped all the time?"

"Yes, the same actress, but a different sort of mother. She — she's more enterprising; she's a sort of chemist, in a way; puts up preserves and jellies for the hotel. She never touches a mop in the whole piece and dresses neat from start to finish."

"And does the cross-eyed man play in it? Sometimes, in scenes with him, I'd get the idea I wasn't really doing my best."

"Yes, yes, I know." Baird waved a sympathetic hand. "Poor old Jack. He's trying hard to do something worthwhile, but he's played in those cheap comedy things so long it's sort of hard for him to get out of it and play serious stuff, if you know what I mean."

"I know what you mean," said Merton.

"And he's been with me so long I kind of hate to discharge him. You see, on account of those eyes of his, it would be hard for him to get a job as a serious actor, so I did think I'd give him another part in this piece if you didn't object, just to sort of work him into the worthwhile things. He's so eager for the chance. It was quite pathetic how grateful he looked when I told him I'd try him once more in one of the better and finer things. And a promise is a promise."

"Still, Merton, you're the man I must suit in this cast; if you say the word I'll tell Jack he must go, though I know what a blow it will be to him —"

"Oh, no, Mr. Baird," Merton interrupted fervently, "I wouldn't think of such a thing. Let the poor fellow have a chance to learn something better than the buffoonery he's been doing. I'll do everything I can to help him. I think it is very pathetic, his wanting to do the better things; it's fine of him. And maybe some day he could save up enough to have a good surgeon fix his eyes right. It might be done, you know."

"Now that's nice of you, my boy. It's kind and generous. Not every actor of your talent would want Jack working in the same scene with him. And perhaps, as you say, some day he can save up enough from his wages to have his eyes fixed. I'll mention it to him. And this reminds me, speaking of the cast, there's another member who might bother some of these fussy actors. She's the girl who will take the part of your city sweetheart. As a matter of fact, she isn't exactly the type I'd have picked for the part, because she's rather a large, hearty girl, if you know what I mean. I could have found a lot who were better lookers; but the poor thing has a bedridden father and mother and a little crippled brother and a little sister that isn't well, and she's working hard to send them all to school — I mean the children, not her parents; so I saw the chance to do her a good turn, and I hope you'll feel that you can work harmoniously with her. I know I'm too darned human to be in this business —" Baird looked aside to conceal his emotion.

"I'm sure, Mr. Baird, I'll get along fine with the young lady, and I think it's fine of you to give these people jobs when you could get better folks in their places."

"Well, well, we'll say no more about that," replied Baird gruffly, as one who had again hidden his too-impressionable heart. "Now ask in the outer office where that Wayne film is today and catch it as often as you feel you're getting any of the Edgar Wayne stuff. We'll call you up when work begins."

He saw the Edgar Wayne film, a touching story in which the timid, diffident country boy triumphed over difficulties and won the love of a pure New York society girl, meantime protecting his mother from the insulting sneers of the idle rich and being made to suffer intensely by the apparent moral wreck of his dear little sister whom a rich scoundrel lured to the great city with false promises that he would make a fine lady of her. Never before had he studied the acting method of Wayne with a definite aim in view. Now he watched until he himself became the awkward country boy. He was primed with the Wayne manner, the appealing ingenuousness, the simple embarrassments; the manly regard for the old mother, when word came that Baird was ready for him in the new piece.

This drama was strikingly like the Wayne piece he had watched, at least in its beginning. Baird, in his striving for the better things, seemed at first to have copied his model almost too faithfully. Not only was Merton to be the awkward country boy in the little hillside farmhouse, but his mother and sister were like the other mother and sister.

Still, he began to observe differences. The little sister — played by the Montague girl — was a simple farm maiden as in the other piece, but the mother was more energetic. She had silvery hair and wore a neat black dress, with a white lace collar and a cameo brooch at her neck, and she embraced her son tearfully at frequent intervals, as had the other mother; but she carried on in her kitchen an active business in canning fruits and putting up jellies, which, sold to the rich people at the hotel, would swell the little fund that must be saved to pay the mortgage. Also, in the present piece, the country boy was to become a great inventor, and this was different. Merton felt that this was a good touch; it gave him dignity.

He appeared ready for work on the morning designated. He was now able to make up himself, and he dressed in the country-boy costume that had been provided. It was perhaps not so attractive a costume as Edgar Wayne had worn, consisting of loose-fitting overalls that came well above his waist and were fastened by straps that went over the shoulders; but, as Baird remarked, the contrast would be greater when he dressed in rich city clothes at the last. His hair, too, was no longer the slicked-back hair of Parmalee, but tousled in country disorder.

For much of the action of the new piece they would require an outside location, but there were some interiors to be shot on the lot. He forgot the ill-fitting overalls when shown his attic laboratory where, as an ambitious young inventor, sustained by the unfaltering trust of mother and sister, he would perfect certain mechanical devices that would bring him fame, fortune, and the love of a pure New York society girl. It was a humble little room containing a work-bench that held his tools and a table littered with drawings over which he bent until late hours of the night.

At this table, simple, unaffected, deeply earnest, he was shown as the dreaming young inventor, perplexed at moments, then, with brightening eyes, making some needful change in the drawings. He felt in these scenes that he was revealing a world of personality. And he must struggle to give a sincere interpretation in later scenes that would require more action. He would show Baird that he had not watched Edgar Wayne without profit.

Another interior was of the neat living room of the humble home. Here were scenes of happy family life with the little sister and the fond old mother. The Montague girl was a charming picture in her simple print dress and sunbonnet beneath which hung her braid of golden hair. The mother was a sweet old dear, dressed as Baird had promised. She early confided to Merton that she was glad her part was not to be a mopping part. In that case she would have had to wear knee-pads, whereas now she was merely, she said, to be a tired business woman.

Still another interior was of her kitchen where she busily carried on her fruit-canning activities. Pots boiled on the stove and glass jars were filled with her product. One of the pots, Merton noticed, the largest, had a tightly closed top from which a slender tube of copper went across one corner of the little room to where it coiled in a bucket filled with water, whence it discharged its contents into bottles.

This, it seemed, was his mother's improved grape juice, a cooling drink to tempt the jaded palates of the city folks up at the big hotel.

The laboratory of the young inventor was abundantly filmed while the earnest country boy dreamed hopefully above his drawings or tinkered at metal devices on the work-bench. The kitchen in which his mother toiled was repeatedly shot, including close-ups of the old mother's ingenious contrivances — especially of the closed boiler with its coil of copper tubing — by which she was helping to save the humble home.

And a scene in the neat living room with its old-fashioned furniture made it all too clear that every effort would be required to save the little home. The cruel money-lender, a lawyer with mean-looking whiskers, confronted the three shrinking inmates to warn them that he must have his money by a certain day or out they would go into the streets. The old mother wept at this, and the earnest boy took her in his arms. The little sister, terrified by the man's rough words, also flew to this shelter, and thus he defied the intruder, calm, fearless, dignified. The money would be paid and the intruder would now please remember that, until the day named, this little home was their very own.

The scoundrel left with a final menacing wave of his gnarled hand; left the group facing ruin unless the invention could be perfected, unless Mother could sell an extraordinary quantity of fruit or improved grape juice to the city folks, or, indeed, unless the little sister could do something wonderful.

She, it now seemed, was confident she also could help. She stood apart from them and prettily promised to do something wonderful. She asked them to remember that she was no longer a mere girl, but a woman with a woman's determination. They both patted the little thing encouragingly on the back.

The interiors possible on the Holden lot having been finished, they motored each day to a remote edge of the city where outside locations had been found for the humble farmhouse and the grand hotel. The farmhouse was excellently chosen,

Merton thought, being the neat, unpretentious abode of honest, hard-working people; but the hotel, some distance off, was not so grand, he thought, as Baird's new play seemed to demand. It was plainly a hotel, a wooden structure with balconies; but it seemed hardly to afford those attractions that would draw wealthier element from New York. He forebore to warn Baird of this, however, fearing to discourage a manager who was honestly striving for the serious in photodrama.

His first exterior scene saw him, with the help of Mother and little sister, loading the one poor motor car which the family possessed with Mother's products. These were then driven to the hotel. The Montague girl drove the car, and scenes of it in motion were shot from a car that preceded them.

They arrived before the hotel; Merton was directed to take from the car an iron weight attached to a rope and running to a connection forward on the hood. He was to throw the weight to the ground, plainly with the notion that he would thus prevent the car from running away. The simple device was, in fact, similar to that used, at Gashwiler's strict orders, on the delivery wagon back in Simsbury, for Gashwiler had believed that Dexter would run away if untethered. But of course it was absurd, Merton saw, to anchor a motor car in such a manner, and he was somewhat taken aback when Baird directed this action.

"It's all right," Baird assured him. "You're a simple country boy, and don't know any better, so do it plumb serious. You'll be smart enough before the show's over. Go ahead, get out, grab the weight, throw it down, and don't look at it again, as if you did this every time. That's it. You're not being funny; just a simple country boy like Wayne was at first." He performed the action, still with some slight misgiving. Followed scenes of brother and sister offering Mother's wares to the city folks idling on the porch of the hotel. Each bearing a basket they were caught submitting the jellies and jams. The brother was laughed at, even sneered at, by the supercilious rich, the handsomely gowned women and the dissipated looking men. No one appeared to wish his jellies.

The little sister had better luck. The women turned from her, but the men gathered about her and quickly bought out the stock. She went to the car for more and the men followed her. To Merton, who watched these scenes, the dramatist's intention was plain. These men did not really care for jellies and jams, they were attracted solely by the wild-rose beauty of the little country girl. And they were plainly the sort of men whose attentions could mean no good to such as she.

Left on the porch, he was now directed to approach a distinguished looking old gentleman, probably a banker and a power in Wall Street, who read his morning papers. Timidly he stood before this person, thrusting forward his basket. The old gentleman glanced up in annoyance and brutally rebuffed the country boy with an angry flourish of the paper he read.

"You're hurt by this treatment," called Baird, "and almost discouraged. You look back over your shoulder to where sister is doing a good business with her stuff, and you see the old mother back in her kitchen, working her fingers to the bone — we'll have a flash of that, see? — and you try again. Take out that bottle in the corner of the basket, uncork it, and try again. The old man looks up — he's smelled something. You hold the bottle toward him and you're saying so-and-so, so-and-so, so-and-so, 'Oh, Mister, if you knew how hard my poor old mother works to make this stuff! Won't you please take a little taste of her improved grape juice and see if you don't want to buy a few shillings' worth' — so-and-so, so-and-so, so-and-so — see what I mean? That's it, look pleading. Think how the little home depends on it."

The old gentleman, first so rude, consented to taste the improved grape juice. He put the bottle to his lips and tilted it. A camera was brought up to record closely the look of pleased astonishment that enlivened his face. He arose to his feet, tilted the bottle again, this time drinking abundantly. He smacked his lips with relish, glanced furtively at the group of women in the background, caught the country boy by a sleeve and drew him farther along the porch.

"He's telling you what fine stuff this grape juice is," explained Baird; "saying that your mother must be a wonderful old lady, and he'll drop over to meet her; and in the meantime he wants you to bring him all this grape juice she has. He'll take it; she can name her own price. He hands you a 10 dollar bill for the bottle he has and for another in the basket — that's it, give it to him. The rest of the bottles are jams or something. You want him to take them, but he pushes them back. He's saying he wants the improved grape juice or nothing. He shows a big wad of bills to show he can pay for it. You look glad now — the little home may be saved after all."

The scene was shot. Merton felt that he carried it acceptably. He had shown the diffident pleading of the country boy that his mother's product should be at least tasted, his frank rejoicing when the old gentleman approved of it. He was not so well satisfied with the work of the Montague girl as his innocent little sister. In her sale of Mother's jellies to the city men, in her acceptance of their attentions, she appeared to be just the least bit bold. It seemed almost as if she wished to attract their notice. He hesitated to admit it, for he profoundly esteemed the girl, but there were even moments when, in technical language, she actually seemed to "vamp" these creatures who thronged about her to profess for her jams and jellies an interest he was sure they did not feel.

He wondered if Baird had made it plain to her that she was a very innocent little country girl who should be unpleasantly affected by these advances. The scene he watched shot where the little sister climbed back into the motor car, leered at by the four New York club-men, he thought especially distasteful. Surely the skirt of her print dress was already short enough. She needed not to lift it under this evil regard as she put her foot up to the step.

It was on the porch of the hotel, too, that he was to have his first scene with the New York society girl whose hand he won. She proved to be the daughter of the old gentleman who liked the improved grape juice. As Baird had intimated, she was a large girl; not only tall and stoutly built, but somewhat heavy of face. Baird's heart must have been touched indeed when he consented to employ her, but Merton remembered her bedridden father and mother, the little crippled brother, the little sister who was also in poor health, and resolved to make their scenes together as easy for her as he could.

At their first encounter she appeared in a mannish coat and riding breeches, though she looked every inch a woman in this attire.

"She sees you, and it's a case of love at first sight on her part," explained Baird. "And you love her, too, only you're a bashful country boy and can't show it the way she can. Try out a little first scene now."

Merton stood, his basket on his arm, as the girl approached him. "Look down," called Baird, and Merton lowered his gaze under the ardent regard of the social butterfly. She tossed away her cigarette and came nearer. Then she mischievously pinched his cheek as the New York men had pinched his little sister's. Having done this, she placed her hand beneath his chin and raised his face to hers.

"Now look up at her," called Baird. "But she frightens you. Remember your country raising. You never saw a society girl before. That's it — look frightened while she's admiring you in that bold way. Now turn a little and look down again. Pinch his cheek once more, Lulu. Now, Merton, look up and smile, but kind of scared — you're still afraid of her — and offer her a bottle of Ma's preserves. Step back a little as you do it, because you're kind of afraid of what she might do next. That's fine. Good work, both of you."

He was glad for the girl's sake that Baird had approved the work of both. He had been afraid she was overdoing the New York society manner in the boldness of her advances to him, but of course Baird would know.

His conscience hurt him a little when the Montague girl added her praise to Baird's for his own work. "Kid, you certainly stepped neat and looked nice in that love scene," she warmly told him. He would have liked to praise her own work, but could not bring himself to. Perhaps she would grow more shrinking and modest as the drama progressed.

A part of the play now developed as he had foreseen it would, in that the city men at the hotel pursued the little sister to her own door-step with attentions that she should have found unwelcome. But even now she behaved in a way he could not approve. She seemed determined to meet the city men halfway.

"I'm to be the sunlight arc of this hovel," she announced when the city men came, one at a time, to shower gifts upon the little wild rose.

Later it became apparent that she must in the end pay dearly for her too-ready acceptance of these favors. One after another the four city men, whose very appearance would have been sufficient warning to most girls, endeavored to lure her up to the great city where they promised to make a lady of her. It was a situation notoriously involving danger to the simple country girl, yet not even her mother frowned upon it.

The mother, indeed, frankly urged the child to let all of these kind gentlemen make a lady of her. The brother should have warned her in this extremity; but the brother was not permitted any share in these scenes. Only Merton Gill, in his proper person, seemed to feel the little girl was all too cordially inviting trouble.

He became confused, ultimately, by reason of the scenes not being taken consecutively. It appeared that the little sister actually left her humble home at the insistence of one of the villains, yet she did not, apparently, creep back months later broken in body and soul. As nearly as he could gather, she was back the next day. And it almost seemed as if later, at brief intervals, she allowed herself to start for the great city with each of the other three scoundrels who were bent upon her destruction. But always she appeared to return safely and to bring large sums of money with which to delight the old mother.

It was puzzling to Merton. He decided at last — he did not like to ask the Montague girl — that Baird had tried the same scene four times, and would choose the best of these for his drama.

Brother and sister made further trips to the hotel with their offerings, only the sister now took jams and jellies exclusively, which she sold to the male guests, while the brother took only the improved grape juice which the rich old New Yorker bought and generously paid for.

There were other scenes at the hotel between the country boy and the heavy-faced New York society girl, in which the latter was an ardent wooer. Once she was made to snatch a kiss from him as he stood by her, his basket on his arm. He struggled in her embrace, then turned to flee.

She was shown looking after him, laughing, carelessly slapping one leg with her riding crop.

"You're still timid," Baird told him. "You can hardly believe you have won her love."

In some following scenes at the little farmhouse it became impossible for him longer to doubt this, for the girl frankly told her love as she lingered with him at the gate.

"She's one of these new women," said Baird. "She's living her own life. You listen — it's wonderful that this great love should have come to you. Let us see the great joy dawning in your eyes."

He endeavored to show this. The New York girl became more ardent. She put an arm about him, drew him to her. Slowly, almost in the manner of Harold Parmalee, as it seemed to him, she bent down and imprinted a long kiss upon his lips. He had been somewhat difficult to rehearse in this scene, but Baird made it all plain. He was still the bashful country boy, though now he would be awakened by love.

The girl drew him from the gate to her waiting automobile. Here she overcame a last reluctance and induced him to enter. She followed and drove rapidly off.

It was only now that Baird let him into the very heart of the drama.

"You see," he told Merton, "you've watched these city folks; you've wanted city life and fine clothes for yourself; so, in a moment of weakness, you've gone up to town with this girl to have a look at the place, and it sort of took hold of you. In fact, you hit up quite a pace for awhile; but at last you go stale on it —"

"The blight of Broadway," suggested Merton, wondering if there could be a cabaret scene.

"Exactly," said Baird. "And you get to thinking of the poor old mother and little sister back here at home, working away to pay off the mortgage, and you decide to come back. You get back on a stormy night; lots of snow and wind; you're pretty weak. We'll show you sort of fainting as you reach the door. You have no overcoat nor hat, and your city suit is practically ruined. You got a great chance for some good acting here, especially after you get inside to face the folks. It'll be the strongest thing you've done, so far."

It was indeed an opportunity for strong acting. He could see that. He stayed late with Baird and his staff one night and a scene of the prodigal's return to the door of the little home was shot in a blinding snow-storm. Baird warmly congratulated the mechanics who contrived the storm, and was enthusiastic over the acting of the hero. Through the wintry blast he staggered, half falling, to reach the door where he collapsed. The light caught the agony on his pale face. He lay a moment, half-fainting, then reached up a feeble hand to the knob of the door.

It was one of the annoyances incident to screen art that he could not go in at that moment to finish his great scene. But this must be done back on the lot, and the scene could not be secured until the next day.

Once more he became the pitiful victim of a great city, crawling back to the home shelter on a wintry night. It was Christmas eve, he now learned. He pushed open the door of the little home and staggered in to face his old mother and the little sister. They sprang forward at his entrance; the sister ran to support him to the homely old sofa. He was weak, emaciated, his face an agony of repentance, as he mutely pled forgiveness for his flight.

His old mother had risen, had seemed about to embrace him fondly when he knelt at her feet, but then had drawn herself sternly up and pointed commandingly to the door. The prodigal, anguished anew at this repulse, fell weakly back upon the couch with a cry of despair. The little sister placed a pillow under his head and ran to plead with the mother. A long time she remained obdurate, but at last relented. Then she, too, came to fall upon her knees before the wreck who had returned to her.

Not many rehearsals were required for this scene, difficult though it was. Merton Gill had seized his opportunity. His study of agony expressions in the film course was here rewarded. The scene closed with the departure of the little sister. Resolutely, showing the light of some fierce determination, she put on hat and wraps, spoke words of promise to the stricken mother and son, and darted out into the night. The snow whirled in as she opened the door.

"Good work," said Baird to Merton. "If you don't hear from that little bit you can call me a Swede."

Some later scenes were shot in the same little home, which seemed to bring the drama to a close. While the returned prodigal lay on the couch, nursed by the forgiving mother, the sister returned in company with the New York society girl who seemed aghast at the wreck of him she had once wooed. Slowly she approached the couch of the sufferer, tenderly she reached down to enfold him. In some manner, which Merton could not divine, the lovers had been reunited.

The New York girl was followed by her father — it would seem they had both come from the hotel — and the father, after giving an order for more of Mother's grape juice, examined the son's patents. Two of them he exclaimed with delight over, and at once paid the boy a huge roll of bills for a 10th interest in them.

Now came the grasping man who held the mortgage and who had counted upon driving the family into the streets this stormy Christmas eve. He was overwhelmed with confusion when his money was paid from an ample hoard, and slunk, shame-faced, out into the night. It could be seen that Christmas day would dawn bright and happy for the little group.

To Merton's eye there was but one discord in this finale. He had known that the cross-eyed man was playing the part of hotel clerk at the neighboring resort, but he had watched few scenes in which the poor fellow acted; and he surely had not known that this man was the little sister's future husband. It was with real dismay that he averted his gaze from the embrace that occurred between these two, as the clerk entered the now happy home.

One other detail had puzzled him. This was the bundle to which he had clung as he blindly plunged through the storm. He had still fiercely clutched it after entering the little room, clasping it to his breast even as he sank at his mother's feet in physical exhaustion and mental anguish, to implore her forgiveness. Later the bundle was placed beside him as he lay, pale and wan, on the couch.

He supposed this bundle to contain one of his patents; a question to Baird when the scene was over proved him to be correct.

"Sure," said Baird, "that's one of your patents." Yet he still wished the little sister had not been made to marry the cross-eyed hotel clerk.

And another detail lingered in his memory to bother him. The actress playing his mother was wont to smoke cigarettes when not engaged in acting. He had long known it. But he now seemed to recall, in that touching last scene of reconciliation, that she had smoked one while the camera actually turned. He hoped this was not so. It would mean a mistake. And Baird would be justly annoyed by the old mother's carelessness.

CHAPTER XVI

OF SARAH NEVADA MONTAGUE

They were six long weeks doing the new piece. The weeks seemed long to Merton Gill because there were so many hours, even days, of enforced idleness. To pass an entire day, his face stiff with the make-up, without once confronting a camera in action, seemed to him a waste of his own time and a waste of Baird's money. Yet this appeared to be one of the unavoidable penalties incurred by those who engaged in the art of photodrama. Time was needed to create that world of painted shadows, so swift, so nicely consecutive when revealed, but so incoherent, so brokenly inconsequent, so meaningless in the recording.

How little an audience could suspect the vexatious delays ensuing between, say, a knock at a door and the admission of a visitor to a neat little home where a fond old mother was trying to pay off a mortgage with the help of her little ones. How could an audience divine that a wait of two hours had been caused because a polished city villain had forgotten his spats? Or that other long waits had been caused by other forgotten trifles, while an expensive company of artists lounged about in bored apathy, or smoked, gossiped, bantered?

Yet no one ever seemed to express concern about these waits. Rarely were their causes known, except by some frenzied assistant director, and he, after a little, would cease to be frenzied and fall to loafing calmly with the others. Merton Gill's education in his chosen art was progressing. He came to loaf with the unconcern, the vacuous boredom, the practiced nonchalance, of more seasoned artists.

Sometimes when exteriors were being taken the sky would overcloud and the sun be denied them for a whole day. The Montague girl would then ask Merton how he liked Sunny Cafeteria. He knew this was a jesting term that would stand for sunny California, and never failed to laugh.

The girl kept rather closely by him during these periods of waiting. She seemed to show little interest in other members of the company, and her association with them, Merton noted, was marked by a certain restraint. With them she seemed no longer to be the girl of free ways and speech. She might occasionally join a group of the men who indulged in athletic sports on the grass before the little farmhouse — for the actors of Mr. Baird's company would all betray acrobatic tendencies in their idle moments — and he watched one day while the simple little country sister turned a series of hand-springs and cart-wheels that evoked sincere applause from the four New York villains who had been thus solacing their ennui.

But oftener she would sit with Merton on the back seat of one of the waiting automobiles. She not only kept herself rather aloof from other members of the company, but she curiously seemed to bring it about that Merton himself would have little contact with them. Especially did she seem to hover between him and the company's feminine members. Among those impersonating guests at the hotel were several young women of rare beauty with whom he would have been not unwilling to fraternize in that easy comradeship which seemed to mark studio life. These were far more alluring than the New York society girl who wooed him and who had secured the part solely through Baird's sympathy for her family misfortunes.

They were richly arrayed and charmingly mannered in the scenes he watched; moreover, they not too subtly betrayed a pleasant consciousness of Merton's existence. But the Montague girl noticeably monopolized him when a better acquaintance with the beauties might have come about. She rather brazenly seemed to be guarding him. She was always there.

This very apparent solicitude of hers left him feeling pleasantly important, despite the social contacts it doubtless deprived him of. He wondered if the Montague girl could be jealous, and cautiously one day, as they lolled in the motor car, he sounded her.

"Those girls in the hotel scenes — I suppose they're all nice girls of good family?" he casually observed.

"Huh?" demanded Miss Montague, engaged with a pencil at the moment in editing her left eyebrow. "Oh, that bunch? Sure, they all come from good old Southern families — Virginia and Indiana and those places." She tightened her lips before the little mirror she held and renewed their scarlet. Then she spoke more seriously. "Sure, Kid, those girls are all right enough. They work like dogs and do the best they can when they ain't got jobs. I'm strong for 'em. But then, I'm a wise old trouper. I understand things. You don't. You're the real country wild rose of this piece. It's a good thing you got me to ride herd on you. You're far too innocent to be turned loose on a comedy lot.

"Listen, boy —" She turned a sober face to him — "the straight lots are fairly decent, but get this: a comedy lot is the toughest place this side of the bad one. Any comedy lot."

"But this isn't a comedy lot. Mr. Baird isn't doing comedies any more, and these people all seem to be nice people. Of course some of the ladies smoke cigarettes —"

The girl had averted her face briefly, but now turned to him again. "Of course that's so; Jeff is trying for the better things; but he's still using lots of his old people. They're all right for me, but not for you. You wouldn't last long if mother here didn't look out for you. I'm playing your dear little sister, but I'm playing your mother, too. If it hadn't been for me this bunch would have taught you a lot of things you'd better learn some other way. Just for one thing, long before this you'd probably been hopping up your reindeers and driving all over in a Chinese sleigh."

He tried to make something of this, but found the words meaningless. They merely suggested to him a snowy winter scene of Santa Claus and his innocent equipage. But he would intimate that he understood.

"Oh, I guess not," he said knowingly. The girl appeared not to have heard this bit of pretense.

"On a comedy lot," she said, again becoming the oracle, "you can do murder if you wipe up the blood. Remember that."

He did not again refer to the beautiful young women who came from fine old Southern homes. The Montague girl was too emphatic about them.

At other times during the long waits, perhaps while they ate lunch brought from the cafeteria, she would tell him of herself. His old troubling visions of his wonder-woman, of Beulah Baxter the daring, had well-nigh faded, but now and then they would recur as if from long habit, and he would question the girl about her life as a double.

"Yeah, I could see that Baxter business was a blow to you, Kid. You'd kind of worshiped her, hadn't you?"

"Well, I — yes, in a sort of way —"

"Of course you did; it was very nice of you —" She reached over to pat his hand. "Mother understands just how you felt, watching the films back there in Gooseberry" — He had quit trying to correct her as to Gashwiler and Simsbury. She had hit upon Gooseberry as a working composite of both names, and he had wearily come to accept it — "and I know just how you felt" — Again she patted his hand — "that night when you found me doing her stuff."

"It did kind of upset me."

"Sure it would! But you ought to have known that all these people use doubles when they can — men and women both. It not only saves 'em work, but even where they could do the stuff if they had to — and that ain't so often — it saves 'em broken bones, and holding up a big production two or three months. Fine business that would be. So when you see a woman, or a man either, doing something that someone else could do, you can bet someone else is doing it. What would you expect? Would you expect a high-priced star to go out and break his leg?

"And at that, most of the doubles are men, even for the women stars, like Kitty Carson always carries one who used to be a circus acrobat. She couldn't hardly do one of the things you see her doing, but when old Dan gets on her blonde transformation and a few of her clothes, he's her to the life in a long shot, or even in mediums, if he keeps his map covered.

"Yeah, most of the doublers have to be men. I'll hand that to myself. I'm about the only girl that's been doing it, and that's out with me hereafter, I guess, the way I seem to be making good with Jeff. Maybe after this I won't have to do stunts, except of course some riding stuff, prob'ly, or a row of flips or something light. Anything heavy comes up — me for a double of my own." She glanced sidewise at her listener. "Then you won't like me any more, hey, Kid, after you find out I'm using a double?"

He had listened attentively, absorbed in her talk, and seemed startled by this unforeseen finish. He turned anxious eyes on her. It occurred to him for the first time that he did not wish the Montague girl to do dangerous things any more. "Say," he said quickly, amazed at his own discovery, "I wish you'd quit doing all those — stunts, do you call 'em?"

"Why?" she demanded. There were those puzzling lights back in her eyes as he met them. He was confused.

"Well, you might get hurt."

"Oh!"

"You might get killed sometime. And it wouldn't make the least difference to me, your using a double. I'd like you just the same."

"I see; it wouldn't be the way it was with Baxter when you found it out."

"No; you — you're different. I don't want you to get killed," he added, rather blankly. He was still amazed at this discovery.

"All right, Kid. I won't," she replied soothingly.

"I'll like you just as much," he again assured her, "no matter how many doubles you have."

"Well, you'll be having doubles yourself, sooner or later — and I'll like you, too." She reached over to his hand, but this time she held it. He returned her strong clasp. He had not liked to think of her being mangled perhaps by a fall into a quarry when the cable gave way — and the camera men would probably keep on turning!

"I always been funny about men," she presently spoke again, still gripping his hand. "Lord knows I've seen enough of all kinds, bad and good, but I always been kind of afraid even of the good ones. Any one might not think it, but I guess I'm just natural-born shy. Man-shy, anyway."

He glowed with a confession of his own. "You know, I'm that way, too. Girl-shy. I felt awful awkward when I had to kiss you in the other piece. I never did, really —" He floundered a moment, but was presently blurting out the meager details of that early amour with Edwina May Pulver. He stopped this recital in a sudden panic fear that the girl would make fun of him. He was immensely relieved when she merely renewed the strength of the handclasp.

"I know. That's the way with me. Of course I can put over the acting stuff, even vamping, but I'm afraid of men off-stage. Say, would you believe it, I ain't ever had but one beau. That was Bert Stacy. Poor old Bert! He was lots older than me; about 30, I guess. He was white all through. You always kind of remind me of him. Sort of a feckless dub he was, too; kind of honest and awkward — you know. He was the one got me doing stunts. He wasn't afraid of anything. Didn't know it was even in the dictionary. That old scout would go out night or day and break everything but his contract. I was 12 when I first knew him and he had me doing twisters in no time. I caught on to the other stuff pretty good. I wasn't afraid, either, I'll say that for myself. First I was afraid to show him I was afraid, but pretty soon I wasn't afraid at all.

"We pulled off a lot of stuff for different people. And of course I got to be a big girl and three years ago when I was 18 Bert wanted us to be married and I thought I might as well. He was the only one I hadn't been afraid of. So we got engaged. I was still kind of afraid to marry any one, but being engaged was all right. I know we'd got along together, too, but then he got his with a motorcycle.

"Kind of funny. He'd do anything on that machine. He'd jump clean over an auto and he'd leap a 30-foot ditch and he was all set to pull a new one for Jeff Baird when it happened. Jeff was going to have him ride his motorcycle through a plate-glass window. The set was built and everything ready and then the merry old sun don't shine for three days. Every morning Bert would go over to the lot and wait around in the fog. And this third day, when it got too late in the afternoon to shoot even if the sun did show, he says to me, 'c'mon, hop up and let's take a ride down to the beach.' So I hop to the back seat and off we start and on a ninety-foot paved boulevard what does Bert do but get caught in a jam? It was an ice wagon that finally bumped us over. I was shook up and scraped here and there. But Bert was finished. That's the funny part. He'd got it on this boulevard, but back on the lot he'd have rode through that plate-glass window probably without a scratch. And just because the sun didn't shine that day, I wasn't engaged any more. Bert was kind of like some old sea-captain that comes back to shore after risking his life on the ocean in all kinds of storms, and falls into a duck-pond and gets drowned."

She sat a long time staring out over the landscape, still holding his hand. Inside the fence before the farmhouse three of the New York villains were again engaged in athletic sports, but she seemed oblivious of these. At last she turned to him again with an illumining smile.

"But I was dead in love once before that, and that's how I know just how you feel about Baxter. He was the preacher where we used to go to church. He was a good one. Pa copied a lot of his stuff that he uses to this day if he happens to get a preacher part. He was the loveliest thing. Not so young, but dark, with wonderful eyes and black hair, and his voice would go all through you. I had an awful case on him. I was 12, and all week I used to think how I'd see him the next Sunday. Say, when I'd get there and he'd be working — doing pulpit stuff — he'd have me in kind of a trance.

"Sometimes after the pulpit scene he'd come down right into the audience and shake hands with people. I'd almost keel over if he'd notice me. I'd be afraid if he would and afraid if he wouldn't. If he said 'And how is the little lady this morning?' I wouldn't have a speck of voice to answer him. I'd just tremble all over. I used to dream I'd get a job workin' for him as extra, blacking his shoes or fetching his breakfast and things.

"It was the real thing, all right. I used to try to pray the way he did — asking the Lord to let me do a character bit or something with him. He had me going all right. You must 'a' been that way about Baxter. Sure you were. When you found she was married and used a double and everything, it was like I'd found this preacher shooting hop or using a double in his pulpit stuff."

She was still again, looking back upon this tremendous episode.

"Yes, that's about the way I felt," he told her. Already his affair with Mrs. Rosenblatt seemed a thing of his childhood. He was wondering, rather, if the preacher could have been the perfect creature the girl was now picturing him. It would not have displeased him to learn that this refulgent being had actually used a double in his big scenes, or had been guilty of mere human behavior at odd moments. Probably, after all, he had been just a preacher. "Uncle Sylvester used to want me to be a preacher," he said, with apparent irrelevance, "even if he was his own worst enemy." He added presently, as the girl remained silent, "I always say my prayers at night." He felt vaguely that this might raise him to the place of the other who had been adored. He was wishing to be thought well of by this girl.

She was aroused from her musing by his confession. "You do? Now ain't that just like you? I'd have bet you did that. Well, keep on, son. It's good stuff."

Her serious mood seemed to pass. She was presently exchanging tart repartee with the New York villains who had perched in a row on the fence to be funny about that long — continued holding of hands in the motor car. She was quite unembarrassed, however, as she dropped the hand with a final pat and vaulted to the ground over the side of the car.

"Get busy, there!" she ordered. "Where's your understander — where's your top-mounter?" She became a circus ringmaster. "Three up and a roll for yours," she commanded. The three villains aligned themselves on the lawn. One climbed to the shoulders of the other and a third found footing on the second. They balanced there, presently to lean forward from the summit. The girl played upon an imaginary snare drum with a guttural, throaty imitation of its roll, culminating in the "boom!" of a bass-drum as the tower toppled to earth. Its units, completing their turn with somersaults, again stood in line, bowing and smirking their acknowledgments for imagined applause.

The girl, a moment later, was turning hand-springs. Merton had never known that actors were so versatile. It was an astounding profession, he thought, remembering his own registration card that he had filled out at the Holden office. His age, height, weight, hair, eyes, and his chest and waist measures; these had been specified, and then he had been obliged to write the short "No" after ride, drive, swim, dance — to write "No" after "Ride?" even in the artistically photographed presence of Buck Benson on horseback!

Yet in spite of these disabilities he was now a successful actor at an enormous salary. Baird was already saying that he would soon have a contract for him to sign at a still larger figure. Seemingly it was a profession in which you could rise even if you were not able to turn hand-springs or were more or less terrified by horses and deep water and dance music.

And the Montague girl, who, he now fervently hoped, would not be killed while doubling for Mrs. Rosenblatt, was a puzzling creature. He thought his hand must still be warm from her enfolding of it, even when work was resumed and he saw her, with sunbonnet pushed back, stand at the gate of the little farmhouse and behave in an utterly brazen manner toward one of the New York clubmen who was luring her up to the great city. She, who had just confided to him that she was afraid of men, was now practically daring an undoubted scoundrel to lure her up to the great city and make a lady of her. And she had been afraid of all but a clergyman and a stunt actor! He wondered interestingly if she were afraid of Merton Gill. She seemed not to be.

On another day of long waits they ate their lunch from the cafeteria box on the steps of the little home and discussed stage names. "I guess we better can that 'Clifford Armytage' stuff," she told him as she seriously munched a sandwich. "We don't need it. That's out. Merton Gill is a lot better name." She had used "we" quite as if it were a community name.

"Well, if you think so —" he began regretfully, for Clifford Armytage still seemed superior to the indistinction of Merton Gill.

"Sure, it's a lot better," she went on. "That 'Clifford Armytage' — say, it reminds me of just another such feckless dub as you that acted with us one time when we all trouped in a rep show, playing East Lynne and such things. He was just as wise as you are, and when he joined out at Kansas City they gave him a whole book of the piece instead of just his sides. He was a quick study, at that, only he learned everybody's part as well as his own, and that slowed him. They put him on in Waco, and the manager was laid up, so they told him that after the third act he was to go out and announce the bill for the next night, and he learned that speech, too.

"He got on fine till the big scene in the third act. Then he went bloody because that was as far as he'd learned, so he just left the scene cold and walked down to the foots and bowed and said, 'Ladies and gentlemen, we thank you for your attendance here this evening and tomorrow night we shall have the honor of presenting Lady Audley's Secret.'

"With that he gave a cold look to the actors back of him that were gasping like fish, and walked off. And he was like you in another way because his real name was Eddie Duffy, and the lovely stage name he'd picked out was Clyde Maltravers."

"Well, Clifford Armytage is out, then," Merton announced, feeling that he had now buried a part of his dead self in a grave where Beulah Baxter, the wonder-woman, already lay interred. Still, he was conscious of a certain relief. The stage name had been bothersome.

"It ain't as if you had a name like mine," the girl went on. "I simply had to have help."

He wondered what her own name was. He had never heard her called anything but the absurd and undignified "Flips." She caught the question he had looked.

"Well, my honest-to-God name is Sarah Nevada Montague; Sarah for Ma and Nevada for Reno where Ma had to stop off for me — she was out of the company two weeks — and if you ever tell a soul I'll have the law on you. That was a fine way to abuse a helpless baby, wasn't it?"

"But Sarah is all right. I like Sarah."

"Do you, Kid?" She patted his hand. "All right, then, but it's only for your personal use."

"Of course the Nevada —" he hesitated. "It does sound kind of like a geography lesson or something. But I think I'll call you Sarah, I mean when we're alone."

"Well, that's more than Ma ever does, and you bet it'll never get into my press notices. But go ahead if you want to."

"I will, Sarah. It sounds more like a true woman than 'Flips.'"

"Bless the child's heart," she murmured, and reached across the lunch box to pat his hand again.

"You're a great little patter, Sarah," he observed with one of his infrequent attempts at humor.

On still another day, while they idled between scenes, she talked to him about salaries and contracts, again with her important air of mothering him.

"After this picture," she told him, "Jeff was going to sew you up with a long-time contract, probably at 150 per. But I've told him plain I won't stand for it. No five-year contract, and not any contract at that figure. Maybe three years at 250, I haven't decided yet. I'll wait and see —" she broke off to regard him with that old puzzling light far back in her eyes — "wait and see how you get over in these two pieces.

"But I know you'll go big, and so does Jeff. We've caught you in the rushes enough to know that. And Jeff's a good fellow, but naturally he'll get you for as little as he can. He knows all about money even if he don't keep Yom Kippur. So I'm watching over you, son — I'm your manager, see? And I've told him so, plain. He knows he'll have to give you just what you're worth. Of course he's entitled to consideration for digging you up and developing you, but a three-year contract will pay him out for that. Trust mother."

"I do," he told her. "I'd be helpless without you. It kind of scares me to think of getting all that money. I won't know what to do with it."

"I will; you always listen to me, and you won't be camping on the lot any more. And don't shoot dice with these roughnecks on the lot." "I won't," he assured her. "I don't believe in gambling." He wondered about Sarah's own salary, and was surprised to learn that it was now double his own. It was surprising, because her acting seemed not so important to the piece as his. "It seems like a lot of money for what you have to do," he said.

"There," she smiled warmly, "didn't I always say you were a natural-born trouper? Well, it is a lot of money for me, but you see I've helped Jeff dope out both of these pieces. I'm not so bad at gags — I mean the kind of stuff he needs in these serious dramas. This big scene of yours, where you go off to the city and come back a wreck on Christmas night — that's mine. I doped it out after the piece was started — after I'd had a good look at the truck driver that plays opposite you."

Truck driver? It appeared that Miss Montague was actually applying this term to the New York society girl who in private life was burdened with an ailing family. He explained now that Mr. Baird had not considered her ideal for the part, but had chosen her out of kindness.

Again there flickered far back in her eyes those lights that baffled him. There was incredulity in her look, but she seemed to master it.

"But I think it was wonderful of you," he continued, "to write that beautiful scene. It's a strong scene, Sarah. I didn't know you could write, too. It's as good as anything Tessie Kearns ever did, and she's written a lot of strong scenes."

Miss Montague seemed to struggle with some unidentified emotion. After a long, puzzling gaze she suddenly said: "Merton Gill, you come right here with all that make-up on and give mother a good big kiss!"

Astonishingly to himself, he did so in the full light of day and under the eyes of one of the New York villains who had been pretending that he walked a tight-rope across the yard. After he had kissed the girl, she seized him by both arms and shook him. "I'd ought to have been using my own face in that scene," she said. Then she patted his shoulder and told him that he was a good boy.

The pretending tight-rope walker had paused to applaud. "Your act's flopping, Bo," said Miss Montague. "Work fast." Then she again addressed the good boy: "Wait till you've watched that scene before you thank me," she said shortly.

"But it's a strong scene," he insisted.

"Yes," she agreed. "It's strong."

He told her of the other instance of Baird's kindness of heart.

"You know I was a little afraid of playing scenes with the cross-eyed man, but Mr. Baird said he was trying so hard to do serious work, so I wouldn't have him discharged. But shouldn't you think he'd save up and have his eyes straightened? Does he get a very small salary?"

The girl seemed again to be harassed by conflicting emotions, but mastered them to say, "I don't know exactly what it is, but I guess he draws down about 1250 a week."

"Only 12 dollars and 50 cents a week!"

"Twelve *hundred* and 50," said the girl firmly.

"1,250 dollars a week!" This was monstrous, incredible. "But then why doesn't he have his eyes —"

Miss Montague drew him to her with both her capable arms. "My boy, my boy!" she murmured, and upon his painted forehead she now imprinted a kiss of deep reverence. "Run along and play," she ordered. "You're getting me all nervous." Forthwith she moved to the center of the yard where the tight-rope walker still endangered his life above the heads of a vast audience.

She joined him. She became a performer on the slack wire. With a parasol to balance her, she ran to the center of an imaginary wire that swayed perilously, and she swung there, cunningly maintaining a precarious balance. Then she sped back to safety at the wire's end, threw down her parasol, caught the handkerchief thrown to her by the first performer, and daintily touched her face with it, breathing deeply the while and bowing.

He thought Sarah was a strange child — "One minute one thing and the next minute something else."

CHAPTER XVII

MISS MONTAGUE USES HER OWN FACE

Work on the piece dragged slowly to an end. In these latter days the earnest young leading man suffered spells of concern for his employer. He was afraid that Mr. Baird in his effort to struggle out of the slough of low comedy was not going to be wholly successful. He had begun to note that the actors employed for this purpose were not invariably serious even when the cameras turned. Or, if serious, they seemed perhaps from the earnestness of their striving for the worthwhile drama, to be a shade too serious. They were often, he felt, over-emphatic in their methods. Still, they were, he was certain, good actors. One could always tell what they meant.

It was at these times that he especially wished he might be allowed to view the "rushes." He not only wished to assure himself for Baird's sake that the piece would be acceptably serious, but he wished, with a quite seemly curiosity, to view his own acting on the screen. It occurred to him that he had been acting a long time without a glimpse of himself. But Baird had been singularly firm in this matter, and the Montague girl had sided with him. It was best, they said, for a beginning actor not to see himself at first. It might affect his method before this had crystallized; make them self-conscious, artificial.

He was obliged to believe that these well-wishers of his knew best. He must not, then, trifle with a screen success that seemed assured. He tried to be content with this decision. But always the misgivings would return. He would not be really content until he had watched his own triumph. Soon this would be so securely his privilege that not even Baird could deny it, for the first piece in which he had worked was about to be shown. He looked forward to that.

It was toward the end of the picture that his intimacy with the Montague girl grew to a point where, returning from location to the studio late, they would dine together. "Hurry and get ungreased, Son," she would say, "and you can take an actress out to dinner." Sometimes they would patronize the cafeteria on the lot, but oftener, in a spirit of adventure, they would search out exotic restaurants. A picture might follow, after which by street-car he would escort her to the Montague home in a remote, flat region of palm-lined avenues sparsely set with new bungalows.

She would disquiet him at these times by insisting that she pay her share of the expense, and she proved to have no mean talent for petty finance, for she remembered every item down to the street-car fares. Even to Merton Gill she seemed very much a child once she stepped from the domain of her trade. She would stare into shop windows wonderingly, and never failed to evince the most childish delight when they ventured to dine at an establishment other than a cafeteria.

At times when they waited for a car after these dissipations he suffered a not unpleasant alarm at sight of a large-worded advertisement along the back of a bench on which they would sit. "You furnish the Girl, We furnish the House," screamed the bench to him above the name of an enterprising tradesman that came in time to bite itself deeply into his memory.

Of course it would be absurd, but stranger things, he thought, had happened. He wondered if the girl was as afraid of him as of other men. She seemed not to be, but you couldn't tell much about her. She had kissed him one day with a strange warmth of manner, but it had been quite publicly in the presence of other people. When he left her at her door now it was after the least sentimental of partings, perhaps a shake of her hard little hand, or perhaps only a "S'long — see you at the show-shop!"

It was on one of these nights that she first invited him to dine with the Montague family. "I tried last night to get you on the telephone," she explained, "but they kept giving me someone else, or maybe I called wrong. Ain't these six-figured Los Angeles telephone numbers the limit? When you call 208972 or something, it sounds like paging a box-car. I was going to ask you over. Ma had cooked a lovely mess of corned beef and cabbage. Anyway, you come eat with us tomorrow night, will you? She'll have something else cooked up that will stick to the merry old slats. You can come home with me when we get in from work."

So it was that on the following night he enjoyed a home evening with the Montagues. Mrs. Montague had indeed cooked up something else, and had done it well; while Mr. Montague offered at the sideboard a choice of amateur distillations and brews which he warmly recommended to the guest. While the guest timidly considered, having had but the slightest experience with intoxicants, it developed that the confidence placed in his product by the hospitable old craftsman was not shared by his daughter.

"Keep off it," she warned, and then to her father, "Say, listen, Pa, have a heart; that boy's got to work tomorrow."

"So be it, my child," replied Mr. Montague with a visible stiffening of manner. "Sylvester Montague is not the man to urge strong drink upon the reluctant or the over-cautious. I shall drink my aperitif alone."

"Go to it, old Pippin," rejoined his daughter as she vanished to the kitchen.

"Still, a little dish of liquor at this hour," continued the host suggestively when they were alone.

"Well" — Merton wished the girl had stayed — "perhaps just a few drops."

"Precisely, my boy, precisely. A mere dram." He poured the mere dram and his guest drank. It was a colorless, fiery stuff with an elusive taste of metal. Merton contrived an expression of pleasure under the searching glance of his host. "Ah, I knew you would relish it. I fancy I could amaze you if I told you how recently it was made. Now here" — He grasped another bottle purposely — "is something a full 10 days older. It has developed quite a bouquet. Just a drop —"

The guest graciously yet firmly waved a negation.

"Thanks," he said, "but I want to enjoy the last — it — it has so much flavor."

"It has; it has, indeed. I'll not urge you, of course. Later you must see the simple mechanism by which I work these wonders. Alone, then, I drink to you."

Mr. Montague alone drank of two other fruits of his loom before the ladies appeared with dinner. He was clean — shaven now and his fine face glowed with hospitality as he carved roast chickens. The talk was of the shop: of what Mr. Montague scornfully called "grind shows" when his daughter led it, and of the legitimate hall-show when he gained the leadership. He believed that moving pictures had sounded the knell of true dramatic art and said so in many ways.

He tried to imagine the sensations of Lawrence Barrett or Louis James could they behold Sylvester Montague, whom both these gentlemen had proclaimed to be no mean artist, enacting the role of a bar-room rowdy five days on end by reclining upon a sawdust floor with his back supported by a spirits barrel. The supposititious comments of the two placed upon the motion-picture industry the black guilt of having degraded a sterling artist to the level of a peep-show mountebank. They were frankly disgusted at the spectacle, and their present spokesman thought it as well that they had not actually lived to witness it — even the happier phases of this so-called art in which a mere chit of a girl might earn a living wage by falling downstairs for a so-called star, or the he-doll whippersnapper — Merton Gill flinched in spite of himself — could name his own salary for merely possessing a dimpled chin.

Further, an artist in the so-called art received his payment as if he had delivered groceries at one's back door. "You, I believe," — The speaker addressed his guest — "are at present upon a pay-roll; but there are others, your elders-possibly your betters, though I do not say that —"

"You better not," remarked his daughter, only to be ignored.

"— others who must work a day and at the close of it receive a slip of paper emblazoned 'Talent Pay Check.' How more effectively could they cheapen the good word 'talent'? And at the foot of this slip you are made to sign, before receiving the pittance you have earned, a consent to the public exhibition for the purpose of trade or advertising, of the pictures for which you may have posed. Could tradesmen descend to a lower level, I ask you?"

"I'll have one for 1,250 tomorrow night," said Mrs. Montague, not too dismally. "I got to do a duchess at a reception, and I certainly hope my feet don't hurt me again."

"Cheer up, old dears! Pretty soon you can both pick your parts," chirped their daughter. "Jeff's going to give me a contract, and then you can loaf forever for all I care. Only I know you won't, and you know you won't. Both of you'd act for nothing if you couldn't do it for money. What's the use of pretending?"

"The chit may be right, she may be right," conceded Mr. Montague sadly.

Later, while the ladies were again in the kitchen, Mr. Montague, after suggesting, "Something in the nature of an after-dinner cordial," quaffed one for himself and followed it with the one he had poured out for a declining guest who still treasured the flavor of his one aperitif.

He then led the way to the small parlor where he placed in action on the phonograph a record said to contain the ravings of John McCullough in his last hours. He listened to this emotionally.

"That's the sort of technique," he said, "that the so — called silver screen has made but a memory." He lighted his pipe, and identified various framed photographs that enlivened the walls of the little room. Many of them were of himself at an earlier age.

"My dear mother-in-law," he said, pointing to another. "A sterling artist, and in her time an ornament of the speaking stage. I was on tour when her last days came. She idolized me, and passed away with my name on her lips. Her last request was that a photograph of me should be placed in her casket before it went to its final resting place."

He paused, his emotion threatening to overcome him. Presently he brushed a hand across his eyes and continued, "I discovered later that they had picked out the most wretched of all my photographs — an atrocious thing I had supposed was destroyed. Can you imagine it?"

Apparently it was but the entrance of his daughter that saved him from an affecting collapse. His daughter removed the record of John McCullough's ravings, sniffed at it, and put a fox-trot in its place.

"He's got to learn to dance," she explained, laying hands upon the guest.

"Dancing — dancing!" murmured Mr. Montague, as if the very word recalled bitter memories.

With brimming eyes he sat beating time to the fox-trot measure while Merton Gill proved to all observers that his mastery of this dance would, if ever at all achieved, be only after long and discouraging effort.

"You forget all about your feet," remarked the girl as they paused, swaying to the rhythm. "Remember the feet — they're important in a dance. Now! —" But it was hard to remember his feet or, when he did recall them, to relate their movements even distantly to the music. When this had died despairingly, the girl surveyed her pupil with friendly but doubting eyes.

"Say, Pa, don't he remind you of someone? Remember the squirrel that joined out with us one time in the rep show and left 'East Lynne' flat right in the middle of the third act while he went down and announced the next night's play — the one that his name was Eddie Duffy and he called himself Clyde Maltravers?"

"In a way, in a way," agreed Mr. Montague dismally. "A certain lack of finish in the manner, perhaps."

"Remember how Charlie Dickman, the manager, nearly murdered him for it in the wings? Not that Charlie didn't have a right to. Well, this boy dances like Eddie Duffy would have danced."

"He was undeniably awkward and forgetful," said Mr. Montague. "Well do I recall a later night. We played Under the Gaslight; Charlie feared to trust him with a part, so he kept the young man off stage to help with the train noise when the down express should dash across. But even in this humble station he proved inefficient. When the train came on he became confused, seized the cocoanut shells instead of the sand-paper, and our train that night entered to the sound of a galloping horse. The effect must have been puzzling to the audience. Indeed, many of them seemed to consider it ludicrous. Charlie Dickman confided in me later. 'Syl, my boy,' says he, 'this bird Duffy has caused my first gray hairs.' It was little wonder that he persuaded young Duffy to abandon the drama. He was not meant for the higher planes of our art. Now our young friend here" — he pointed to the perspiring Merton Gill — "doesn't even seem able to master a simple dance step. I might say that he seems to out-Duffy Duffy — for Duffy could dance after a fashion."

"He'll make the grade yet," replied his daughter grimly, and again the music sounded. Merton Gill continued unconscious of his feet, or, remembering them, he became deaf to the music. But the girl brightened with a sudden thought when next they rested.

"I got it!" she announced. "We'll have about 200 feet of this for the next picture — you trying to dance just the way you been doing with me. If you don't close to a good hand I'll eat my last pay-check."

The lessons ceased. She seemed no longer to think it desirable that her pupil should become proficient in the modern steps. He was puzzled by her decision. Why should one of Baird's serious plays need an actor who forgot his feet in a dance?

There were more social evenings at the Montague home. Twice the gathering was enlarged by other members of the film colony, a supper was served and poker played for inconsiderable stakes. In this game of chance the Montague girl proved to be conservative, not to say miserly, and was made to suffer genuinely when Merton Gill displayed a reckless spirit in the betting. That he amassed winnings of 98 cents one night did not reassure her. She pointed out that he might easily have lost this sum.

She was indeed being a mother to the defenseless boy. It was after a gambling session that she demanded to be told what he was doing with his salary. His careless hazarding of poker-chips had caused her to be fearful of his general money sense.

Merton Gill had indeed been reckless. He was now, he felt, actually one of the Hollywood set. He wondered how Tessie Kearns would regard his progress. Would she be alarmed to know he attended those gay parties that so often brought the film colony into unfavorable public notice? Jolly dinners, dancing, gambling, drinking with actresses — for Mr. Montague had at last turned out a beer that met with the approval not only of his guests but of his own more exacting family. The vivacious brew would now and again behave unreasonably at the moment of being released, but it was potable when subdued.

It was a gay life, Merton felt. And as for the Montague girl's questions and warnings about his money, he would show her! He had, of course, discharged his debt to her in the first two weeks of his work with Baird. Now he would show her what he really thought of money.

He would buy her a gift whose presentation should mark a certain great occasion. It should occur on the eve of his screen debut, and would fittingly testify his gratitude. For the girl, after all, had made him what he was. And the first piece was close to its premiere. Already he had seen advance notices in the newspapers. The piece was called *Hearts On Fire*, and in it, so the notices said, the comedy manager had at last realized an ambition long nourished. He had done something new and something big: a big thing done in a big way. The Montague girl would see that the leading man who had done so much to insure the success of Baird's striving for the worthwhile drama was not unforgetful of her favors and continuous solicitude.

He thought first of a ring, but across the blank brick wall of the jewelry shop he elected to patronize was an enormous sign in white: The House of Lucky Wedding Rings. This staring announcement so alarmed him that he not only abandoned the plan for a ring-any sort of ring might be misconstrued, he saw-but in an excess of caution chose another establishment not so outspoken. If it kept wedding rings at all, it was decently reticent about them, and it did keep a profusion of other trinkets about which a possible recipient could entertain no false notions. Wrist watches, for example. No one could find subtle or hidden meanings in a wrist watch.

He chose a bauble that glittered prettily on its black silk bracelet, and was not shocked in the least when told by the engaging salesman that its price was a sum for which in the old days Gashwiler had demanded a good 10 weeks of his life. Indeed it seemed rather cheap to him when he remembered the event it should celebrate. Still, it was a pleasing trifle and did not look cheap.

"Do you warrant it to keep good time?" he sternly demanded.

The salesman became diplomatic, though not without an effect of genial man-to-man frankness. "Well, I guess you and I both know what women's bracelet-watches are." He smiled a superior masculine smile that drew his customer within the informed brotherhood. "Now here, there's a platinum little thing that costs 750, and this one you like will keep just as good time as that one that costs 600 more. What could be fairer than that?"

"All right," said the customer. "I'll take it." During the remaining formalities attending the purchase the salesman, observing that he dealt with a tolerant man of the world, became even franker. "Of course no one," he remarked pleasantly while couching the purchase in a chaste bed of white satin, "expects women's bracelet-watches to keep time. Not even the women."

"Want 'em for looks," said the customer.

"You've hit it, you've hit it!" exclaimed the salesman delightedly, as if the customer had expertly probed the heart of a world-old mystery.

He had now but to await his great moment. The final scenes of the new piece were shot. Again he was resting between pictures. As the date for showing the first piece drew near he was puzzled to notice that both Baird and the Montague girl curiously avoided any mention of it. Several times he referred to it in their presence, but they seemed resolutely deaf to his "Well, I see the big show opens Monday night."

He wondered if there could be some recondite bit of screen etiquette which he was infringing. Actors were superstitious, he knew. Perhaps it boded bad luck to talk of a forthcoming production. Baird and the girl not only ignored his reference to Hearts on Fire, but they left Baird looking curiously secretive and the Montague girl looking curiously frightened. It perplexed him. Once he was smitten with a quick fear that his own work in this serious drama had not met the expectations of the manager.

However, in this he must be wrong, for Baird not only continued cordial but, as the girl had prophesied, he urged upon his new actor the signing of a long-time contract. The Montague girl had insisted upon being present at this interview, after forbidding Merton to put his name to any contract of which she did not approve. "I told Jeff right out that I was protecting you," she said. "He understands he's got to be reasonable."

It appeared, as they set about Baird's desk in the Buckeye office, that she had been right. Baird submitted rather gracefully, after but slight demur, to the terms which Miss Montague imposed in behalf of her protege. Under her approving eye Merton Gill affixed his name to a contract by which Baird was to pay him a salary of 250 dollars a week for three years.

It seemed an incredible sum. As he blotted his signature he was conscious of a sudden pity for the manager. The Montague girl had been hard — hard as nails, he thought — and Baird, a victim to his own good nature, would probably lose a great deal of money. He resolved never to press his advantage over a man who had been caught in a weak moment.

"I just want to say, Mr. Baird," he began, "that you needn't be afraid I'll hold you to this paper if you find it's too much money to pay me. I wouldn't have taken it at all if it hadn't been for her." He pointed an almost accusing finger at the girl.

Baird grinned; the girl patted his hand. Even at grave moments she was a patter. "That's all right, Son," she said soothingly. "Jeff's got all the best of it, and Jeff knows it, too. Don't you, Jeff?"

"Well —" Baird considered. "If his work keeps up I'm not getting any the worst of it."

"You said it. You know very well what birds will be looking for this boy next week, and what money they'll have in their mitts.

"Maybe," said Baird.

"Well, you got the best of it, and you deserve to have. I ain't ever denied that, have I? You've earned the best of it the way you've handled him. All I'm here for, I didn't want you to have too much the best of it, see? I think I treated you well."

"You're all right, Flips."

"Well, everything's jake, then?"

"Everything's jake with me."

"All right! And about his work keeping up — trust your old friend and well-wisher. And say, Jeff —" Her eyes gleamed reminiscently. "You ain't caught him dancing yet. Well — wait, that's all. We'll put on a fox-trot in the next picture that will sure hog the footage."

As this dialogue progressed, Merton had felt more and more like a child in the presence of grave and knowing elders. They had seemed to forget him, to forget that the amazing contract just signed bore his name. He thought the Montague girl was taking a great deal upon herself. Her face, he noted, when she had stated terms to Baird, was the face she wore when risking a small bet at poker on a high hand. She seemed old, indeed. But he knew how he was going to make her feel younger. In his pocket was a gift of rare beauty, even if you couldn't run railway trains by it. And pretty things made a child of her.

Baird shook hands with him warmly at parting. "It'll be a week yet before we start on the new piece. Have a good time. Oh, yes, and drop around some time next week if there's any little thing you want to talk over — or maybe you don't understand."

He wondered if this were a veiled reference to the piece about to be shown. Certainly nothing more definite was said about it. Yet it was a thing that must be of momentous interest to the manager, and the manager must know that it would be thrilling to the actor.

He left with the Montague girl, who had become suddenly grave and quiet. But outside the Holden lot, with one of those quick transitions he had so often remarked in her, she brightened with a desperate sort of gaiety.

"I'll tell you what!" she exclaimed. "Let's go straight down town — it'll be six by the time we get there — and have the best dinner money can buy: lobster and chicken and vanilla ice-cream and everything, right in a real restaurant — none of this tray stuff — and I'll let you pay for it all by yourself. You got a right to, after that contract. And we'll be gay, and all the extra people that's eating in the restaurant'll think we're a couple o' prominent film actors. How about it?" She danced at his side.

"We'll have soup, too," he amended. "One of those thick ones that costs about 60 cents. Sixty cents just for soup!" he repeated, putting a hand to the contract that now stiffened one side of his coat.

"Well, just this once," she agreed. "It might be for the last time."

"Nothing like that," he assured her. "More you spend, more you make — that's my motto."

They waited for a city-bound car, sitting again on the bench that was so outspoken. "You furnish the girl, we furnish the home," it shouted. He put his back against several of the bold words and felt of the bracelet-watch in his pocket.

"It might be the last time for me," insisted the girl. "I feel as if I might die most any time. My health's breaking down under the strain. I feel kind of a fever coming on right this minute."

"Maybe you shouldn't go out."

"Yes, I should."

They boarded the car and reached the real restaurant, a cozy and discreet resort up a flight of carpeted stairs. Side by side on a seat that ran along the wall they sat at a table for two and the dinner was ordered. "Ruin yourself if you want to," said the girl as her host included celery and olives in the menu. "Go on and order prunes, too, for all I care. I'm reckless. Maybe I'll never have another dinner, the way this fever's coming on. Feel my hand."

Under the table she wormed her hand into his, and kept it there until food came. "Do my eyes look very feverish?" she asked.

"Not so very," he assured her, covering an alarm he felt for the first time. She did appear to be feverish, and the anxiety of her manner deepened as the meal progressed. It developed quickly that she had but scant appetite for the choice food now being served. She could only taste bits here and there. Her plates were removed with their delicacies almost intact. Between courses her hand would seek his, gripping it as if in some nameless dread. He became worried about her state; his own appetite suffered.

Once she said as her hot hand clung to his, "I know where you'll be tomorrow night." Her voice grew mournful, despairing. "And I know perfectly well it's no good asking you to stay away."

He let this pass. Could it be that the girl was already babbling in delirium?

"And all the time," she presently went on, "I'll simply be sick a-bed, picking at the covers, all blue around the gills. That'll be me, while you're off to your old motion picture — 'the so-called art of the motion picture,'" she concluded with a careful imitation of her father's manner.

He tried to determine whether she were serious or jesting. You never could tell about this girl. Whatever it was, it made him uneasy.

Outside he wished to take her home in a taxi-cab, but she would not hear to this. "We'll use the town-car, Gaston," she announced with a flash of her old manner as she waved to an on-coming street-car. During the long ride that followed she was silent but restless, tapping her foot, shifting in her seat, darting her head about. The one thing she did steadily was to clutch his arm.

During the walk from the car to the Montague house she twice indulged in her little dance step, even as she clung to the arm, but each time she seemed to think little of it and resumed a steady pace, her head down. The house was dark. Without speaking she unlocked the door and drew him into the little parlor.

"Stand right on that spot," she ordered, with a final pat of his shoulder, and made her way to the dining room beyond where she turned on a single light that faintly illumined the room in which he waited. She came back to him, removed the small cloth hat, tossed it to a chair, and faced him silently.

The light from the other room shone across her eyes and revealed them to him shadowy and mysterious. Her face was set in some ominous control. At last she looked away from him and began in a strained voice, "If anything happens to me —"

He thought it time to end this nonsense. She might be feverish, but it could be nothing so serious as she was intimating. He clutched the gift. "Sarah," he said lightly, "I got a little something for you — see what I mean?" He thrust the package into her weakly yielding hands.

She studied it in the dusk, turning it over and over. Then with no word to him she took it to the dining room where under the light she opened it. He heard a smothered exclamation that seemed more of dismay than the delight he expected, though he saw that she was holding the watch against her wrist. She came back to the dusk of the parlor, beginning on the way one of her little skipping dance steps, which she quickly suppressed. She was replacing the watch on its splendid couch of satin and closing the box.

"I never saw such a man!" she exclaimed with an irritation that he felt to be artificial. "After all you've been through, I should think you'd have learned the value of money. Anyway, it's too beautiful for me. And anyway, I couldn't take it — not tonight, anyway. And anyway —" Her voice had acquired a huskiness in this speech that now left her incoherent, and the light revealed a wetness in her eyes. She dabbed at them with a handkerchief. "Of course you can take it tonight," he said in masterful tones, "after all you've done for me."

"Now you listen," she began. "You don't know all I've done for you. You don't know me at all. Suppose something came out about me that you didn't think I'd 'a' been guilty of. You can't ever tell about people in this business. You don't know me at all-not one little bit. I might 'a' done lots of things that would turn you against me. I tell you you got to wait and find out about things. I haven't the nerve to tell you, but you'll find out soon enough —"

The expert in photoplays suffered a sudden illumination. This was a scene he could identify — a scene in which the woman trembled upon the verge of revealing to the man certain sinister details of her past, spurred thereto by a scoundrel who blackmailed her. He studied the girl in a new light. Undoubtedly, from her words, he saw one panic-stricken by the threatened exposure of some dreadful complication in her own past. Certainly she was suffering.

"I don't care if this fever does carry me off," she went on. "I know you could never feel the same toward me after you found out —"

Again she was dabbing at her eyes, this time with the sleeve of her jacket. A suffering woman stood before him. She who had always shown herself so competent to meet trouble with laughing looks was being overthrown by this nameless horror. Suddenly he knew that to him it didn't matter so very much what crime she had been guilty of.

"I don't care what you've done," he said, his own voice husky. She continued to weep.

He felt himself grow hot. "Listen here, Kid" — He now spoke with more than a touch of the bully in his tone — "stop this nonsense. You — you come here and give me a good big kiss — see what I mean?"

She looked up at him from wet eyes, and amazingly through her anguish she grinned. "You win!" she said, and came to him.

He was now the masterful one. He took her protectingly in his arms. He kissed her though with no trace of the Parmalee technique. His screen experience might never have been. It was more like the dead days of Edwina May Pulver.

"Now you stop it," he soothed —"all this nonsense!" His cheek was against hers and his arms held her. "What do I care what you've done in your past — what do I care? And listen here, Kid" — There was again the brutal note of the bully in his voice — "don't ever do any more of those stunts — see what I mean? None of that falling off streetcars or houses or anything. Do you hear?"

He felt that he was being masterful indeed. He had swept her off her feet. Probably now she would weep violently and sob out her confession. But a moment later he was reflecting, as he had so many times before reflected, that you never could tell about the girl. In his embrace she had become astoundingly calm. That emotional crisis threatening to beat down all her reserves had passed. She reached up and almost meditatively pushed back the hair from his forehead, regarding him with eyes that were still shadowed but dry. Then she gave him a quick little hug and danced away. It was no time for dancing, he thought.

"Now you sit down," she ordered. She was almost gay again, yet with a nervous, desperate gaiety that would at moments die to a brooding solemnity. "And listen," she began, when he had seated himself in bewilderment at her sudden change of mood, "you'll be off to your old motion picture tomorrow night, and I'll be here sick in bed —"

"I won't go if you don't want me to," he put in quickly.

"That's no good; you'd have to go sometime. The quicker the better, I guess. I'll go myself sometime, if I ever get over this disease that's coming on me. Anyway, you go, and then if you ever see me again you can give me this —" She quickly came to put the watch back in his hands. "Yes, yes, take it. I won't have it till you give it to me again, if I'm still alive." She held up repulsing hands. "Now we've had one grand little evening, and I'll let you go." She went to stand by the door.

He arose and stood by her. "All this nonsense!" he grumbled. "I — I won't stand for it — see what I mean?" Very masterfully again he put his arms about her. "Say," he demanded, "are you afraid of me like you said you'd always been afraid of men?"

"Yes, I am. I'm afraid of you a whole lot. I don't know how you'll take it." "Take what?"

"Oh, anything — anything you're going to get."

"Well, you don't seem to be afraid of me."

"I am, more than anyone."

"Well, Sarah, you needn't be — no matter what you've done. You just forget it and give me a good big —"

"I'm glad I'm using my own face in this scene," murmured Sarah.

Down at the corner, waiting for his car, he paced back and forth in front of the bench with its terse message — "You furnish the girl, we furnish the house" — Sarah was a funny little thing with all that nonsense about what he would find out. Little he cared if she'd done something — forgery, murder, anything.

He paused in his stride and addressed the vacant bench: "Well, I've done my part."

CHAPTER XVIII

"FIVE REELS, 500 LAUGHS"

It occurred to him the next morning that he might have taken too lightly Sarah's foreboding of illness. Reviewing her curious behavior he thought it possible she might be in for something serious.

But a midday telephone call at the Montague home brought assurances from the mother that quieted this fear. Sarah complained of not feeling well, and was going to spend a quiet day at home. But Mrs. Montague was certain it was nothing serious. No; she had no temperature. No fever at all. She was just having a spell of thinking about things, sort of grouchy like. She had been grouchy to both her parents. Probably because she wasn't working. No, she said she wouldn't come to the telephone. She also said she was in a bad way and might pass out any minute. But that was just her kidding. It was kind of Mr. Gill to call up. He wasn't to worry.

He continued to worry, however, until the nearness of his screen debut drove Sarah to the back of his mind. Undoubtedly it was just her nonsense. And in the meantime, that long-baffled wish to see himself in a serious drama was about to be gratified in fullest measure. He was glad the girl had not suggested that she be with him on this tremendous occasion. He wanted to be quite alone, solitary in the crowd, free to enjoy his own acting without pretense of indifference.

The Pattersons, of course, were another matter. He had told them of his approaching debut and they were making an event of it. They would attend, though he would not sit with them. Mr. Patterson in his black suit, his wife in society raiment, would sit downstairs and would doubtless applaud their lodger; but he would be remote from them; in a far corner of the topmost gallery, he first thought, for Hearts on Fire was to be shown in one of the big down-town theaters where a prominent member of its cast could lose himself.

He had told the Pattersons a little about the story. It was pretty pathetic in spots, he said, but it all came right in the end, and there were some good Western scenes. When the Pattersons said he must be very good in it, he found himself unable to achieve the light fashion of denial and protestation that would have become him. He said he had struggled to give the world something better and finer. For a moment he was moved to confess that Mrs. Patterson, in the course of his struggles, had come close to losing ten dollars, but he mastered the wild impulse. Some day, after a few more triumphs, he might laughingly confide this to her.

The day was long. Slothfully it dragged hours that seemed endless across the company of shining dreams that he captained. He was early at the theater, first of early comers, and entered quickly, foregoing even a look at the huge lithographs in front that would perhaps show his very self in some gripping scene.

With an empty auditorium to choose from, he compromised on a balcony seat. Down below would doubtless be other members of the company, probably Baird himself, and he did not wish to be recognized. He must be alone with his triumph. And the loftier gallery would be too far away.

The house filled slowly. People sauntered to their seats as if the occasion were ordinary; even when the seats were occupied and the orchestra had played, there ensued the annoying delays of an educational film and a travelogue. Upon this young actor's memory would be forever seared the information that the conger eel lays 15 million eggs at one time and that the inhabitants of Upper Burmah have quaint native pastimes. These things would stay with him, but they were unimportant. Even the prodigal fecundity of the conger eel left him cold.

He gripped the arms of his seat when the cast of *Hearts on Fire* was flung to the screen. He caught his own name instantly, and was puzzled. "Clifford Armytage — By Himself." Someone had bungled that, but no matter. Then at once he was seeing that first scene of his. As a popular screen idol he breakfasted in his apartment, served by a valet who was a hero worshipper.

He was momentarily disquieted by the frank adoration of the cross-eyed man in this part. While acting the scene, he remembered now that he had not always been able to observe his valet. There were moments when he seemed over-emphatic. The valet was laughed at. The watcher's sympathy went out to Baird, who must be seeing his serious effort taken too lightly.

There came the scene where he looked at the photograph album. But now his turning of the pages was interspersed with close-ups of the portraits he regarded so admiringly. And these astonishingly proved to be enlarged stills of Clifford Armytage, the art studies of Lowell Hardy. It was puzzling. On the screen he capably beamed the fondest admiration, almost reverent in its intensity — and there would appear the still of Merton bidding an emotional farewell to his horse. The very novelty of it held him for a moment — Gashwiler's Dexter actually on the screen! He was aroused by the hearty laughter of an immense audience.

"It's Parmalee," announced a hoarse neighbor on his right. "He's imitatin' Harold! Say, the kid's clever!"

The laughter continued during the album scene. He thought of Baird, somewhere in that audience, suffering because his play was made fun of. He wished he could remind him that scenes were to follow which would surely not be taken lightly. For himself, he was feeling that at least his strong likeness to Parmalee had been instantly admitted. They were laughing, as the Montague girl had laughed that first morning, because the resemblance was so striking. But now on the screen, after the actor's long fond look at himself, came the words, "The Only Man He Ever Loved."

Laughter again. The watcher felt himself grow hot. Had Baird been betrayed by one of his staff?

The scene with the letters followed. Clothes baskets of letters. His own work, as he opened a few from the top, was all that he could have wished. He was finely Harold Parmalee, and again the hoarse neighbor whispered, "Ain't he got Parmalee dead, though?"

"Poor, silly little girls!" the screen exclaimed, and the audience became noisy. Undoubtedly it was a tribute to his perfection in the Parmalee manner. But he was glad that now there would come acting at which no one could laugh. There was the delicatessen shop, the earnest young cashier and his poor old mother who mopped. He saw himself embrace her and murmur words of encouragement, but incredibly there were giggles from the audience, doubtless from base souls who were impervious to pathos. The giggles coalesced to a general laugh when the poor old mother, again mopping on the floor, was seen to say, "I hate these mopping mothers. You get took with house-maid's knee in the first reel."

Again he was seized with a fear that one of Baird's staff had been clumsy with subtitles. His eyes flew to his own serious face when the silly words had gone.

The drama moved. Indeed the action of the shadows was swifter than he supposed it would be. The dissolute son of the proprietor came on to dust the wares and to elicit a laugh when he performed a bit of business that had escaped Merton at the time. Against the wire screen that covered the largest cheese on the counter he placed a placard, "Dangerous. Do not Annoy."

Probably Baird had not known of this clowning. And there came another subtitle that would dismay Baird when the serious young bookkeeper enacted his scene with the proprietor's lovely daughter, for she was made to say: "You love above your station. Ours is 125th Street; you get off at 59th."

He was beginning to feel confused. A sense of loss, of panic, smote him. His own part was the intensely serious thing he had played, but in some subtle way even that was being made funny. He could not rush to embrace his old mother without exciting laughter.

The robbery of the safe was effected by the dissolute son, the father broke in upon the love scene, discovered the loss of his money, and accused an innocent man. Merton felt that he here acted superbly. His long look at the girl for whom he was making the supreme sacrifice brought tears to his own eyes, but still the witless audience snickered. Unobserved by the others, the old mother now told her son the whereabouts of the stolen money, and he saw himself secure the paper sack of bills from the ice-box. He detected the half-guilty look of which he had spoken to Baird. Then he read his own incredible speech — "I better take this cool million. It might get that poor lad into trouble!" Again the piece had been hurt by a wrong subtitle. But perhaps the audience laughed because it was accustomed to laugh at Baird's productions. Perhaps it had not realized that he was now attempting one of the worthwhile things. This reasoning was refuted as he watched what occurred after he had made his escape.

His flight was discovered, policemen entered, a rapid search behind counters ensued. In the course of this the wire screen over the biggest cheese was knocked off the counter. The cheese leaped to the floor, and the searchers, including the policemen, fled in panic through the front door. The Montague girl, the last to escape, was seen to announce, "The big cheese is loose — it's eating all the little ones!"

A band of intrepid firemen, protected by masks and armed with axes, rushed in. A terrific struggle ensued. The delicatessen shop was wrecked. And through it all the old mother continued to mop the floor. Merton Gill, who had first grown hot, was now cold. Icy drops were on his chilled brow. How had *Hearts on Fire* gone wrong?

Then they were in the great open spaces of the Come All Ye dance hall. There was the young actor in his Buck Benson costume, protecting his mother from the brutality of a Mexican, getting his man later by firing directly into a mirror — Baird had said it would come right in the exposure, but it hadn't. And the witless cackled.

He saw his struggle with the detective. With a real thrill he saw himself bear his opponent to the ground, then hurl him high and far into the air, to be impaled upon the antlers of an elk's head suspended back of the bar. He saw himself lightly dust his sleeves after this feat, and turn aside with the words, "That's one Lodge he can join."

Then followed a scene he had not been allowed to witness. There swung Marcel, the detective, played too emphatically by the cross-eyed man. An antler point suspended him by the seat of his trousers. He hung limply a moment, then took from his pocket a saw with which he reached up to contrive his release. He sawed through the antler and fell. He tried to stand erect, but appeared to find this impossible. A subtitle announced: "He had put a permanent wave in Marcel."

This base fooling was continuously blown upon by gales of stupid laughter. But not yet did Merton Gill know the worst. The merriment persisted through his most affecting bit, the farewell to his old pal outside — how could they have laughed at a simple bit of pathos like that? But the watching detective was seen to weep bitterly.

"Look a' him doin' Buck Benson," urged the hoarse neighbor gleefully. "You got to hand it to that kid — say, who is he, anyway?"

Followed the thrilling leap from a second-story window to the back of the waiting pal. The leap began thrillingly, but not only was it shown that the escaping man had donned a coat and a false mustache in the course of his fall, but at its end he was revealed slowly, very slowly, clambering into the saddle!

They had used here, he saw, one of those slow cameras that seem to suspend all action interminably, a cruel device in this instance. And for his actual escape, when he had ridden the horse beyond camera range at a safe walk, they had used another camera that gave the effect of intense speed. The old horse had walked, but with an air of swiftness that caused the audience intense delight.

Entered Marcel, the detective, in another scene Merton had not watched. He emerged from the dance hall to confront a horse that remained, an aged counterpart of the horse Merton had ridden off. Marcel stared intently into the beast's face, whereupon it reared and plunged as if terrified by the spectacle of the cross-eyed man.

Merton recalled the horse in the village that had seemed to act so intelligently. Probably a shot-gun had stimulated the present scene. The detective thereupon turned aside, hastily donned his false mustache and Sherlock Holmes cap, and the deceived horse now permitted him to mount. He, too, walked off to the necromancy of a lens that multiplied his pace a thousandfold. And the audience rocked in its seats.

One horse still remained before the dance hall. The old mother emerged. With one anguished look after the detective, she gathered up her disreputable skirts and left the platform in a flying leap to land in the saddle. There was no trickery about the speed at which her horse, belabored with the mop-pail, galloped in pursuit of the others. A subtitle recited: "She has watched her dear ones leave the old nest flat. Now she must go out over the hills and mop the other side of them!"

Now came the sensational capture by lasso of the detective. But the captor had not known that, as he dragged his quarry at the rope's end, the latter had somehow possessed himself of a sign which he later walked in with, a sign reading, "Join the Good Roads Movement!" nor that the faithful old mother had ridden up to deposit her inverted mop-pail over his head.

Merton Gill had twice started to leave. He wanted to leave. But each time he found himself chained there by the evil fascination of this monstrous parody. He remained to learn that the Montague girl had come out to the great open spaces to lead a band of train-robbers from the "Q.T. ranch."

He saw her ride beside a train and cast her lasso over the stack of the locomotive. He saw her pony settle back on its haunches while the rope grew taut and the train was forced to a halt. He saw the passengers lined up by the wayside and forced to part with their valuables. Later, when the band returned to the ranch with their booty, he saw the dissolute brother, after the treasure was divided, winning it back to the family coffers with his dice. He saw the stricken father playing golf on his bicycle in grotesque imitation of a polo player.

And still, so incredible the revealment, he had not in the first shock of it seemed to consider Baird in any way to blame. Baird had somehow been deceived by his actors. Yet a startling suspicion was forming amid his mental flurries, a suspicion that bloomed to certainty when he saw himself the ever-patient victim of the genuine hidalgo spurs.

Baird had said he wanted the close-ups merely for use in determining how the spurs could be mastered, yet here they were. Merton Gill caught the spurs in undergrowth and caught them in his own chaps, arising from each fall with a look of gentle determination that appealed strongly to the throng of lackwits. They shrieked at each of his failures, even when he ran to greet his pictured sweetheart and fell headlong. They found the comedy almost unbearable when at Baird's direction he had begun to toe in as he walked. And he had fallen clumsily again when he flew to that last glad rendezvous where the pair were irised out in a love triumphant, while the old mother mopped a large rock in the background. An intervening close-up of this rock revealed her tearful face as she cleansed the granite surface. Above her loomed a painted exhortation to "Use Wizard Spine Pills." And of this pathetic old creature he was made to say, even as he clasped the beloved in his arms — "Remember, she is my mother. I will not desert her now just because I am rich and grand!"

At last he was free. Amid applause that was long and sincere he gained his feet and pushed a way out. His hoarse neighbor was saying, "Who is the kid, anyway? Ain't he a wonder!"

He pulled his hat down, dreading he might be recognized and shamed before these shallow fools. He froze with the horror of what he had been unable to look away from. The ignominy of it! And now, after those spurs, he knew full well that Baird had betrayed him. As the words shaped in his mind, a monstrous echo of them reverberated through its caverns — the Montague girl had betrayed him!

He understood her now, and burned with memories of her uneasiness the night before. She had been suffering acutely from remorse; she had sought to cover it with pleas of physical illness. At the moment he was conscious of no feeling toward her save wonder that she could so coolly have played him false. But the thing was not to be questioned. She — and Baird — had made a fool of him.

As he left the theater, the crowd about him commented approvingly on the picture: "Who's this new comedian?" he heard a voice inquire. But "Ain't he a wonder!" seemed to be the sole reply.

He flushed darkly. So they thought him a comedian. Well, Baird wouldn't think so — not after tomorrow. He paused outside the theater now to study the lithograph in colors. There he hurled Marcel to the antlers of the elk. The announcement was "*Hearts on Fire*! A Jeff Baird Comedy. Five Reels, 500 Laughs."

Baird, he sneeringly reflected, had kept faith with his patrons if not with one of his actors. But how he had profaned the sunlit glories of the great open West and its virile drama! And the spurs, as he had promised the unsuspecting wearer, had stood out! The horror of it, blinding, desolating!

And he had as good as stolen that money himself, taking it out to the great open spaces to spend in a bar-room. Baird's serious effort had turned out to be a wild, inconsequent farrago of the most painful nonsense.

But it was over for Merton Gill. The golden bowl was broken, the silver cord was loosed. Tomorrow he would tear up Baird's contract and hurl the pieces in Baird's face. As to the Montague girl, that deceiving jade was hopeless. Never again could he trust her.

In a whirling daze of resentment he boarded a car for the journey home. A group seated near him still laughed about Hearts on Fire. "I thought he'd kill me with those spurs," declared an otherwise sanely behaving young woman — "that hurt, embarrassed look on his face every time he'd get up!"

He cowered in his seat. And he remembered another ordeal he must probably face when he reached home. He hoped the Pattersons would be in bed, and walked up and down before the gate when he saw the house still alight. But the light stayed, and at last he nerved himself for a possible encounter. He let himself in softly, still hoping he could gain his room undiscovered; but Mrs. Patterson framed herself in the lighted door of the living room and became exclamatory at sight of him.

And he who had thought to stand before these people in shame to receive their condolences now perceived that his trial would be of another but hardly less-distressing sort. For somehow, so dense were these good folks, that he must seem to be not displeased with his own performance. Amazingly they congratulated him, struggling with reminiscent laughter as they did so.

"And you never told us you was one of them funny comedians," chided Mrs. Patterson. "We thought you was just a beginner, and here you got the biggest part in the picture! Say, the way you acted when you'd pick yourself up after them spurs threw you — I'll wake up in the night laughing at that."

"And the way he kept his face so straight when them other funny ones was cutting their capers all around him," observed Mr. Patterson.

"Yes! wasn't it wonderful, Jed, the way he never let on, keeping his face as serious as if he'd been in a serious play?"

"I like to fell off my seat," added Mr. Patterson.

"I'll tell you something, Mr. Armytage," began Mrs. Patterson with a suddenly serious manner of her own, "I never been one to flatter folks to their faces unless I felt it from the bottom of my heart — I never been that kind; when I tell a person such-and-such about themselves they can take it for the truth's own truth; so you can believe me now — I saw lots of times in that play tonight when you was even funnier than the cross-eyed man."

The young actor was regarding her strangely; seemingly he wished to acknowledge this compliment but could find no suitable words. "Yes, you can blush and hem and haw," went on his critic, "but any one knows me I'll tell you I mean it when I talk that way — yes, sir, funnier than the cross-eyed man himself. My, I guess the neighbors'll be talking soon's they find out we got someone as important as you be in our spare-room — and, Mr. Armytage, I want you to give me a signed photograph of yourself, if you'll be so good."

He escaped at last, dizzy from the maelstrom of conflicting emotions that had caught and whirled him. It had been impossible not to appear, and somehow difficult not to feel, gratified under this heartfelt praise. He had been bound to appear pleased but incredulous, even when she pronounced him superior, at times, to the cross-eyed man — though the word she used was "funnier."

Betrayed by his friends, stricken, disconsolate, in a panic of despair, he had yet seemed glad to hear that he had been "funny." He flew to the sanctity of his room. Not again could he bear to be told that the acting which had been his soul's high vision was a thing for merriment.

He paced his room a long time, a restless, defenseless victim to recurrent visions of his shame. Implacably they returned to torture him. Reel after reel of the ignoble stuff, spawned by the miscreant, Baird, flashed before him; a world of base painted shadows in which he had been the arch offender.

Again and again he tried to make clear to himself just why his own acting should have caused mirth. Surely he had been serious; he had given the best that was in him.

And the groundlings had guffawed!

Perhaps it was a puzzle he could never solve. And now he first thought of the new piece.

This threw him into fresh panic. What awful things, with his high and serious acting, would he have been made to do in that? Patiently, one by one, he went over the scenes in which he had appeared. Dazed, confused, his recollection could bring to him little that was ambiguous in them. But also he had played through *Hearts on Fire* with little suspicion of its low intentions.

He went to bed at last, though to toss another hour in fruitless effort to solve this puzzle and to free his eyes of those flashing infamies of the night. Ever and again as he seemed to become composed, free at last of tormenting visions, a mere subtitle would flash in his brain, as where the old mother, when he first punished her insulter, was made by the screen to call out, "Kick him on the knee-cap, too!"

But the darkness refreshed his tired eyes, and sun at last brought him a merciful outlet from a world in which you could act your best and still be funnier than a cross-eyed man.

He awakened long past his usual hour and occupied his first conscious moments in convincing himself that the scandal of the night before had not been a bad dream. The shock was a little dulled now. He began absurdly to remember the comments of those who had appeared to enjoy the unworthy entertainment. Undoubtedly many people had mentioned him with warm approval. But such praise was surely nothing to take comfort from. He was aroused from this retrospection by a knock on his door. It proved to be Mr. Patterson bearing a tray. "Mrs. P. thought that you being up so late last night mebbe would like a cup of coffee and a bite of something before you went out." The man's manner was newly respectful. In this house, at least, Merton Gill was still someone.

He thanked his host, and consumed the coffee and toast with a novel sense of importance. The courtesy was unprecedented. Mrs. Patterson had indeed been sincere. And scarcely had he finished dressing when Mr. Patterson was again at the door.

"A gentleman downstairs to see you, Mr. Armytage. He says his name is Walberg but you don't know him. He says it's a business matter."

"Very well, I'll be down." A business matter? He had no business matters with any one except Baird.

He was smitten with a quick and quite illogical fear. Perhaps he would not have to tear up that contract and hurl it in the face of the manager who had betrayed him. Perhaps the manager himself would do the tearing. Perhaps Baird, after seeing the picture, had decided that Merton Gill would not do. Instantly he felt resentful. Hadn't he given the best that was in him? Was it his fault if other actors had turned into farce one of the worthwhile things?

He went to meet Mr. Walberg with this resentment so warm that his greeting of the strange gentleman was gruff and short. The caller, an alert, businesslike man, came at once to his point. He was, it proved, not the representative of a possibly repenting Baird. He was, on the contrary, representing a rival producer. He extended his card — The Bigart Comedies.

"I got your address from the Holden office, Mr. Armytage. I guess I routed you out of bed, eh? Well, it's like this, if you ain't sewed up with Baird yet, the Bigart people would like to talk a little business to you. How about it?"

"Business?" Mr. Armytage fairly exploded this. He was unhappy and puzzled; in consequence, unamiable.

"Sure, business," confirmed Mr. Walberg. "I understand you just finished another five-reeler for the Buckeye outfit, but how about some stuff for us now? We can give you as good a company as that one last night and a good line of comedy. We got a gag man that simply never gets to the end of his string. He's doping out something right now that would fit you like a glove — and say, it would be a great idea to kind 'a' specialize in that spur act of yours. That got over big. We could work it in again. An act like that's good for a million laughs."

Mr. Armytage eyed Mr. Walberg coldly. Even Mr. Walberg felt an extensive area of glaciation setting in.

"I wouldn't think of it," said the actor, still gruffly.

"Do you mean that you can't come to the Bigart at all — on any proposition?"

"That's what I mean," confirmed Mr. Armytage.

"Would 350 a week interest you?"

"No," said Mr. Armytage, though he gulped twice before achieving it.

Mr. Walberg reported to his people that this Armytage lad was one hard-boiled proposition. He'd seen lots of 'em in his time, but this bird was a wonder.

Yet Mr. Armytage was not really so granitic of nature as the Bigart emissary had thought him. He had begun the interview with a smoldering resentment due to a misapprehension; he had been outraged by a suggestion that the spurs be again put to their offensive use; and he had been stunned by an offer of 350 dollars a week. That was all.

Here was a new angle to the puzzles that distracted him. He was not only praised by the witless, but he had been found desirable by certain discerning overlords of filmdom. What could be the secret of a talent that caused people, after viewing it but once, to make reckless offers?

And another thing — why had he allowed Baird to "sew him up"? The Montague girl again occupied the foreground of his troubled musings. She, with her airs of wise importance, had helped to sew him up. She was a helpless thing, after all, and false of nature. He would have matters out with her this very day. But first he must confront Baird in a scene of scorn and reprobation.

On the car he became aware that far back in remote caverns of his mind there ran a teasing memory of some book on the shelves of the Simsbury public library. He was sure it was not a book he had read. It was merely the title that hid itself. Only this had ever interested him, and it but momentarily. So much he knew. A book's title had lodged in his mind, remained there, and was now curiously stirring in some direct relation to his present perplexities.

But it kept its face averted. He could not read it. Vaguely he identified the nameless book with Tessie Kearns; he could not divine how, because it was not her book and he had never seen it except on the library shelf.

The nameless book persistently danced before him. He was glad of this. It kept him at moments from thinking of the loathly Baird.

CHAPTER XIX

THE TRAGIC COMEDIAN

Penetrating the Holden lot he was relieved to find that he creat-
ed no immediate sensation. People did not halt to point derisive
fingers at him; he had half feared they would. As he approached
the office building he was almost certain he saw Baird turn in
ahead of him. Yet when he entered the outer room of the Buckeye offices a young woman looked up from her typewriter to tell
him that Mr. Baird was not in.

She was a serious-eyed young woman of a sincere manner;
she spoke with certainty of tone. Mr. Baird was not only out, but
he would not be in for several days. His physician had ordered
him to a sanitarium.

The young woman resumed her typing; she did not again,
glance up. The caller seemed to consider waiting on a chance
that she had been misinformed. He was now sure he had seen
Baird enter the building, and the door of his private office was
closed. The caller idled outside the railing, absently regarding
stills of past Buckeye atrocities that had been hung upon the
walls of the office by someone with primitive tastes in decora-
tion. He was debating a direct challenge of the young woman's
veracity.

What would she say if told that the caller meant to wait right
there until Mr. Baird should convalesce? He managed some appraising side-glances at her as she bent over her machine. She
seemed to believe he had already gone.

Then he did go. No good talking that way to a girl. If it had been a man, now — "You tell Mr. Baird that Mr. Gill's got to see him as soon as possible about something important," he directed from the open door.

The young woman raised her serious eyes to his and nodded. She resumed her work. The door closed. Upon its closing the door of Baird's private office opened noiselessly to a crack that sufficed for the speaking voice at very moderate pitch to issue.

"Get Miss Montague on the phone," directed the voice. The door closed noiselessly. Beyond it Mr. Baird was presently speaking in low, sweet tones.

"'Lo, Sister! Listen; that squirrel just boiled in here, and I ducked him. I told the girl I wasn't to be in unless he was laughing all over, and he wasn't doing the least little thing that was anywheres near laughing. See what I mean? It's up to you now. You started it; you got to finish it. I've irised out. Get me?"

On the steps outside the rebuffed Merton Gill glanced at his own natty wrist-watch, bought with some of the later wages of his shame. It was the luncheon hour; mechanically he made his way to the cafeteria. He had ceased to rehearse the speech a doughtier Baird would now have been hearing.

Instead he roughly drafted one that Sarah Nevada Montague could not long evade. Even on her dying bed she would be compelled to listen. The practicing orator with bent head mumbled as he walked. He still mumbled as he indicated a choice of foods at the cafeteria counter; he continued to be thus absorbed as he found a table near the center of the room.

He arranged his assortment of viands. "You led me on, that's what you did," he continued to the absent culprit. "Led me on to make a laughing-stock of myself, that's what you did. Made a fool of me, that's what you did."

"All the same, I can't help thinking he's a harm to the industry," came the crisp tones of Henshaw from an adjoining table. The rehearsing orator glanced up to discover that the director and the sunny-faced brown and gray man he called Governor were smoking above the plates of their finished luncheon.

"I wouldn't worry too much," suggested the cheerful governor.

"But see what he does: he takes the good old reliable, sure-fire stuff and makes fun of it. I admit it's funny to start with, but what'll happen to us if the picture public ever finds that out? What'll we do then for drama — after they've learned to laugh at the old stuff?"

"Tush, tush, my boy!" The Governor waved a half — consumed cigarette until its ash fell. "Never fear. Do you think a thousand Jeff Bairds could make the picture public laugh at the old stuff when it's played straight? They laughed last night, yes; but not so much at the really fine burlesque; they guffawed at the slapstick stuff that went with it. Baird's shrewd. He knows if he played straight burlesque he'd never make a dollar, so notice how he'll give a bit of straight that is genuine art, then a bit of slapstick that any one can get. The slapstick is what carries the show. Real burlesque is criticism, my boy; sometimes the very high-browest sort. It demands sophistication, a pretty high intelligence in the man that gets it.

"All right. Now take your picture public. Twenty million people every day; not the same ones every day, but with same average cranial index, which is low for all but about seven out of every hundred. That's natural because there aren't 20 million people in the world with taste or real intelligence — probably not five million. Well, you take this 20 million bunch that we sell to every day, and suppose they saw that lovely thing last night — don't you know they'd all be back tonight to see a real mopping mother with a real son falsely accused of crime — sure they'd be back, their heads bloody but unbowed. Don't worry; that reliable field marshal, old General Hokum, leads an unbeatable army."

Merton Gill had listened to the beginning of this harangue, but now he savagely devoured food. He thought this so-called Governor was too much like Baird.

"Well, Governor, I hope you're right. But that was pretty keen stuff last night. That first bit won't do Parmalee any good, and that Buck Benson stuff — you can't tell me a little more of that wouldn't make Benson look around for a new play."

"But I do tell you just that. It won't hurt Parmalee a bit; and Benson can go on Bensoning to the end of time — to big money. You keep forgetting this 20-million audience. Go out and buy a picture magazine and read it through, just to remind you. They want hokum, and pay for it. Even this thing of Baird's, with all the saving slapstick, is over the heads of a good half of them. I'll make a bet with you now, anything you name, that it won't gross two thirds as much as Benson's next Western, and in that they'll cry their eyes out when he kisses his horse good-bye. See if they don't. Or see if they don't bawl at the next old gray-haired mother with a mop and a son that gets in bad.

"Why, if you give 'em hokum they don't even demand acting. Look at our own star, Mercer. You know as well as I do that she not only can't act, but she's merely a beautiful moron. In a world where right prevailed she'd be crowned queen of the morons without question. She may have an idea that two and two make four, but if she has it's only because she believes everything she hears. And look at the mail she gets. Every last one of the 20 million has written to tell her what a noble actress she is. She even believes that.

"Baird can keep on with the burlesque stuff, but his little old two-reelers'll probably have to pay for it, especially if he keeps those high-priced people. I'll bet that one new man of his sets him back 750 a week. The Lord knows he's worth every cent of it. My boy, tell me, did you ever in all your life see a lovelier imitation of a perfectly rotten actor? There's an artist for you. Who is he, anyway? Where'd he come from?" Merton Gill again listened; he was merely affecting to busy himself with a fork. It was good acting.

"I don't know," replied Henshaw. "Some of the crowd last night said he was just an extra that Baird dug up on the lot here. And, on the subject of burlesque, they also said Baird was having him do some Edgar Wayne stuff in a new one."

"Fine!" The Governor beamed. "Can't you see him as the honest, likable country boy? I bet he'll be good to his old mother in this one, too, and get the best of the city slickers in the end. For heaven's sake don't let me miss it! This kid last night handed me laughs that were better than a month's vacation for this old carcass of mine. You say he was just an extra?"

"That's what I heard last night. Anyway, he's all you say he is as an artist. Where do you suppose he got it? Do you suppose he's just the casual genius that comes along from time to time? And why didn't he stay 'straight' instead of playing horse with the sacred traditions of our art? That's what troubled me as I watched him. Even in that wild business with the spurs he was the artist every second. He must have tricked those falls but I couldn't catch him at it. Why should such a man tie up with Baird?"

"Ask me something hard. I'd say this bird had been tried out in serious stuff and couldn't make the grade. That's the way he struck me. Probably he once thought he could play Hamlet — one of those boys. Didn't you get the real pathos he'd turn on now and then? He actually had me kind of teary a couple of times. But I could see he'd also make me laugh my head off any time he showed in a straight piece.

"To begin with, look at that low-comedy face of his. And then — something peculiar — even while he's imitating a bad actor you feel somehow that it isn't all imitation. It's art, I grant you, but you feel he'd still be a bad actor if he'd try to imitate a good one. Somehow he found out his limits and decided to be what God meant him to be. Does that answer you? It gives you acting-plus, and if that isn't the plus in this case I miss my guess."

"I suppose you're right — something like that. And of course the real pathos is there. It has to be. There never was a great comedian without it, and this one is great. I admit that, and I admit all you say about our audience. I suppose we can't ever sell to 20 million people a day pictures that make any demand on the human intelligence. But couldn't we sell something better to one million — or a few thousand?"

The Governor dropped his cigarette end into the dregs of his coffee. "We might," he said, "if we were endowed. As it is, to make pictures we must make money. To make money we must sell to the mob. And the mob reaches full mental bloom at the age of 15. It won't buy pictures the average child can't get."

"Of course the art is in its infancy," remarked Henshaw, discarding his own cigarette.

"Ours is the Peter Pan of the arts," announced the Governor, as he rose.

"The Peter Pan of the arts —"

"Yes. I trust you recall the outstanding biological freakishness of Peter."

"Oh!" replied Henshaw.

When Merton Gill dared to glance up a moment later the men were matching coins at the counter. When they went out he left a half-eaten meal and presently might have been observed on a swift-rolling street-car. He mumbled as he blankly surveyed palm-bordered building sites along the way. He was again rehearsing a tense scene with the Montague girl. In actor parlance he was giving himself all the best of it. But they were new lines he mumbled over and over. And he was no longer eluded by the title of that book he remembered on the library shelf at Simsbury. Sitting in the cafeteria listening to strange talk, lashed by cruel memories, it had flashed upon his vision with the stark definition of a screened subtitle. He rang the Montague bell twice before he heard a faint summons to enter. Upon the parlor couch, under blankets that reached her pillowed head, lay Sarah. She was pale and seemed to suffer. She greeted him in a feeble voice, lids fluttering over the fires of that mysterious fever burning far back in her eyes.

"Hullo, Kid," he began brightly. "Here's your watch." Her doubting glance hovered over him as he smiled down at her. "You giving it to me again, Merton?" She seemed unable to conquer a stubborn incredulity.

"Of course I'm giving it to you again. What'd you think I was going to do?"

She still surveyed him with little veiled glances. "You look so bright you give me Kleig eyes," she said. She managed a wan smile at this.

"Take it," he insisted, extending the package. "Of course it won't keep Western Union time, but it'll look good on you."

She appeared to be gaining on her incredulity, but a vestige of it remained. "I won't touch it," she declared with more spirit than could have been expected from the perishing, "I won't touch it till you give me a good big kiss."

"Sure," he said, and leaned down to brush her pale cheek with his lips. He was cheerfully businesslike in this ceremony.

"Not till you do it right," she persisted. He knelt beside the couch and did it right. He lingered with a hand upon her pale brow.

"What you afraid of?" he demanded.

"You," she said, but now she again brought the watch to view, holding it away from her, studying its glitter from various angles. At last she turned her eyes up to his. They were alive but unrevealing. "Well?"

"Well?" he repeated coolly.

"Oh, stop it!" Again there was more energy than the moribund are wont to manifest. There was even a vigorous impatience in her tone as she went on, "You know well enough what I was afraid of. And you know well enough what I want to hear right now. Shoot, can't you?"

He shot. He stood up, backed away from the couch to where he could conveniently regard its stricken occupant, and shot gaily.

"Well, it'll be a good lesson to you about me, this thing of your thinking I was fooled over that piece. I s'pose you and Baird had it between you all the time, right down to the very last, that I thought he was doin' a serious play. Ho, ho!" He laughed gibingly. It was a masterful laugh. "A serious play with a cross-eyed man doing funny stuff all through. I thought it was serious, did I? Yes, I did!" Again the dry, scornful laugh of superiority. "Didn't you people know that I knew what I could do and what I couldn't do? I should have thought that little thing would of occurred to you all the time. Didn't you s'pose I knew as well as any one that I got a low-comedy face and couldn't ever make the grade in a serious piece?

"Of course I know I got real pathos — look how I turned it on a couple o' times in that piece last night — but even when I'm imitating a bad actor you can see it ain't all acting. You'd see soon enough I was a bad actor if I tried to imitate a good one. I guess you'd see that pretty quick. Didn't you and Baird even s'pose I'd found out my limits and decided to be what God meant me to be?

"But I got the pathos all right, and you can't name one great comedian that don't need pathos more'n he needs anything else.

He just has to have it — and I got it. I got acting-plus; that's what, I got. I knew it all the time; and a whole lot of other people knew it last night. You could hear 50 of 'em talking about it when I came out of the theater, saying I was an artist and all like that, and a certain Los Angeles society woman that you can bet never says things she don't mean, she told me she saw lots of places in this piece that I was funnier than any cross-eyed man that ever lived. And what happens this morning?" Hands in pockets he swaggered to and fro past the couch.

"Well, nothing happens this morning except people coming around to sign me up for 350 a week. One of 'em said not an hour ago — he's a big producer, too — that Baird ought to be paying me 750 because I earned every cent of it. Of course I didn't want to say anything the other day, with you pretending to know so much about contracts and all that — I just thought I'd let you go on, seeing you were so smart — and I signed what you told me to. But I know I should have held off — with this Bamberger coming over from the Bigart when I was hardly out of bed, and says will 350 a week interest me and promising he'll give me a chance to do that spur act again that was the hit of the piece —"

He broke off, conscious suddenly that the girl had for some time been holding a most peculiar stare rigidly upon him. She had at first narrowed her right eye at a calculating angle as she listened; but for a long time now the eyes had been widened to this inexplicable stare eloquent of many hidden things.

As he stopped his speech, made ill at ease by the incessant pressing of the look, he was caught and held by it to a longer silence than he had meant to permit. He could now read meanings. That unflinching look incurred by his smooth bluster was a telling blend of pity and of wonder.

"So you know, do you," she demanded, "that you look just enough too much like Harold Parmalee so that you're funny? I mean," she amended, seeing him wince, "that you look the way Parmalee would look if he had brains?"

He faltered but made a desperate effort to recover his balance.

"And besides, what difference does it make? If we did good pictures we'd have to sell 'em to a mob. And what's a mob? It's 15 years old and nothing but admirers, or something like that, like

Muriel Mercer that wouldn't know how much are two times two if the neighbors didn't get it to her —"

Again he had run down under her level look. As he stopped, the girl on the couch who had lain with the blankets to her neck suddenly threw them aside and sat up. Surprisingly she was not garbed in sick-bed apparel. She seemed to be fully dressed.

A long moment she sat thus, regarding him still with that slow look, unbelieving yet cherishing. His eyes fell at last.

"Merton!" he heard her say. He looked up but she did not speak. She merely gave a little knowing nod of the head and opened her arms to him. Quickly he knelt beside her while the mothering arms enfolded him. A hand pulled his head to her breast and held it there. Thus she rocked gently, the hand gliding up to smooth his hair. Without words she cherished him thus a long time. The gentle rocking back and forth continued.

"It's — it's like that other time you found me —" His bluster had gone. He was not sure of his voice. Even these few words had been hard. He did not try more.

"There, there, there!" she whispered. "It's all right, everything's all right. Your mother's got you right here and she ain't ever going to let you go — never going to let you go."

She was patting his head in rhythm with her rocking as she snuggled and soothed him. There was silence for another interval. Then she began to croon a song above him as she rocked, though the lyric was plainly an improvisation.

"Did he have his poor old mother going for a minute? Yes, he did. He had her going for a minute, for a minute. Yes, he had her going good for a minute.

"But oh, he won't ever fool her very long, very long, not very long, because he can't fool his dear old mother very long, very long; and he can bet on that, bet on that, so he can, bet a lot of money on that, that, that!" Her charge had grown still again, but she did not relax her tightened arms.

"Say," he said at last.

"Well, honey."

"You know those benches where we wait for the cars?"

"Do I know them?" The imperative inference was that she did.

"I looked at the store yesterday. The sign down there says 'Himebaugh's dignified system of deferred payments.'"

"Yes, yes, I know."

"Well, I saw another good place — it says 'The house of lucky rings' — you know — rings!"

"Sure, I know. That's all right."

"Well," he threw off the arms and got to his feet. She stood up then.

"Well, all right!"

They were both constrained now. Both affected an ease that neither felt. It seemed to be conceded without words that they must very lightly skirt the edges of Merton Gill's screen art. They talked a long tune volubly of other things: of the girl's illness from which she now seemed most happily to have recovered, of whether she was afraid of him — she professed still to be — of the new watch whose beauties were newly admired when it had been adjusted to its owner's wrist; of finances they talked, and even, quite simply, of accessible homes where two could live as cheaply as one.

It was not until he was about to go, when he stood at the door while the girl readjusted his cravat, smoothed his hair, and administered a final series of pats where they seemed most needed, that he broke ever so slightly through the reserve which both had felt congealing about a certain topic.

"You know," he said, "I happened to remember the title of a book this morning; a book I used to see back in the public library at home. It wasn't one I ever read. Maybe Tessie Kearns read it. Anyway, she had a poem she likes a lot written by the same man. She used to read me good parts of it. But I never read the book because the title sounded kind of wild, like there couldn't be any such thing. The poem had just a plain name; it was called 'Lucile,' but the book by the same man was called *The Tragic Comedians*. You wouldn't think there could be a tragic comedian would you? — well, look at me."

She looked at him, with that elusive, remote flickering back in her eyes, but she only said, "Be sure and come take me out to dinner. Tonight I can eat. And don't forget your overcoat. And listen — don't you dare go into Himebaugh's till I can go with you."

One minute after he had gone the Montague girl was at the telephone.

"Hello! Mr. Baird, please. Is this Mr. Baird? Well, Jeff, everything's jake. Yeah. The poor thing was pretty wild when he got here. First he began to bluff. He'd got an earful from someone, probably over on the lot. And he put it over on me for a minute, too. But he didn't last good. He was awful broke up when the end came. Bless his heart. But you bet I kissed the hurt place and made it well. How about him now? Jeff, I'm darned if I can tell except he's right again. When he got here he was some heartbroke and some mad and some set up on account of things he hears about himself. I guess he's that way still, except I mended the heartbreak. I can't quite make him out — he's like a book where you can't guess what's coming in the next chapter, so you keep on reading. I can see we ain't ever going to talk much about it — not if we live together 20 years. What's that? Yeah. Didn't I tell you he was always getting me, somehow? Well, now I'm got. Yeah. We're gonna do an altar walk. What? Oh, right away. Say, honest, Jeff, I'll never have an easy minute again while he's out of my sight. Helpless! You said it. Thanks, Jeff. I know that, old man. Good-bye!"

CHAPTER XX

ONWARD AND UPWARD

At the first showing of the Buckeye company's new five-reel comedy — Five Reels, 500 Laughs — entitled *Brewing Trouble*, two important members of its cast occupied balcony seats and one of them throughout the piece brazenly applauded the screen art of her husband. "I don't care who sees me," she would reply ever and again to his whispered protests.

The new piece proved to be a rather broadly stressed burlesque of the type of picture drama that has done so much to endear the personality of Edgar Wayne to his public. It was accorded a hearty reception. There was nothing to which it might be compared save the company's previous *Hearts on Fire*, and it seemed to be felt that the present offering had surpassed even that masterpiece of satire.

The Gills, above referred to, watched the unwinding celluloid with vastly different emotions. Mrs. Gill was hearty in her enjoyment, as has been indicated. Her husband, superficially, was not displeased. But beneath that surface of calm approval — beneath even the look of bored indifference he now and then managed — there still ran a complication of emotions, not the least of which was honest bewilderment. People laughed, so it must be funny. And it was good to be known as an artist of worth, even if the effects of your art were unintended.

It was no shock to him to learn now that the mechanical appliance in his screen-mother's kitchen was a still, and that the grape juice the honest country boy purveyed to the rich New Yorker had been improved in rank defiance of a constitutional amendment. And even during the filming of the piece he had suspected that the little sister, so engagingly played by the present Mrs. Gill, was being too bold. With slight surprise, therefore, as the drama unfolded, he saw that she had in the most brazen manner invited the attentions of the city villains.

She had, in truth, been only too eager to be lured to the great city with all its pitfalls, and had bidden the old home farewell in her simple country way while each of the villains in turn had awaited her in his motor-car. What Merton had not been privileged to watch were the later developments of this villainy. For just beyond the little hamlet at a lonely spot in the road each of the motor-cars had been stopped by a cross-eyed gentleman looking much like the clerk in the hotel, save that he was profusely bewhiskered and bore side-arms in a menacing fashion.

Declaring that no scoundrel could take his little daughter from him, he deprived the villains of their valuables, so that for a time at least they should not bring other unsuspecting girls to grief. As a further precaution he compelled them to abandon their motor-cars, in which he drove off with the rescued daughter. He was later seen to sell the cars at a wayside garage, and, after dividing their spoils with his daughter, to hail a suburban trolley upon which they both returned to the home nest, where the little girl would again languish at the gate, a prey to any designing city man who might pass.

She seemed so defenseless in her wild-rose beauty, her longing for pretty clothes and city ways, and yet so capably pro by this opportune father who appeared to foresee the moment of her flights.

He learned without a tremor that among the triumphs of his inventive genius had been a machine for making 10-dollar bills, at which the New York capitalist had exclaimed that the state right for Iowa alone would bring 100,000 dollars. Even more remunerative, it would seem, had been his other patent — the folding boomerang. The manager of the largest boomerang factory in Australia stood ready to purchase this device for 10 million dollars. And there was a final view of the little home after prosperity had come to its inmates so long threatened with ruin. A sign over the door read "Ye Olde Fashioned Gifte Shoppe," and under it, flaunted to the wayside, was the severely simple trade-device of a high boot.

These things he now knew were to be expected among the deft infamies of a Buckeye comedy. But the present piece held in store for him a complication that, despite his already rich experience of Buckeye methods, caused him distressing periods of heat and cold while he watched its incredible unfolding. Early in the piece, indeed, he had begun to suspect in the luring of his little sister a grotesque parallel to the bold advances made him by the New York society girl. He at once feared some such interpretation when he saw himself coy and embarrassed before her down-right attack, and he was certain this was intended when he beheld himself embraced by this reckless young woman who behaved in the manner of male screen idols during the last dozen feet of the last reel. But how could he have suspected the lengths to which a perverted spirit of satire would lead the Buckeye director?

For now he staggered through the blinding snow, a bundle clasped to his breast. He fell, half fainting, at the door of the old home. He groped for the knob and staggered in to kneel at his mother's feet. And she sternly repulsed him, a finger pointing to the still open door.

Unbelievably the screen made her say, "He wears no ring. Back to the snow with 'em both! Throw 'em Way Down East!"

And Baird had said the bundle would contain one of his patents!

Mrs. Gill watched this scene with tense absorption. When the mother's iron heart had relented she turned to her husband. "You dear thing, that was a beautiful piece of work. You're set now. That cinches your future. Only, dearest, never, never, never let it show on your face that you think it's funny. That's all you'll ever have to be afraid of in your work."

"I won't," he said stoutly.

He shivered — or did he shudder? — and quickly reached to take her hand. It was a simple, direct gesture, yet somehow it richly had the quality of pleading.

"Mother understands," she whispered. "Only remember, you mustn't seem to think it's funny."

"I won't," he said again. But in his torn heart he stubbornly cried, "I don't, I don't!"

Some six months later that representative magazine, *Silver Screenings*, emblazoned upon its front cover a promise that in the succeeding number would appear a profusely illustrated interview by Augusta Blivens with that rising young screen actor, Merton Gill.

The promise was kept. The interview wandered amid photographic reproductions of the luxurious Hollywood bungalow, set among palms and climbing roses, the actor and his wife in their high-powered roadster (Mrs. Gill at the wheel); the actor in his costume of chaps and sombrero, rolling a cigarette; the actor in evening dress, the actor in his famous scene of the Christmas eve return in *Brewing Trouble*; the actor regaining his feet in his equally famous scene of the malignant spurs; the actor and his young wife, on the lawn before the bungalow, and the young wife aproned, in her kitchen, earnestly busy with spoon and mixing bowl.

"It is perhaps not generally known," wrote Miss Blivens, "that the honor of having discovered this latest luminary in the stellar firmament should be credited to Director Howard Henshaw of the Victor forces. Indeed, I had not known this myself until the day I casually mentioned the Gills in his presence. I lingered on a set of *Island Love*, at present being filmed by this master of the unspoken drama, having but a moment since left that dainty little reigning queen of the celluloid dynasty, Muriel Mercer. Seated with her in the tiny bijou boudoir of her bungalow dressing room on the great Holden lot, its walls lined with the works of her favorite authors — for one never finds this soulful little girl far from the books that have developed her mentally as the art of the screen has developed her emotionally — she had referred me to the director when I sought further details of her forthcoming great production, an idyll of island romance and adventure. And presently, when I had secured from him the information I needed concerning this unique little drama of the great South Seas, I chanced to mention my approaching encounter with the young star of the Buckeye forces, an encounter to which I looked forward with some dismay.

"Mr. Henshaw, pausing in his task of effecting certain changes in the interior of the island hut, reassured me. 'You need have no fear about your meeting with Gill,' he said. 'You will find him quite simple and unaffected, an artist, and yet sanely human.' It was now that he revealed his own part in the launching of this young star. 'I fancy it is not generally known,' he continued, 'that to me should go the honor of having "discovered" Gill. It is a fact, however. He appeared as an extra one morning in the cabaret scene we used in Miss Mercer's tremendous hit, *The Blight of Broadway*. Instantly, as you may suppose, I was struck by the extraordinary distinction of his face and bearing. In that crowd composed of average extra people he stood out to my eye as one made for big things. After only a moment's chat with him I gave him a seat at the edge of the dancing floor and used him most effectively in portraying the basic idea of this profoundly stirring drama in which Miss Mercer was to achieve one of her brightest triumphs.

"'Watch that play today; you will discover young Gill in many of the close-ups where, under my direction, he brought out the psychological, the symbolic — if I may use the term — values of the great idea underlying our story. Even in these bits he revealed the fine artistry which he has since demonstrated more broadly under another director.

"'To my lasting regret the piece was then too far along to give him a more important part, though I intended to offer him something good in our next play for Muriel Mercer — you may recall her gorgeous success in *Her Father's Wife* — but I was never able to find the chap again. I made inquiries, of course, and felt a really personal sense of loss when I could get no trace of him. I knew then, as well as I know now, that he was destined for eminence in our world of painted shadows. You may imagine my chagrin later when I learned that another director was to reap the rewards of a discovery all my own.'

"And so," continued Miss Blivens, "it was with the Henshaw words still in my ears that I first came into the presence of

Merton Gill, feeling that he would — as he at once finely did — put me at my ease. Simple, unaffected, modest, he is one whom success has not spoiled. Both on the set where I presently found him — playing the part of a titled roué in the new Buckeye comedy — to be called, one hears, *Nearly Sweethearts or Something* — and later in the luxurious but homelike nest which the young star has provided for his bride of a few months-she was 'Flips' Montague, one recalls, daughter of a long line of theatrical folk dating back to days of the merely spoken drama-he proved to be finely unspoiled and surprisingly unlike the killingly droll mime of the Buckeye constellation. Indeed one cannot but be struck at once by the deep vein of seriousness underlying the comedian's surface drollery. His sense of humor must be tremendous; and yet only in the briefest flashes of his whimsical manner can one divine it.

"'Let us talk only of my work,' he begged me. 'Only that can interest my public.' And so, very seriously, we talked of his work.

"'Have you ever thought of playing serious parts?' I asked, being now wholly put at my ease by his friendly, unaffected ways.

"He debated a moment, his face rigidly set, inscrutable to my glance. Then he relaxed into one of those whimsically appealing smiles that somehow are acutely eloquent of pathos. 'Serious parts — with this low-comedy face of mine!' he responded. And my query had been answered. Yet he went on, 'No, I shall never play Hamlet. I can give a good imitation of a bad actor but, doubtless, I should give a very bad imitation of a good one.

"Et vailet, Messieurs." I remarked to myself. The man with a few simple strokes of the brush had limned me his portrait. And I was struck again with that pathetic appeal in face and voice as he spoke so confidingly. After all, is not pure pathos the hallmark of great comedy? We laugh, but more poignantly because our hearts are tugged at. And here was a master of the note pathetic.

"Who that has roared over the Gill struggle with the dreadful spurs was not even at the climax of his merriment sympathetically aware of his earnest persistence, the pained sincerity of his repeated strivings, the genuine anguish distorting his face as he senses the everlasting futility of his efforts? Who that rocked with laughter at the fox-trot lesson in Object, Alimony, could be impervious to the facial agony above those incompetent, disobedient, heedless feet?

"Here was honest endeavor, an almost prayerful determination, again and again thwarted by feet that recked not of rhythm or even of bare mechanical accuracy. Those feet, so apparently aimless, so little under control, were perhaps the most mirthful feet the scored failure in the dance. But the face, conscious of their clumsiness, was a mask of fine tragedy.

"Such is the combination, it seems to me, that has produced the artistry now so generally applauded, an artistry that perhaps achieved its full flowering in that powerful bit toward the close of *Brewing Trouble* — the return of the erring son with his agony of appeal so markedly portrayed that for the moment one almost forgot the wildly absurd burlesque of which it formed the joyous yet truly emotional apex. I spoke of this.

"'True burlesque is, after all, the highest criticism, don't you think?' he asked me. 'Doesn't it make demands which only a sophisticated audience can meet — isn't it rather high-brow criticism?' And I saw that he had thought deeply about his art.

"'It is because of this,' he went on, 'that we must resort to so much of the merely slapstick stuff in our comedies. For after all, our picture audience, 20 million people a day — surely one can make no great demands upon their intelligence.' He considered a moment, seemingly lost in memories of his work. 'I dare say,' he concluded, 'there are not 20 million people of taste and real intelligence in the whole world.'

"Yet it must not be thought that this young man would play the cynic. He is superbly the optimist, though now again he struck a note of almost cynic whimsicality. 'Of course our art is in its infancy —' He waited for my nod of agreement, then dryly added, 'We must, I think, consider it the Peter Pan of the arts. And I dare say you recall the outstanding biological freakishness of Peter.' But a smile — that slow, almost puzzled smile of his — accompanied the words.

"'You might,' he told me at parting, 'call me the tragic comedian.' And again I saw that this actor is set apart from the run of his brethren by an almost uncanny gift for introspection. He has ruthlessly analyzed himself. He knows, as he put it, 'what God meant him to be.' Was here a hint of poor Cyrano?

"I left after some brief reference to his devoted young wife, who, in studio or home, is never far from his side. 'It is true that I have struggled and sacrificed to give the public something better and finer,' he told me then; 'but I owe my real success all to her.' He took the young wife's hand in both his own, and very simply, unaffectedly, raised it to his cheek where he held it a moment, with that dreamy, remembering light in his eyes, as of one striving to recall bits of his past.

"'I think that's all,' he said at last. But on the instant of my going he checked me once more. 'No, it isn't either.' He brightened. 'I want you to tell your readers that this little woman is more than my wife — she is my best pal; and, I may also add, my severest critic.'"